A GRAVES COMMITMENT

A GRAVES COMMITMENT

By J.A. Lesser

Published by Sandia Press
Copyright © 2024 Jonathan A. Lesser

Cover illustration by Nancy Twinem
Design by Cindy Monroe

ISBN: 978-0-9859749-4-7

Printed in the U.S.A.

Chapter 1

The morning dawned deceptively peaceful as sunlight filtered into my bedroom. Formerly somnolent birds sang loudly in the nearby trees, cattle in the back pasture lowed for their hay, Pedro the rooster crowed, and Daisy, Uncle Bill's *sombrero*-doffed, twenty-five stone porcine companion, grunted from her station upon the *portal* of the ranch house.

Spring had arrived in the village of Vaca Seca, located deep in the Valle de los Lobos in far northern New Mexico, and as removed from civilisation as the heart of darkness in deepest Africa.

Once dressed, I stumbled into the kitchen, the olfactory keenly aware of the boiled, tar-like substance Uncle Bill called cowboy coffee.

"Mornin', pard'ner," he said with excessive cheer for such an early hour. "Coffee's hot."

"Thanks," I replied, a cavernous yawn escaping the jaws. I glided over to the cupboard and retrieved a large mug. After three years of living with Uncle Bill, an aromatic Earl Grey was but a dim memory of my former London life, with its banking career, comely ex-wife Cynthia, and spacious flat in Kensington. Then again, a cuppa would be no match for the challenges—both the four- and two-legged variety—each day brought.

As I have relayed previously, my arrival in the village, which was, came about owing to two unpleasant events Fate dropped on my head like large melons. First, I was sacked from my position as a banker to make way for the Chairman's dim-witted and mannequin-fondling nephew. Shortly thereafter, I was sacked from the position of husband after my then spouse, Cynthia, fell under the spell of a swarthy and silken-tongued Spanish co-worker, Rodrigo Lopreso de Vargas, whose whisperings, she informed the self, made her feel as if she was floating in a beautiful garden of geraniums.

When Fate biffs one with mannequin-fondling nephews and whispering geraniums, one is left with little recourse but to raise the white flag. So, rather than remain in London and despite my father's stern rejoinder that I was a nincompoop for abandoning ship, I set sail for the far side of the world, where Uncle Bill had long resided.

He himself had been cast out by the Graves family for his general worship of what was deemed the boorish cowboy lifestyle of Zane Grey novels and, especially, for an ill-timed "Howdy, pard'ner!" slap on the back of Lord Admiral Sir Henry Throckmorton, a self-important boor, but one whose connections to the Admiralty had demanded fawning respect from all persons Graves. The slap, and the resultant running aground of the over-whiskyed Sir Henry onto a table filled with expensive champagne, was poorly received by Uncle Bill's father, who summarily expelled Uncle Bill from London society. Only too happy to comply, Uncle Bill departed England, ultimately weighing anchor at his current abode.

The town had only recently recovered from two tempests, of which I have previously described. The first was Roger Victory—a fluorescent-toothed, famous Hollywood director, actor, and lecherous cad—had arrived intent upon creating a film about the rebirth of the Dos Abuelas cafe, which I helped resurrect from its long slide into decrepitude caused by the eponymous *abuelas*, the vituperative sisters, Esperanza and Maria.

Roger left a stream of broken promises and unpaid bourses, which resulted in a greater than usual number of the locals complaining to the self about untrustworthy *gringos*. When he departed, he took with him the second tempest that had laid waste to the town: Sunflower, a voluptuous and Joan of

Arc-shaming Siren who had arrived with her then paramour, one Sky Blue, intending to open the Siddhartha restaurant, art gallery, and spiritual centre. Sunflower's rather casual view of fidelity, along with her tactile fondness for the male sex, including the self, was viewed quite unfavourably by the entirety of the local females, including Loretta Alvarez, to whom I was now officially engaged.

Ultimately, Sunflower's and Sky Blue's entrepreneurial efforts came to naught, owing to the vagaries of remodelling the worn-down building owned by the avaricious Joe Garcia, which was to be Siddhartha's home, and which Joe hoped to sell whatever goods they required from his general store at stratospheric prices. On Siddhartha's opening night, Sunflower became convinced the building was haunted, assisted by Roger's ghostly voice.

The *coup de grace* was delivered by a rather emboldened mouse that resided in the building and which had managed to weigh anchor on Sunflower, who was deathly afraid of rodents. When the rodentary invader breached her blouse, Sunflower screamed and tore off the garment, to the great pleasure of the male diners present, and dashed out into the night. She soon found comfort in Roger's Moby Dick-like white bus, and in his arms, leaving Sky Blue aground. Sunflower departed Vaca Seca with Roger and became his new Hollywood starlet, one Veronica Lee. A dejected Sky Blue returned to New York City, to resume his career as a stockbroker. And Loretta ultimately forgave the self for being led towards temptation.

After their sudden departure, life in Vaca Seca returned to what qualified as normal for the town. The repairs to Rudy's Bar and Package Liquors, into which Nestor Martinez had crashed his lorry to raid the large, beer-laden cooler one evening, had finished in record time, such was the importance placed on restoring Vaca Seca's most important institution.

Paco, Nestor's urine-spewing, ill-tempered, and barkative canine, continued to wander the streets, cleverly avoiding the numerous motorists who wished to send him to his final reward.

Maria cooked tirelessly whilst occasionally enhancing her recipes with ash from her ever-present cigarette. As for Esperanza, she remained her recalcitrant, scheming, and complaining self, whether it was the allegedly sore back that made it impossible for her to assist in the kitchen or complaints that the self, whom she addressed as *Pendejito,* was undeserving of her's and Maria's niece Loretta, with whom I was engaged to be married.

I sat down heavily, retrieved a letter from my shirt pocket, and placed it on the kitchen table. Uncle Bill glanced at it over his coffee cup. "That a new letter from your mother? How's she doin'? I still can't believe you never told her you're getting married. Now, not inviting your father, that pompous brother of mine, *that* I can understand. But not your mother."

I shook my head. "No, this is the letter she sent in early January. I've received nothing from her since; no responses to the letters I've sent and nothing from my father. It is rather disconcerting."

Uncle Bill grunted. "I'm sure everything's fine, Bennie. Maybe she got upset when she read about the wedding?"

"M-hem," I replied with a pronounced clearing of the throat. "I, er, never informed her of the blessed event. As I have explained previously, Mother is quite Church of England. One doubts she would approve of my marriage in a Catholic church. Besides, her reaction to the local environs and its inhabitants surely would be like Cynthia's."

After Rodrigo had abandoned Cynthia for fresher game, she had ventured to Vaca Seca in hopes of resuscitating our failed marriage. She then experienced a cultural shock, especially after being confronted by Coronado de Vaca, the rodentary-eyed and rotund local who had been my first introduction to the townspeople and who claimed to be the ancestor of the Spanish conquistador Álvar Núñez Cabeza de Vaca.

A good-hearted, but minimally-witted soul, Coronado always meant well. Invariably, however, one's dealings with Coronado induced headaches and a noticeable increase in blood pressure. My first encounter with him occurred moments after I decamped from the bus that brought me to Vaca Seca. Espying the self, an inebriated Coronado offered to chauffeur me to Uncle Bill's ranch and promptly vomited on my trousers.

Uncle Bill took a large, shark-like bite from a well-buttered *tortilla*. "Well, it's your wedding, pard'ner, but it ain't the cowboy way." Uncle Bill believed firmly in the cowboy code of behaviour. And although he had not followed the Fifth Commandment, he was determined for me to do so.

"Perhaps you are correct, Uncle Bill. I shall write Mother this evening and inform her of the blessed event. Of course, the marriage will have taken place by the time she receives the letter."

"What kind of excuse you gonna come up with for not telling her before?"

"Er, yes, that will require some additional thought. I gather using the excuse of—what is the expression—'shotgun wedding,' should be avoided."

Uncle Bill laughed. "You got something to tell me, Bennie?"

"Gah! I mean, no, of course not."

"Big day's coming up pretty soon, ain't it?"

"One week from Thursday. Loretta confirmed the date with Father Castillo."

Uncle Bill raised an eyebrow. "You gonna convert, Bennie? Father Castillo won't want a heathen in his church."

"The subject has yet to be broached with the good Father. Nor, more importantly, with Loretta's mother, although I am sure she will not mind if I retain my Church of England status, however tenuous. And I suspect I can convince Maria, at least after she has been disarmed of any chef's knives. As for Satan's spawn, Esperanza surely will insist on my conversion, if only to heighten the likelihood that Father Castillo will find me unworthy."

Uncle Bill laughed. "Yep. You tell your mother that Loretta's Catholic?"

"M-hem, no. I believe that presenting it to her as a *fait accompli* will be easier, although perhaps I will admit that fact from the letter I shall write."

Uncle Bill grunted his affirmation. He drained his coffee cup, stood up, and retrieved the pot off the stove. "You want another cup of coffee?" he asked.

"Thank you, no." Although I was long used to the consistency and taste of Uncle Bill's tar-like cowboy brew, the stomach threatened to mutiny after two cups.

"Okay. Well, I gotta go to Joe's store and get some Farm Calm."

Miller's Concentrated Farm Calm, advertised as "for the distressed animal," was the local's preferred veterinary solution. It was a sweetened mixture containing large quantities of grain alcohol that did indeed calm the local populace, both two and four-legged.

Uncle Bill looked down at me and grinned. "Oh, don't forget, Marjorie's stall needs mucking out."

Marjorie was Uncle Bill's obstreperous and ill-tempered equine. Despite, or perhaps because Uncle Bill had entrusted me with her maintenance since my arrival, she took a sadistic delight in making my life miserable – especially well-aimed kicks that would on occasion strike me amidships. I would approach her with the utmost care whilst she glared malevolently, waiting for her morning repast. Fortunately, consuming the mash of oats, molasses, and hay usually appealed to her more than striking out at her keeper. But mucking out her stall required she be let out, which invited unprovoked attacks.

"Er, I would be pleased to dose Daisy should you care to deal with Marjorie."

"I keep tellin' you, Bennie, she's as gentle as a lamb."

I lifted my shirt and displayed the large, fading bruise above my waist, a casualty of Marjorie's last successful attack. "Perhaps the cafe should serve 'lamb' stew one of these evenings," I replied.

Uncle Bill wagged his finger at me. "You just got to be more understanding, Bennie. She'll change her mind."

"On the contrary, Uncle Bill, I understand that equine sociopath only too well."

"Oh, hell, Bennie. Just remember, Loretta won't like you complaining all the time. Now, we both got work to do."

Later that morning, having survived yet another episode of Marjorie's equine disdain for the self, I sat down at the kitchen table and composed a letter to my mother.

Dearest Mother,

It has been quite some time since your letter of 3 January. I have written you twice in the interim, so you will understand my increasing concern about your well-being. I do hope you are well, but if not, please let me know or have Father do so. (I hope Father has recovered from the gout attack you mentioned.)

All is well here. I continue to manage the cafe. I recently engaged some additional kitchen help, a young-ish chap named Ernie Chacon, who seems unbothered by both Esperanza's yelling and washing dishes. Surprisingly, Maria has taken him under her wing, so to speak. She has even begun to instruct him in the culinary arts, including a Lord Nelson-like approach to chopping onions—straight at 'em and vicious chopping.

I do have news for you. By the time you receive this letter, Loretta and I will be married. (The wedding shall take place on 17 June, eight days from now.) It will be a small, informal ceremony, given we have both been married previously.

I apologise for not informing you sooner, but I did not wish you and Father to undertake an arduous

*journey out of any obligation. We hope to visit London in
the not-too-distant future to see you and Father. I have
promised Loretta a grand tour of Europe, including, naturally, Cannes.*

> *Your loving son,*
>
> *Benjamin*

I re-read the letter, hoping she would not be offended by
receiving the connubial news after-the-fact. Mother had been
quite fond of Cynthia and, I suspect, harboured a belief that
Rodrigo's successful entrapment of Cynthia was due in part to
some unknown failure on my part. I imagined that, if I told her
of the marriage to Loretta, she would respond by saying, "Best
not to allow yourself to be cuckolded again, dear," or words
to that effect. As for my father, he would be offended by the
marital announcement, if only because taking offense at the
"nincompoop who darkens my doorway" had been his *raison
d'être*. Fortunately, the Graves stiff upper lip had long ago prevailed, and had been further stiffened by Esperanza's constant
name-calling and repeated use of her middle finger.

Confident in the knowledge that whatever tempest the
news of the wedding would cause in London would not roil
the waters, I inserted the letter into an envelope, addressed it,
and retrieved the necessary postage from a small drawer in the
kitchen.

Fate had a very different view.

Chapter 2

I bid Uncle Bill a good morning and readied myself for the day's exertions. I stepped out the front door, lorry keys in hand. Daisy eyed me somnolently from beneath her *sombrero* but did not rouse herself.

I walked over to the lorry Uncle Bill had bequeathed to the self, opened the door, and sat down. As I was about to place the key in the ignition, I heard the roar of an engine coming up the road. Then, glancing at the rearview mirror, I observed a dirt-covered white lorry on a collision course.

"Gah!" I screamed and braced for impact. I heard a loud squealing of brakes and then felt a large thud as the lorry engaged my rear bumper.

"Bloody hell!" I sat motionless for a few moments. Then, convinced I had not been physically damaged, I exited the front seat and almost tripped over Daisy, who had come to investigate the disturbance to her post-breakfast slumber. "What do you think you're—"

I eyed the lorry, which appeared to be empty. "Eh?" I muttered. Then, I heard a loud grunt, as the lorry's corpulent driver sat upright, opened the driver door, and swung his frame onto the ground.

"Ah, it's you, Coronado."

I shook my head and walked towards the back of my lorry, then sighed deeply upon surveying the damage. The right-side taillight, what was left of it, hung limply from a small white wire. The bumper was bent downwards towards the right rear tyre.

"Sorry, Señor Graves," Coronado said, surveying the damage, "I was gonna fix my brakes, but I kinda forgot."He pointed at the dismembered taillight. "You want me to fix that?"

"God no," I muttered under my breath. "That is, thank you for the offer, Coronado. I need to see Luis anyway. I am quite sure he can repair the damage."

"Okay, Señor Graves. But if Luis can't fix it, I can do it for you. I like to help."

"Er, yes, I know," I replied dully.

Daisy approached Coronado, sniffed at his trouser pocket, and grunted. "Sorry, Daisy," he said apologetically, "I already ate my *burrito*."

"M-hem. Although I'm sure Daisy appreciates your contrition, dare I enquire as to the reason for this sudden, er, encounter?"

"Huh?"

"Why are you here? Has another white bus mysteriously appeared?" Coronado's last unannounced arrival had occurred in the middle of the night to alert me of the presence of a mysterious white bus owned by Roger Victory, as I was to discover. "Are flames engulfing the cafe? Perhaps a herd of elephants has trampled Windsor Castle?"

"Oh, no, Señor Graves. I haven't seen Señor Victory's bus again. And I think the cafe is okay." He scratched his head. "What's Winter Castle? Is it a zoo? I've never seen an elephant. Have you, Señor Graves?"

I groaned.

Presently, he reached into the same trouser pocket that Daisy's olfactory had detected the presence of a *burrito* and retrieved a soiled and grease-stained envelope. "Señora Flores told me to give this to you right away, 'cause it's from London."

Señora Flores was the town's postmistress. The local post office was a small, dilapidated building next to Luis Chavez's' Texaco station. She interpreted the American saying of "neither rain, nor snow, nor dead of night" to mean those times when the post office was to be closed. As for sunny days, she would perform her postal duties when she was so inclined, which was infrequently. And on those occasions, her demeanour was, to be charitable, so off-putting that even Esperanza could be left stammering.

Coronado handed me the letter. "Sorry, Señor Graves. My *burrito* kinda spilled on it." The self's name and address had been scratched out and the words "Deliver to *gringo*" scrawled in their stead.

"Here's another letter, too, Señor Graves."

He handed me the second letter. Whilst not grease-stained, it was encrusted with mud and reeked of stale alcohol, and there appeared to be a set of bite marks below the stamps bearing the Queen's profile.

"Did both of these arrive from London this morning?" I queried. "Rather odd."

"Uh, not exactly, Señor Graves," Coronado said, his right foot now arcing a trench into the gravel. "Sorry."

I goggled at him and held up the masticated envelope, pointing accusatively at the toothmarks. "This letter has been gnawed upon."

"Sorry, Señor Graves," replied Coronado, shifting his gaze towards the newly dug trench. "Señora Flores gave me that letter a while ago."

"How long, exactly, qualifies as 'a while ago?'"

Coronado began to count slowly on his corpulent fingers. "I dunno. I think it was before that big snow we got. I couldn't get my truck out for two days."

The big snow—several feet of it—had struck in the third week of February. The back ached at the mere recall of the hours of shovelling it had endured, which included time spent clearing away the avalanche that had slid off the barn roof and blocked the sliding door, entombing Marjorie inside. Although I would have preferred to leave well enough alone, Uncle Bill's misplaced equine sentimentality required several hours of shovelling to enable her to escape, with Marjorie expressing her gratitude as per usual. I was fortunate she connected only with the shovel and not my shin.

The jaw dropped. "Do you mean you've possessed this letter since February?" I shouted.

Coronado shrugged. "Uh, I guess so. It was on the floor of my truck. I found a mouse nest behind my seat. Maybe they chewed on it. I got some in my house, too. Joe gave me some of those wire things to catch them, but every time I try to—"

"Please, Coronado," I interrupted, raising the right hand whilst resisting the urge to bang the now throbbing skull against the side of the lorry. "Why didn't you bring me this letter when Señora Flores gave it to you?"

Coronado shrugged again. "I meant to give it to you, Señor Graves." He nodded sheepishly. "Is it real important?"

"How would I know you bloody—I mean, never mind." An image of keel-hauling Coronado materialised within the grey matter. I tore open the first letter, which was dated the first of May, and began to read.

Dearest Benjamin,

You will recall I told you how I wished to see you again, as well as meet your Uncle William, whom you have told me so much about. I said I was going to meet with the travel agent to make the arrangements.

Well, the arrangements are now complete! I am sorry to tell you that Father's Parliamentary duties are too pressing for him to accompany. He insisted I not go alone. So, I have invited your cousin, Archie, who is most eager to go, in his place. We leave for Albuquerque on the 10th of next month. The travel agent told us there is a bus that stops in your town the following day. I am looking forward to dining at that charming café you manage. (I am quite sure you will have improved the wine list. Perhaps you will have managed to stock the Château Bouscaut Grand Cru Classé we enjoyed in Cannes? Of course, one can hope!)

"Gah!" I shouted.

"Must be good news, huh, Señor Graves," said Coronado whilst nodding his head.

"Gah," I whimpered.

Presently, I espied Uncle Bill walking towards us. He glanced at Coronado, then at the two lorries. "What's all the dang commotion about, Bennie?" he asked. Then, he walked behind my lorry and shook his head.

"*Buenos días*, El Vaquero," said Coronado. "I kinda hit your truck. Sorry."

Although Uncle Bill initially was referred to as the *gringo*, his hard work, including help with the previous incarnation of the cafe, which was owned by Ernesto Morales and run under the watchful eye of Uncle Bill's wife Celestina. With his ever-present cowboy hat and cowboy mannerisms, which were inspired by the many Zane Grey novels he had read, Uncle Bill became known as "the *gringo* who thinks he's a vaquero" and ultimately just "El Vaquero."

Uncle Bill looked at the lorry. He rubbed his chin, looked at Coronado, then rubbed his chin a second time. "Brakes not working again, Coronado?"

"Not real good, El Vaquero," replied Coronado.

"Okay," said Uncle Bill, a note of resignation in his voice. "How about you ask Luis to fix them this time? I'll even pay for it."

"Thanks, El Vaquero," said Coronado. "That's real nice of you."

"My pleasure," said Uncle Bill. He turned to the self and slapped the right shoulder. "Well, pard'ner, it could be worse. Guess I'll head to town now." He turned and began to walk back to the house.

"Er, I say, Uncle Bill, might I have a word before you depart? Rather important and all that."

"Sure, Bennie."

I turned to Coronado. "Eh, would you mind telling Maria I shall be delayed?" I glanced at my watch. "You may tell her I expect to be at the cafe by half ten, I mean, ten-thirty."

"Okay, Señor Graves." Coronado waddled back to his lorry and hoisted himself onto the driver's seat. As he began to back up, the front bumper, which apparently had wedged itself under my lorry's rear one, pulled the latter off completely. It fell to the ground with a loud thud, raising a cloud of dust. Coronado peered out of his window. "Sorry, Señor Graves." Before I could respond, he turned his lorry around and sped off.

I eyed the now defenestrated bumper, sighed, and trudged back towards the house, attempting to grasp the blow Fate had delivered. I walked past Daisy, who had returned to her slumber on the porch, stepped inside, and closed the front door. Uncle Bill was in the kitchen, downing another cup of coffee. He looked at me and smiled.

"Why the hang-dog look, pard'ner?"

"Fate has dealt a crushing blow, Uncle Bill, delivering not the usual vicissitudes, but a veritable hurricane salivating over the opportunity to swamp the Graves' ship. The self's impending nuptials, nay, very survival, are at stake."

"C'mon, Bennie, the truck ain't that bad. Luis can fix it."

"Yes, well, you did not witness the defenestration of the entire rear bumper. However, that is not the maelstrom to which I refer." I handed him Mother's most recent letter. He read it quickly and smiled.

"Dorothy's coming here? Well, I'll be damned." He continued to read the letter. "Says she is arriving on the tenth. I guess she's gonna miss the wedding after all. You better send that letter to her and explain everything. Be a lot harder if you have to explain it to her face."

"Er, as to the timing, Uncle Bill, perhaps you do not realise—"

"Does Dorothy really think the cafe serves French wine?" he asked, laughing. "Can you imagine her asking Esperanza for a wine list?"

"One would not describe Esperanza as an oenophile," I replied, imagining her erupting in paroxysms of anger if asked for a *Chateau Beychevelle* or a *Grand Cru Bourgogne.* "Should you examine the date of Mother's letter more carefully, you will see that she arrives tomorrow."

Uncle Bill's eyebrows rocketed upwards. "Tomorrow!" He looked carefully at the date on the letter. "Damn, pard'ner. Guess we've got some housecleaning to get done. You better hoof it home tonight as soon as you can." He shook his head. "I hope Dorothy will understand you not telling her about the wedding."

"Er, yes," I groaned. "And I must inform Loretta of this. I hope she understands, too."

"Oh, hell, Bennie, of course she will. Stop your bellyaching. Anyway, Dorothy's gonna be real glad she can attend your wedding. You've got nothing to worry about."

"M-hem, yes," I coughed.

"Says she's bringing her nephew, Archie. Guess that makes him my nephew, too. What's he like? Good kid?"

"Archie? By comparison, Esperanza is almost angelic."

"C'mon, nobody can be that bad tempered," replied Uncle Bill. "Can he?"

"Eh, what? Bad-tempered? Oh, no, quite the opposite. I dare say one will never meet anyone more charming than Archie. I don't suppose you correspond regularly with Aunt Constance, his mother?"

"Can't say I do. I never understood why she married that pompous idiot brother of mine. Well, you know all about me and my family."

I coughed again. "Yes, well, once you meet the lad, you may require something more bracing in your morning coffee."

"Eh? What do you mean? For God's sake, Bennie, spit it out."

"The words ne'er-do-well, wastrel, and reprobate come to mind. Allow me to offer several examples. In sixth form, Archie was expelled from Eaton for pinching the Headmaster's Jaguar."

Uncle Bill laughed. "Hell, those little toffs are always doing that sort of thing. I remember some of the older boys when I was in school. One night, they removed one of the dormitory toilets and put it in front of the head's house, along with a large sign that said, 'Head of the class.' Harmless fun."

"M-hem, yes," I replied. "In this instance, the Jaguar, or more accurately what remained of it, was recovered by the police one week later in a rather seedy part of the East End. The boot and bonnet were battered, the engine, seats, and tyres had been removed, and the vehicle was filled with a large quantity of odoriferous rubbish, including the remains of several canines. The Head was not amused, especially when the insurance company informed him that, owing to his having left the keys in the ignition, he had failed to secure the vehicle in a prudent manner. They declined recompense."

"Archie did that? How did the Head find out?"

"Apparently, not having absorbed the wisdom of 'silence is golden,' Archie bragged about his efforts to several of his friends, who quite naturally spoke to their friends, and so forth. The day after the vehicle was recovered, the Head burst into Archie's maths class, grabbed him by the nearest ear, and marched him to the door. He also presented a bill to Aunt Constance for a replacement vehicle, in exchange for not having Archie tossed in gaol. I gather the sum was deducted from Archie's trust."

Uncle Bill grunted. "Anything else?"

I coughed. "There are rather numerous examples. The following year, Archie 'borrowed' fifty pounds from Aunt Constance, allegedly for purchasing several business textbooks he claimed would benefit his preparation for Oxford, which he used to bet on numerous horses. It was only when Uncle Arthur offered to provide Archie with unpaid work at his firm and asked to see the textbooks Archie had purchased that the truth came out. Well, that and the inconvenient fact that Archie used Uncle Arthur's bookmaker and happened to drop in when the latter was himself placing a large sum on a race."

Uncle Bill grunted disdainfully. "Sounds like my brother."

Chapter 3

The next morning, the alarm chimed. I groaned, having spent much of the previous night in a frenzy of spic-and-spanning the house. Dressing quickly, I staggered into the kitchen, detecting the aroma of percolating coffee and warm *tortillas*.

"Morning, pard'ner," chirped Uncle Bill. "Thanks for tidying up last night. Place looks real good. You get much sleep?"

"Perhaps a few hours," I said as a cavernous yawn escaped the jaws. "The bus arrives at, what, ten o'clock?"

Yep.'Course, that driver doesn't care much about a schedule. You gonna go meet them?"

"Yes, unless you would prefer the honour."

"Nope. I've got to head up to Ernesto Morales' ranch this morning. He's got a tractor I might buy. I'm thinking of expanding the herd and a bigger tractor would come in real handy." Ernesto was a friendly-giant sort of chap who owned a large ranch north of town, and from whom Uncle Bill frequently purchased hay for the cattle. "Then I gotta drive up to Alamosa to buy more fencing. That goddamn bull has done a real number on some of it. Joe doesn't have much in stock and I wouldn't pay what he charges anyway."

One could not accurately describe Joe Garcia, the eponymous owner of the local store and Loretta's uncle, as merely avaricious, despite the nickels in his cash register crying out in distress over how hard he squeezed them. He was also a vindictive sort, having once binned a rattlesnake into the kitchen of the cafe as punishment for my refusal to pay the exorbitant prices he intended to charge for supplies we needed to open, then subsequently attempting to set fire to the cafe on opening night.

"You bring your mother and Archie back here. Tell 'em to make themselves at home and that I'll be back a little later this afternoon. There's plenty of food in the icebox."

"Thanks, Uncle Bill. I informed everyone last night about their arrival. Esperanza began complaining about arriving early to assist Maria, who merely expelled a large cloud of cigarette smoke and waved her chef's knife threateningly at the self. All ship-shape, in other words." I paused. "What about Daisy? They may be nonplussed by the sight of a *sombrero*-clad pig on the porch."

"Just tell your mother not to let Daisy into the house. And you better take their luggage around the back. You remember what happened when you arrived, don't you?"

"I still grieve over the lost bottle of single malt." When I first arrived, Daisy espied my valises. In a fit of rage, she destroyed them, including the bottle I had so carefully wrapped.

"And make damn sure the front door is latched."

Unbeknownst to Uncle Bill and the self, a gust of wind had blown the front door open the previous spring, allowing Daisy to saunter inside. She raided the icebox, which we later found empty and lying on its side next to the fireplace. Then, sated with an unexpected repast that included cannibalising a large pork roast, she proceeded to nap in Uncle Bill's bed, which collapsed under her 25-stone weight.

"Is Loretta nervous about meeting your mother?"

"Yes, although I assured her that mother will be favourably disposed based on the angelic descriptions of Loretta I wrote in my letters."

"You tell her about Archie?"

"Er, I chose not to convey the more explicit details of his criminal past, if that's what you mean. I did advise her that Archie was a bit of a bounder. She laughed and asked if Archie was as much a 'ladies' man' as the self. Although Loretta assured me she could look after herself, Archie's ability to charm the fairer sex puts Roger Victory to shame."

"Don't worry, Bennie. Loretta isn't the flighty type. She stuck with you, after all, even after you slobbered over that Sunflower gal."

"I did not 'slobber' over Sunflower, as you put it. Besides," I added, placing the right hand over the heart, "*semper fidelis* is the Graves' motto regarding the fairer sex. And as you well know, Cynthia was unfaithful to the self."

Uncle Bill struggled to avoid geysering the coffee he had just swallowed. "Right you are, Bennie. Remind me to tell you about your uncles sometime. Now, I gotta get going. Oh, don't forget to feed and water Marjorie. She's always faithful to you." He laughed heartily, stood up from the table, and disappeared out the back door, leaving me to contemplate the joyous occasion when Marjorie would be found in a tin or bottle of glue.

Presently, I found myself in the barn, performing the morning ablutions for the cantankerous and vindictive equine. I avoided Marjorie's usual "good morning" hoof and slid the barn door shut. I mucked out her stall, a job I looked forward to having Archie perform, and placed the soiled hay in a wheelbarrow. I then mixed her oats and mash into a large bucket, whilst she loitered impatiently outside in her corral, doubtless plotting a surprise attack. I walked over to the barn door, engaged the handle in my right hand, and pushed. The door did not move. I strained, using both hands, leaning in as if battling a gale. The door remained immobile. "Bloody, hell," I shouted. "What have you done?"

Not being the chatty type, Marjorie remained silent, presumably still somewhere in the corral and doubtless torn between glee at my entombment and sorrow at the absence of her morning oats. I put the bucket of oats down and began rummaging through the barn for a crowbar or a hammer— anything that would enable me to pry open the door. Finding none, I reefed unsuccessfully on the door yet again. Then I attempted to push it outward. Finally, in Marjorie's finest tradition, I kicked at it, hoping to loosen several boards and crawl through. But lacking Marjorie's femoral prowess, this, too, failed.

Although light streamed in through various small holes in the wooden walls, the barn was windowless. I walked around the base of the walls to see if there were any openings I could squeeze through. Finding none larger than sized for the local mice, I looked upwards. Some of the metal roofing was loose and might be amenable to being pushed open. However, the ladder lay outside the barn and I was incapable of high-jumping to the rafters and then to-ing and frow-ing from them like a chimpanzee to reach any loose panels.

I sat down on an old stool and contemplated the situation anew. I checked my watch, which read half nine. I would arrive a few minutes before the bus if I left now. I stood up, walked over to the door, and heaved in a last futile gesture.

Knackered by the previous night's cleaning and my unsuccessful efforts at escape, I wandered over to the side of the barn and sat down on the dirt floor, resting my back on the wall. Fate, it seemed, had decided I should remain trapped inside. I could only hope that one of the locals would espy Archie and my mother wandering aimlessly about and provide them aid and comfort. I then fell sound asleep.

Several hours later, I was awakened by the roaring of a vehicle driving up to the house. "Hullo!" I shouted. "Is that you, Uncle Bill? I'm trapped inside the barn! Can you please get me out!"

There was no response. Then, I heard footsteps approach and, moments later, what sounded like a metal bucket dropping onto the dirt. Presently, the barn door slid open, and bright sunshine streamed inside. I stood up, rubbed the oculars, blinked several times, and stared into the light.

"What-ho and pip, pip, old man!" said the silhouette towering above me. "Hiding from your guests, oh cousin of mine?"

"Eh? How did you open the door, Archie?"

He lifted the crushed remains of a metal bucket. "This was jammed against it," he said calmly, before tossing it aside. "How could that have possibly happened when you were inside?"

The jaw dropped and then hoisted itself closed. "Bloody satanic equine," I mouthed silently. "I, er, I'm not sure exactly. Thanks for the rescue."

Presently, my mother stepped into the doorway. She wore a royal blue dress, along with white heels, a pillbox hat, and a string of pearls. "My dear boy," she said as she kissed the self's cheek. "It's been so long. How are you, dear?"

"I'm fine, Mother, other than nonplussed that I was trapped inside. But how did you get here? Uncle Bill drove up to Colorado. I intended to meet you when you arrived but, as you can see, I was trapped inside the bloody barn."

"Well, after the bus driver retrieved our valises, we waited. After ten minutes, a man came to our rescue. At first, I thought he was a taxi driver, until—"

"Gah!" I cried. "Coronado brought you here?"

"No, that's not his name," said Mother. "Perhaps you know him."

I stepped outside. Rudy Sandoval, the eponymous owner of Rudy's Bar and Liquors, stood in the corral. He smiled and tipped his cowboy hat. "Can't even greet your mother, huh Bennie? And after she travelled halfway around the world to see you get married."

"Er, yes. Thank you, Rudy," I replied.

"I saw Coronado walking towards them," he said. "Figured they were relatives of yours. I remember you telling me what happened when he brought you out here for the first time, so I ran over. Told Coronado Joe needed him."

"No need to remind me," I groaned.

"I say, that Coronado chap looked rather like a beady-eyed hippopotamus," said Archie. "He kept smiling at us and nodding his head. He also asked if we would like a *burrito*, whatever that is. Then, he shoved his hand into his pocket and removed a greasy mass wrapped in paper. The smell reminded me of a rubbish bin."

I wondered how Archie and Mother would take to the Dos Abuelas menu, which featured several types of *burritos*, though admittedly we did not offer *burrito dans une poche sale*. "If Rudy hasn't done so already, I shall be happy to expound on some of the locals for you, including Coronado. In the meantime, Mother, you must be exhausted. Would you care to lie down?"

"Yes, Benjamin," she said, stifling a yawn. "I had no idea how far from civilisation you were. Your letters didn't do it justice."

"End of the bloody earth, if you ask me," added Archie. "One cannot head to the club for a snifter and rarefied conversation, can one?"

"No, but Rudy's establishment is quite pleasant," I said. I nodded at Rudy, who rolled his eyes.

"Well, I gotta get back, Bennie," said Rudy. "You know I don't like to leave Antonio manning the bar for too long. Some of the regulars still try and take advantage of him." Antonio was Rudy's fourteen-year-old grandson, whom I first encountered soon after arriving in Vaca Seca. Even then he was a sound publican.

"Nice to meet you, Mrs. Graves, Archie," said Rudy, doffing his hat. "I hope you enjoy your stay. A little different than where you come from, but we like it."

"Thank you again, Rudy," I said. "Would you mind stopping at the cafe and letting them know I will be there as soon as possible?"

"Sure, Bennie." He doffed his cowboy hat, strode back to his lorry, and was soon motoring away.

As the sound of Rudy's lorry faded, I approached Mother. "Let's get you settled in the house first."

"What about the valises?" asked Mother.

"I, er, I will come back and help Archie retrieve them," I said. By now, Marjorie was standing next to him. He reached up and petted the side of her head. "Be careful," I cautioned. She enjoys nothing more than launching hoofed artillery at anyone nearby."

"Really?" he said. "Seems quite friendly to me." Archie turned back and looked at Marjorie, who eyed me disdainfully. He patted the horse's forehead. "What's her name?"

"Marjorie," I replied, through gritted molars. "She belongs to Uncle Bill."

Archie walked over to the valises and picked up two of the smaller ones. "Right, ho," he said. "Lead the way, cousin."

Terrified that Daisy would espy the valises, I motioned for Archie to wait. "Er, we can bring everything around to the back door," I said, pointing towards the right side of the house. "A bit closer and all that."

After settling Mother in Uncle Bill's bedroom and shutting the door, I sat down at the kitchen table with Archie. "My apologies, but I am overdue at the cafe. Uncle Bill should be returning soon. Would you care for something to eat?"

"Quite. I'm famished, old man. I don't suppose you have something to, er, clear the pallet, as it were?"

I glanced at the watch. "A bit early for that, isn't it?"

"Well, it's seven hours later in London. Right now, I should be enjoying a whisky at the club."

"Whisky, eh? Well, perhaps a small tipple to wash the dust down." I retrieved a bottle of Dusty Trail from the cabinet and poured a stiff dose into a glass. "Here you are. It's Uncle Bill's favourite whisky."

"Thanks, old chap," he said, as he raised the glass. "Cheers." He downed the contents in one swallow, then proceeded to gasp and cough uncontrollably. "My God, what was that?"

"It's called Dusty Trail," I replied, suppressing a grin.

Archie grabbed the bottle and coughed several times more. "The whisky cowboys ask for by name," he read. "Cowboys must be completely daft. Frankenstein's monster would recoil from this swill."

"It does take some getting used to. But Uncle Bill enjoys it, so you may wish to be careful with your description around him."

"All right, old man," said Archie. "I need a glass of water." He walked over to the sink, rinsed out the glass, filled it with water from the tap, and drank it down greedily. "Ugh. I don't think I've ever tasted anything so horrid."

"I rather doubt you have. And would you please stop calling me 'old man'. It's rather grating."

Archie slapped my shoulder. "You always were a bit of a stuffed shirt, cousin."

I grunted. "Er, perhaps a cheese sandwich?" I asked.

"Thanks, old m—, that is, yes, please."

After devouring the sandwich, Archie leaned back in his chair. "What possessed Uncle Bill to decamp to here of all places?" he asked. "And what possessed you to come here?"

"It's rather a long story. Has no one ever told you what happened to Uncle Bill?"

"As a matter of fact, I don't recall his name ever being mentioned. Father never spoke of him at home and Aunt Dorothy refused to speak about the matter on our journey. She would say only that there was an 'incident' many years ago when Uncle Bill was a lad."

"Best to ask Uncle Bill himself about the 'incident," as Mother put it." I then proceeded to provide a highly abridged version of how Uncle Bill came to reside in Vaca Seca and the cafe's history.

"I never read any Zane Grey novels," Archie said, after I had finished. "Aunt Dorothy said you own the cafe."

"No. I am merely the unfortunate sod who 'manages' it, to use that term loosely."

"Not going to receive any Michelin stars, what?"

I laughed. "I suspect no Michelin reviewers will be arriving any time soon."

"But surely you would have preferred living in a cosmopolitan location like New York City and a respectable position."

"A respectable position landed me in the soup. After all, I was made redundant because to the bank Chairman could provide his mannequin-fondling nephew, a twit of the highest order, with gainful employment."

"What? I hadn't heard that. Uncle Gerald told me that you fell apart after your divorce. Called you a—"

"Nincompoop?" I sighed. "Father took my losing Cynthia to a Spaniard named Rodrigo, whom she claimed whispered to geraniums, and my being made redundant at the bank as moral failings that had tarnished the Graves' name and reputation. He even resurrected an incident that took place when I was twelve years old: falling out of a tree I had climbed to drop water-filled balloons on Thomas Parkingham—a larded goose of a child who had a disgusting habit of sitting on the self and breaking wind. My father claimed that, but for that fall and the resulting gammy knee, I would have been an officer in the Royal Grenadiers and inherited his seat in Parliament. Although Mother came to my defence, the ensuing row between them was unpleasant: my father accusing her of mollycoddling me. Mother, for her part, suggested I travel to Cannes rather than New Mexico, which she viewed as no different from Conrad's *Heart of Darkness* in deepest Africa."

Archie coughed. "Well, that and a blight on the family like Uncle William. Still, no reason to abandon ship for—" he glanced around and shuddered, er, "this."

I offered a half-hearted shrug of the shoulders. The *paterfamilias* had long viewed the world as one overrun with nincompoops, idiots, and twits, and considered the self to be a combination of all three. But a Graves maintains a stiff upper lip, even in the heaviest of weather. "Uncle Bill has rather different views on the Graves, including my father. In any case, I must dash. I've missed the luncheon crowd at the cafe and there is no telling what damage Esperanza may have done."

"Esperanza? Who is that?"

"She is one of the two eponymous *abuelas*—the word means 'grandmother.' I must warn you, though, you will discover that she is not of the cuddly, 'how about a nice cup of tea and hot buttered scone, dear,' variety. She is rather like an ill-tempered cobra."

"Yow. What about the other grandmother?"

"Ah." I paused, whilst the grey matter considered the appropriate adjectives. "One would not describe Maria as ill-tempered, well, not always. More like a smouldering volcano: quiet most of the time, but prone to cataclysmic eruptions on short notice."

Archie hoisted an eyebrow. "Sound like quite the pair." He paused. "Say, how about I come along?" asked Archie. "Aunt Dorothy will probably be asleep for a while. She and Uncle William will want to catch up after he returns and I may as well get to know the natives a bit more whilst I'm here, including your aboolas."

"M-hem. Er, I suppose you can. But Esperanza and Maria may be especially foul-tempered this afternoon."

"Never fear, Cousin. I shall win them over with my charm."

Chapter 4

As we stopped in front of the cafe, I espied Paco, barking and torpedoing his way across the road to drench one or more of the lorry's tyres in urine. "Avast, you bloody cur," I shouted, as I opened the door and slid down to the macadam. I attempted a kick, but unlike Marjorie, the self's aim was far wide of the mark. The dog continued to bark madly as it dashed under the lorry and ran towards Rudy's.

"Nice dog," said Archie, as he watched Paco disappear behind the bar.

"That would be Paco. He belongs to Nestor Martinez, whom you will likely find inebriated in Rudy's bar." I pointed to Nestor's dented and dirt-encrusted lorry. "That's his lorry parked out front."

"Looks rather worse for wear," said Archie.

"The bonnet is actually new. Nestor drove the lorry through Rudy's front door one morning last year. He then helped himself to the beer in the cooler. In any case, his dog is a barkative, urine-spewing menace, who is especially fond of doorways, shoes, and trouser legs. I should exercise extreme vigilance."

"Right, then. Your little slice of paradise has—" Archie paused and counted on his fingers, "a beady-eyed hippopotamus, grandmothers out of a Grimm's fairy tale, a drunkard who drives his lorry through front doors, and a stealthy, urinating dog. Anything else one should know about?"

"One admits the locals—two-legged and four—do take rather some getting used to. Now, if you will excuse me, I really must attend to the cafe before Esperanza and Maria explode.

Would you care to meet them?" I glanced at the watch. "Loretta should be here by four o'clock. Although we are not serving lunch presently, I'm sure Maria would be willing to prepare something for you, if you still feel peckish. Or, you can wait until the dinner crowd arrives, beginning at five. Uncle Bill presumably shall motor in with Mother for dinner."

Archie cast an eye towards Rudy's. "Er, perhaps I will go for a stroll first. Take in the local colour and all that, such as it is. I do have rather a thirst. Must be the alpine air. I gather Rudy will have something more palatable than that cowboy swill— what did you call it?"

"Dusty Trail, the whisky cowboys ask for by name."

Archie shuddered. "Ugh. Horrid. Well, cheerio, old chap. I shall return anon to meet the two aboolas and your betrothed." He turned, set course for Rudy's, and sailed away, disappearing through the bar's front door.

"How come you're late, *Pendejito*," Esperanza growled, as I stepped inside the cafe. "You think you don't got to work here no more? My back hurts real bad."

"And a very good day to you, too, Esperanza. I was, er, unavoidably delayed. As you know, my mother and cousin arrived this morning. Uncle Bill decamped to Colorado for some fencing supplies. So, I settled them in."

Esperanza waved her left hand dismissively, tracing an arc of cigarette smoke. "More *gringos*, huh? They as crazy as you, *Pendejito*? After Loretta meets them, maybe she's gonna decide she don't want no *gringo* relatives and call the wedding off."

I had learned long ago that the only suitable approach to dealing with Esperanza was to return heavy fire. "Sod off," I replied. "If you don't want to work here, just say the word and you can march out the front door. Well?"

"¡*Vete a la chingada!*" Esperanza shouted. She held up the middle finger of her left hand and then disappeared into the kitchen.

"Bloody nuisance," I muttered, before entering the kitchen. "*Buenas tardes*, Maria," I warbled. "Apologies for being tardy. As

I attempted to explain to your sister, I was getting my mother and cousin settled in."

Maria shrugged. She waved a chef knife-wielding hand for me to come over to the counter, whilst she stirred a large pot. "You got to chop some more onions for me. Then cook more chicken for the *enchiladas*. Loretta said she would be back soon. Josefa's sick, so I made some soup for her."

Josefa was Loretta's mother. A few years after Uncle Bill's wife Celestina had died unexpectedly, he and Josefa had dated briefly, but the memory of Celestina was too strong. Years later, Josefa met a chap from Albuquerque, whom I gathered she still saw occasionally.

I retrieved an apron and stepped over to the counter, whereupon I commenced battle with the onions. "My cousin, Archie, would like to meet you and Esperanza. He was going to walk around the town for a bit and looks forward to sampling some of your best."

"Just don't you let him come into my kitchen," Maria growled, pointing her knife at the self amidship.

"No need for concern, Maria," I said, raising my hands in mock surrender. "Archie is the perfect gentleman. I shall make sure he sits quietly at the table and does not set foot in the kitchen."

She grunted an affirmation and resumed stirring a large pot violently and emitting puffs steam engine-like puffs of cigarette smoke that curled over the pot.

"Right, then," I said.

An hour or so later, Loretta strolled into the kitchen. "Hi, Bennie. Hi, *Tía* Maria," she said whilst walking to a corner where several stained aprons hung. After tying one around her waist, she approached the self and proffered a quick kiss, then glided over to Maria. "Smells good."

Maria tossed the remains of her cigarette onto the floor and crushed them violently. "How's Josefa? Is she feeling better?"

Loretta shrugged. "A little. She really liked your soup."

"The universal cure," I added.

"Are your mother and cousin at the ranch?" asked Loretta. "Have you spoken to them about the wedding?"

"Ah," I replied, after a moment's pause. "Yes, they are, although I was, er, unavoidably detained. Rudy was kind enough to rescue them from Coronado's clutches and transport them safely to Uncle Bill's."

Loretta shook her head and began to laugh. "What happened?"

"The equine nemesis happened. Whilst I was inside the barn preparing her morning meal, she jammed a metal bucket under the lower part of the door. Try as I might, I could not open it."

Loretta burst out laughing. "Only you could get locked in a barn by a horse, Bennie."

"That's 'cause El Vaquero's horse knows you're a *pendejito*," shouted Esperanza from the storage room off the kitchen. Maria merely turned around and shook her head silently before re-engaging battle with the large pot on the stove.

"And what about our wedding?" asked Loretta.

"Er, well, Mother was quite fatigued and required a lie-down. I intend to broach the subject this evening."

"And when will you introduce me to my future mother-in-law?" Loretta asked.

"Oh, er, quite soon, although Mother is not yet privy to our wedding plans."

"What? You never told her we were getting married?"

"M-hem, no," I mumbled. "Er, perhaps we should step into the dining room and discuss this privately."

"No, we will discuss it right here," growled Loretta. She eyed me suspiciously. "Why haven't you told your mother we are getting married? Are you ashamed of me? Not good enough for your family? Still thinking about that *chichona*?"

"Gah! I mean, no, of course not. I was merely planning on presenting the marriage as a *fait accompli* to her at a later date to avoid, er—"

"Avoid what?" Loretta asked icily. Her eyes narrowed, the ocular daggers aimed and ready.

"You ashamed of my niece, *Pendejito*," Esperanza growled, pointing an accusatory finger towards the self. "We ain't good enough for you *gringos?*"

"No, of course not," I said with increased volume. "As I am trying to explain—to Loretta, mind—I did not anticipate my mother would be in attendance in case there was any, er, unpleasantness regarding the ceremony and so forth."

Loretta's eyes narrowed even further. "What do you mean, 'unpleasantness'?"

Beads of sweat were forming rapidly on the Graves brow. "Well, my mother has an, er, more cosmopolitan take on life, as it were. Given the local environs, I wished to avoid any, er, upset associated with the small church wedding. It has nothing to do with you, Loretta. I did write my mother about you. She wrote back, stating, and I quote, 'She sounds like a charming young lady.' Mother also expressed the hope to meet you one day, which you shall in—" I glanced at the watch, "several hours, as Uncle Bill shall be escorting her here for dinner."

"I dunno, Loretta," said Esperanza, as she emerged from the storage room. "Sounds like more bullshit to me."

"No one asked you, Esperanza," I replied, "and God help anyone who relies on your marital counsel." I raised a middle finger to her, then turned back towards Loretta. "There is nothing to be upset about. Mother is already prepossessed to think you are a wonderful, kind-hearted soul, which you are, of course. I simply wished to avoid the inevitable nuptial complexities. Mother interjected herself into the ceremonial minutiae at my previous wedding, down to the colours and placement of the flower arrangements. As Cynthia's mother had her own strongly held views on appropriate wedding flora, it was a wonder there were no fisticuffs during the ceremony. I do not want our wedding to be burdened similarly."

"What about your father?" Loretta asked.

"Ah. This is the rare instance where Father was quite reasonable. "He considers me unworthy of marrying anyone and expressed his sympathy for the betrothed, along with the hope that she would come to her senses and abandon ship, as it were."

"Your father knows you real good, *Pendejito*," laughed Esperanza.

I sighed but said nothing. Loretta shook her head and stowed the ocular daggers. "Okay, Bennie. I think I understand. Are you going to tell her when she gets here?"

"I thought it best if I inform her of the blessed event later this evening at the ranch."

"Would you like me to be there with you?"

The grey matter pondered momentarily. "Er, perhaps it would be best if I did so alone. Although I expect the announcement will be uncontroversial, one never knows how the *materfamilias* will behave in the presence of the bride-to-be."

"Okay. But if you change your mind, let me know."

"Thanks."

"Does your cousin know about the wedding?"

"Archie? Not yet. No need to worry about him, though. I suspect Archie's concern will be confined to the available spirits. He tried the Dusty Trail and was singularly unimpressed."

Loretta laughed. "Is he at the ranch now?"

"No. He chose to wander about the town, although I suspect his wanderings will have begun and ended at Rudy's."

"What's he like, Bennie?" asked Loretta. "A stuffed shirt like someone I know."

"M-hem, yes," I said. "Archie's a bit of a rogue but I am sure you will find him charming."

"A rogue, huh? Like you, perhaps?" She laughed again.

"Well, Archie has always been quick to forgive his own trespasses, even if others were less so." I paused. "Do you really consider me a rogue, Loretta?"

"She thinks you're a *Pendejito*!" shouted Esperanza, who again burst into hyena-like laughter.

"One would think your list of insults would extend beyond '*Pendejito*'," I replied coldly. "Then again, perhaps not."

"I got lots of things I can call you," Esperanza hissed. "You want me to tell you?"

"*Basta, hermana*," Maria said firmly, pointing her chef's knife towards Esperanza. "I can't cook like this. *No más*."

"Okay," said Esperanza, somewhat chastened. "What else do you want me to do, *hermana?*"

"By all means, allow me to provide you with a list," I said. "Have you ensured the tables in the dining room are set? Cleaned all the chairs? Swept the floor? Oh, and doubtless Paco has left his unique calling card by the front door, which will want scrubbing."

Esperanza raised her middle finger, silently mouthing the words I knew only too well, and stormed into the dining room.

"You know she doesn't mean it," said Loretta.

"Eh? Of course she bloody well means it. She ought to partner with Marjorie. They could call themselves 'The Satan Sisters,' 'The Devil's Spawn,' or "The Fiend and the Filly."

"She's my aunt, Bennie," Loretta said. "You should take the high road."

"One wonders if she was switched at birth or raised by vituperative wolves."

"Bennie!"

"I know, I know. Turn the other cheek and all that. Spinning tops have turned less."

Loretta wiped a lock of hair from her forehead. "Maybe the United Nations can negotiate a truce between the two of you."

"Well, the League of Nations, was supposed to prevent all future wars. Failed rather miserably, as the kindly Mr. Hitler could attest."

Loretta's eyes darkened. "My aunt is not a Nazi, whatever you think of her. I don't want my wedding—our wedding— ruined, Bennie. Can you please, *please* ignore her."

Although I wished to point out that Esperanza would have made an excellent Gestapo officer, the more diplomatic neurons counselled verbal restraint. "Say no more, my love. All cheeks ready to come about."

I continued my *sous* chef work for Maria whilst Loretta constructed tamales and Esperanza banged away in the dining room. At four o'clock, I heard the front door open and a sloppy voice bellow. "What-ho! Is this the cousin's Michelin-starred cafe? Where are you, old chap? I'm ready for those ensheeladas you spoke of."

"Oh, no," I groaned.

Esperanza bulldozed into the kitchen, followed by an overly lubricated Archie, beer bottle clutched firmly in hand. "This your brother, *Pendejito?*" she said, raising a thumb in his direction.

"Cousin, actually."

"But surely I am like a brother to you, eh, cousin?" Archie said, as he absentmindedly waved the bottle in the air. "I must say cousin, you've got some capital chaps here. Really capital. Even the hippopotamus."

Loretta turned to me. "Hippopotamus?" she asked.

Just as I was about to respond, Coronado lolled through the kitchen door. "*Hola,*" he slurred, whilst glancing about. "*Hola,* Señor Graves. *Hola,* Loretta. *Hola,* Maria. Me and Señor Archie are real hungry. Can we have some *enchiladas,* Maria?"

"Ensheeladas sound wonderful," Archie slurred, "whatever they are. And ser-serveeza, too."

Maria turned around slowly, eyed the self, and emitted a large cloud of cigarette smoke. "Get outta my kitchen, both of you," she growled, pointing her knife menacingly. "*Ahora mismo.*"

"Oh, okay. Sorry, Maria," Coronado replied. He reversed course, wobbled dangerously, and staggered through the kitchen door.

"Indeed, quite sorry, Maria," added Archie. He bowed and then weighed anchor onto the floor.

Maria stared silently at the inert mass, then pointed her knife at me and waved it towards the door.

I shrugged, then walked over and hoisted Archie onto his feet. "Come along, cousin," I said, escorting him towards the door. "Loretta, would you prepare a fresh pot of coffee? An especially strong one. I doubt my mother will want to see Archie in this condition.

"I'm not in any condition, cousin," Archie replied.

The olfactory detected something amiss. "What is that smell?" I looked around and espied a small brownish disc next to Archie's right shoe. "Oh, bloody hell, Archie."

"What's wrong, cousin?"

I looked over my shoulder at Esperanza. "Did you not clean up Paco's *ofrenda* on the porch as you were supposed to?"

"There wasn't nothing in front of the door, *Pendejito*," she said. "Uh, Paco must have just done that."

"No doubt," I replied. "Well, whatever Paco's delivery hour, would you mind cleaning it up off the floor *before* we open for dinner?"

"You know I can't bend over 'cause of my back," Esperanza replied, holding her right hand to her hip. "Besides, it was your *gringo* brother who stepped in it."

Despite a fervent desire to launch a carronade's worth of epithets and a nearby rolling pin at Esperanza, I remained silent and escorted Archie back into the dining room. I sat him down at a corner table. "Give me your shoes, you bloody idiot."

"Why?" he asked, leaning back in the chair.

"Because our patrons will be put off if they detect an *odeur de merde*, courtesy of Paco."

"You mean the little yellowish cur I saw before?"

"That would be the offending canine," I said, as I removed Archie's shoes. "Gah," I groaned. "Just wait here and do not move." I took his shoes outside, opened the spigot for the nearby hose, and doused them thoroughly, along with the porch. When I returned inside with the clean, but dripping, shoes, I espied Loretta mopping the floor, which now smelled like disinfectant, and Archie, head bowed and nursing a cup of coffee at a nearby table.

"Thanks, Loretta," I said. "The porch is now ship-shape."

"At least you didn't scream at my aunt," she replied, whilst to-ing and fro-ing the mop.

"Er, yes."

"Your bird is quite comely," Archie whispered, his eyes focused on Loretta. "Well done, old chap."

"Finish your bloody coffee," I growled. "Do you want my mother to see you in this condition?"

"Calm yourself, cousin. A momentary lapse. Perhaps it's the altitude. Less oxygen to the brain enhances the effects of alcohol and all that, or so I am told."

Presently, Loretta strode in, bearing another cuppa. "Here, Archie," she said.

"You're an angel of mercy," replied Archie, with a wink. "Compared to you, Florence Nightingale is the merest bit of stuff."

"Thanks, uh, I guess," Loretta replied. "Um, I need to get back to the kitchen. Let me know if you want any more coffee." She turned and quickly disappeared through the kitchen door.

"Sober up, Archie," I growled. "You've made a bloody fool of yourself."

"It shan't happen again, old chap," he said. "Scout's honour. Not that I ever was a scout, but whatever it is they do, it must be honourable."

I paused as the grey matter constructed a strategy. "Animals," I said.

"What?"

"Animals. The care and feeding of Uncle Bill's four-legged's. An honourable activity fit for a scout or the wayward inebriate."

"Afraid I don't know anything about them. Animals, that is, although I dated a bird at Oxford who liked horses. I would accompany her to her father's stables. We would ride out for a picnic and, well—no need for details."

"I would prefer not to be enlightened, thank you. Although, feel free to ride Marjorie to any nearby picnics. She tolerates Uncle Bill as a passenger, but as far as I can ascertain, no one else. I certainly have no intention of putting her to the test."

"Er, what sort of menagerie does Uncle Bill possess?"

"Besides Marjorie, there are numerous cattle, including a somewhat cantankerous bull named Malcolm. And there is Daisy, of course."

"Who, or should I say what, is Daisy?"

"Daisy is Uncle Bill's twenty-five stone, *sombrero*-wearing pig. One usually finds her alighted on the front porch."

"Eh?"

"She's a pig who wears a *sombrero*. It's a large hat of sorts."

Archie draw dropped slightly. He glanced at the now empty mug he held. "Perhaps I need more coffee. I distinctly heard you say a pig that wears a large hat."

"Quite."

"What did you call it? A *sombrero*? Is that like a bowler?"

"Of course not. A bowler would provide limited protection from the sun. Anyway, you'll see her soon enough."

"A hat-wearing pig," Archie muttered. "Do the cattle wear hats, too? Perhaps the ten-gallon ones everyone wears in those John Wayne westerns?"

"No, none of the bovines are hatted. Just Daisy."

"And you want me to take care of all of them?"

"Indeed. Feed and water Marjorie, muck out her stall, and provide clean bedding. Make sure the cattle have water and alfalfa. That sort of thing. I will demonstrate for you anon."

Archie grimaced. "Muck out? As in, er, manure?"

"I gather you've some experience with muck. Something about the Eaton head's Jaguar?"

Archie stiffened. "I had nothing to do with that. I nicked the car, yes, but was blamed unfairly for the car's ultimate condition. Some thug stole it from me and, well, presumably you know the rest of the story."

"Well, Jaguar or no, you'll soon become quite familiar with manure. Marjorie produces copious quantities of the stuff."

Archie grunted. "Aunt Dorothy said this would be a nice vacation for me. Better than Cannes. I hardly think mucking out a stall qualifies."

"One needs to earn one's keep whilst domiciled at the ranch." I paused, then added, "old chap."

"Very well. And speaking of keep, I'm feeling rather peckish. Any chance of a meal?

I glanced at the watch. "Well, we open for dinner at five o'clock. But as it's half four already, I will ask Maria. I'm sure she could construct a plate of *enchiladas*."

Immediately after I said the word "*enchiladas*," I perceived a tapping on the left shoulder. I turned around. Two rodentary eyes stared back at the self.

"I gather you would like a plate of *enchiladas*, too, Coronado?" I asked.

"Thanks, Señor Graves. I'm real hungry." He sniffed at the air. "Smells real good." Although I detected only the scent of disinfectant, when it came to the presence of comestibles, Coronado would make even the most acute bloodhound jealous.

I sighed. "Very well. Can you pay this time?"

He reached into his trouser pocket and extracted a handful of greasy coins, a torn dollar bill, and an obviously used mouse trap. He slowly counted out a dollar's worth of coins and then dropped them, along with the dollar bill, on the table. "Here you go, Señor Graves. I got two dollars."

I had learned long ago not to enquire about Coronado's oddities, including the contents of his trouser pockets, and thus did not ask why he was carrying a mousetrap. Instead, I gave silent thanks that the mousetrap was *sans* rodent, then scraped the lucre off the table and into my hand. "Right, then. Two plates of *enchiladas*."

Ten minutes later, having survived Maria's volcanic rumbling about Archie's trespasses and Esperanza's complaint about how much money *El Gordo*, as she called Coronado, owed the cafe, I returned with two steaming plates and set them down on the table. "Here you are, Archie. Maria's *enchiladas*. They are *non-pareil*." But whilst Coronado hoovered his *enchiladas* and *refritos* like a starving lion, Archie merely stared at the plate and grimaced. "Something the matter?" I asked.

"Er, no, I mean, what *is* this exactly?"

"Rolled *enchiladas*. They contain a mixture of chicken, onions, and cheese. Maria smothers them in her red chile sauce, sprinkles a bit more cheese on top, and places it under the broiler. '*Muy sabrosa*,' as the locals like to say. As you can observe, Coronado is quite the fan."

"*Sí*, Señor Graves," Coronado replied, scraping his now-empty plate. "They're real good, Señor Archie."

Archie handed his untouched plate to Coronado. "Here you go, old chap. The stomach is feeling a bit unsettled."

"You sure, Señor Archie?" Coronado asked with a hopeful gleam in his eyes.

"Quite, old chap. I know a trencherman when I see one."

"Huh?"

"Never mind, Coronado," I said as he began hoovering the second plate with a voraciousness that rivalled Daisy's.

"I don't suppose you have anything a bit easier on the digestion, cousin," Archie said. "Perhaps a digestive biscuit?"

"You do have rather a greenish hue," I said. "You're not going to—"

I was interrupted by a sudden geyser onto the trousers. "Gah!" I shouted, eyeing the damage, which was now dripping onto the floor.

"Sorry, old chap," said Archie, wiping his mouth with a serviette. "I do feel better. Perhaps I had one too many."

I goggled the ruined trousers and groaned softly. "More than that, I should think. We must get this cleaned before five." I grimaced, hastened back to the kitchen, and set course for the sink.

As I burst through the door, Loretta looked up from the stove. "What happened, Bennie—oh my God, your pants!" she shouted. "Coronado again?"

"No," I replied through clenched molars. "My cousin. He went green and then, well, you can see for yourself. I'm afraid the dining room floor wants cleaning again."

"We can smell it, too, *Pendejito*," Esperanza shouted. "Get out! You're gonna ruin all the food."

"As you're so concerned about ruination, Esperanza," I replied icily, "please take a mop and bucket and swab the dining room floor, lest our forthcoming guests turn away." Before she could respond with an upturned middle finger,

I located several rags, rinsed them with scalding water, and stepped outside into the alleyway to repair the damage to the raiment.

Loretta followed me outside. "You okay, Bennie? I'm sorry I laughed about Marjorie locking you in the barn, but it's pretty funny. I guess you're having a bad day."

I sat down on a tattered chair near the door. A small pool of water began to form as water dripped off the bottoms of the trousers. "Fate has been rather vicious today." I stood up. "Well, the Graves pride may be wounded—to say nothing of the trousers—but the Graves spirit remains indomitable." I glanced down at the pool of water. "I really must change. Can you manage whilst I motor back to the ranch? I should be back within the hour."

Loretta smiled and kissed me gently. "You are something else, Benjamin Graves," she said. "By the way, try not to get locked in the house by Daisy."

"M-hem, yes."

On the way home, I encountered Uncle Bill and my mother, who were motoring into town. Rather than describe the emetic experience with Archie, I merely stated I had spilt something on my trousers and required a quick change.

Upon my return, I stepped inside and counted a dozen patrons. Uncle Bill was sitting with Archie and my mother at a table near the back wall. As I proceeded towards them, I espied "Tiny" Roybal, the well-larded, oaf-like, and execrable county sheriff, and his equally well-larded and oaf-like family.

"Hey, *gringo*," he shouted whilst motioning me towards his table. I sighed and walked towards him slowly, anticipating the usual torrent of invective about poor service that had begun on the cafe's opening night, after which I informed him of his keen resemblance to Daisy.

"Yes, er, sheriff?"

"Who are them *gringos* with El Vaquero? Is that old lady his date? And that young one looks kinda like you, just not as ugly." He laughed heartily at the feeble humour.

"The 'young one' is my cousin, Archie, and the 'old lady' is my mother. Whilst you may direct whatever invective you wish towards me, if I hear you say anything derogatory about my mother, then—"

"Then *what, gringo?*" He crossed his large arms. The spawn, having observed their patriarch do so, crossed their arms in ape-like imitation.

"Then you shan't set foot here again. No more of Maria's *enchiladas, tamales, posole*—or *sopapillas*. Then again, given the collective *avoirdupois* around the table, that may be to your benefit." A look of horror came across the spawn, who glanced hungrily at their father.

"Ow!" he cried suddenly, glaring at his wife, who had delivered a deft blow to his ankle with her shoe. "Uh, okay. Sorry, *gringo*, I didn't know she was your mother. I didn't mean nothing." He extended a large paw towards me, which I shook reluctantly.

Although the grey matter offered a menu of invective for the vocal cords to deliver, the Graves *noblesse oblige* prevailed. "Apology accepted. Now, if you'll excuse me, I must attend to my mother."

I glided over to the table where she, Uncle Bill and Archie sat. "How are you, Mother?" I asked. "Were you able to get some rest?"

"Oh, yes, dear, I did. Your Uncle and I have been catching up."

"Er, catching up, I mean, of course, you are." I eyed Uncle Bill, who shook his head in the negative, which informed me he had not yet mentioned the impending nuptials. "Yes, well, I'm glad you like it. Have you ordered?"

"Not yet. William explained you don't serve wine."

"Er, no, sorry. However, I can retrieve a bottle for you from Rudy if you like. I am sure he has a bottle of white wine sequestered somewhere on the premises, although I doubt it will meet the *Chassagne-Montrachet* or *Chateau d'Yquem* standard."

"Is he also your *sommelier*?" she asked.

Uncle Bill suppressed a laugh.

"Er, not really," I replied. "Rudy, the chap who escorted you to the ranch this morning, owns the eponymous bar and liquor store across the road. I am afraid the locals are not what one would characterise as oenophiles. They prefer beer. Isn't that right, Archie?"

"Quite, old chap," he said with a slight grin.

Mother's expression revealed palpable disappointment. "No need to bother with wine, dear," she said. "A glass of water will be fine." She paused. "Is it safe to drink?" she asked in a whisper. "I've heard one should never drink the water in undeveloped countries."

"Er, I believe the water is fine Mother. There is a deep well that provides drinking water for the town."

"Oh, all right then," she said.

"Has Uncle Bill explained the menu to you?" I asked.

"Yes, but it all seems so . . . foreign," she said warily. "What would you suggest dear?"

An image of Archie's previous emetic geyser rose in the grey matter. "May I suggest a *tamale*? Maria's *tamales* are quite delectable and not overly spicy."

"All right, dear. I once ate escargot in France. This sounds almost as exotic."

I had tried escargot once myself, with difficulty. Why the French considered a common garden pest to be a delicacy was beyond the self's comprehension. "I'm sure you will enjoy it, Mother. Uncle Bill? Your usual?"

"Yep. Green chile *enchiladas*, pard'ner," he said. "And maybe a *relleno*, too. I could eat a horse."

Although I wished to suggest a specific equine on which he could dine, I refrained from saying so to avoid offending Mother. "Right," I said. "How about you, Archie?"

Archie's countenance began to develop its previous greenish hue. "Er, perhaps just a *tamale*."

"Very well. I shall bring *sopapillas* for everyone, too."

I returned to the kitchen and informed Maria of their order, then turned to Loretta, who was placing several plates on a tray. "Did you introduce yourself to my mother?" I asked.

"I did." Loretta scowled. "She asked if we were dating. Then she mentioned your ex-wife and told me you have very high standards. What is that supposed to mean? Does your mother think I won't meet those high standards of yours?"

"Eh, what? No, I mean, of course not," I stammered. "Mother is just being, well, motherly, one supposes. Surely your mother was unsure whether I would meet your standards."

"You don't meet nobody's standards, *Pendejito*," said Esperanza, laughing. "Paco's got higher standards than you."

"*Hermana*," Maria growled. "I told you, *no más*."

"I still can't believe you never told your mother about our wedding," hissed Loretta.

"Yes, I know," I said apologetically, "but when I tell her this evening she will be delighted."

"You're marrying her?" Mother shouted when we all were seated around the fireplace back at the house. "And you never thought to inform us? This is outrageous and contemptible, Benjamin. What will your father say?"

I was quite sure that my father would utter some combination of the words "nincompoop," "wastrel," and "disappointment," before returning to his perusal of the *Times*. "I, er, that is, I meant to tell you, Mother. It, uh, slipped my mind, what with the goings-on at the ranch and such."

"Piffle, Benjamin," she replied. "I can always tell when you are shading the truth. I hesitate to ask, but do you have to marry her? If so, there is no need to toss your life away. The family has dealt with such delicate matters in the past."

"What? No, of course not."

"I know these things happen, Benjamin," she said matter-of-factly, whilst ignoring what I had just said, "even in the best of families like ours."

I stood up and folded my arms defiantly. "This is not a 'shotgun wedding' Mother," I said. "I believe that is the colloquial term used, is it not, Uncle Bill?"

"Yep," he said. "C'mon, Dorothy. Loretta's a real nice gal. There's been no hanky-panky goin' on between them."

In fact, there had been a bit of 'hanky-panky,' as Uncle Bill called it, but a Graves is not one to kiss and tell, as it were, least of all to one's mother.

Mother eyed me suspiciously. "Don't you think you should marry a nice British girl? She asked. "I could make enquiries."

I espied Archie suppressing a laugh. "This is not the eighteenth century, Mother," I said sharply. "Besides, you may recall that I *was* married to a nice British girl, who decamped with a Spanish lothario because he conversed with geraniums or some such nonsense."

"There is no need to raise your voice to me, Benjamin," she said. "Marrying below your station in life is never a good idea."

"My station in life? Mother, I was cuckolded, then unceremoniously made redundant in favour of the bank Chairman's dim-witted, mannequin-fondling nephew. Had my station fallen any further, it would have been beneath the ocean."

"Your father offered to place you in a position in New York."

"I had quite enough of banking, Mother," I sighed. "I like living here, even though I sometimes wonder whether the locals are from another planet. I intend to marry Loretta, whether you and Father approve or not."

"Where are you to be married?" she asked icily.

"The local church."

"What type of ceremony shall you be having?"

"Ceremony?" I gulped. "I mean, the usual sort. You know, 'do you, so and so, take this woman, such and such, to be your wife,' etcetera, etcetera, then, 'I pronounce you husband and wife.'"

"I am familiar with the words spoken, Benjamin. Which church?"

"The church?" I repeated. "Well, I can show you it tomorrow, if you like. Rather a quaint old building."

"Don't be an ass, Benjamin. I mean, what religion?"

"Oh, yes. It is a Catholic church. Neither Loretta nor her mother would approve of a civil ceremony."

"Is Loretta Catholic?" she asked, eyes widening.

"Er, yes. Most of the locals are, to varying degrees."

Mother shook her head. "She could convert to the Church of England. Then you can both return to London and be married in a proper church."

"I doubt Loretta would convert and her mother would certainly not approve."

"She could still be married in the church back home, where you and Cynthia were married."

"Gah," I groaned softly. "We are not returning to London for our wedding, Mother."

"Very well," Mother replied, pursing her lips tightly. "Another consequence of marrying below your station." She raised her hand quickly before I could respond. "Your fall from graces was unfortunate, Benjamin. Nevertheless, you remain a Graves. There are standards, after all."

"Indeed, Mother," I said, "and I shan't be violating them by marrying Loretta in the local Catholic church."

"C'mon, Dorothy," Uncle Bill said. "None of that highfalutin' stuff's important."

"What does that mean, William?" asked Mother.

"It means high society," I answered. "And Uncle Bill is correct. It really doesn't matter."

"Very well, Benjamin," she said. "May I at least speak with her before the wedding?"

"You spoke to her in the cafe," I replied.

Mother scowled and emitted a low harrumph. "She did not mention marriage. I mean a proper discussion. I wish to know her intentions."

"Her intentions?" I asked. "What do you mean?"

"I mean is she marrying you for money?" said Mother. "You will inherit the bulk of the family estate, after all."

I sighed. "I doubt Father wishes to leave me tuppence, much less the family estate."

"Nonsense, Benjamin," she said before standing up slowly. "Now, I am quite tired and shall say goodnight to everyone. We will continue this discussion in the morning."

"Good night, Mother," I said.

"Good night, Aunt Dorothy," said Archie. "As the Bard wrote, 'when love speaks, the voice of all the gods make heaven drowsy with the harmony.'"

"Piffle," replied Mother, as she exited stage left and down the hall to her bedroom.

I raised an eyebrow. "I never knew you were an aficionado of Shakespeare, Archie."

"I'm not," he replied. "But that particular passage did wonders for convincing a few birds of, well—"

"Say no more," I said quickly.

"Well, I'm gonna hit the hay, too, young fellas," said Uncle Bill. He stood up, stretched, and yawned. "Don't you worry, Benny. Loretta will win your mother over real fast."

"I do hope so, Uncle Bill," I said. "In any event, thank you for helping to soothe the maternal beast."

"Sure thing, pard'ner," he said with a grin. "Now, you two better get some shut-eye, too. Archie, you're gonna get a taste of ranch life in the mornin'."

"Right, then, old chap," said Archie. "Off I go."

With Mother having been appeased, if only somewhat, a calm descended over the grey matter before I drifted off. Archie had behaved himself, even if only out of self-preservation, after the afternoon's trespasses. Mother had said nothing especially untoward about Loretta. Tiny's brief and unexpected expression of humility to the self was yet another victory. The Graves ship was sailing over smooth waters. Only Fate, never one for kind hearts or coronets when it came to the goings-on in Vaca Seca, at least those involving the self, was ready to despatch heavy weather.

Chapter 5

The next morning harkened bright and sunny; the local birds sang gaily to one other and the cattle lowed. Even Marjorie had absorbed the bucolic air, allowing me to approach her without despatching a hoof at the self's leg. God indeed was in his heaven; all was right with the world. After a breakfast featuring a fine marmalade Mother had brought, I educated a grumbling Archie on the care and feeding of the menagerie and motored to the cafe whistling a happy tune.

When I arrived, Maria was already in the kitchen and holding a bag of onions at knifepoint whilst she puffed away like a locomotive. Maria informed me that Loretta was still Florence Nightingaling Josefa, and would arrive late morning. She also said that Esperanza had motored to Santa Fe to see her oafish boyfriend, Hector Castillo—the very thought of whom caused a shudder through the Graves keel—as I had once encountered Esperanza at her home, entertaining Hector. She was dressed in a short, pink satin robe, which was tied loosely about her waist. Try as the neurons might, they had never been able to erase that terrifying image. No doubt Lucifer himself would assure new arrivals that, whilst they might spend eternity burning in pools of magma, even he would not resort to such a cruel punishment

I retrieved the broom and dustpan and returned to the porch. Paco had deposited his usual gift, and the steps were also covered with dirt and several discarded serviettes. I swept the steps from top to bottom and stepped onto the ground. Feeling a presence, I turned around. Before me stood a large, oval-shaped figure whom I had never seen. Despite the warmth and sunshine, she wore a full-length yellow mackintosh, along with a matching hat and rubber boots, which made her resemble an overfed goldfish standing on its tail. As I goggled her, she screamed, moved towards me, and struck the left shoulder with a large umbrella.

"Gah!" I shouted. "What the bloody—?"

"¡*Diablo*! ¡*Diablo*!" she screamed and began swinging the umbrella at me again, this time landing a blow on the right arm.

Angered, I snatched the weapon from her hands. "Are you barking mad?" I shouted whilst backing away. "Who are you? Why are you striking me?"

"Give me my umbrella!" She thrust out a pudgy hand, which anchored itself onto the tip, and ripped it from my hand.

"Sod off, you bloody madwoman."

She lowered the umbrella and stared at me blankly. Then she turned around and began walking down the road.

Shaken by the encounter, I despatched the self into the relative safety of Rudy's. Inside, I espied the eponymous owner behind the bar, drying glasses.

"You okay, Bennie?" Rudy said, eyeing me lazily. "You look like you've seen a ghost."

"Unless the local ghosts have taken to striking people with umbrellas, then no. I was sweeping the steps outside the front door of the cafe when a madwoman appeared out of nowhere. She began shouting wildly and then struck my shoulder with her umbrella."

"Umbrella?" Rudy laughed as he glanced out the window. "Looks sunny to me."

"Not just an umbrella. She looked like a member of the National Lifeboat."

"Huh?" Rudy asked. "What's that?"

"It's a British association. Volunteers who man lifeboats to rescue mariners and such."

"Do they use umbrellas?"

"Eh, what? No, that is, I don't believe so. I mean, she was dressed like one of the volunteers. She wore a yellow mackintosh and hat—"

"What's a 'mackintosh'?"

"A raincoat."

Rudy stiffened and his eyes widened. "Did you say she was wearing a raincoat?"

"Yes."

"Did she have on rubber boots, too?"

"Yes, as a matter of fact, she did. How did you know?"

"*Dios mio!*" he shouted, "It's *La Loca.*"

"*La Loca*? An apt description, I should think. You know this woman?"

Rudy moaned and rubbed the back of his neck. Although it was still morning, he retrieved two glasses and poured generous doses of one of his better whiskies into each. "Here name's Porfiria Alcalde," he moaned. "I didn't think she would ever come back." Rudy shook his head, then emptied his glass. Pouring a second, he walked over to a table, pulled out a chair, sat down heavily, and motioned me over. "Sit down, Bennie. You think Esperanza is bad. She's a saint compared to Porfiria."

I sat as instructed and grimaced. "Worse than Esperanza? Granted, I admit Esperanza has never attempted to biff me with an umbrella, although she has lobbed tins of hominy at me. Oh, and once a frozen pork shoulder."

"Like I said, Porfiria is something else. She grew up here. She was always a little strange, and as she got older, she got worse. Her mother, Adela, spoiled her. When Porfiria was a little girl, she would dig up everyone's flowers and throw them into the road. People would complain, but Adela just shrugged and said 'Porfiria has a very delicate sense of smell. The scent of flowers upsets her.'"

Thoughts of Rodrigo drifted through the grey matter.

Rudy continued. "Like I said, things got a lot worse as she got older. She would sometimes sit in the middle of the road—right outside the bar—and start shouting."

"At whom?" I asked.

"Nobody," Rudy said. "That was what was so strange. She would be out there having a conversation with herself. So, everybody started calling her '*La Loca*.' If a woman walked by, she would turn away. But if it was a guy, she would shout, '¡*Diablo!*' and attack them. Happened to me once. If she was anywhere near the bar, nobody would come in, not even Nestor."

I rubbed my still-sore shoulder and raised the eyebrows. "That is what she shouted at me before launching her attack. But why does she hate the male of the species? Spurned highschool romance, that sort of thing?"

"You mean other than because she's crazy?"

"Well, compared with my encounter, a March hare is a paragon of sanity. At least they do not attack passers-by with umbrellas."

"Anyway, a few months after Porfiria's older sister Consuela was born, her father, Ramón Alcalde, passed away. Adela was never the same. Everybody tried to help her. They would bring her meals, vegetables from their gardens, that sort of thing.

"At first, Adela accepted the help. But after a few months, she wouldn't even answer the door. She would tell them to go away. People would leave the stuff by the door and that's where it would stay. Adela wouldn't even take it. So, people stopped bringing things over.

"Then she left. She didn't tell anybody where she was going. But Nestor was in Santa Fe one day and he ran into Adela in a grocery store, where she was working as a cashier. He asked how she was doing, but she didn't even answer him."

"About three years later, Adela walks into Joe's store, like she had never left. She had moved back with Consuela and now had little Porfiria, too. Adela wouldn't say who Porfiria's father was. She found a rundown old adobe outside of town, a little past where Nestor lives. She lived there for almost ten years. Adela would come into town and go to Joe's store to buy what she needed. Maybe she went to Española, too. Nobody knew where she got her money.

"The girls went to school here. People would ask Consuela how her mother was, but all she would ever say was, "She's okay." Porfiria would just stand next to Consuela but wouldn't say anything. Even Joe felt sorry for them. He would give them candy. One winter, they came to school without coats, so Joe gave them each a big winter coat."

"Joe Garcia offered charity?" I asked incredulously, as Joe had never hinted of being the loaves and fishes sort.

Rudy continued. "Yeah, well, by the time Porfiria was in high school, she was always wearing that same outfit you saw. If you asked her why, she would start screaming and run away. People asked Adela why, but Adela just shrugged. Her older sister, Consuela, said that Porfiria was afraid of signals coming from the Sun and the Moon."

"Eh, what? Signals? Do you mean from space aliens?"

Rudy shrugged. "I dunno. The boys were terrified of her. She was big and real strong."

I rubbed my right arm. "Indeed," I muttered.

Rudy nodded. "Back then, Maria worked part-time at the school as a janitor. She told me that she was cleaning a classroom one afternoon after school when Porfiria walked in. Porfiria grabbed some chalk and threw it at Maria. Maria picked the chalk up off the floor but didn't say anything. She just put the chalk back on the blackboard. Then she walked over to Porfiria, looked her in the eye, and said '*No más.*' You know that look, Bennie."

"Er, yes, only too well," I said. "A charging rhinoceros on the receiving end of one of Maria's looks would pull up short and apologise profusely."

Rudy laughed. "Yeah, that's the one. I've gotten it a few times."

"Did Maria tell you what happened after that?"

"She said Porfiria never gave her any more trouble. If Porfiria saw Maria, she would just lower her head. Then one day, about a year after Consuela had graduated and moved away, Adela and Porfiria just disappeared. Nobody ever saw them again. But five years later, Porfiria gets off the bus with a suitcase, wearing her raincoat and hat."

"By herself? Where did she live?"

"She moved back into that same old adobe," Rudy replied. "Adela, or maybe it was Consuela, sent her money every month. Luis felt bad for her and fixed up an old car he had at the Texaco station. Most days, she would park the car up the road and walk around town. Sometimes she would sit outside the bar. If anyone tried to talk to her, she would stick out her arm and say, 'Don't talk to me.' Like I said, even Nestor was afraid to come inside."

"Biffing chaps with her umbrella then, as well?"

"No. That's new. She didn't have an umbrella then. About a year later, she disappeared again. We just assumed Adela or Consuela had put her into the state mental hospital in Las Vegas."

"You mean the loony bin?" I asked.

Rudy raised an eyebrow. "Don't you have them back home?" he asked.

"Oh, yes. No shortage of nutters, although I never encountered one shouting '*Diablo*' at the locals. I do recall one rather odd chap when Cynthia and I were living in Kensington. Every day, he would walk about the neighbourhood holding his mother's hand."

"What's wrong with that?"

"Nothing really, except that he insisted she was an invisible kangaroo. He would boast about her pugilistic abilities, too. Claimed his mother had once knocked out Dick Richardson in the third round."

Rudy shook his head. "Whoa. At least he wasn't violent."

"And now Porfiria has returned to cry '¡*Diablo*!' and let slip the umbrellas of war," I said. "In England, the local constabulary can toss nutters into the loony bin, at least temporarily. Perhaps we should ask Tiny to escort her to Las Vegas?"

Rudy laughed and shook his head. "Tiny? Are you kidding? You know what he's like. Besides, he tried once. She was outside the bar yelling. Tiny was in the bar. He came out, told her to shut up, and grabbed her arm. She swung around and hit him. Knocked him out cold. From then on, if he saw her, he would run the other way. And I mean run. You ever see Tiny run?"

I laughed. "No, although I have observed him waddling towards the cafe whilst holding his belt, which I assume prevents his stomach from dragging across the macadam. I would have quite enjoyed seeing Porfiria's knockout punch."

"Yeah. Maybe Porfiria could have knocked out your Dick Richardson."

Presently, the front door burst open and Coronado walked inside. He sat down on a bar stool, removed his cap, and rubbed the top of his head. "Rudy, you gotta come quick. ¡*Hijole*! It's *La Loca*. She's come back. She hit me on the head." He rubbed his head again, then turned and stared at me blankly. "*Hola*, Señor Graves. Did *La Loca* hit you, too?"

"She did indeed, Coronado," I said. "Landed several blows before retreating into the shadows. Rudy was recounting the rather bizarre history."

Coronado eyed me blankly, then turned to Rudy. "Can I have a beer?"

Rudy opened a bottle and placed it on the bar before Coronado. "Thanks." He raised the bottle to his lips and drained it entirely, then put the now empty bottle on top of the bar. "Can I have one more, Rudy? I'm real thirsty."

"All right," said Rudy. "Do you have any money today?"

Coronado stuffed a pudgy hand into his right pocket and retrieved the used mousetrap I had seen previously. "Sorry, Rudy," he said whilst examining the contents in his hand. "But I can pay you later this week after Joe pays me."

Coronado was employed, to use the term loosely, by Joe Garcia at the general store, presumably because no one else in the town was willing to labour under Joe's mercurial wrath and *de minimis* wages. Coronado seemed not to mind. Joe would yell at Coronado, who would smile and say, "Sorry, Joe." Joe would then storm away, cursing, and Coronado would continue blithely doing whatever it was that had caused Joe to erupt. It seemed an ideal arrangement.

Rudy shook his head. "One more, Coronado. Jesus, you must owe me a couple hundred bucks by now."

Coronado shrugged, then quickly drained the entire contents of the second bottle.

I stood up. "Well, thanks for the history, Rudy. Now, I must return to the cafe. With any luck, *La Loca* will have wandered off by now. Does she tend to enter buildings or just loiter outside?"

"She's never come in here if that's what you're asking," Rudy said. "But she never hit people with umbrellas, either. So, who knows what she's gonna do now? But look on the bright side, Bennie. You should be able to outrun her."

"M-hem, yes," I replied. "Well as they say, the valiant die only one death whilst cowards die a thousand." I opened the front door slowly and peered up and down the road in search of the enemy. "Right then, over the top and into battle." I stepped onto the *portal*, which was deserted, then bounded across the road to the cafe, dashed up the front steps, and entered the relative safety of the dining room.

Inside, I espied Loretta preparing the dining room for the luncheon onslaught. "Hullo, dearest one," I chirped.

She glanced up from the table where she was placing silverware. "Hi, Bennie. Where have you been? It's almost lunchtime."

"Er, sorry. I was attacked earlier this morning by a raincoat-wearing, umbrella-biffing woman who looks like an overfed goldfish. After the attack, I dashed into Rudy's. He relayed the sordid history of this woman, whom I gather the town refers to as '*La Loca*.'"

Loretta's eyes widened. "She's back? Oh, no! When?"

I glanced at the watch. "About an hour ago. I was sweeping the steps outside."

"No, I mean, when did she come back here?"

"Ah. Afraid I don't know that. Presumably, not long ago, as no one else has mentioned any umbrella attacks. I take it you have encountered her previously?"

Loretta nodded. "I was in high school the last time. She would come inside and go to the principal's office to complain that students were smoking and drinking outside. She said she could smell the smoke at her house."

"Eh? Rudy said she was living in an old adobe near where Nestor now lives. Isn't the high school in Ojo Madera? That must be, what, twenty miles from here and in the opposite direction?"

Loretta shook her head slowly. "Uh-huh. After the third time, the principal started locking the school doors. So, she waited until the end of the day. When he came out, she would start complaining to him again."

"Rudy also informed me that Tiny will be of no help. Apparently, her pugilistic abilities were sufficient to deliver a knock-out blow to him."

Loretta laughed. "Yeah, everybody knew about that. Even the little kids in town would come up to him and say, 'Want to fight, *perderdor*? I bet I can knock you out like that girl.' He would tell them to shut up and then walk away."

"*Perderdor*? What does that mean?"

"Sorry, Bennie. It means 'loser.'"

"Ah, the perceptiveness of youth. Rather like the emperor with no clothes, although the visual image of Tiny *sans* raiment is not one to be entertained lightly. What finally happened? Did anyone stop her?"

"After a few weeks, she just stopped. Never came to the school again."

I paused. "She must have encountered your aunts at some point. Unstoppable force meets immovable objects."

Loretta's eyes narrowed. "*Tia* Esperanza always avoided Porfiria. Believe it or not, back then she wasn't as, well, you know—"

"Say no more," I interrupted, raising the right hand. "I gather your aunt stored up her a life's worth of vituperation like one of those large dams, only to release it upon the self's arrival. Anyway, what about Maria?"

"Only once. I think it was on a *tamale* day. Porfiria had been standing in line, waiting like everyone else, but *Tía* Maria ran out before she could get any. So, Porfiria came up to *Tía* Maria and started shouting. *Tía* Maria picked up one of her knives, turned around to face Porfiria and shook her head slowly. She didn't say one word. Porfiria walked away and never went near *Tía* Maria again."

"The strong, silent type, our Maria. Should I tell her Porfiria has returned?"

"Maybe after lunch, Bennie."

"Quite. One would not wish to upset Maria whilst she prepares meals for the customers. Right then, let me help you with the dining room preparation and then I will assess our supplies. That should do it."

"Benjamin Graves," Loretta said slowly, "you haven't said anything about last night. What did your mother say about the wedding?"

"Ah. Well, she was rather surprised, of course, and questioned whether it was what Uncle Bill terms a 'shotgun wedding.' By the end of the evening, however, she was satisfied."

"She thought you were marrying me because you *had* to," Lorretta rumbled.

"What? No, I mean, of course not," I stammered, attempting to calm the looming eruption. "Mother was—"

"Go on," said Loretta.

I decided to omit Mother's concern about Loretta's being Catholic. "Er, nothing really. She would like to speak with you later today. Why don't you come up to the ranch this afternoon? I can stay here and assist Maria."

"Is that all she told you?" Loretta growled.

I gulped. "Er, yes. Why?"

"I'm sorry, Bennie. I guess I'm just nervous. I'm sure your mother is very nice. I know it was hard for you to speak with my mother."

I took Loretta's hand in mine. "I think you will like her. Mother has always been kind and level-headed."

"Okay, Bennie," she replied as she kissed me quickly.

At around half three, I was in the kitchen assisting Maria by constructing *tamales*. My initial forays after I had first arrived had been less than successful, described as looking like horse-shit by Esperanza, much to her amusement. Of course, given my extensive experience mucking out Marjorie's stall, I now knew that Esperanza's description was inaccurate.

Presently, the kitchen door burst open, admitting Loretta, who steamed inside and over to the counter where I was assembling the *tamales*. Without warning, she launched a fist into the right shoulder.

"Gah!" I cried. "What was that for?"

"She asked me if *I* was going to convert."

I groaned. "Mother asked you to convert?"

"She said it would be better for *me*. What's that supposed to mean?"

"Why don't we discuss this in the dining room," I said, taking Loretta's hand to escort her out of the kitchen.

"You stay here and tell us, *Pendejito*," said Esperanza. "We're family."

"Sod off, Esperanza," I said calmly.

"*Hermana*," said Maria, interrupting her pot-stirring, "leave them alone."

A temporarily chastened Esperanza raised her middle finger, then turned away.

We sat down at one of the tables. "There's no need for you to convert, Loretta. The Graves have always been Church of England types, but none have been what one might term 'fire and brimstone' about it, as I recall. Mother would attend services every Sunday, but my father rarely did, especially after he discovered the local priest voted Labour. And you know it matters not one whit to me."

"Did you tell your mother we are getting married in a Catholic church?"

"Yes. I informed her we were to be married in the local Catholic church."

"Did you tell her the rest?" asked Loretta.

"Eh? I don't understand. Are we not getting married in the local church?"

"We are, but there's a problem."

I goggled at Loretta. "I still don't understand."

"We can't get married in the church unless you convert."

"Gah! You mean *I* must convert?"

"Uh-huh," said Loretta, nodding her head. "Besides, my mother insists on it. So does *Tía* Esperanza. *Tío* Joe said he doesn't care. He said you're going to burn in hell anyway, so it doesn't matter whether you convert."

"Always the open-minded chap, your uncle," I said. "I always assumed your mother would be indifferent to the matter. As for Esperanza—"

"That's right, *Pendejito*," chortled Esperanza, who had opened the kitchen door stealthily and listening in. "No conversion, no Loretta, and no nothing else. ¿*Comprende?*" She began making a rude gesture with her fingers.

"*Tía* Esperanza, that's horrible," shouted Loretta.

"Sorry, Loretta," she replied, insincerely. "*Pendejito* understands."

I glared at Esperanza.

"Please don't say it, Bennie," begged Loretta, wagging her index finger. "Can't you two get along, at least until after the wedding?"

Esperanza shrugged her shoulders, grunted, and retreated back to the kitchen. I shook my head in resignation. "Very well. Are you quite sure Josefa would not be a bit more, forgiving, as it were?"

"Not when it comes to my marriage," Loretta said. "Besides, Father Castillo won't marry us unless you convert."

Father Castillo was what Uncle Bill called a "circuit riding" priest who served numerous small towns and villages over a large area that extended into southern Colorado. He held services in the town's small church every eighth Sunday. On other Sundays, services were led by various locals, including, oddly enough, Joe Garcia, who presumably never preached about the second deadly sin. I knew Loretta attended these occasionally, but I had never met the good Father.

"Yes, but we've both been married previously," I said. "Besides, I was given to understand that divorce was one of those 'thou shalt not's' for Catholics, with penalties of excommunication, burning in Hell, and all that."

"I know, but my mother said Father Castillo would understand because of how Jaime treated me."

"Ah, yes. I had forgotten about that blackguard."

Jaime was Loretta's ex-husband. On our first date, Loretta had confided to me about their marriage, or rather its unravelling. They had lived in Santa Fe, where he worked at the local lumber yard. He was also a drunkard who hit her, something completely foreign to the Graves code. She sensibly divorced him, despite the religious prohibitions.

"I understand Father Castillo's providing dispensation for you. But I rather doubt he would provide the same for one whose wife was swept away by a geranium-whispering cad. As for my mother, her position on the matter is clear. Granted, my father will not care; Catholic, Protestant, or Druid, he will still think me a nincompoop."

"You need to confront your mother," said Loretta. "We can't get married unless you convert, Bennie. It doesn't mean you have to go to church every week. Besides, what else can we do?"

"I recall suggesting the local magistrate's office. Or eloping, which one imagines comes to the same thing."

"I couldn't do that to my mother. She would be heartbroken. I'm all she has." Tears began to well up in Loretta's eyes.

I groaned internally. Even the most battle-hardened Graves would melt in the presence of tears produced by the fairer sex. "All right, Loretta," I said, squeezing her hand. I shall reach some form of *modus vivendi* with my mother." I paused. "Perhaps if I convince her that my conversion will be the Potemkin Village sort," I said, half to myself.

"Huh? What's that mean?" asked Loretta.

"How you gonna convert in some village, *Pendejito?*" asked Esperanza, who had scurried back into the dining room like a roach. "You got to do it here with Father Castillo."

"It means a fraudulent, er, well, anyway, during the reign of Catherine the Great, Grigoriy Potemkin was charged with—"

"What the fuck are you talking about?" growled Esperanza. "You gonna convert or not?"

"Er, yes," I mumbled. "I will inform my mother."

Loretta wrapped her arms around me. "Oh, Bennie, thank you. It will mean a lot to *my* mother and everyone else here."

I was fortunate that Loretta could not see my bulging eyes and dropped jaw whilst she embraced the self. Between an umbrella-biffing loon who believed I was the Devil and my impending conversion, the grey matter pondered whether an exorcism was soon to follow. It was then an idea surfaced in the grey matter, like that of a spouting whale. "Er, Loretta, it occurs to me that I will need to discuss this with Father Castillo himself. I mean, he will want to know about my marriage to Cynthia and such, will he not? Plus, he will surely wish to provide some sort of menu of tasks I will need to perform. You know, how many 'Hail Mary's' and 'Our Father's' to recite, that sort of thing."

Loretta released her embrace and sat upright. "Yes, he will want to speak with you about it and tell you what you need to do. Don't worry, Bennie. I already told him about your previous marriage. "But he will want you to attend confession."

"Confession? What am I supposed to confess to?"

"You know. You tell Father Castillo your sins and then he offers you absolution."

"Maybe he won't, *Pendejito,*" said Esperanza. "He don't like *gringos.*"

"Will you please just sod off," I said, exasperated. "After Loretta and I have finished, I promise I shall return to the kitchen where you may hurl additional epithets at the self. Until then, sod off!"

"Okay, *Pendejito,*" said Esperanza. "No way Father Castillo's gonna accept your confession. You sin just 'cause you're here."

Rather than respond to Esperanza, I turned yet another cheek until it was ready to snap. Esperanza, apparently needing to recharge her epithets, then returned to the kitchen. I whispered in Loretta's ear. "Have we not, er, 'sinned' *in re*: the upcoming marriage? Isn't that punishable by keelhauling or hanging from the nearest yardarm?" Loretta accelerated a fist into the right shoulder. "Gah! That's the precise spot where you biffed me earlier."

"Be quiet," Loretta hissed softly. "Don't say anything about that. I don't want the whole town to know."

"Isn't what one tells one's priest held in the strictest confidence?" I asked.

Loretta gave me one of those "You cannot possibly be that dim-witted" looks the fairer sex is well known for. "It's a small town, Bennie—*very* small."

"Right-ho. Priestly gossip and all that."

"And don't *ever* say anything to my mother."

"To Josefa? Fear not, Loretta. One never speaks of such things to any mother. Nor does one ever contemplate one's parents' past behaviour that led to one's existence," I added, shuddering. "As for Father Castillo, I take it I should merely confess minor sins?"

Her eyes narrowed. "Are there any other kind I should know about?"

"What? No, of course not. I mean, during my Cambridge days I engaged in some laddish behaviour like most of the chaps, but that was many years ago."

"I meant more recent behaviour. Like Sunflower recent." Loretta's eyes narrowed further whilst she readied the ocular daggers for mass firing.

I made the sign of the cross. "We've been through all of that, Loretta," I said, raising the right hand. "Nothing happened, despite Sunflower's entreaties. You have my word as a gentleman, which a Graves does not give lightly."

Loretta stowed the ocular daggers. "All right, Bennie. I believe you."

"Anything else I need to know about the good Father?"

"He wants to baptise you, too."

"What? You mean hold-the-chap-under-the-water and what-not? I believe I was previously submerged at a tender age, then Father-Son-and-Holy-Ghosted."

"It doesn't matter. Father Castillo said you have to be baptised as a Catholic. That's part of your conversion."

I groaned. "Is a Catholic baptism that different from the Church of England version? Will he see how long I can hold my breath underwater?"

"It's not different," Loretta replied. "I know it all sounds silly, but it's mostly just to please my mother."

I rubbed my forehead, which was beginning to ache. "All right. At least promise that Paco won't allowed near the baptismal basin."

Chapter 6

The remainder of the afternoon proceeded on course. There were no further sightings of Porfiria, although news of her reappearance had spread quickly. The locals appeared to be waiting in anticipation for an unseen enemy whom they thought would reappear at any moment, and the *viejos* who normally sat on Rudy's *portal* instead disappeared to the relative safety of the bar.

Nestor staggered into the cafe and was immediately interrogated—had he seen *La Loca* at the old adobe?—but he only shrugged before sitting down with a six-pack he had purchased from Rudy and ordering *tamales*. Each time the cafe's front door opened, everyone turned towards it fearfully. Anyone about to depart would open the front door slowly and peer up and down the road before exiting. Even Paco appeared to be exercising greater caution. On his normal afternoon micturition rounds, which left few vehicles and doorways untouched, I espied him peering out cautiously from underneath the lorries before dashing to his next target.

Uncle Bill brought Mother and Archie back to the cafe for dinner. Archie offered to procure a bottle of wine for Mother as soon as they were seated, but she declined politely. He then announced he was setting course for Rudy's to secure a bottle of beer and would return shortly, before sprinting out the front door.

"How are you, Mother?" I asked. "Did you and Loretta have a nice chat. Are you and Uncle Bill catching up?"

"She seems to be a pleasant young lady," said Mother, who then sighed. "I suggested she convert, for your sake, but I am not hopeful." Mother now pointed to Uncle Bill. "I've tried to convince William to write to your father. And you should too, Benjamin. Gerald is quite proud of you."

The eyebrows rocketed upwards. "Did you say, 'Father is proud of me?' I sputtered. "I rather doubt that, as the words 'nincompoop' and 'pride' are rather incompatible with one another."

"You must forgive him, dear. He means well. And so should you, William."

Uncle Bill glanced at me, then turned back to my mother. "Look, Dorothy," he began. "I've been here since before the war. It's home. I don't want that high falutin' life. Never did. And having Bennie here has been a blessing." He arced his arm around the room. "Celestina worked here. It meant a lot to her. After she died, everything went to hell. If it wasn't for Bennie, we wouldn't be sitting here. I know it ain't much, but I can almost see Celestina whenever I come here."

"You never told me that, William. And neither did you, Benjamin. Of course, your father will be proud of you for doing this. I expect you to write him tomorrow."

"Er, yes, Mother," I said, sheepishly. "Now, what would you like for dinner?"

"I think I will have those *enchiladas* William ate yesterday. They did smell good. But not too spicy. Your father and I tried some of that new East Indian food a few months ago. I can't remember what it was called, but it left us both with dyspepsia."

"Mild *enchiladas*, it is then," I said. "What about you, Uncle Bill?"

"How about Maria's *tacos* tonight, pard'ner?"

"Your wish is my command, Uncle Bill." I glanced at the watch. "Archie seems to have been delayed. Would you like me to dash over to Rudy's and retrieve him, Mother?"

"That's all right, dear. He's an adult. I'm sure he's making new friends. You know how gregarious your cousin is."

I assumed Archie would be several gregarious sheets to the wind before his return and hoped my trousers would avoid any resulting emetic entanglements. "Er, yes, he is that."

The dinner crowd was above average in numbers. After delivering Mother's and Uncle Bill's meals to them, I was fully occupied to-ing and fro-ing between the kitchen and dining room. As Esperanza continued to complain about her back, Loretta took over waitressing duties. Meanwhile, each time I entered the kitchen, I espied Esperanza standing next to Maria and jabbering away, whilst adding the odd rude gesture in my direction.

After we closed for the evening, Loretta and I spiffed the dining room. Archie never returned, so I assumed he had either secured a lift back to the ranch or was still in the bar. I bid Loretta goodnight, closed and locked the front door, descended the steps, and was immediately set upon by Porfiria.

"¡*Diablo!*" she screamed, readying her umbrella for a strike. "Don't look at me, *gringo*. ¡*Diablo!*"

"Avast, you madwoman!" I shouted, as I dodged the swinging umbrella and hoofed it towards Rudy's. I opened the door, ran inside, slammed the door shut, and locked it. Six pairs of eyes, including those belonging to Nestor, Joe Garcia, and Archie goggled me. "She's out there again. Keep the door locked."

The doorknob rattled, followed by a loud pounding on the door. "I know you're in there *Diablo*," she yelled. Finally, after several excruciating minutes, the pounding ceased.

"Gah, why me?" I whimpered.

Archie raised his bottle. "I say, old chap. The wicked witch after you again? How about a snifter to take the edge off?"

I sat down heavily on one of the bar stools. "A large Dusty Trail, if you please, Antonio," I said.

"Sure, Señor Graves." He placed a glass in front of me and poured a large dose. I reached into my trouser pocket, extracted a dollar bill, and set it down on the bar. "Is your grandfather in the back office?"

"No. He said he had to do some stuff at home and asked me to lock up."

"Very well. Thank you, Antonio." I downed the Dusty Trail and stood up. "Right, Archie. Let's return you to the ranch. I need to speak with Mother."

"It's not even nine o'clock, cousin."

"Yes, but the four-legged's will want attention early in the morning. You know, early bird, worm, and such."

"Can they not get their own worms?" he asked, before standing up and stretching. "Very well, cousin." He turned to the seated patrons. "Well, good night, chaps," he said, raising an imaginary class. "I mustn't turn into a pumpkin at midnight, or perhaps nine o'clock."

"*Buenos noches*, Archie," they replied in unison, whilst raising empty beer bottles. "Thanks for buying the drinks."

"Hey, *gringo*," Joe shouted, pointing an empty beer bottle at me, "how come you don't buy nobody drinks like your cousin, here?" The others nodded.

"I shall be happy to do so, Joe, immediately after you do the same."

Joe grunted. "I give you lots of money to you, *gringo*. You don't pay full price for stuff."

"And I shan't do so. Unless, of course, you would prefer I took the cafe's business elsewhere. To Sabrosa Foods, perhaps?"

Joe muttered something untoward under his breath but said nothing further.

"Right, Archie, let us be off." I unlocked the front door and surveilled the surroundings to see if Porfiria was still present. Determining that the coast was clear, Archie and I dashed back to the lorry, which was parked around the side of the cafe, and motored back to the ranch.

"Drinking one's dinner, eh, Archie?"

"No worries, cousin. The young publican provided some sandwiches and Joe Garcia brought several bags of crisps. That older chap's yellow cur was inside the bar for most of the evening. A friendly little beast. Seems to like crisps."

"Bloody dog is a menace," I replied. "One hopes it will soon meet its heavenly reward."

"Now, now, cousin, we must always be kind to animals," said Archie, yawning. "Perhaps you are right about the early bird. I am rather knackered this evening." He soon nodded off and I drove the remainder of the way in silence.

Arriving at the ranch, Archie awakened with a start. He slid out of his seat and walked slowly onto the portal by the front door. Daisy grunted. "Sorry to disturb you, old girl," he said, doffing an invisible hat.

Inside, Mother and Uncle Bill were sitting by the fireplace. Archie announced he was retiring for the night and slouched towards the self's bedroom, where Uncle Bill had set out a mattress.

"Busy evening, dear?" Mother asked.

"Rather," I answered, as I sat down heavily on the sofa. "I hope you enjoyed your dinner."

"It was quite good, thank you. Although I do wish you could serve wine."

"Yes, well, one must cater to the clientele, Mother."

Uncle Bill arose from his chair and stretched. "Well, all, I'm gonna mosey off to bed, too. Got to get an early start tomorrow. Bennie, will you take care of the fire before you go to bed?"

"Of course, Uncle Bill. Good night."

"Goodnight, William," said Mother.

"Goodnight, Dorothy."

Uncle Bill disappeared down the hall and closed his bedroom door.

"Now, dear, I wish to discuss the wedding with you," said Mother, eying the self suspiciously.

I gulped. "Er, yes?"

"Have you asked Loretta to convert? I can only imagine what Gerald will say if he has a Catholic daughter-in-law."

"Er, yes, the subject did come up and Loretta and I agreed."

"Good, then it's settled."

"M-hem. Well, the wedding will be held in the local church and presided over by Father Castillo. You must understand, Mother, that most of the townspeople are Catholic, as is Loretta's mother and her other relatives."

"I suppose the actual ceremony doesn't matter," said Mother, sighing. "And it's good that this Father Castillo doesn't mind you're not being Catholic. Will the ceremony be non-denominational?"

"Non-denominational? Er, not exactly."

"What do you mean, Benjamin, and why are you turning red?"

"Eh, red? Merely the heat of the fireplace, I should think." I fanned the self's face and felt beads of perspiration forming above the brow.

"You haven't answered my question, Benjamin."

"The ceremony? I, er, my understanding is that it will follow the Catholic tradition. A mere formality, one imagines, what?"

"You're perspiring, dear. I can always tell you aren't being fully truthful when you perspire." She folded her hands together and placed them in her lap. "Now, let's have it."

"Er, well, as I mentioned, it shall be a Catholic ceremony. There are a few minor items to be taken care of beforehand."

Mother tilted her head downward and eyed the self from over her reading glasses. "Such as?"

"M-hem, yes. Loretta has informed me I shall need to meet with the good Father before the ceremony. Assess my *bona fides*, vis-à-vis the matrimonial bond with Loretta, that sort of thing.

"Just a meeting with the priest? Nothing else, Benjamin?"

There are times when Fate takes the tide at flood, enabling the enemy's cannons to be fired at point-blank range. This was one such time. "Er, I gather my presence will be required in the priestly confessional. Not that I have any sins needing absolution, other than perhaps wishing Marjorie to be converted into tinned meat. I mean, I rather doubt the good Father is expecting a complete catalogue of sins since I wore short pants."

"Confession?" shouted Mother, her eyes goggling me. "Next you will tell me you are going to be baptised."

"Er, only in spirit."

"Only in spirit, Benjamin," shouted Mother. "What else is there? I'm beginning to understand why your father called you a nincompoop. You are not thinking this through."

It was one thing for the *paterfamilias* to describe the self as a "nincompoop." That was in keeping with his other descriptors, including ass, buffoon, carbuncle, and several others of a cruder nature. But when one's mother resorts to hurling slings and arrows, then presumably one has excavated a deep hole and binned oneself into it with a shovel.

Fortunately, before I could continue my verbal excavation with an untoward remark, I was rescued by Uncle Bill, who walked into the sitting room. "What's all the commotion?" he asked, stifling a yawn.

"William," Mother said sternly, "my son—your nephew—intends to convert. He will also be baptised by the priest who will marry them. You simply must bring him to his senses."

Uncle Bill rubbed his chin and stifled a second yawn. He eyed me warily. "Loretta asked you to convert and be baptised, Bennie?"

"Er, in a manner of speaking, Uncle Bill. Loretta informed me that Mrs. Alvarez was rather insistent, as was Father Castillo. I had always assumed Mrs. Alvarez was more the 'live and let live' type, but apparently not, at least when it comes to the marriage of her daughter. So, if we are to be married in the local church, which Loretta and her mother both insist on, then that is the butcher's bill one must pay."

"Yep, I guess so," Uncle Bill said, nodding.

"I did suggest the registrar's office as an alternative or elopement. However, as you may well imagine, the suggested secular alternatives were not well-received. They are quite set upon a church wedding."

Uncle Bill nodded. "I told you that Celestina and I were married by a Justice of the Peace. But I never told you that her mother, who was also Catholic, wanted to shoot me because of it."

"The marriage or that you absconded with her daughter?" I asked.

He laughed. "Both. Not many mothers think their daughter's husband-to-be measures up. You want me to talk to Josefa? I might get her to change her mind."

"You absolutely should, William," said Mother. "Better yet, I will speak with her. No son of mine is going to become a Catholic."

"Gah!" I exclaimed. "I mean, that is most kind of you to offer Mother, but I see no need for you to become a latter-day Henry VIII. Nor do I wish to be excommunicated."

"Stuff and nonsense, Benjamin," replied Mother. "You cannot be excommunicated if you don't belong to the church."

"I was speaking of excommunication from the town," I said. "Not to mention a distinct likelihood of tar and feathers. I can think of several locals, including Loretta's aunt, Esperanza, who would gleefully assist with such an endeavour."

"He's right, Dorothy," Uncle Bill said. "Folks here are pretty set in their ways. They've accepted Bennie, but it hasn't been easy for him. Wasn't easy for me, either. It took a long time, and I was lucky to have Celestina with me. She smoothed a whole lot of ruffled feathers."

Mother eyed Uncle Bill before turning towards the self. "Your father is going to erupt when he hears about this," she said.

"Merely one more item to include in his ledger of my failings," I said, waving my hand dismissively. "May I suggest discretion as the better part of valour in this instance, Mother, and ask that you not speak with Mrs. Alvarez or any of the locals about this?"

"Very well," she said through anchored molars. "But I refuse to attend your so-called baptism." Mother sighed. "Your great-grandfather Mansfield Graves, who was the rector at St. Paul's at the turn of the century, will surely be rolling in his grave. I hope you are happy, Benjamin. Now, if you will excuse me, I am going to bed." She stood up, glowered at the self, and then marched off to her bedroom.

"She'll come around, pard'ner," said Uncle Bill emphatically after Mother had closed her bedroom door. "It's that dang family pride. You just do what you gotta do to make Loretta happy. You sure you don't want me to have a word with Josefa? Get her to back off a little?"

"A most gracious offer, Uncle Bill, but no. The wedding is barely a week away. No sense roiling the waters any more than they already are. A Graves must endure the slings and arrows of misfortune. Granted, were my father present, I suspect there would be a great deal more slinging and arrowing."

"Heh. You're right about that. Well, I gotta get me some shut-eye. I'll see you in the morning."

"Right-ho, Uncle Bill. Good night."

I followed him down the hall and opened the door to my bedroom slowly, negotiated the floor so as not to step on Archie, and sat down on the bed.

"Becoming a Fenian, eh, old chap?" Archie said. "Aunt Dorothy is none too pleased, from the sounds of it."

"No, she is not," I said. "I explained to her that I consider it to be merely a *pro forma* conversion to appease Loretta's mother. I mean, the entire process is daft."

Archie laughed. "The conversion and baptism of Benjamin Graves. No doubt the entire town will turn out; the highlight of the social season, and all that. When is the blessed event?"

I groaned. "There are several. First, my baptismal ceremony and then my confession, in which I gather my Catholic bona fides will be established. Loretta and her mother will speak with Father Castillo to set the precise date and time. It's all nonsense and a bloody nuisance. Not that I would characterise it as such to either of them."

"Of course not, old chap."

"Moreover, Loretta's other relatives would be displeased, which regrettably includes Esperanza."

"Not a fan of yours, eh, cousin?"

"I'm not sure who is worse, Esperanza or that madwoman."

"Will everyone attend the conversion ceremony?"

"Gah! I hope to keep the entire baptism a secret, with just Loretta and her mother there." Images of the Roman Coliseum and the self being devoured by lions bubbled to the top of the grey matter. "If word leaks out, it will be a circus—or worse. So, please, no word to anyone."

"I shall maintain it in the strictest of confidence, cousin. You need not worry."

Chapter 7

The following morning began peacefully. I lingered over my coffee, which Uncle Bill had brewed to an even more tar-like in consistency than usual, whilst observing the cattle in the back pasture. Knowing that Archie would be caring for the four-leggeds, especially, Marjorie, put a spring in the Graves step.

The travails of the previous evening had receded, if only temporarily. I intended to apprise Loretta of Mother's acceptance of the religious goings-on-to-be and ask her to establish the various appointments with Father Castillo for the following week.

Archie staggered into the kitchen as I drained my cuppa, looking as if he had been beaten about the head and shoulders: tousled hair, half-shut-eyes, and a noticeable scowl.

"Top of the morning, Archie," I said at enhanced volume.

"Oh, please, God, let there be coffee," he mumbled as he approached the cabinet where Uncle Bill stored the coffee cups.

"A bit of excess at Rudy's last night, Archie? You seemed all right when we discussed my conservation with Mother last night."

"The after-effects had not hit," Archie said. "That hippopotamus chap, Coronado, suggested I try something called tequila, mixed with beer. Apparently, one places the glass of tequila into the glass of beer and then drinks the mixture as quickly as possible. Well, it seemed innocuous enough and I downed several."

"Rather like an unexploded bomb that decided to go off?"

He walked over to the coffee pot and poured the mixture into the cup he had secured. "God, what is this stuff? It smells like burning tyres."

"That is Uncle Bill's 'cowboy' coffee. He made it especially strong this morning. I suggest you add a large quantity of milk and several sugars if you prefer the digestive system not to rebel."

Archie placed the cup on the table, retrieved the milk from the fridge, and sat down. He poured milk into the cup until it overflowed, picked it up, grunted, and took a large swallow. "Uggh. That is well and truly awful."

"True. However, as Uncle Bill is fond of saying, it helps cowboys get up and do what needs to be done."

"Does that include vomiting?"

"If it does, I would appreciate a timely warning. And speaking of what needs to be done, I do hope you are in eager anticipation of feeding and watering the four-legged's this morning."

Archie eyed me from beneath his cup, which presently he was holding to his forehead. "All right. Do you intend to supervise?"

"I shall indeed. We do want to avoid any unnecessary unpleasantness—chased by Malcolm, kicked by Marjorie, stepped on by Daisy—that sort of thing."

"Malcolm?"

I pointed out the window towards the pasture. "Do you see that bull?"

"They all look rather the same to me, old chap."

"Yes, well, you may notice that the third one from the left is rather heftier than the others and has a ring through its nose. That is Malcolm."

"I take it Malcolm is foul-tempered. How wonderful."

"No, he isn't especially foul-tempered, well, not always. One does not want to place oneself between him and one of the heifers when he is ready to, er, do his duty, as it were. Otherwise, he is relatively docile. Nevertheless, I suggest you not approach him too closely."

"Right. Avoid the bull. I already know about Marjorie, although as I mentioned, she was quite ladylike when we rescued you from the barn."

"M-hem, yes. As for Daisy, the biggest danger is that, whilst you pour her breakfast into the trough she will step on you. One needs to be fleet of foot. Now, would you like something to eat before we venture forth?"

"Afraid the stomach is reeling a bit from the coffee, although I am beginning to feel livelier. Why don't you show me what needs to be done? I will breakfast afterwards with your mother."

A while later, having reviewed with Archie the care and feeding particulars and having bid good morning to Mother, who was still smouldering, I motored into town and parked the lorry in its usual spot around the side of the cafe. I periscoped the nearby environs to determine whether Porfiria was lurking about. Finding the coast clear, I exited the lorry and quickly ran into the cafe, locking the door behind me.

I turned around and was confronted with two pairs of goggling eyes belonging to Esperanza and Coronado.

"*Felicitaciones*, Señor Graves," said Coronado, nodding. He waddled towards the self and extended a dirty hand for me to shake. "Can I come to your baptism and confession? Maybe there's gonna be something to eat."

"What? How can you possibly know about the baptism and confession?" I asked.

"Luis told me when I got gas for my truck this morning," said Coronado.

"Luis told *you*?" I spluttered. "How did he find out?"

"I dunno, Señor Graves. He said Nestor told him when he came in to get a new tyre for his truck," Coronado replied.

"Nestor?" I shouted. I grasped my head with both hands, ready to rip clumps of hair out. "Nestor is rarely conscious before noon. This is madness."

"I made sure the whole town knows about it, *Pendejito*," said Esperanza, laughing loudly. She drew on her cigarette and chimneyed a large cloud of smoke towards me. "But we wanna hear you confess your sins first. Maybe Father Castillo won't baptise you because you got too many of them. Then no marriage to Loretta."

"Can I come to your confession, too, Señor Graves?" asked Coronado. "Once, Father Castillo told Old Joe he had to confess in front of the whole town because he stole one of Manny Ramirez's goats. Then Father Castillo told Old Joe to pay ten dollars to Manny and say he was sorry."

The grey matter reeled. I had entered yet another circle of Hell. "I was given to understand that confession is a private matter between priest and supplicant, Coronado. I do not intend it to become a public spectacle for the town's amusement."

Coronado blinked his rodentary eyes. "Huh? What's a 'supplicant'?"

"It's the bloody person who is confessing," I shouted. I pointed towards the front door. "Out, Coronado! Out before I go into the kitchen and return with one of Maria's knives."

Coronado lowered his head and retreated slowly. "Sorry, Señor Graves."

I exhaled loudly. "It is I who should apologise to you, Coronado. I should not have erupted. Would you do me a small favour?"

"Sure, Señor Graves. I like to help."

"Will you tell everyone the confession will take place one week from, er, Friday at—" I paused to glance at the watch "two o'clock?"

"Okay, Señor Graves," said Coronado.

"Don't listen to him, *Gordo*," said Esperanza. "That's after the wedding."

"How come Father Castillo wants you to confess after the wedding, Señor Graves?" asked Coronado.

"He, that is—never mind, Coronado," I said, whilst scowling at Esperanza.

"You better confess that you were screwing Sunflower," said Esperanza, making the usual rude gesture with her thumb and forefinger to emphasise the accusation. "Father Castillo's gonna want to hear all about that. My Loretta should know it, too. Maybe then she'll understand that she shouldn't marry no *gringo*. Or maybe he'll hold your head underwater real long."

Coronado smiled and nodded. "I liked Señora Flower. Did you invite her to the wedding, Señor Graves?"

By now, the blood pressure had risen to the point of nuclear detonation. "Gah!" I screamed. I paused to inhale a large breath of air. "Esperanza," I hissed whilst attempting to loosen my closed jaws, "I suggest you return to the kitchen before I pick up one of the dining room chairs and break it over your head."

Esperanza's eyes widened. She raised her middle finger, turned around, and disappeared through the kitchen door. I turned and eyed Coronado, who was standing mouth agape. "Señora Flower will not be attending the wedding, Coronado, nor will she be attending my baptism, nor my confession, which I gather will take place whilst I am in the stocks. Do you understand?"

"What are stocks, Señor Graves?" he asked.

I groaned inwardly. "Just a figure of speech, Coronado. Now, shouldn't you be getting back to the store? Surely, Joe will want you there."

"I guess so." He began to waddle towards the front door. Before he opened it, he stopped and turned towards me. "Señor Graves," he said quietly, "Joe said you shot somebody in London. Are you gonna confess that to Father Castillo?"

"Joe said what?" I shouted. "I mean, no, Coronado, I will not confess. Because the shooting took place in London, it is, er, out of Father Castillo's jurisdiction. I can confess to the good Father only those things that have happened in Vaca Seca. Also, I already confessed the event to a priest in England and have been absolved. It is as if the shooting never happened."

"Oh, okay, Señor Graves," replied Coronado, apparently satisfied with my logic. "When I go to confession, do I have to tell Father Castillo I owe Rudy a lot of money?"

"Er, how much do you owe?"

"I dunno. Rudy said a couple hundred bucks, but Joe thinks it's more."

I raised an eyebrow. "Perhaps you should ask Rudy. Or, better yet, you could ask Father Castillo whether you should discuss it in the confession."

"Okay, Señor Graves. That's a real good idea. Thanks." He waddled to the front door, opened it, and disappeared down the steps.

I pulled a chair out from the nearest table and sat down heavily, resisting the urge to bang the now throbbing skull on the tabletop repeatedly. After several immobile minutes, I stood up and walked into the kitchen. Esperanza was jabbering to Maria, who was stirring the filling for her *tamales*. As the door opened, they both looked at me, cigarettes dangling from their mouths. "Not one bloody word, Esperanza," I growled. "Not one. I don't know what you have been telling Loretta or Mrs. Alvarez—"

"I didn't say nothing, *Pendejito*," she said angrily. "Everybody in town knows, including Loretta."

"There's nothing to know because nothing bloody happened," I seethed. "Nothing. Do you understand what the word 'nothing' means? It is an absence, a void, very much like the inside of your skull."

"¡*Vete a la chingada, Pendejito!*" shouted Esperanza.

"*No más, hermana*," Maria said sternly. "I don't want to hear no more." Maria then turned to me. "Loretta told us this morning you were gonna convert so you two can be married in the church. She and Josefa are real happy now. *Hermana*, don't say nothing more about Bennie and that *chichona*. If he says nothing happened, then okay."

Esperanza shook her head. "You really want our Loretta to marry a *gringo*?"

"She ain't our Loretta. She wants to marry Bennie. I don't like Hector, but it ain't up to me to tell you not to see him no more."

"What's wrong with Hector?" Esperanza asked, jutting her chin out.

Maria shrugged but remained silent. I decided not to remind Esperanza that Hector was a drunken, lecherous oaf who had sought to paw Loretta and, but for stepping into a hole and crashing to the ground, would have succeeded.

"Er, thank you, Maria," I mumbled. "I have assured Loretta repeatedly that I have always been faithful. That is part of the Graves code."

"I don't care about no code," Maria said. "I gotta finish making the *tamales*."

Later that morning, Loretta walked into the cafe with a spring in her step and a smile on her face. "Hi, Bennie," she said gaily, as I was finishing the dining room preparations. "It's all arranged. On Tuesday morning, Father Castillo will meet with us to discuss the wedding. Then, on Wednesday afternoon, he will baptise you and hear your confession. It's scheduled for two o'clock, when the cafe is closed."

"Why not hear my confession on Tuesday?"

"Tuesday's meeting is about the wedding service. He's going to ask you questions about your faith and then tell you what's involved in converting. There's a ceremony."

"Eh? Ceremony?"

"That's right. It's part of the service when your baptism will take place."

"I thought the baptism would be private, with only you and your mother in attendance."

"Oh, no, everyone is encouraged to attend. It's meant to be a celebration of your joining the faith."

I thought of Esperanza's earlier remarks about my baptismal submersion and groaned softly.

"What's wrong, Bennie?"

"Er, nothing my love," I gargled. "Merely contemplating the blessed events to come. Coronado mentioned a previous incident when Old Joe was forced to confess publicly to stealing Manny Ramirez's goat."

"I must not have been here when that happened. That doesn't sound like Old Joe."

"Well, Coronado may be mistaken about the details, including who nicked what, if anything, from whom. One never knows."

Loretta laughed. "Have you stolen any goats, Benjamin Graves?"

"None that I recall. Although you may wish to ask Coronado to be sure. I am more concerned about the supposedly public aspect of Old Joe's confession before the good Father. I was given to understand that confession was rather a private matter."

"It is. I never heard of a priest having a public confession. Would you like me to show you the confessional in the church? It's two very small rooms. You will sit in one and Father Castillo will sit in the one next to it. You don't even see him."

I waved my hand to dismiss the suggestion. "No need. It sounds straightforward."

The luncheon crowd was steady, but uneventful. Even Esperanza managed to wait tables without erupting.

Around half twelve, Archie strolled in. "What-ho and pip-pip, all," he said, doffing a tan cowboy hat lent to him by Uncle Bill. Espying the self, he walked over and sat down at the table I was clearing. "Hullo, cousin. Beautiful day isn't it?"

"You seem to be in a cheerful mood," I said. "Any hidden bruises from the animals?"

"Not a one, old chap, although one does not stand between that hat-wearing pig of yours and its breakfast. Oh, and Marjorie was as gentle as a lamb. I retrieved an old carrot, which she took from my hand. And she did not attempt to lock me in the barn."

"M-hem," I grunted. "Yes, well, would you care for lunch or is the stomach still reeling from Uncle Bill's coffee?"

"No, I feel fine." He rubbed his hands together. "Famished, actually. What would you recommend?"

"The chicken *enchiladas* are a favourite, but one cannot go wrong with any menu item, although I might suggest you avoid the *menudo*."

"Eh, *menudo*? What's that? I am feeling adventurous."

"*Menudo* is a stew of sorts. The celebratory ingredient is tripe made from a cow's stomach."

Archie's eyes widened. "Ugh. No offence to your *chef de cuisine*, but I'm not feeling quite that adventurous, old chap. I believe I shall stick to the *enchiladas*."

"A wise choice—old chap. I shall return anon."

I walked into the kitchen. Loretta was assisting Maria with the meal preparations. Esperanza had disappeared, her whereabouts unknown. A small cloud of bluish-grey smoke floated over Maria's head and ash dangled precariously from the end of her cigarette over a plate of *tamales*.

"One plate of chicken *enchiladas*, if you please, Maria. It's for my cousin, so perhaps you should use the milder chile."

Maria grunted.

"Okay, Bennie," Loretta said. I'll have it ready in two minutes."

"Thanks. I shall wait here."

"Are you and Esperanza getting along?" Loretta asked whilst she prepared the *enchiladas*.

"Er, no major battles this morning," I lied. "She even stepped aside once and allowed me to pass by unmolested. Perhaps she is ill."

"Oh, stop it, Bennie," said Loretta. "Be thankful for the peace."

"Er, yes, of course I am," I said. "But one must treat a courteous Esperanza like a coiled cobra that is ready to strike."

Loretta sighed and shook her head gently, then handed me a plate with steaming *enchiladas*, *refritos*, and rice. "All right, Bennie. Here you go. And be nice."

"I always endeavour to do so," I replied. I entered the dining room bearing Archie's lunch and set course for his table. Presently, I heard the front door open. There was an audible gasp and then a silence descended onto the room as all eyes focused on the door.

Standing athwart the entry was Porfiria. Her raincoat was unbuttoned, revealing too-tight black shorts and a white blouse, which made her look like an obese penguin. She looked around the room, took off her rain hat, sat down at a nearby table, and placed her umbrella on the floor.

"Gah," I moaned, as Archie's plate of *enchiladas* crashed to the floor.

Porfiria glared at the self but said nothing. The other patrons began to abandon ship, streaming out the front door. "We'll pay you later," several shouted.

Presently, only she and Archie remained.

"Gimme a menu," she said calmly.

I retreated slowly towards the table with the cash register where we kept the menus. Retrieving one, I approached her with trepidation. I dangled the menu in front of her, which she grabbed like a hungry lion securing a large piece of raw meat.

"Er, would you like anything to drink?" I mumbled, whilst slowly backing away beyond the reach of the umbrella

She glared at the self. "Get me a Coke," she commanded. Her eyes slowly scanned the interior of the dining room. "What happened to this place? And how come you talk funny?"

I feared the mental slow match had been kindled in her brain and was now burning towards an inevitable outburst. "We, er, remodelled several years ago," I replied warily, whilst continuing to inch backward.

"Looks different." She raised her voice. "I don't like it." She goggled Archie, who goggled back. "How come that *gringo* looks like you? Does he talk funny, too?"

"Er, he is my cousin. Now, if you will excuse me, I shall retrieve your Coke."

I turned around and accelerated into the kitchen, followed by Archie. The radio was blaring, and Loretta was washing dishes. Esperanza, who had reappeared, was jabbering with Maria by the stove.

Maria looked at Archie and pointed her chef's knife. "I said he can't come into my kitchen," she growled.

"Er, yes, Maria. Exigent circumstances and all that," I replied loudly.

"Huh? Can't you speak regular English?" asked Maria.

"Could you please lower the volume on the wireless, I mean, the radio?" I shouted.

Esperanza reached over to the counter and lowered the volume. "What's wrong, *Pendejito?*" she asked. "You see your *chichona?*"

I sighed and pointed towards the dining room. "No. It's Porfiria. She is sitting in the dining room.

Esperanza's eyes widened. "¡*Dios mio!*" she said. "How come she's sitting in there?"

"One presumes to have lunch," I replied. "As soon as she entered, the other customers fled. Without paying, I might add."

Loretta walked over to the door and opened it a crack. "She's just sitting there staring out the window. What should we do?"

"Well, she requested a Coke," I said. "Perhaps you or Esperanza can take it to her."

"I ain't goin' out there, *Pendejito*," Esperanza said. "She asked you. You do it."

"Yes, but at our last encounter, the madwoman screamed that I was the Devil and biffed me with that umbrella of hers."

"I'll go," Loretta said warily. "She won't remember me."

"Allow me," said Archie, with a deep bow. "I would not want any harm to come to an angel like yourself. Now, if one of you will provide me with her Coke, I shall proceed forthwith."

I rolled my eyes at Archie's exaggerated chivalry and readied the glass. "Here you are, cousin," I said. "Be vigilant. You may also wish to ask her what she wishes to order."

"Never fear, old chap," he said, taking the glass in hand. "Besides, anyone of that bulk is unlikely to move quickly."

"She is quite capable of moving her umbrella-grasping arm quickly," I replied.

Archie raised the glass to his forehead. "Well, into the breach, as they say." He glided through the kitchen door as Loretta, Esperanza, and I observed discreetly through a narrow opening in the doorway.

"Here you are, madam," said Archie as he placed the glass on the table. "Now, what would you care to order?"

She stared at him and blinked. "I want the *posole*. And bring me some *sopapillas*, too."

"Very good, madam."

He glided back into the kitchen. "*Posole* and something called a soap pillow for our mackintosh-wearing intruder," he announced. "What is a soap pillow? It sounds ghastly."

"It's pronounced *sopapilla*, Archie," I said. "You should try one."

"Speaking of which, cousin, I believe my luncheon is still on the dining room floor."

"Oh, yes, right. Why don't you sit in that chair in the corner? Unless, of course, you would prefer to sit in the dining room again?"

"How come you dropped the *enchiladas*, *Pendejito*?" crowed Esperanza. "You scared?"

"Of course not. Merely taken aback by Porfiria's presence. Besides, you seem to be cowering in here. Perhaps you are afraid of her."

"I ain't scared of her," she replied angrily. "I gotta stay in here and help Maria."

I decided to let the matter drop. Painful experience had demonstrated the general futility of arguments with Esperanza, which quickly devolved into shouting matches. As tempted as I was to resort to Esperanza's preferred epithets, I knew that doing so would upset Loretta. My experience with Cynthia had shown that, as her wedding date approached, the female of the species resembled an agitated wasp, ever more ready to attack the intended, whether with verbal stings or nearby crockery. Consequently, discretion was called for.

I turned away from Esperanza and motioned Archie towards the chair in the corner.

"The chair will be fine," Archie said. "Would you prefer I deliver the *posole* and *sopapillas* to her? Unless, of course, you intend to drop those onto the floor as well?"

"No," I muttered. In what appeared to be a choreographed dance, Loretta dropped the sopapillas into the fryer, placed the bowl of posole onto a tray, removed the now redolent sopapillas from said fryer, placed them into a wax-paper-lined basket, and placed the basket onto the tray.

"You okay, Bennie?" asked Loretta. "I can take it to her."

"A Graves never shirks from his sacred duty, Loretta," I said. I picked up the tray and slowly approached the door. As I went through, I espied Porfiria sipping on her drink and staring out the front window. "Here you are, madam. *Posole* and *sopapillas*."

"Where's the nice *gringo*?" she asked. Her eyes narrowed. "Didn't I see you yesterday?"

"Er, the nice chap? Ah, well, he is in the kitchen at present. As for seeing me yesterday, er, no, I fear you are mistaken—"

"¡*Diablo*! Get away from me!" she shouted. I retreated quickly and turned towards the kitchen door as the bowl of posole hurtled past the right ear and crashed into the wall separating the dining room from the kitchen.

"Gah!" I exclaimed upon reaching the relative safety of the kitchen.

"What happened, Bennie?" Loretta asked, whilst maintaining a weather eye on the kitchen door.

"That madwoman launched her *posole* at me."

Presently, the kitchen door flew open and Porfiria stepped inside.

"Where's the *gringo*?" she demanded, banging the tip of her umbrella on the floor.

Although I was not one for displays of false bravado, nor one to threaten physical harm to the female of the species, the Graves magnanimity had by now jumped through the kitchen window and sprinted down the road. I retrieved one of Maria's nearby knives and turned towards her.

"Get out, you harridan!" I shouted. "If you attack me with your umbrella, I shall defend myself."

"Not you," she said calmly, "the nice *gringo*."

The grey matter was thoroughly nonplussed. I had expected her to shout "¡*Diablo!*" and biff me with the umbrella. "Er, she means you, Archie," I said, pointing the knife towards him. He is sitting in the corner."

Archie, who was consuming a plate of *enchiladas*, relinquished his fork to the floor. "Eh?"

Porfiria goggled Archie. "How come you didn't bring me my *posole*?" she asked.

"What? Well, I don't work here, actually," he babbled.

"How come?" she asked.

"Ah. Just visiting to attend my cousin's wedding," he replied, pointing towards the self. "Then it's back to civilisation—I mean, London, where I live."

Porfiria fell momentarily silent. "Is that how come you talk so funny? I saw somebody from London on TV. He talked like you." She turned towards the self.

I raised the chef's knife, anticipating an outburst.

"You're the one getting married," she said matter-of-factly.

"How do you know that?" I asked.

"Poor girl," she said, shaking her head. "She must be real desperate or just stupid."

Although I was long accustomed to verbal slings and arrows, Loretta was not, especially when they were directed towards her upcoming nuptials.

"Get out of here, Porfiria!" Loretta shouted. She crossed her arms to her chest and stepped forward, ready to let slip the dogs of war, but was stopped by Maria, who put a restraining hand on Loretta's shoulder.

"You remember me, Porfiria?" Maria asked calmly. "From the high school?"

Porfiria shook her head slowly. "Um, no."

"You sure you don't remember throwing chalk at me, Porfiria?" asked Maria. "I remember."

Porfiria's eyes suddenly widened. Then she lowered her head, turned around, and quickly exited the kitchen. Loretta walked over to the kitchen door and opened it.

"She's gone," Loretta said, wiping a wisp of hair from her brow. "Thank you, *Tía* Maria. What was that about chalk?"

Maria shrugged but did not answer. Instead, she restored the cigarette to her lips, inhaled, and released a large cloud of smoke. "*No más*, Loretta," she muttered softly, patting Loretta's arm, before returning to her stove to stir a bubbling pot of *frijoles*. I even espied a slight, if brief, upturn in the corners of her mouth, which for Maria constituted an exhibition of jocularity *in extremis*.

I placed the knife back on the counter and walked over to Loretta. "Rudy told me the story," I whispered. "I shall relay it later."

Loretta nodded.

I went into the storeroom, where I retrieved a bucket, several dishcloths, and a large sponge. "Right," I announced. "The dining room wants cleaning. Care to assist, Archie?"

Archie stood up quickly and walked towards the self. "Lead on, cousin," he said. "And afterwards, I intend to retire to Rudy's. I am in desperate need of a large restorative whisky, even if it's that swill you and Uncle Bill drink."

"As am I," I replied quietly. "I will inform Loretta and then join you."

After spic-and-spanning the dining room, Archie trotted over to Rudy's. I returned to the kitchen and deposited the soiled implements into the sink.

"Maria, thank you for defusing that rather volatile situation," I said.

She grunted and continued to stir the *frijoles*.

"Are you all right, Loretta?" I asked.

"Yes," she replied. "Would you really have used that knife, Bennie?"

"I might have used it to parry an umbrella blow, but otherwise, no. Of course, a Graves will always defend a damsel in distress from physical harm, as Archie said earlier."

"If she says anything more about me, you may have to protect *her*," said Loretta.

"At the ready to leap over the gunwales and do battle, eh?"

"If someone tells me I'm desperate or stupid, I am," she replied.

"What about the wedding?" I asked hesitantly.

"What do you mean?" asked Loretta.

"Well," I began, "one would prefer not to have the 'I dos' interrupted by screams of '¡*Diablo!*'"

I espied Esperanza shaking her head. "Okay by me," she muttered. "You still got time to change your mind, Loretta."

"Stop it, *Tía* Esperanza. I'm not changing my mind."

"Okay," she grumbled. She shielded her upraised middle finger from Loretta's view.

"I didn't think about that. What should we do, Bennie?"

"Can the door to the church be locked?"

"No. There's no lock on the door."

"Presumably, manned guard towers, landmines, and patrols of ravenous dogs are out of the question. Perhaps Rudy has an idea. I desperately require a restorative and shall ask him."

"Okay. I better go check on my mother. I'll see you in an hour."

We walked outside and parted. As I watched Loretta disappear down the road, I could only wonder what Fate had planned as its wedding gift.

Chapter 8

I stepped into Rudy's. As the eyes adjusted to the dim light, I espied Archie sitting beside Coronado and Joe Romero at the bar.

"Hey, Bennie," Rudy said. "I hear there were some fireworks at the cafe."

"Indeed," I replied. "Porfiria launched a bowl of *posole* at the self, if that's what you mean."

He laughed and placed a beer next to me. "Archie said you threatened to stab her."

I retrieved the bottle and took a long pull. "Thanks," I said. "Yes, she barged into the kitchen with that bloody umbrella. I retrieved one of Maria's knives as an *épée* to parry any umbrella-thrusts. That woman is barking mad."

"My cousin was about to defend the honour of his bride-to-be," said Archie. "Quite the nobleman."

"Loretta was about to defend her own honour," I replied. "You would have been proud, too, Rudy. Maria calmly restrained Loretta. She then mentioned the chalk-tossing incident you told me about at the high school. Porfiria stood down immediately before retreating to parts unknown."

"That's my *querida*," said Rudy. "A woman of action and few words."

"Er, yes," I replied. "But short of stationing Maria at the church door, how can we prevent Porfiria from bursting in during the ceremony?"

"I know how, *gringo*," said Joe. "Don't have no wedding."

"Are you suggesting your niece elope?" I asked.

He paused, presumably to allow his cranial cash register to tote up the receipts. "Save me some money if she did because I wouldn't have to get no wedding gift. But it would be better if you just called it off. You ain't good enough for her."

"I previously suggested we elope," I said, ignoring the insult, "which would allow me to avoid the upcoming baptism, confession, and conversion to your faith. Alas, Loretta's mother insists on my converting, and they both insist on a church wedding. Hence, I am afraid you shall be sorely disappointed Joe. Of course, you can suggest that Loretta call the wedding off."

"I already tried that," grumbled Joe. "That girl don't know what's good for her and especially what ain't good for her."

I shook my head but said nothing.

Coronado, who had been resting his head on the bar in front of four empty beer bottles, now raised it. "I got you and Loretta a wedding gift, Señor Graves," he said. "You wanna see?" Coronado shoved a pudgy hand into his trouser pocket and retrieved several coins, a grease-stained serviette, and the ever-present mousetrap. He stared at the contents in his hand. "I guess I don't have it. Sorry, Señor Graves. You got any mice? You can have this." He thrust the mousetrap towards the self.

I waved him off. "Er, no, quite all right, Coronado. We have an ample supply of mousetraps at the ranch."

"Maybe you need one for the cafe, Señor Graves," he said. "Remember the mouse that was on Señora Flower and she took her shirt off in the cafe?"

Rudy and Joe nodded. "That was one real lucky mouse," said Joe, who smiled absently at the memory of Sunflower.

"Yes, well, a rather unique situation, Coronado. Er, besides, I am quite certain that particular mouse is no longer inside the cafe."

Archie raised his eyebrows. "This sounds like a most interesting story, cousin. Who, pray tell, is this Señora Flower who, ah, doffed her blouse for a mouse, so to speak?"

Both Joe and Rudy laughed.

"That was some girl, Bennie," Rudy said. "¡Híjole!"

"Oh, I must hear about this," said Archie.

"No, you must not," I replied.

Joe cupped his hands in front of his chest. "She was a *chichona*, Archie. You never saw a girl like that." He pointed an accusatory finger towards me. "Your cousin was all over her like flies on honey."

"Indeed? Was this pre-Loretta, old chap?" asked Archie slyly.

"No," said Joe, before I could respond. "Your *gringo* cousin was two-timing my Loretta. That's one reason he don't deserve her."

"I was not 'two-timing' Loretta, Joe" I said angrily. "I told you that long ago. Nothing untoward happened between Sunflower and the self." I turned to Archie. "Sunflower, whom Coronado refers to as "Señora Flower,' had rather an—"

"I'm all ears, cousin," interrupted Archie, who was smiling broadly. "This Sunflower of yours sounds like a rare bird. Was that her name?"

Beads of perspiration had gathered above the brow. "I mean, Sunflower—her Christian name was Jane—was rather, er, tactile with members of the opposite sex and oozed a sort of fecundity, if you know what I mean. This predilection caused, shall we say, some friction between Loretta and the self."

"I never thought of you as the Casanova sort," said Archie. "I stand corrected."

"Who's this Casanova?" asked Joe.

"He was an Italian chap who lived in the eighteenth century," replied Archie. "Rather a rogue, who had numerous affairs with all sorts of women." Archie wagged his index finger. "Tsk, tsk, Benjamin Graves."

"Sorry to disappoint, Archie," I said, "but despite Joe's claim, I behaved honourably at all times. As you should know, the words on the Graves coat-of-arms read '*Vires–Fidelitas–Honoris*.'"

"From what I know of our relatives, old chap, none of those hold, especially *fidelitas*. Anyway, what happened to Jane-Sunflower?" asked Archie.

"She ran off with a film director named Roger Victory. He had come to Vaca Seca to make a film about the cafe, God only knows why. In any case, after leaving a trail of wreckage and unpaid debts, as I am sure both Rudy and Joe can attest, he wooed Sunflower from her then-boyfriend Sky Blue with a promise of a career in Hollywood."

"Sky Blue?" Archie asked. "A chap named Sky Blue? Surely, you're joking."

"I cannot recall his Christian name. Sky Blue changed her name to Sunflower in a renaming ceremony."

"Renaming ceremony," said Archie, shaking his head. "My God, they sound barking mad."

"Yeah," said Joe, "but I made some real good money from that *gringo* Sky Blue. I even sold him a building down the street."

"The Sky was the limit, so to speak?" asked Archie.

"I dunno," said Joe, "I didn't own it." He smiled absently and drained the bottle in his hand. "That *gringo* was real stupid."

Archie turned to the self. "So, this Roger chap was going to make a movie about the little cafe of yours? What possible reason—"

"A rather long and painful story," I said.

Joe nodded. "That Victory *gringo* still owes me two hundred bucks," growled Joe.

"Me, too," said Rudy.

"Was Sunflower in the movie?" Archie asked.

"No," I said. "There was no movie. Roger promised rather more than he delivered."

"So, this Victory chap lured Sunflower away with false promises?" asked Archie.

"Not entirely," I said. "One day, Loretta and I were walking in Santa Fe. As we passed by the El Farol, the local cinema, we both espied a poster for a film—I don't recall the title now—with a picture of a scantily dressed and even more voluptuous Sunflower. The poster read, 'Introducing Veronica Lee.' Whether she made any additional films, I cannot say."

"I am sorry I could not make her acquaintance," said Archie, raising a beer bottle to his lips.

Presently, an idea congealed in the grey matter. "She appears to have taken rather a shine to you, Archie," I said.

"Who?" he asked.

"Porfiria," I replied.

Archie geysered a mouthful of beer onto the bar. "Er, sorry, Rudy," he said.

"That's the solution," I said.

"Spewing beer on her?" asked Archie, who was now mopping up beer off the top of the bar.

"No. You can entertain Porfiria during the wedding ceremony," I said matter-of-factly.

"What? Look, cousin, if you think I shall 'entertain' that madwoman during your wedding, then you're as barking mad as she is. Why not have the police nick her and bung her into the loony bin for the day?"

"I gather that was tried once before," I answered. "Do you recall my encounter yesterday with Tiny Roybal, the county sheriff?"

"The chap with almost as much excess tonnage as—I mean, yes," said Archie.

"According to Rudy, Tiny confronted Porfiria once to do just that," I said. "Apparently, she knocked him out."

"It's true," said Rudy. "Porfiria has a pretty good right hook. At least, she used to."

"Aren't there laws against biffing policemen here?" asked Archie.

"Sure there are," Rudy answered. "But all we got is Tiny and he's afraid to go near her."

Coronado raised his head up off the bar again. "I got an idea, Señor Graves. You can—"

"Never mind, Coronado," I interrupted, not wishing to hear another of Coronado's bizarre notions. "I am sure we shall arrive at a solution."

"Okay, Señor Graves," Coronado said. "I guess you couldn't lock her inside El Vaquero's barn like you were when Señor Archie got here?"

A silence descended in the bar as various pairs of eyes looked at one another.

Rudy was the first to break the silence. "I gotta admit, Bennie, that could work."

"Indeed, cousin," said Archie, "Uncle Bill's horse was able to lock you in. Surely you could do the same to her."

Joe burst into gales of laughter. "Huh? El Vaquero's horse locked you in the barn? That's either a real smart horse or a real stupid *gringo*. And horses ain't smart."

"M-hem," I grunted, as steam poured out from the ears. "Whilst I agree the idea of incarcerating Porfiria has merit—and thank you, Coronado, for the suggestion—allow me to point out a slight complication: how precisely would she be lured into the barn? One doubts an offer of alfalfa and a bucket of oats will succeed."

"I could give her a *burrito*," said Coronado. "If somebody told me I could have a *burrito* I'd go into El Vaquero's barn."

"A snake," said Joe.

I goggled Joe. "Eh? Are you suggesting we lure her into the barn with a snake?"

"No, *estupido*," hissed Joe. "I put a rattlesnake in her house. It bites her and we move her body into the barn."

Now Rudy erupted in laughter. The self's jaw dropped onto the floor and rolled under a table.

"What's so funny, Rudy?" asked Joe. "You got a better idea?"

Rudy, who was now doubled over laughing, waved his hand dismissively. "You gonna murder her, Joe?" he said, after catching his breath. "I don't think even Tiny will let you get away with that."

"Well, I ain't heard nobody come up with a better idea," growled Joe. He jerked his thumb towards Coronado. "*El Gordo* wants to lure her with a *burrito*. You gonna hook one on a fishing pole and drive out to El Vaquero's ranch?"

"What if she's hungry, Joe?" Coronado said. He paused and looked at the ceiling. "I'm kinda hungry now."

"Not a *burrito*, Coronado, but Archie," I said triumphantly.

Archie straightened himself on the bar stool. "Eh? I say, are you comparing me to a *burrito*, cousin? I may be compared to many things, but surely a *burrito* is not one of them."

I smiled. "You can be the lure, Archie. The bait on the hook, so to speak."

"What are you talking about?" Archie asked.

"She likes you, Archie," I said. "You can lure her to the barn."

"Surely not," replied Archie.

"Don't you remember earlier this afternoon? She asked for the 'nice *gringo*.'" I paused. "That's you."

"What?" he stammered. "Are you suggesting—gads, you're as loony as she is. First, you suggest I 'entertain' this mad-woman. Now you wish me to what, sweep her off her feet, which by the way would require a large crane, and lure her into Uncle Bill's barn with the promise of a *tête-à-tête*?"

"Something like that," I replied calmly.

"No!" Archie shouted, shaking his head vigorously. "A thousand times no. I have no intention of being a sacrificial lamb. Nor shall I woo—the mere thought is revolting. I second the snake."

"All right, all right," I said, as the grey matter struggled to find a solution. "Rudy, can you think of anyone in the town who could lure her? Anyone from years ago?"

Rudy scratched his head. "I dunno, Bennie," he said. "I remember she would sometimes see Nestor with his dog. She liked to pet him."

"Nestor?" asked Archie.

"No, the dog," said Rudy.

"Ah, right," said Archie.

"Are you saying she enjoyed petting Paco?" I asked incredulously.

"No, that was before Paco," said Rudy. "It was some sort of mutt, a little bigger than Paco. Nestor just called it Perro."

"I don't understand," I said. "Did she pet the dog and then scream at Nestor?"

"I don't remember her screaming at him," Rudy said. "Do you, Joe?"

Joe shook his head. "No. I only scream at Nestor when he leaves my store without paying."

"At least he never motored through the shop's front door," I said.

Joe looked at Rudy's post-Nestor front door and shrugged. "Yeah, I guess so," he said.

"Very well," I said. "If Porfiria likes dogs, then Archie first secures Paco and asks her to hide the dog in Uncle Bill's barn for safekeeping. She takes Paco into the barn, whereupon Archie closes and locks the door, and Bob's your uncle."

"Who's Uncle Bob, Señor Graves?" asked Coronado. "I got three uncles: *Tío* Manuel, *Tío* Ramón, and *Tío* Felipe. *Tío* Felipe died a long time ago when he was stealing Roberto Mondragon's' bull. It kicked him and—"

"How interesting, Coronado," I interrupted, not wishing to hear the entire saga of the uncle-knackering bull. "It is a figure of speech that means—oh, never mind."

"Okay, Señor Graves," said Coronado. "Are you gonna use Uncle Bob's truck? You can use mine if you want instead."

I resisted the growing urge to manoeuvre to the nearest wall and biff my head against it. "Er, thank you, Coronado. I shall keep your kind offer in mind."

"I dunno, Bennie," said Rudy. "I remember Perro. He was a real nice dog. Anybody could pet him. You know what Paco's like."

"M-hem," I gargled. "That does present a problem. Paco is not the most pliant of canines." I slapped my forehead. "Of course!"

"What?" said Rudy.

"Farm Calm," I said. "A bracing dose will render Paco malleable."

"I say," chirped Archie, "what is 'Farm Calm?'"

"A veterinary draught," I said. "Its main ingredients are grain alcohol and sugar, to be prescribed, as the bottle reads, for 'the distressed animal.' The two-legged locals consume as much of the stuff as the four-legged ones."

"Yeah," said Joe, "I sell lots of that stuff. I gotta raise my price."

Archie placed his left elbow on the bar and then set his head into his left hand. "Let me see if I understand," he said, gazing around the bar. "You wish to inebriate Paco with this Farm Calm draught, bin him into a lorry, and lock him in Uncle Bill's barn. Then, you intend to return to town, lure the madwoman into said lorry on the pretence of rescuing said inebriated dog, motor with her to Uncle Bill's ranch, then tell her that the dog is in the barn and can only be rescued by her, whereupon she summons her inner RSPCA, enters the barn, and is locked inside."

I nodded uncertainly. "Well, yes, that is an apt description of the sequence of events."

Archie continued, "And you intend that I shall be the one luring her into the lorry, and so forth."

"Quite," I said.

Archie shook his head, which was still cradled in his left hand. "Stark raving bloody mad," he muttered.

"Do you have a better idea?" I asked.

"Yes," he replied, jerking a thumb towards Joe. "I recommend the rattlesnake. Far more reasonable."

Joe nodded his head. "Your cousin is a lot smarter than you, *gringo*."

I sighed, resisting the erupting urge to tell him to sod off. "Very well, Joe. Shall I inform Loretta of your intentions? Or better still, perhaps I should inform Maria? After all, she has direct experience with your rattlesnake-binning efforts."

Joe took a long pull from the beer bottle in front of him. "Okay, okay, no rattlesnake. It was just an idea."

"You can supply the Farm Calm," I said. "I shall even pay you extra for the bottle."

"How much extra?" he said, his eyes lighting up.

"Er, double," I said. "Will that be satisfactory?"

"Sure," Joe said, his eyes lighting up.

"What if Paco doesn't like Farm Calm, Señor Graves?" asked Coronado. "I tried to give some to a rooster once, but it wouldn't drink none. Then it pecked me real hard."

I resisted the urge to ask Coronado why he had attempted to dose a rooster with Farm Calm. "I was under the impression that all animals hoovered up the stuff," I said.

"Paco likes beer, Bennie," Rudy said, "almost as much as Nestor. We can mix some Farm Calm with beer. I'm sure the dog will drink that."

"An excellent suggestion, Rudy," I said. "I believe the plan is coming to fruition."

Archie coughed. "What about the madwoman?" he asked.

"I don't understand," I replied.

"She appears at random times, does she not," he said. "How do you ensure she is present after you've inebriated the dog?"

"Ah," I gargled.

"Ah, indeed," said Archie.

I drummed my fingers on the bar. "That does put a spanner into the plan," I said. "But surely, there must be a way."

Archie and Joe reached for the beer bottles before them, whilst Rudy walked over to the cooler.

"You want another beer, Bennie?" he asked.

"Thank you, no," I said.

Coronado eyed Rudy plaintively and Rudy retrieved two bottles, offering one to Coronado.

"Thanks, Rudy," Coronado said, latching onto the bottle like an overweight gorilla grasping a banana.

I glanced at the watch. "Damn and blast. I must return to the cafe. Perhaps all of you can think of something."

"We will," they said in unison, laughing.

"Gah," I muttered.

Chapter 9

I dashed back into the cafe and set course for the kitchen. As I entered, Loretta, Esperanza, and Maria turned around. "Sorry," I mumbled. "I was, er, discussing the wedding logistics with Archie."

"Is he going to be your best man, Bennie?" asked Loretta. "He's family, after all."

"I confess I had not given it any thought," I said. In truth, I was sceptical of Archie as best anything. Entrusting him with Loretta's wedding ring, especially as Uncle Bill had insisted Loretta wear the ring he had given Celestina, seemed a bridge too far.

"Well, you had better decide soon," said Loretta.

"M-hem, yes." I glanced at the watch. "Heavens, look at the time. Is there anything else to do at present?"

"No, *Pendejito*," said Esperanza. "I think I got arthritis in my hands now from setting the tables." She held up both hands for me to view, then curled all but the middle fingers of each down.

"How droll, Esperanza," I said.

"Stop it, *Tía* Esperanza," yelled Loretta.

"Okay," said Esperanza. "Why don't I stay in the kitchen and help Maria? You can wait tables with *Pendej*—uh, Bennie."

"All right," said Loretta. "What do you think, Bennie? We can dance with our trays."

"Er, yes," I said. "You seem quite cheerful, Loretta."

"I am. My mother is feeling much better. She's coming here tonight. Your mother can meet her."

I gulped. Mother had expressed her intent to confront Josefa regarding my forthcoming conversion. I was afraid their meeting suddenly beforehand would set match to fuse. "Er, yes, of course," I said, "Mother has expressed a desire to meet your mother and, er, get to know her better."

"Good," said Loretta. "I saved that nice table in the back for everyone. When will they be here? I can tell my mother to be here at the same time."

"I suspect between half five and six o'clock. Uncle Bill gets quite peckish by early evening."

"Okay," said Loretta as she undid her apron and placed it in my hand. "I'll be back in five minutes. I'll tell my mother to be here at six. Will Archie be coming, too?"

"I, uh, yes, I believe he shall join my mother and Uncle Bill," I said. Presently, Archie is at Rudy's."

Loretta kissed me and dashed out the front door.

Esperanza eyed me suspiciously. "What's wrong, *Pendejito*? You think Josefa ain't good enough for your *gringa* mother?"

"I've told you before, Esperanza, you can insult me as much as you wish, but do not insult my mother."

"*Sí, hermana*," Maria said, not looking up from the stove, "don't say nothing bad about Bennie's mother."

"Okay," growled Esperanza. She raised her middle finger silently, then turned around and walked into the storeroom.

The dining crowd was relatively placid. At six, Uncle Bill walked inside with my mother. Loretta espied them, retrieved three menus, and then escorted them to a table towards the back corner. Several minutes later, Loretta's mother walked in.

"Hullo, Mrs. Alvarez," I said, escorting her to the table where Uncle Bill and my mother were seated. "I am delighted to hear you are feeling much better. Allow me to introduce you to my mother."

"Mother," I said, "this is Loretta's mother, Josefa Alvarez."

"Hello," said Mrs. Alvarez, extending her right hand towards my mother. "It's nice to meet you."

My mother took the extended hand in hers and shook it gently. "Thank you. It's nice to meet you, too. Your daughter and my son make a lovely couple."

Mrs. Alvarez looked at me and sat down. "Yes, Bennie and my Loretta are a good match. I'm so glad he is conv—"

"Excuse the interruption," I said loudly. "What may I bring you to drink? Josefa?"

"Oh, I'll have iced tea," Josefa answered. "But not much ice, Bennie."

"Iced tea with only a dash of ice," I said. "Mother?"

"Just a glass of water for me, dear, thank you."

"Uncle Bill?"

He pulled out two bottles of beer from a paper bag. "Just need a glass, pard'ner. Got to be civilised for your mother."

"Right, then," I said. "One iced tea, one water, and one glass. Mother, you may wish to sample Maria's *rellenos* this evening. They are most flavourful and not overly spicy."

I sped into the kitchen, hoping that the subject of my conversion would not come up.

"Your mother arrived, Loretta," I said. "I've seated her with Uncle Bill and my mother."

"Are they getting along?" she asked.

"Er, yes, they appear to be, although your mother started to raise the topic of conversion almost immediately. I interrupted for fear of a clash of civilisations, so to speak."

"I thought you said you had explained everything to your mother."

"I have. She is not pleased, of course, but appears to have accepted my explanation regarding the necessity of the situation."

"All right. I just don't want any arguments."

"Nor I. Thankfully, Mother is quite adept with strangers. With my father in Parliament, she has much practice maintaining a civil tongue."

"Okay, Bennie. I'm sorry to be so defensive about it. I just want everything to go smoothly for the wedding."

I patted Loretta's arm. "We shall have fair-weather sailing, my love. I promise."

Presently, there was a loud noise in the dining room, followed by a shout. I dashed towards the door and was about to enter the dining room when Coronado burst through and collided with me.

"Gah!" I shouted crashing to the floor and pinned underneath his bulk. "Get off me, Coronado," I said, struggling to speak. "I cannot breathe!"

"Sorry, Señor Graves," he said, punishing the olfactory with breath that reeked of beer and whatever he had just consumed. As he attempted to right himself, his knee pushed into my left thigh.

"Gah!" I shouted again. "My leg, you're breaking it!"

Loretta rushed to my aide. She tried to push Coronado off me but had no more success than someone attempting to roll a beached whale. Esperanza joined Loretta.

"Get off!" shouted Esperanza. She heaved on Coronado's arm, whilst Loretta pushed his side. Together, they rolled him off my chest.

I gasped for air. "Thank—thank you," I said.

"You okay, Bennie?" asked Loretta.

"I think so." I extended my right hand towards her. "Would you please help me up? I fear he has damaged my leg."

Loretta pulled my right arm whilst Esperanza, in an unusual display of public spiritedness, grasped my left arm. Together, they restored me to the vertical.

"Er, thank you, Esperanza," I said, still sucking in lungfulls of air.

"I don't like you, *Pendejito*, but nobody deserves to be squashed by *El Gordo*."

"Yes, well, whatever the reason, I am most appreciative."

"Can you walk, Bennie?" asked Loretta.

"The leg appears to be undamaged," I said, after taking a trepidatious step. I goggled Coronado. "Why did you rush in here?"

"It's your mom, Señor Graves," he said. "She and Josefa started fighting. Your mom shouted something at Josefa and then Josefa grabbed a plate and threw it at her." Coronado smiled. "It's kinda funny when ladies fight."

Loretta's eyes widened. She rushed towards the dining room, closely followed by Esperanza and a limping self. As I entered the dining room, the jaw dropped. Customers were lined up against both walls grinning like hyenas. Mother and Josefa stood perhaps ten feet apart facing each other, each holding a dinner plate. Uncle Bill was sitting at the table rubbing his head. His glass of beer was on its side, the contents having spilt on the table and onto the floor.

"Mother!" Loretta and I shouted simultaneously. Loretta ran to her mother's side whilst I limped to my mother's. Loretta then escorted her mother into the kitchen.

"What is going on?" I hissed, as I retrieved the dinner plate from her hand. "Have you gone mad?"

"I was defending your honour," she said. "The nerve of that woman."

"By smashing crockery? What are you talking about?"

"Loretta's mother had not sat down for a minute before telling me that her priest would determine whether you and our entire family are worthy. If not, she would not allow Loretta to marry you." Mother paused. "Not worthy, indeed. I have never heard such nonsense, and I was not about to let our family's history be denigrated. I told her in no uncertain terms that any Catholic girl was unworthy of my son and so was any idiot priest. Loretta's mother then picked up a plate and threw it at me. So, I did the same." Mother harrumphed loudly. "I forbid this marriage, Benjamin. She may be a nice girl, but *she* is not worthy of *you*."

I groaned. "All right, Mother. Calm down. Perhaps we should step outside for a few minutes. What happened to Uncle Bill? Is he all right?"

"William attempted to intervene, but someone's arm smashed into his head."

"'Someone's arm,' you say?" I asked. "Did you strike Uncle Bill, Mother?"

"Well, everyone's arms were waving about. It was an accident, of course."

"Very well," I said. "I think it best if I escort you back to the ranch now."

"Yes, dear. Please take me away from this . . . this place."

I opened the front door. Mother stepped outside onto the *portal* and I followed. As I was about to descend the steps, Porfiria suddenly appeared in the road, fully mackintoshed and waving her *umbrella*.

"¡*Diablo!*" she shouted, pointing the umbrella towards me.

"Oh, please, not again," I moaned.

"Who is that woman?" my mother asked. "She appears to be disturbed."

"Mad as a March hare," I said. "If you would stay on the porch here, that would be best. She wields that umbrella of hers like a broadsword."

I turned towards Porfiria. "Leave me alone," I shouted, "or I shall thrash you with that bloody umbrella."

She looked at me and lowered it. Presently, I espied Archie. He had exited Rudy's and was approaching her.

"I say, er, Porfiria is it? Remember me? You called me the nice *gringo*. I brought you a Coke earlier this afternoon."

She eyed Archie. "Yeah, I remember you. Can I have another Coke?"

"Of course, you may. But first, why don't you let my cousin and his mother pass by? Then we shall go inside where you can have your Coke and something to eat. How does that sound?"

Archie pointed surreptitiously towards the left, indicating an escape route.

"Okay," she said, aiming an accusatory forefinger at the self. "But I don't want him near me."

"He won't be there," Archie said smoothly. He motioned again for us to exit stage left.

"That's right," I said, "we are about to—"

"Don't talk to me," screamed Porfiria.

I raised my hands. "Let's go, Mother," I whispered, "before this brief window of sanity closes."

I hustled Mother down the stairs and towards the back of the cafe, where my lorry was parked. I helped her into her seat, stepped inside, shut the door, and breathed out heavily.

"My God, what a nightmare," I said.

"Who is that woman, Benjamin, and why is she wearing a macintosh?"

"Her name is Porfiria Alcalde. It is a very long story, which I would prefer not to relate at the present time. I will leave you at the ranch and then return to the cafe. When I return home later this evening, I will provide you with the details. That is, after I pour myself a large whisky.

I returned to the cafe about one hour later, feeling thoroughly knackered. Afraid Porfiria might still be lurking inside the dining room, I stepped into the kitchen via the back door and espied Maria and Esperanza, sitting around a table, chimneying away.

"What is the situation?" I asked them. "Is she still here?"

"No," Esperanza said. "She came in with your cousin. Then everybody else left real fast. He got her a Coke and some *enchiladas*. She ate. Then she left. Maybe a half-hour ago."

"Where is Archie?" I asked.

"After she left, he and El Vaquero went to Rudy's," Esperanza replied. "El Vaquero said he needed a drink."

"Ah," I said. "And Loretta?"

"She took Josefa home," said Esperanza. "I told her she didn't have to come back tonight. Your mom better not start no more fights in the cafe, *Pendejito*."

"I believe it was Josefa who instigated the, er, altercation," I said.

"I can't cook no more," said Maria, whose face had taken on a greyish hue and was shaking her head. "We got fighting, we got *La Loca* and *El Gordo* coming into my kitchen. I'm too old for this shit, Bennie."

I sighed. "I understand, Maria," I said. "Archie brought Porfiria into the cafe this evening because it allowed me to escape to safety. She was screaming as per usual at me. Did she have any, er, outbursts whilst here?"

"No," said Esperanza. "But everybody left after she came in. I didn't get no tips and people didn't pay their bill. Nobody pays and we got no money to stay open."

"I understand, but we cannot prevent her from coming in here, unless you can convince Tiny to bin her into the state hospital."

"You know he ain't gonna do nothing," said Esperanza.

"Yes, well, I suspect you are correct," I said. "What about her sister? Perhaps she has some influence."

"Nobody knows where Consuela is," said Esperanza.

"Perhaps Tiny could use his official status to locate Consuela," I said.

Esperanza and Maria both eyed the self. "You think he would do that?" Esperanza asked.

"One would hope he would." I replied, "Although if anyone can evade his duty, it is Tiny. Perhaps if we offered him a few free meals in exchange?"

Esperanza nodded. "For a *gringo*, you got a good idea," she said.

"Damned with faint praise again, eh, Esperanza," I said.

"Huh?"

I waved my hand dismissively. "Not important. Which one of you intends to speak with him?"

"Esperanza and me will talk to him," Maria said, releasing a large cloud of blue-grey smoke.

"Perhaps we should shutter the cafe until after the wedding, Maria. That will give you some time to rest. Calm things down, what?"

Maria nodded. "Yeah, okay, that sounds good. But we gotta have everybody here for the wedding *fiesta*."

"That's most kind of you, Maria. But there is really no need."

"It ain't for you, *Pendejito*, it's for Loretta," chimed Esperanza. "'Course if she don't marry you, then we're gonna have a lot bigger *fiesta*."

I sighed and shook the head, which felt as if an axe had been despatched into it. "I must say, Esperanza, you remind me of Lord Nelson. 'Never mind manoeuvres,' he would say, 'go straight at them.' Well, if we are to shutter the cafe, I will post a sign on the door tomorrow morning. In the meantime, can you lock up the evening?"

Esperanza shrugged. "Yeah, okay."

Maria waved her hand and ever-present cigarette but said nothing.

"Thank you," I said. "Now, if you will excuse me, I must speak with Loretta's mother and see if we can maintain some form of temporary armistice."

I walked out the back door, reconnoitred the area to determine if Porfiria and her umbrella were lurking about, and then walked to the lorry. Once inside, I laid my head against the steering wheel. Fate was enjoying itself far too much at the self's expense.

Chapter 10

I motored to Mrs. Alvarez's home, parked the lorry, and knocked on the door. The dog, Chata, began barking loudly. Presently, Mrs. Alvarez opened the door. Chata rushed out, tail wagging, and nuzzled my hand.

"Hullo, Chata," I said, patting her head. "May I speak with you, Mrs. Alvarez?"

"Come in, Bennie," she replied coolly. "Loretta's inside."

I walked into the sitting room and espied Loretta on the sofa. Her eyes were red and swollen.

"Hi, Bennie," Loretta said. "Is everything okay at the cafe?"

"Everything is fine. We decided to close the cafe until after the wedding. Maria is exhausted and she appears to be rather at wit's end."

Loretta nodded. "That's probably a good idea. What about Porfiria?"

"She didn't scream at anyone if that is what you mean. I gather she consumed her *enchiladas* and left. Unfortunately, most of the other patrons left when she arrived, without paying. Our financial position is becoming increasingly perilous. Esperanza is especially angry about her lost gratuities, although one wonders why anyone would provide her one."

Loretta smiled. "That sounds like *Tía* Esperanza. What about the other thing?"

"What other thing?" I asked.

"The fight," Loretta mumbled.

"Oh, yes, the crockery-smashing," I said.

"I'm sorry, Bennie," said Loretta's mother, "but I could not let your mother's accusations go unanswered."

"Accusations, Mrs. Alvarez?"

"She insulted the Pope and called me a religious nut for wanting you to convert before marrying Loretta. She then said my Loretta was not worthy of you. How dare she. If anything, you're not worthy of my Loretta."

I imagined Fate was relaxing somewhere nearby, reclining in a leather wing chair and sipping a well-aged single malt, thoroughly enjoying my predicament. Having heard both parties' accusations of unworthiness, I began to doubt how we would reach a marital *modus vivendi* other than via elopement.

I sat down next to Loretta. "Mrs. Alvarez," I said haltingly, "please understand. My mother is upset. She dislikes the idea of my converting but has accepted it as a *fait accompli*. However, there is no reason this should become a dispute of Shakespearean proportion."

"There is no dispute," Josefa replied sternly. "If you marry Loretta, you must first convert. Why can't your mother understand that? Is she stupid?"

Loretta's eyes widened and she placed a hand over her mouth.

The Graves honour was now under direct fire, and a vigorous response was required. The eyebrows raised and the molars clenched. "I would thank you not to insult my mother, Mrs. Alvarez."

"There's no need to take that tone with me, Benjamin," she huffed. "Father Castillo will decide whether you are worthy. If he does, and only if he does, will the wedding proceed. But I won't allow your mother to attend."

The jaw weighed anchor. "What did you say?"

"I won't allow your mother to attend the wedding," she repeated sternly.

"Because she is not of the faith?" I asked. "Do you also forbid my cousin and Uncle Bill to attend?"

"They haven't insulted me like your mother did. She's just another rich *gringa*."

"What did you say?" I stammered.

"That's enough, both of you!" shouted Loretta. "Mother, it's my wedding, not yours. Unless you want me to elope, you won't exclude anyone. Is that clear?" Presently, Loretta turned and directed fire towards the self. "Bennie, I understand you're upset by what my mother said. But, please, please, I just want a nice, quiet wedding. I don't want it to turn into the gunfight at the OK Corral."

"Neither do I," I replied.

"Okay," muttered Loretta's mother.

"Look, Mrs. Alvarez," I said, fatigue creeping into my voice, "I must contend with Esperanza and Joe, neither of whom want the wedding to proceed because I am a *gringo*. I must contend with a swivel-eyed loon who enjoys attacking me with her umbrella because she believes me to be the Devil. Then there is my mother, who is suffering from cultural shock—Vaca Seca being rather different than London, after all—and for whom a Catholic wedding might as well be conducted by Martians. Plus, the cafe's finances are taking on water, so to speak, and I am supposed to keep it afloat for Uncle Bill.

"I have agreed to convert, and I shall ensure my mother behaves at the wedding. Is that not sufficient? If not, then I shall escort Loretta to Santa Fe and marry her in a civil ceremony, church and town be damned."

"Well, Mother?" growled Loretta. "As much as I want a church wedding, I agree with Bennie."

Loretta's mother paused and raised both hands in surrender. "Okay, okay," she said. "I just want what's best for my daughter."

"As do I, Mrs. Alvarez. I trust avoiding a full-scale battle meets that criterion."

"I guess so," she replied, "but I don't want to sit next to your mother."

"I quite agree. One must always separate match from gunpowder." I glanced at the watch, which read half eight. "Now, if you will excuse me, I must return to the ranch and attempt to placate my mother."

Loretta walked outside with me to the parked lorry. "Thanks, Bennie," she said quietly. "I never imagined things could get this crazy."

I laughed. "In Vaca Seca? The entire town is a loony bin. I shouldn't be surprised if there is a rattlesnake in the church the day of the wedding. Or maybe your uncle will try to burn it down, as he did with the cafe. As for Esperanza—"

"Okay, okay," Loretta said, "I know they complain, but they really do like you."

I raised an eyebrow. "If your uncle's attempts to coerce a rattlesnake to sink its fangs into the self and torch the cafe are expressions of favour, one shudders to think what his expressions of disfavour would be."

"*Tío* Joe apologised for that. And you know what *Tía* Esperanza is like."

I grimaced. "Only too well."

"*Tía* Maria won't let her do anything stupid."

"Whilst I admire Maria, her control over her sister seems limited, especially outside of the cafe. However, we shall meet what Fate presents head-on, just as Lord Nelson would."

I bent down and kissed Loretta. "Now, I must return to the ranch and steady my mother. Perhaps we should dose them both with Farm Calm. We could modify the label to say, 'for the distressed animal, including mothers of bride and groom.'"

Loretta laughed. "Maybe we should get them both drunk. My mother just falls asleep when she's had too much to drink. What happens to your mother?"

The grey matter whirled momentarily. "Hmm. I cannot recall ever having seen her three sheets to the wind. My father is quite another matter. When over-whiskyed, he becomes even louder and more pompous than usual. I suspect my mother would react like yours and just fall asleep, although one never knows."

Loretta eyed me silently and offered a Cheshire cat-like smile.

"Are you suggesting—?" I said, gaping.

She nodded vigorously.

I pondered Loretta's idea, then kissed her. "Loretta Alvarez, I stand before you in awe. It is a brilliant idea. However, mounting a successful campaign will require a level of deviousness I do not possess. Fortunately, I know someone who does."

Shortly thereafter, I arrived back at the ranch. As I climbed the steps of the portal, Daisy grunted and raised her head.

"Hullo, Daisy," I said, scratching her ears under the *sombrero*. The sow grunted again and lowered her head down. I opened the front door and stepped into the sitting room. Uncle Bill and Archie were nursing glasses of Dusty Trail. Mother appeared to be drinking tea.

"Good evening, all," I chirped.

"Howdy, pard'ner," said Uncle Bill.

"What-ho, old chap," said Archie.

"Did you deal with that horrible woman?" asked Mother.

I glided over to the sideboard and poured a bracing glass of Dusty Trail. "There are numerous candidates, Mother, although Esperanza and Porfiria currently are the leading contenders. To whom are you referring?

"I was referring to Loretta's mother," she replied. "Did you speak with her?"

"I did. She has agreed to an armistice."

"What does that mean?" asked my mother.

"First, it means there shall be no more bunging of crockery, *objet d'art*, or any other heavy objects at one another, and anyone who happens to be in the line of fire. Second, it means that you and Mrs. Alvarez shall be kept apart from one another, including at the wedding. Third, there shall be no shouting of epithets, gnashing of teeth, rending of garments, or other displays of intemperance, *especially* at the wedding ceremony."

Mother emitted a sound between a harrumph and a low growl. "Very well, Benjamin. But I am disappointed you are not defending the Graves honour more vigorously."

"Well, I would prefer to avoid a formal duel," I said, "even if some of the Graves ancestors enjoyed them. I suggest discretion is the better part of valour in this instance."

"I agree, Aunt Dorothy," said Archie. "Nothing good will come of a feud."

"The boys are right, Dorothy," added Uncle Bill. "Folks around here are pretty set in their ways. Have been for a long, long time."

Mother eyed the self with an expression of disdain and resignation, then turned to face Uncle Bill. "I don't understand how both of you live in this . . . this, I don't know the word for it."

"It grows on you, Dorothy," said Uncle Bill. "But it sure ain't for everybody."

"It most definitely is not for me," said Mother. "You don't even speak the Queen's English anymore, William."

"I am most capable of doing so, Dorothy," replied Uncle Bill in a full Oxbridge accent. "But I don't talk that way anymore. Prefer talking like a cowboy, because that's what I am."

Mother sighed. "All right. I survived the Blitz. I can certainly survive another week of this."

"That's the Graves spirit, Aunt Dorothy," said Archie, raising his now empty whisky glass.

"Here, here," said Uncle Bill.

"Right-ho, Mother," I added.

"Pah. I'm going to bed," said Mother.

When her bedroom door closed, I turned to Archie. "Loretta and I need your advice," I said.

"My advice, old chap?" asked Archie. "Happy to oblige." He rose from his chair, walked over to the sideboard, and poured another glass of Dusty Trail. "This swill you call whisky grows on one."

"Easy, pard'ner," said Uncle Bill. "It'll sneak up on you."

"Thanks for the warning, Uncle," said Archie, "Are you speaking about getting pissed or that it will destroy the lining of one's stomach."

"Both, if you ain't careful," replied Uncle Bill.

"Right, then," said Archie. "Care to share the contents, cousin?" He poured half of the glass into mine.

"Thanks," I said.

"Now, what advice can you and your lovely bride-to-be possibly need from me?" he asked.

"We need our respective mothers three sheets to the wind before the wedding begins."

Archie grimaced. "Granted, my experience is limited, but at the weddings I have attended, it is typically not until after the nuptials that the bride's and groom's relatives become sozzled."

Uncle Bill's eyes narrowed. "What are you aiming at, Bennie?"

"Well, you observed the events at the cafe," I said.

"Yeah, I felt them, too," Uncle Bill replied, rubbing the still-present lump on his forehead.

"So, we employ the Farm Calm strategy," I said.

"They ain't cattle, Bennie," said Uncle Bill.

"Allow me to clarify," I said. "Farm Calm advertises itself as 'for the distressed animal,' does it not? Mother and Josefa are the most distressed animals, wedding-wise, we have. Granted, Esperanza and Joe will be problematic, although I suspect Maria will ensure neither strays too far from acceptable behaviour. If Mother and Josefa are well-lubricated, they will be unlikely to disturb the wedding."

Uncle Bill nodded hesitantly. "I guess that makes sense. Maybe. What time's the wedding again?"

"The ceremony is scheduled for two o'clock," I said.

"Little early in the day for them to be drunk," said Uncle Bill. "If we were talking about Nestor, then it would be easy. But your mother ain't much of a drinker and I don't think Josefa is either."

"That's where Archie comes in," I said.

"I say, cousin," Archie replied, "I participated in a few games at Eaton where the lads would challenge each other to see who could consume the most and remain upright, but I doubt Aunt Dorothy and Loretta's mother are the drinking game type. Besides, I am supposed to nick that Nestor chap's nasty little cur before the wedding, bin it into Uncle's barn, and then convince your *La Loca* to rescue it. Not sure how I can do both."

"No, no," I said, shaking my head. "I need your help in formulating an inebriation strategy."

"Time out, pard'ner," Uncle Bill said. "What's all this about stealin' Paco and puttin' him in my barn?"

"Ah," I coughed. "I am afraid we are fighting a two-front war, wedding-wise, Uncle Bill. Besides the crockery-bunging *materfamilias*, there is the issue of ensuring Porfiria does not barge into the church during the ceremony, scream '¡*Diablo!*' at the self, and then launch an umbrella fusillade."

"So, you aim to lock her in the barn?" asked Uncle Bill.

"M-hem, yes," I said. "According to Rudy, Porfiria is quite fond of dogs. Apparently, whenever she saw Nestor's dog, Perro, she would stop to pet it."

"Yeah, I remember Perro," said Uncle Bill. "Real nice dog. Everybody liked him."

"I gather Perro was quite the amiable canine," I said.

"Paco ain't amiable, pard'ner," said Uncle Bill. "You ought to know that."

"Er, no," I said. "However, as there are no amiable dogs available—I doubt Mrs. Alvarez would appreciate our borrowing Chata—Paco is the obvious choice. I have observed that the other local dogs are quite large and tend to look at one as a starter course."

Uncle Bill's eyes narrowed. "So what's your plan?" he asked.

"We administer a sufficient dose of beer and Farm Calm to make Paco malleable," I said. "Then, because Porfiria considers Archie to be the 'nice *gringo*,' as she says, he informs her of a canine in distress, motors her to the ranch, lures her into the barn where we will have previously deposited Paco, and locks her inside until after the wedding."

Uncle Bill shook his head in disbelief. "Why don't you and Loretta just elope? Be a hell of a lot easier."

"My thoughts, exactly," I said. "However, as the bride and her mother insist on a church wedding, eloping appears out of the question."

Uncle Bill drained his glass and stood up. "Jesus, Bennie, I hope you know what you're doing."

"So do I, Uncle Bill," I muttered, "so do I."

Uncle Bill walked over to the sideboard and placed his glass upon it. "I'll see you in the morning. Gotta get me some shut-eye." He walked down the hall to his bedroom and disappeared.

"Well, cousin," said Archie, after Uncle Bill had shut his bedroom door, "you appear to have yourself quite an undertaking."

"No doubt. I still need your advice on how to inebriate the respective mothers."

"Yes, well, I must ponder that," said Archie. "The difficulty is that it must be done separately. Perhaps you can help Aunt Dorothy along and Loretta can handle her mother."

"I'm not sure how. I cannot command Mother to down a bottle of champagne before the ceremony. And I doubt Loretta can do the same with Josefa."

"They each need a sympathetic barman," declared Archie.

"Eh?"

"Someone to whom they can complain about the wedding whilst that said someone plies them with champagne."

"Rudy is the town's official barman," I said. "Well, he and his grandson Antonio, although I rather doubt that either Mother or Josefa would wish to be plied with champagne by a fourteen-year-old and asked to pour out their disdain for the other. I rather doubt Rudy would like that, either."

"Very well. Then ask Rudy to lubricate one of them."

I thought for a moment. "Hmm. I believe it will be best for Rudy to deal with Mother. She seems to like him, especially as he rescued the both of you from Coronado."

"A true act of divine intervention, cousin," said Archie. "What about Loretta's mother?"

"We need someone who will encourage her to drink and be sympathetic to her complaints about my mother."

"Do you have someone in mind?"

The grey matter whirred silently and arrived at an answer. "Esperanza," I said. "If Mrs. Alvarez complains about the visiting *gringa* disparaging the Catholic faith, then Esperanza will descend like a large vulture ready to gorge itself. The only drawback I foresee is that Esperanza becomes quite surly when inebriated. We will have to trust Maria to keep her sister in check."

Archie raised his empty glass. "Well, here's to a successful strategy on that front, old chap."

Chapter 11

Y ou want me to do what?" shouted Rudy the following afternoon, as Archie and I sat at the bar explaining our plan. "You've already got me helping you to dognap Paco so you can lure Porfiria to rescue him. Now you want me to get your mother drunk, too?"

"Merely trying to avoid fisticuffs during the wedding . . . or worse," I replied. "You seem the natural choice, Rudy. Everyone likes you."

"Doesn't your mother like you?" he asked. "Or your cousin?"

"Well, I presume she does, although she did call me a nincompoop," I said. "But lubricating one's mother with champagne would be rather an incongruous action. As for Archie, he will be otherwise engaged in dognapping."

"I don't know your mother, Bennie," said Rudy. "All I did was drive her to the ranch after she and your cousin arrived. I can't show up with a bottle of champagne and two glasses, knock on the door, and tell her I'm there to get her drunk."

"She just needs a friendly barman to lend an ear," said Archie. "That's what you chaps do best, isn't it?"

Rudy groaned. "How?" he asked. "Do you plan on bringing her into the bar? I doubt that's gonna go over real good with the regulars." He raised a thumb towards the table of four in the corner. "You know how they can get."

"Er, yes," I said. "How about dinner tonight?"

"I thought you closed the cafe until after the wedding."

"We did," I said. "I meant dinner at the ranch. I've become quite proficient at grilling steaks. You can get to know Mother.

Pour on the Sandoval charm that caused four members of the fairer sex to marry you."

Rudy goggled at me. "You do remember they all ended in divorce, don't you?"

"Well, yes, but not immediately," I said. "Mother needs another sympathetic ear, someone to explain how the locals are set in their ways."

"Yeah, they are that," Rudy agreed.

"And as my forthcoming conversion is the proximate cause of my mother's distress, I most certainly am not a sympathetic ear. Rather more like a voracious mosquito buzzing around it."

"Jesus," mumbled Rudy.

"Let us consider other potential candidates," I continued. "Joe Garcia is not especially fond of the self and would likely charge Mother for the champagne. Luis, who, although a most amiable chap when one's lorry requires service or needs a new tyre, would not be a natural choice for a discussion on the Catholic church. Perhaps Nestor, an expert on inebriation after all—"

"Okay, I get it, Bennie," said Rudy.

"She has met Coronado, of course. He might offer—"

"I said I get it, Bennie. I'll come over for dinner—it better be a damn good steak—and I will play the sympathetic bartender for your mother."

"Thank you, Rudy," I said. "Would you perhaps have a decent bottle of wine hiding here? Mother is not one for Dusty Trail."

"Yeah, I got some decent red squirrelled away. I can bring a bottle. But I still don't know what you want me to say."

"Just be your charming, lend-an-ear self," I said. "Mother is not immune to flattery. I shall ask Uncle Bill to conjure some form of ranch 'emergency' requiring him to motor off somewhere before the wedding. He can then suggest you escort her to the wedding. You then arrive with champagne and suggest a pre-wedding glass to calm her nerves, which will surely be wound into steel bands.

"Does Bill know about your plan?" asked Rudy.

"Er, not yet," I said, "but we shall inform him presently."

"Hell of a lot easier if you just eloped," Rudy mumbled. He reached for a glass and poured himself a whisky.

"My thoughts exactly," I said. "Regrettably, the other principals, including Loretta, do not agree."

Rudy drained his glass in one swallow. "Okay. What time do you want me to be there?"

"How about five-ish? That will provide you time to speak with Mother before dinner."

"Why in hell does everything get so complicated when you're involved, Bennie?"

"Fate, I suppose. Or perhaps because Vaca Seca delights in creating unique circles of hell for the self."

"Yeah, I can't argue with that," Rudy said. "So how you gonna get Josefa drunk? I can't be two places at once."

"Er, that is, we intend to recruit Esperanza for that particular task," I said.

Rudy's eyebrows shot skywards. "Huh? You're gonna ask Esperanza to get Josefa drunk before the wedding?"

"Not exactly," I said. "I mean, Esperanza considers the self to be—well, you know what she thinks of me and *gringos* generally. Coupled with my mother's disparagement of the Catholic religion, Esperanza surely will be only too happy to fan the flames, so to speak."

"Sure, Esperanza will pour gasoline on that fire," replied Rudy, "but I don't see how Esperanza gets Josefa drunk."

"M-hem, that detail remains to be addressed," I said. "We are hoping Maria will assist.

"*Mi querida*?" asked Rudy.

"Your what?" asked Archie.

"It is a term of endearment, Archie," I said. "Rudy is rather fond of Maria."

"Maria doesn't drink much, anyway," said Rudy.

"No," I replied, "but if Maria were to suggest they see Josefa before the wedding and suggest they bring some liquid refreshment to calm Josefa, then Esperanza will, I believe, do so gladly."

"Have you talked to Maria about this scheme of yours?" asked Rudy.

"Not yet," I said. "However, as we've shuttered the cafe until after the wedding, I thought we could both speak with her. We could explain the particulars and strategy, and you could describe your role."

Rudy eyed me from above the half-glasses he wore. "It had better be a really big steak, Bennie," said Rudy.

"Right-ho," I said.

"Well, cousin," said Archie, as we returned to the ranch. "What's next for 'Operation Sozzle'?"

"First, we speak with Uncle Bill because it will require his cooperation. Plus, I shall inform him of our dinner guest. Tomorrow, I shall speak with Maria."

"There is one aspect of your plan I don't fully understand, old chap. Nicking the dog is jolly well and good, but how am I to find that madwoman? She seems to appear out of nowhere."

"I have given that some thought. She lives just outside of town, just past where Nestor—recall, he is Paco's owner—resides. If Porfiria is not wandering about the village after you've secured Paco in the barn, then you can motor to where she must be living."

"What if she does not look kindly on strangers knocking at her door?"

"Ah, but you won't be a stranger, Archie. You are the 'nice gringo,' remember? If you identify yourself as such, one assumes she will not respond violently."

"That's all well and good cousin, except the woman is a complete loon. What if she breaks out her umbrella or worse, starts shooting?"

"I hardly think it will come to that. I believe I am the only individual who has been on the receiving end of any umbrella-biffing, at least recently. Besides, surely you are more fleet of foot than Porfiria. As for shooting you, Vaca Seca may be part of Uncle Bill's Wild West, but it is not *that* wild. Well, not usually."

"I should have stayed in Cannes," Archie sighed. "Ah, well, in for a penny, as they say. But if I am maimed . . . or worse, I shall hold you personally responsible."

"Given your history of nicking Jaguars, I should think this will be rather easy."

"Dealing with the police is easy. They may toss you into gaol, but that's about it. Here in, well, I should not call it 'civilisation,' one does not know what to expect."

"Have you ever read any novels by Zane Grey?"

"Never heard of him. Why?"

"Uncle Bill devoured them whilst in his formative years. He still re-reads them. They are all about the Wild West, cowboys and Indians, that sort of thing. Those novels inspired him to leave England and settle here."

"I don't follow you, old chap."

"I mean, whilst not Oxford or Kensington, the Wild West is rather less wild these days. I should think you face more danger from Malcolm than from Porfiria."

"Very well, cousin. But you will need to show me exactly where the madwoman lives. Oh, and I suppose I should have a bit of practice driving your lorry."

"We shall do both tomorrow. Now, onto Uncle Bill."

Soon thereafter, we arrived at the ranch. Daisy greeted us with a loud grunt and encouraged us to scratch behind her *sombrero*-covered ears, which we dutifully performed to her satisfaction. Inside, Mother was in the sitting room reading.

"Hullo, Mother," I said.

"Hello, dear, she said. "Did you two have a nice outing?"

"Quite nice, Aunt Dorothy," said Archie. "Bennie showed me around a bit more. With his cafe closed until after the wedding, he has more free time."

"That's right," I said. "We ran into Rudy. He's going to come out for dinner this evening."

"Rudy?" Mother paused. "Oh, yes, the nice gentleman who drove us here that first day."

"Indeed," added Archie. "Seems like a good egg."

"Excuse me, Mother," I interrupted. "Have you seen Uncle Bill?"

"Yes. He said he needed to repair a fence and went outside." She pointed towards the back where the cattle resided.

"Ah," I said. "Perhaps I will just pop out there. I must speak with him."

"Anything I can help with, dear?" she asked.

"God no," I muttered quietly. "That is, no thank you, Mother. Ranch matters, Marjorie's barn, that sort of thing. Nothing to concern yourself about."

"All right, dear," she said, returning to her book.

"Er, care to accompany me, Archie?" I asked.

"Eh? Oh yes, yes of course I will, old chap," said Archie.

I retrieved three large steaks from the freezer. We then exited out the back door and walked towards the field. Malcolm briefly eyed us, then returned to his grazing.

"Uncle Bill," I shouted.

"Over here," he yelled from beyond the trees on the other side of the field.

We navigated over the fence and walked towards the trees. As we neared them, I espied Uncle Bill further away, wrestling with a wooden fence post and a tangle of barbed wire. He was cursing under his breath.

"Here, let me help Uncle Bill," I said. "What happened?"

"Goddamn Malcolm, that's what," replied Uncle Bill. "He must have been rubbing himself on the post and the whole thing broke. Where is he anyway?"

"Malcolm? Grazing away contentedly on the other side," I said as I jerked the thumb in the bull's direction.

"Okay. Here, Bennie," he said, handing the self a heavy sledgehammer. "I'll hold the post up and you pound it into the ground."

"Anything I can do to help?" asked Archie.

"Yeah," said Uncle Bill. He pointed towards his lorry, which was parked nearby. "There's an extra pair of gloves inside. You go fetch them and then you can hold this damn barbed wire."

Archie offered a mock salute. "Right then. Gloves and hold the barbed wire it is," he said, before trotting towards the lorry.

"How's your mother, Bennie?" asked Uncle Bill. "She's been a might quiet this morning. I guess she's still chewing over that fight with Josefa yesterday."

"No doubt," I said. "Which is why Archie and I must speak with you. We have formulated a plan to deal with both Mother and Mrs. Alvarez to avoid fisticuffs at the wedding."

Uncle Bill turned his head and eyed me suspiciously. "Another plan? You gonna lock them up in my barn, too?" He laughed. "Hell, between the two of them, Porfiria, and Paco, there'd probably be nothing left by the time the wedding's over."

"Er, yes."

Presently, Archie returned and raised his now gloved hands. "Where should I hold the wire, Uncle?" he asked.

Uncle Bill pointed to one of the strands. After Uncle Bill set the post upright, Archie grasped the strand and pulled it taut. I then hammered the top of the post into the ground.

"Thanks, boys," he said. He removed a handkerchief from his back trouser pocket and wiped his forehead. "Maybe Malcolm won't knock it over for a few days. Now, tell me about this plan of yours."

"Yes, well," I coughed, "it begins with Rudy joining us for dinner this evening. I invited him."

Uncle Bill blinked several times. "Okay," he said. "I don't rightly follow what that's got to do with keeping your mother and Josefa from clawing each other's eyes out, but I suppose you're gonna tell me."

"The idea is for Rudy to, er, woo Mother before the wedding," I said.

"What? I may not like that goddamn brother of mine, Bennie, but your mother's married to him."

"No, no," I said. "I mean, the idea is—"

"Allow me to explain," interrupted Archie. "If both Aunt Dorothy and Loretta's mother are, one might say, pacified, before the wedding, then they will be far less likely to erupt like volcanoes during the ceremony. Rudy, an accomplished barman by all appearances, will offer a sympathetic ear to Aunt Dorothy this evening. On the day of the wedding, you will announce some sort of emergency engagement. Rudy will step forward and offer to escort Aunt Dorothy, but before doing so will ply her with copious quantities of champagne, rendering her somnolent and thus indifferent to the religious particulars of the ceremony."

Uncle Bill shook his head in disbelief. "Let me get this straight. While Porfiria is locked in my barn, Rudy's gonna come over to the house to get Dorothy drunk and then drive her to the church, where she will sleep it off during the wedding."

"That seems an apt summary," I said.

"If your mother shows up drunk to the wedding ceremony, Josefa will have a fit," Uncle Bill said.

"Yes, but you see—" I began.

"That's the other part of the plan," interrupted Archie. "The idea is to get Loretta's mother drunk too. Then neither will be any condition to attack the other."

I nodded dully in affirmation.

"Does Rudy get Josefa drunk before or after your mother?" asked Uncle Bill.

"Er, no," I said. "We have identified Esperanza as the appropriate candidate for that particular task."

Uncle Bill's jaw dropped and sought cover in the low grass nearby. "Esperanza? You're kidding?"

"Well, she does enjoy her tipple," I said. "And she will be a most sympathetic ear when Mrs. Alvarez complains about Mother's lack of decorum concerning my forthcoming conversion and subsequent church wedding. Esperanza should also encourage additional complaints regarding Loretta's marriage to a *gringo*, which we trust will encourage additional consumption of spirits.

"I still don't get it, Bennie," said Uncle Bill. "Esperanza won't grease the skids for your wedding. If you ask her for help, that's the last thing she's gonna give you."

"I quite agree, which is why I intend to have Maria to do so."

Uncle Bill's jaw now burrowed underground like an exuberant mole. "You're gonna ask Maria to ask Esperanza to get Josefa drunk before the wedding?" he asked whilst shaking his head. "I need a drink,"

"Not directly," I said. "I shall ask Maria to, shall we say, 'encourage' Esperanza to sit down with Mrs. Alvarez a few hours before the wedding with champagne, and will provide said champagne, which I will have procured for Maria to bestow upon Esperanza. Esperanza, who is not one to turn down an offer of free alcohol, will readily agree. By the time the wedding commences, both should be several sheets to the wind, which will neutralise their innate urges to initiate a confrontation with Mother."

"What's Loretta think about this plan of yours?" asked Uncle Bill.

"Er," I muttered shakily, "perhaps some discretion in that regard is a prudent—"

"Jesus, Bennie," Uncle Bill interrupted. "You ain't gonna tell Loretta what you've got planned?"

"It seems imprudent to tell the bride-to-be of the intent to inebriate her mother before the wedding," I said.

Uncle Bill goggled us silently. He blinked. Then he blinked again. Finally, after a long silence, he turned around and walked towards his lorry whilst shaking his head.

"Wait, Uncle Bill," I cried, as I began trotting after him. "Do you perceive a flaw in this plan?"

He reached the lorry and opened the door, then removed his gloves and deposited them on the seat. "Nope," he said. "I perceive a bushel of 'em, starting with Esperanza. Josefa might just fall asleep when she's had one too many, but you know Esperanza is one mean goddamn drunk. You get her liquored up and she's gonna be loaded for bear when your wedding starts. As for not telling Loretta about this—" Uncle Bill's voice trailed off and he shook his head again.

"Loaded for bear?" I asked.

"Gunnin' for you, like an outlaw," Uncle Bill said. "You may not have to worry about Josefa screaming at your mother because Esperanza will be ten times worse."

"Ah," I said triumphantly, "we have accounted for Esperanza's alcohol-induced temperament. Maria shall be at her side and able to squelch any outbursts."

"Maybe," said Uncle Bill, "and maybe not. I remember something that happened years ago—this was way before you showed up—when I was in Rudy's having a beer. Esperanza burst in spitting fire. She was holding a shotgun. Said she was gonna shoot her sister and wanted to know if she was hiding inside."

"Esperanza threatened to shoot Maria? Why?" I asked.

"Damn right she did," he said. "She was convinced Maria was stealing her boyfriend."

I cringed. "Gah! You mean that dim-witted oaf, Hector? Surely Maria had more common sense than that."

"Nah, this was long before Hector," said Uncle Bill. "Esperanza's boyfriend's name was Miguel. He seemed like a nice guy. Even helped me out a few times at the ranch repairing fences. Didn't take Miguel long to figure out that Esperanza was—"

"An excrescence best run away from," I interrupted.

"Yep, something like that," said Uncle Bill. "Anyway, before Miguel left town, he stopped at Maria's house. He and Esperanza had gone there for dinner a few times, so he thanked her. Told her she was the best cook he had ever known, even better than his mother, and if she was ever in Española, he would buy her dinner. Then he kissed her and drove off."

The grey matter invoked an image of Maria being kissed and shuddered. "I gather Rudy did not approve," I said.

"Rudy was still married then. Lemme see, that would have been wife number two. Or maybe it was number three."

"I am aware of Rudy's history of serial monogamy," I said.

"Well, Esperanza got wind of it and started looking for her sister. That's when she burst into the bar and started waving her shotgun around. Rudy told her Maria wasn't there. He got out the rifle he keeps under the bar and pointed it at Esperanza. Told her to put the shotgun down or he would shoot her. Esperanza lowered the gun and started shouting that Maria had stolen her boyfriend. Well, she used more colourful language, but you get the idea."

"She must have encountered Maria at some point," I said.

"Yep. Later that day. Maria had gotten some stuff for the cafe—it was still open then. Esperanza must have seen her car parked outside. Rudy told me you could hear them both screaming at one another."

"Did Esperanza have her shotgun?" I asked.

"Yeah, Rudy told me she was holding it when she left."

"I take it no shots were fired," I said.

"She fired it all right," said Uncle Bill. "You remember that big hole in the kitchen ceiling when you were fixing up the cafe?"

"Not specifically," I said. "Then again, Coronado almost single-handedly destroyed the cafe when he was attempting to shoot our soon-to-be-overfed skunk, Señor Apestoso." Whilst the cafe was undergoing repairs, the foundation had been raised with numerous house jacks, a skunk had taken up residence underneath. Coronado took it upon himself to eliminate the odoriferous animal and unleashed numerous volleys from his shotgun.

When the dust cleared, both front windows were gone and most of the house jacks had been destroyed. The remaining ones groaned and collapsed, causing the uplifted walls to tumble down and crack the new foundation walls, which were also littered with holes. Whilst we gaped at the destruction Coronado had wrought, the skunk emerged calmly. It shook itself, sniffed, blinked at me with an air of casual indifference, and walked down the street, disappearing into the nearby bushes.

"Yep, I remember," said Uncle Bill. "Anyway, that hole was Esperanza's shotgun. She didn't shoot Maria, but she came close."

"What happened then?" I asked.

"They didn't speak to one another for months. Maria changed the lock on the cafe door so Esperanza couldn't get in. Esperanza would curse Maria if she saw her, but Maria never said a word."

"Well, a *rapprochement* must have occurred at some point," I said.

Uncle Bill shrugged. "About a year later, everything was back to normal. Neither of them said anything about it again."

"A riddle, wrapped in a mystery, inside an enigma, eh?" I replied. "But peace was had eventually."

"Eventually," said Uncle Bill. "But I'm warning you, pard'ner, you're grabbing a tiger by its tail. More like two of them."

"Well, do you have alternative recommendations regarding the best approach to neutralise the potential for a shooting war?" I asked.

Uncle Bill eyed me. "Sure," he said with a laugh. "Elope. Either that or lock Dorothy and Josefa in the barn with Porfiria and Paco."

"M-hem, yes," I said.

Chapter 12

Rudy arrived at the ranch just after five o'clock. I opened the front door and goggled at the impeccably dressed figure that stood before me. He wore a white button-down shirt and a *bolo* tie, a brown sports jacket, freshly pressed denim trousers, highly polished brown cowboy boots, and a white cowboy hat. He had requisitioned two bottles of a cabernet, which he handed to me as he walked inside.

"Thank you, Rudy," I said. "I have never seen you dressed in such finery."

Rudy removed his hat. "Yeah, well, don't get used to it, Bennie. All I know is that steak better be real good."

"Well, whilst I cannot offer you authentic *boeuf a l'anglaise*, I believe the grilled fillet steaks will be to your liking. Please come in. Mother will be out shortly."

Rudy handed me his hat, stepped inside, and sat down on the sofa. Presently, Uncle Bill walked into the sitting room. He, too, was dressed in more formal attire than usual.

"Howdy, Rudy," said Uncle Bill as he extended his hand. Uncle Bill glanced towards the hallway and, as Mother had not emerged from her bedroom, whispered, "You really goin' along with this crazy plan of Bennie's?"

Rudy shook his head in resignation and eyed me. "Yeah, I guess so," he said. "Be a hell of a lot easier if they just eloped."

"Yep," Uncle Bill replied.

I shrugged. "Numerous parties have made that particular suggestion, including Joe Garcia."

"Joe told you to elope?" asked Rudy. "Let me guess. He thought he could save some money by not buying a wedding gift."

"Joe's pecuniary sensitivities are rather acute," I said. "Of course, he clarified that he would prefer the entire wedding to be cancelled because I am not good enough for Loretta."

"You know Joe," said Rudy. "Don't take it personally, Bennie."

"I no longer do," I replied. "Besides, whatever philosophical principles Joe may have, they are outweighed by any opportunities for him to hoover up additional brass. Hence, if I continue to purchase supplies for the cafe from him, the slings and arrows shall be minor."

"Yeah, that's probably true," said Rudy.

Presently, Mother walked into the room. Rudy stood up. "Nice to see you again, Mrs. Graves," he said, extending his hand.

Mother took his hand and shook it mildly. "It's nice to see you, too, Rudy," she said. "Oh, and please, just call me Dorothy."

"Are you enjoying your visit Mrs.—Dorothy?" asked Rudy. "It's nice of you to come so far for your son's wedding. Must have been quite a trip for you and Archie."

"Well, it's quite different than I had imagined. Of course, Benjamin did not inform me he was getting married to Loretta until I was already here," she said, casting a disapproving glance at the self.

"Really? Uh, well, the important thing is that you're here now," said Rudy. "Loretta is a great gal."

Mother shrugged. "She seems pleasant enough, although this nonsense about Benjamin's conversion to Catholicism is quite disconcerting."

"Now, Mother," I interrupted. "Perhaps we should not discuss that now. After all, it's nothing to do with Rudy."

"Very well, Benjamin," she said. "My apologies."

"You know, Mother, Rudy has travelled worldwide," I said. "He's even been to Africa."

Mother's eyes widened. "Africa? Oh, my, did you see any lions? I saw a television programme about them in—now where was that—some plain. Oh yes, the Serengeti Plain, that's it."

Rudy laughed. "Afraid I never saw any lions. I was in the Army during the war, mainly in the desert. All I saw was a lot of camels."

"Have you been to Europe, too?" asked Mother.

"Sure have," said Rudy. "I was stationed in Italy, near Rome. Beautiful city. I wish I had been able to see London."

"Well, London was a horrid place during the war," said Mother. "But everything has been rebuilt. Perhaps you will have a chance to visit someday."

"I hope so," replied Rudy, offering her a smile.

I perceived a distinct thaw in Mother's demeanour towards Rudy. "Is there a Mrs. Salazar?" she asked.

"Uh, well, there was," Rudy said, not revealing there had been a total of four. "Sometimes things don't work out."

"Did something happen during the war?" asked Mother. "Goodness, I hope you were not widowed."

"Huh? Oh, no," Rudy said. "I suppose being overseas for such a long time didn't help. Can't say I blame her."

"You poor man," Mother tut-tutted. "Is there anyone special in your life now?"

Rudy paused, presumably considering whether to reveal his feelings towards Maria, however baffling to the rest of us. "Not really," he said. "Besides, I'm getting too old for all that anyway."

"Nonsense," said Mother. "You and William obviously are highly eligible bachelors."

Uncle Bill laughed. "That's nice of you to say, Dorothy. But I'm a might too set in my ways now."

"Well, you shouldn't be, William," said Mother. "And neither should you, Rudy."

"Perhaps I should commence cooking the steaks," I announced.

"Good idea," said Uncle Bill. "I could eat a horse. And, no, not Marjorie, so don't even think it, Bennie."

"M-hem," I grunted, whilst suppressing a smile at the grey matter's image of Marjorie secured to a large rotating grill.

"Allow me to assist, cousin," said Archie. He sprang up from the sofa and rocketed into the kitchen.

I followed quickly, secured the large plate of steaks, and stepped outside. I had already prepared the grill, which was charcoaling nicely. I placed the steaks on the grill and set the plate down on the table next to it.

"Aunt Dorothy seems quite enamoured with Rudy," said Archie. "I had my doubts, especially after she began discussing your conversion."

"Indeed. I'm relieved he did not mention all four marriages, which likely would have dampened Mother's mood. She was none too pleased when I informed her of my divorce from Cynthia."

"No 'Until death do us part,' eh, old chap?" said Archie, slapping my shoulder.

"Gah! You hit the exact same spot as Loretta and Porfiria. One wonders whether the wing will ever recover."

"Steady on, cousin. Would you like me to tend to the fillets whilst you nurse the injury?"

I shook my head and rubbed my shoulder. "No need. I shall survive. Er, whilst I tend to these, would you decant the wine? You can also place the salad and bread on the table and let everyone know the steaks will be ready in five minutes or so."

"Decant and bread on the table. Aye-aye, Captain," said Archie, offering a mock salute. He spun around in military fashion and marched into the kitchen.

Dinner was a rousing success. Rudy had charmed Mother thoroughly, assisted by the two large glasses of cabernet she had downed.

"My, what a fine meal, Benjamin," said Mother, who had sat down rather heavily on the sofa. "I had no idea you were such an accomplished chef."

"Well, I have learned a few things observing Maria," I said. "Granted, I have not incorporated cigarette ash into my efforts."

"Yeah, real good steak, Bennie," added Rudy, patting his stomach. "Just like you promised."

Presently, Mother turned towards Rudy, who was seated next to her. "Your choice of wine was excellent," she said, patting his hand. "As good as the French varieties I've had. Where did you get it?"

Mother's hand remained on Rudy's. I raised an eyebrow and espied Archie offering a nod of his head to the self.

Rudy smiled. "Got it from a little shop in Albuquerque, called Santiago's Liquors. I don't think Santiago knew much about the stuff. He had an entire case from a winery in California I had read about. It was collecting dust in the back corner of the store. I asked him how much he wanted for the whole case. He told me it had been sitting there for a year and asked me to name a price. I said, 'How about fifty bucks?' thinking he would want at least a hundred, or maybe a hundred and fifty. I would have paid that much, too. But he agreed. Told me that he didn't sell much wine, so he was glad to have the extra space." Rudy laughed softly. "I've still got another half-dozen bottles hidden away."

"Will you be at Benjamin's wedding?" Mother asked.

"Oh, sure," said Rudy. "I wouldn't miss it."

"I'm so glad," she said, sighing. "I wish I could say I am looking forward to it."

"I know you don't like the idea of a Catholic ceremony, Dorothy," Rudy said smoothly, "but they're real nice. Probably not much different than any other. Father Castillo is real down-to-earth, too."

"Well, as long as you will be there, Rudy," Mother said, patting his hand again.

Rudy checked his watch. "Well, I ought to be getting along. I gotta check on Anthony."

"Who is Anthony?" asked Mother.

"He's my grandson," said Rudy. "He's, uh, tending bar while I'm here."

"How kind of him," said Mother. "Well, it was nice of you to come for dinner, Rudy. Will I see you before the wedding?"

"Um, sure, that would be great, Dorothy. How about I take you for a little drive tomorrow up north? Show you some of the countryside."

Mother's eyes lit up. "Oh, I should like that very much," she said.

"Okay. I'll pick you up around nine o'clock." Rudy said. "Or is that too early?"

"Not at all," replied Mother. "The days seem to start at dawn here."

"Even before that, Dorothy," Uncle Bill said. "A cowboy's work is never done."

"Okay," said Rudy. "Then nine it is." He turned to the self. "Thanks again for the steak, Bennie. It was real good."

"Delighted you could attend Rudy," I said, adding an approving nod of the head.

Rudy retrieved his cowboy, offered a courteous doff to Mother, and exited the front door.

I turned towards Archie, who eyed me and smiled discreetly. Although this one aspect of our plan appeared to be on course, I groaned inwardly at the far more challenging waters which lay ahead.

At precisely nine the following morning, Rudy arrived for the promised tour. Hearing him knock, I opened the front door. Rudy was bent down, scratching Daisy behind her ears.

"Ahoy, Rudy," I said. "Do come in. Mother should be ready momentarily. Kind of you to do this. Rather above and beyond, I should think."

"Hey, Bennie," he replied, straightening up with a slight groan. Daisy grunted loudly, displeased by the cessation of ear-scratching activities, but then wandered down the front steps and towards the rear of the house. "I don't mind. I haven't driven around southern Colorado for a while. Might go as far as Salida. I know a little place there that your mother may like."

I laughed. "Should Archie accompany you as chaperone?"

Rudy glared at the self silently.

"Er, yes. Just a spot of humour."

He continued to glare. "What about the rest of your scheme? You gonna speak to Maria today?"

I sighed. "I hope to see her later this morning. I've a few more chores to finish first."

"You sure you don't want to tell Loretta what you've got planned?" he asked.

"I believe discretion to be the better part of valour," I said, "at least until I determine whether Maria is willing to convince Esperanza."

Rudy shook his head. "I would rather juggle some of Joe's rattlesnakes."

Presently, Mother docked in the living room. She wore a pale blue skirt and a white sweater. "Good morning, Rudy," she chirped. "I hope I have not kept you waiting too long."

"Nope. Just arrived, Dorothy." He cleared his throat softly. "You look real nice. Ready for some sightseeing?"

"I am," she said. She then turned towards the self. "Any plans today, Benjamin? With your cafe closed temporarily, you must not have much to do."

I coughed. "Er, yes, Mother. I mean, as Uncle Bill said, there is always work at the ranch that wants doing."

"Well, don't work too hard, dear." She placed her arm within Rudy's. "Shall we go?" she asked him.

Rudy looked at her arm. "Um, sure." He turned to the self. "I promise I'll bring her back safe and sound."

Mother laughed.

"Yes, well, enjoy the outing, Mother. Shall we expect you back for dinner?"

"I don't know, Benjamin." She looked at Rudy and laughed again. "You're not going to take advantage of me, are you? Tell me your lorry has run out of petrol, that sort of thing."

"Gah," I muttered softly.

"What?" Rudy spluttered, untangling his arm from hers. "No, of course not, Dorothy. Well, we had better get going. We should be back by dinner, Bennie."

After they exited the front door, I walked back into the kitchen, poured another cup of Uncle Bill's tar-like coffee, and sat down heavily.

Presently, Archie opened the back door and heaved himself into the kitchen. "That bull of yours is quite cantankerous," he said.

"Malcolm? Did he charge you?"

"Not in so many words. However, he didn't appreciate my bunging hay over the fence. He began snorting loudly and pawing the ground. I decided a hasty retreat was called for."

"A wise decision."

"Why so glum, old chap?"

"Eh? My plan to have Rudy ingratiate himself to Mother may be working too well. She seems quite smitten."

"Indeed? I shouldn't worry about it, cousin. Rudy seems a proper gentleman."

I shook my head. "I'm not concerned about Rudy. It's Mother. She seems quite taken with him."

"Nonsense. Aunt Dorothy is far too proper to allow anything tawdry to take place."

"I hope you are right." I looked at my watch, which read half nine. "I should head to town and speak with Maria."

"Would you like me to attend?"

"Thanks, Archie, but I had best approach Maria myself. Besides, Uncle Bill will be grateful for any assistance you can provide."

"All right, old chap. Best of luck and all that."

"Thanks. I shall need it."

At just after ten o'clock, I parked the lorry in front of Maria's small house. The heart was pounding away as I arrived at the front door and knocked gently. The door opened, revealing to my chagrin a chimneying Esperanza. She removed the cigarette from her mouth and blew a large cloud of smoke into the self's eyes.

"What the fuck you doing here, *Pendejito?*" she growled.

I sighed. "And a good morning to you, too, Esperanza. need to speak with Maria."

"She don't want to talk to you."

"Really? Maria divined I would arrive this morning and told you that she did not wish to speak with me?"

"¡*Vete a la chingada!* Wait here."

Esperanza slammed the front door shut. Inside, I heard her shouting at Maria in Spanish. After waiting for perhaps five minutes, I shook my head and began walking back to the lorry. Presently, the front door opened.

"Sorry, Bennie," said Maria, through lips clenched around her cigarette. "How come you're here? Something happen to the cafe?"

"The cafe? No, everything is fine. Well, other than we are haemorrhaging money. I was, er, hoping to speak with you privately about a matter of some importance. It involves the wedding."

"Did Loretta change her mind? Don't worry none about that. She's just nervous."

"Eh? No, nothing like that. Well, I hope not. I mean, it is the ceremony itself. We may have a problem."

"This about you converting so Father Castillo will marry you?" asked Maria as she motioned the self inside. "Come on in. I got some coffee if you want."

"Er, thank you, but I was rather hoping to speak to you without Esperanza present."

On cue, Esperanza's head appeared behind Maria's left shoulder like a ghostly apparition emerging in the cloud of smoke. "You afraid to talk to me about the wedding, *Pendejito?*" she snarled. "I keep hoping my Loretta will come to her senses."

"Sod off, Esperanza," I said.

"*Cállate, hermana*," hissed Maria. Esperanza raised her middle finger and disappeared. Maria eyed me and shook her head. "I dunno about you two."

"I have tried, Maria."

"You two are like roosters fighting. My sister, she ain't gonna do nothing to screw up the wedding. I told her that already."

"I am most appreciative, Maria. But the matter I wish to speak to you about doesn't involve Esperanza. Rather, it is Mrs. Alvarez."

"Josefa? She ain't said nothing to me about the wedding. She likes you."

"Yes, well, you recall the incident in the cafe, where she and my mother were throwing crockery at one another."

Maria nodded.

"I wish to avoid any, er, incidents like that at the wedding."

"You think they're gonna throw plates at each other in the church?"

"No, of course not." I paused. "Well, one supposes anything is possible. My concern is they will start screaming at one another during the ceremony. Loretta and I merely wish to have a peaceful wedding."

"Okay, but I don't see how I can help. You want me to talk to Josefa?"

"Loretta and I have spoken with her. Although both she and my mother promise they will be civil during the wedding, I am concerned that, without additional measures, those promises will come to nought."

"Huh?"

I sighed. "We thought, that is, Archie and I believe that the only way to ensure domestic tranquillity during the ceremony is if Mrs. Alvarez and my mother are both intoxicated." I made a motion with my thumb and forefinger that signalled drinking.

Maria's eyes widened. "Huh? You want them drunk at the wedding?"

"M-hem, yes. I mean, the hope is that, if they are both sufficiently intoxicated, they will sleep through the ceremony, thus avoiding any altercations. Problem solved, as it were."

"*Híjole*," muttered Maria. "Loretta okay with this?"

"Er, I have not spoken with her about the plan. I was unsure whether she would approve of her mother being in that state during the wedding."

Maria took a long pull from her cigarette and exhaled. "You ever seen Josefa drunk?"

"Well, no. Have you?"

"Once. A long time ago when she was still married. It was in Rudy's. She started yelling at Tomás and then threw a couple of beer bottles at him. He ran out the door and never came back."

"Gah," I moaned, envisioning our intricate plan crumbling into dust. "What happened after he left?"

Maria laughed. "She drank a few more beers. Then she took her shirt off and threw it at the *viejos*. Old Joe caught it. I never seen him smile like that. Then Josefa started dancing. Rudy got her shirt back. He told her to put it on and go back home. Josefa grabbed the shirt and laughed. Then she put it on and walked out. About an hour later, I left. Josefa was asleep in one of the chairs on the *portal*.

My hopes, which had been dashed by the thought of a drunken Josefa dancing shirtless during the wedding, were now restored, although I assumed Father Castillo would be nonplussed by a drunken Josefa removing her raiment in the church.

Maria eyed me suspiciously. "Maybe you and Loretta should elope," she said.

"I assumed you would be opposed to that," I replied.

Maria shrugged. "As long as Loretta's happy, it's okay with me."

"Well, if this feud between my mother and Mrs. Alvarez cannot be resolved, if only for the ceremony, then we may do just that, even though Loretta has her heart set on a church wedding."

"I still don't know how you're gonna get Josefa drunk. Me and Esperanza gonna be cooking for the fiesta in the morning."

"I was hoping you would convince your sister to do so."

Maria's eyes widened. "*Mi hermana*? You want her to get Josefa drunk?"

"I agree it seems far-fetched. You see, Archie and I thought that Esperanza, who would prefer the impending nuptials to crash on a lee shore, would, er, encourage Josefa to drink whilst she, that is, Esperanza, complained bitterly about Loretta marrying the self, and so forth."

"Huh?" Maria asked. "You've seen what she's like when she's drunk. She gets real mean."

I sighed. "Er, yes, I am aware of that fact. In this instance, your sister's mood will, one hopes, encourage Mrs. Alvarez to imbibe more readily until she attains the desired somnolent state."

Maria shook her head again, sucked on her cigarette, and emitted a large cloud of smoke. "I dunno what the fuck you're saying, Bennie. You want me to ask *mi hermana* to get Josefa drunk? And you want me to tell her its 'cause you don't want Josefa and your mom to fight at the wedding? I don't know about Josefa, but if *mi hermana* shows up to your wedding drunk—" Maria paused, took a large draw on her cigarette, exhaled, and shook her head.

"Er, yes, I understand the risk. But one hopes they will both be too inebriated even to attend the ceremony. Rudy has agreed to pacify my mother. In fact, he is giving her a tour around southern Colorado today."

Maria's eyes narrowed and she muttered "*pendejo*" under her breath.

"Excuse me?"

"Huh? Sorry, I was just thinking about Rudy."

"What's he gonna do?"

"He has agreed to bring over champagne before the wedding and ensure my mother is well-oiled before the ceremony begins."

Maria tossed the remains of her cigarette onto the patio. She reached into the pocket of her skirt, extracted a packet, removed one, and lit it angrily. "Just fucking elope," she said, exhaling a steam engine's quantity of smoke.

"As I told everyone, that would be my preference. Alas, it is neither Loretta's nor Josefa's."

"Okay. Let me talk to *mi hermana*. If I tell her it's for Loretta, maybe she'll help."

"Thank you, Maria," I said, exhaling loudly.

"You got another problem."

"Eh? What problem would that be?"

Maria pointed her cigarette towards the road. I turned and espied Loretta exiting her car.

"Gah," I mewled softly.

Chapter 13

H i Bennie," Loretta said, as she walked towards the house. "What's going on?"

"He wants Esperanza to get Josefa drunk before the wedding," said Maria casually.

"*Tía* Esperanza!" Loretta shouted, launching her fist into my beleaguered shoulder. "That's not what I meant."

"Gah!" I yelled, whilst glaring at Maria. "Let me explain."

"You had better explain, Benjamin Graves," growled Loretta. "Now!"

I rubbed the injured wing. "It was your idea, Loretta. If they are both sufficiently inebriated, they will be placid bystanders at the wedding, rather than enemy combatants."

Maria shrugged and continued to chimney away. "Why *Tía* Esperanza?" Loretta asked, eying the self suspiciously.

"She is the logical choice," I said. "Maria will be busy with preparations at the cafe."

"Why not Rudy?" Loretta asked. "My mother has always liked him."

"Alas, I have already engaged Rudy to inebriate my mother," I said. "Hence, the need for an alternate, meaning Esperanza."

"How is Rudy is going to get your mother drunk?" asked Loretta.

"He has agreed to, one might say, 'woo' her," I replied. "Not in an inappropriate manner, of course, but she appears to enjoy his attentions. He was at the ranch last night for dinner and has taken her on a sightseeing trip this morning into southern Colorado. The intent is for him to arrange to escort Mother to the wedding. Rudy will arrive at the ranch before the wedding, whereupon he will 'encourage' Mother with sufficient champagne to render her placid, rather like administering a dose of Farm Calm. Based on the crockery-bunging incident, that seems an apt description of your mother and mine, wedding-wise."

"So, let me see if I understand," said Loretta. "Rudy is going to get your mother drunk and *Tía* Esperanza is supposed to get my mother drunk?"

Presently, the Devil herself appeared at the door. "Loretta," said Esperanza, eyeing the self with her usual quantity of loathing. "You come to your senses yet and tell *Pendejito* you ain't gonna marry him?"

"Stop calling him that, *Tía* Esperanza," said Loretta. "We're getting married, no matter what you think. But if you keep acting this way, then I don't want you at the wedding."

Maria looked at her sister.

"Okay, okay," said Esperanza, waving around her cigarette. "Sorry, *gringo*," she hissed. "That better, Loretta?"

"No, it's not better," replied Loretta. "I love Bennie. You need to call him by his name."

"It's quite all right, Loretta," I said. "The other cheek has turned so often that your sainted aunt's insults have no effect. Although she may find her tasks at the cafe rather more menial, such as cleaning up after Paco every day, along with a reduction in income."

"¡*Veta a la chingada, Pendejito!*" shouted Esperanza. "Maybe I won't work there no more."

"Is that a promise?" I asked. "If so, I accept your resignation, effective immediately."

"*No más*, both of you," said Maria, ending her silence. "*Hermana*, you stop calling Bennie *Pendejito*. And Bennie, you need my sister's help for your plan."

"¿*Que?*" asked Esperanza. "What are you talking about?"

"We need your help, *Tía* Esperanza," Loretta said softly, "to prevent a fight between my mother and Bennie's mother. I don't want my wedding ruined. Please." Loretta's eyes began to water, accentuating the dramatic impact of her statement.

"*Sí*, okay, Loretta," said Esperanza. "Don't cry. I'll make sure *Pendej*— uh, Bennie's mother, don't go to the wedding. No *gringa*, no fight."

"That's not the type of help we seek, Esperanza," I explained. "My mother *will* be in attendance. Hence, we need you to deal with Mrs. Alvarez."

Esperanza's eyes widened. "Loretta, you don't want Josefa at your wedding? That ain't right. She's your mother."

"No, no, you don't understand, *Tía* Esperanza, said Loretta. "Of course I want her there. We just want to make sure she and Bennie's mother don't start fighting during the wedding."

Esperanza shook her head. "How do you want me to do that? You want me to sit between them or something?"

"We need you to, er, ensure Loretta's mother is thoroughly inebriated before the ceremony," I replied.

"Huh? What the fuck does that mean?" asked Esperanza.

"Drunk," I said. "We need you to get her drunk before the wedding."

Esperanza took a large pull off her smouldering cigarette, then exhaled a large cloud of smoke into my eyes. She goggled Loretta. "You want me to get Josefa drunk, Loretta?"

Loretta nodded. "I know it sounds awful, but I agree with Bennie. If they're both drunk, then they won't start fighting and ruin the wedding."

Esperanza turned to Maria and machine-gunned several paragraphs in Spanish that I was unable to comprehend. Maria nodded in affirmation, after which Esperanza turned back towards Loretta and the self. "Okay, Loretta," Esperanza said, shaking her head. "I'll help. But how am I gonna get Josefa drunk? What do I tell her?"

"Um, I'm not sure," replied Loretta. She turned to me. "What does *Tía* Esperanza tell my mother, Bennie? She can't just show up and say, 'I'm supposed to get you drunk before the wedding.'"

"Er, no," I coughed. Presently, the grey matter telegraphed the obvious solution. "Ah, yes. You dislike me, Esperanza, do you not?"

Esperanza laughed. "*Sí, mucho, Pendejito.*"

"And you surely believe Loretta is making a terrible mistake by marrying a *gringo*, especially the self"

"*Sí, Pendejito,*" she said, nodding in agreement. "For somebody stupid, you understand real good."

"Well, there is your *modus operandi*. You offer to escort Mrs. Alvarez to the wedding. Then, on the day of the wedding, you arrive early, accompanied by whatever alcoholic beverage she prefers—I shall pay for it—and begin discussing the self's numerous shortcomings whilst you encourage her to imbibe. In a short time, she will be sozzled and placid."

Esperanza scratched her head and then emitted a hyena-like laugh. "So, you're gonna buy me a case of beer and then you want me to tell Josefa why I don't like you and why she shouldn't let Loretta marry no stupid *gringo*? Esperanza shrugged and turned towards Loretta. "You sure about this, Loretta?"

"I know it sounds crazy, *Tía* Esperanza," replied Loretta, "but it's better than a fight in the church."

"Okay, *bueno,*" said Esperanza. She shook her head again, then returned to the house.

Maria, who had stood silently whilst chimneying away, looked at both of us and nodded disapprovingly. "Maybe my sister's gonna get Josefa drunk. But she's gonna be drunk, too. You know what that means."

"Er, yes," I said. "However, I doubt she will initiate a fight with my mother. Besides, Loretta and I have some experience dealing with Esperanza when she is inebriated."

Maria sighed. "I'm too old for this shit." She walked into the house and slammed the front door.

As Loretta and I walked towards my lorry, a sense of dread grew within the grey matter. An inebriated Esperanza was little different than an enraged scorpion, eager to strike anyone careless enough to come within range. Then again, doing nothing would result in Josefa and my mother circling each other and yowling like angry cats. Scylla and Charybdis surely would be delighted.

"Isn't there any other way, Bennie?" Loretta asked plaintively.

"Well, one assumes murder would be frowned upon, although even Tiny might make an exception regarding your aunt."

She raised her fist and threatened the still-throbbing shoulder.

"Merely a bit of humour to lighten an otherwise distressing situation," I said, raising my hands in mock surrender. "Elopement always remains an option."

"No! I won't do that to my mother or yours," said Loretta. "Nobody in town would forgive us, either."

"Your Uncle Joe would," I replied, "if only to save himself some brass."

"He doesn't really mean that, Bennie. He only says those things to make you mad."

Although Loretta was less familiar with her uncle's pecuniary proclivities than the self, I thought better of arguing the point. I sighed. "Then we have no choice but to navigate the dangerous shoals ahead. At least we know where they lie."

"Don't forget, we still have your conversion, too," added Loretta said.

I groaned inwardly. "Er, yes."

"You promised, Bennie."

"Yes, yes, I know. Thy will be done and such."

We arrived at the lorry. "What are you going to do now?" asked Loretta.

"I must get back to the ranch. Uncle Bill has additional fencing wanting repair, courtesy of Malcolm. And you?"

"My wedding dress needs some alterations. My mother and I are driving to Santa Fe later. There's a shop that will make them."

"Will you model it for me?"

"You know that's bad luck. But don't worry, I think you'll like it."

"I surely will, my love." I bent down and kissed her. "Right, off to Santa Fe for you and back to the ranch for the self."

Loretta waved good-bye and then went back inside the house. I stepped inside the lorry and motored to where it intersected the road that would take me to the ranch. I turned onto it when I spotted a dust-encrusted lorry speeding towards me on a collision course. "Oh, God, please no, not again," I whimpered. I grabbed the steering wheel, closed the oculars tightly, and prepared for the impending carnage.

I heard the roar of its engine and the squeal of tyres, followed by silence. Opening my eyes slowly, I espied two rodentary eyes embedded within a large nodding head, goggling the self from his lorry, which was stopped beside mine.

"*Hola*, Señor Graves," said Coronado. He opened the door of his lorry, crashing it into mine. "Sorry, Señor Graves."

"Would you mind shutting your door and allowing me to exit, Coronado."

After Coronado did so, I stepped out, whereupon I espied a new fissure in the door. "M-hem," I muttered. "How did you know I was here?"

"I dunno, Señor Graves. I just saw your truck. That reminded me I wanted to ask you something."

I raised an eyebrow suspiciously. "Hmm, well?"

"Can I be your best man? I've never been to a wedding before. I saw a movie a couple of years ago. These two people were about to get married in a church. Then, a bad guy comes in and he starts threatening the man with a gun. The best man runs over. He tackles the bad guy and takes his gun away. Then he knocks him out. He saved everybody." Coronado smiled and began to nod.

The jaw dropped involuntarily. "Er, that is most kind of you to offer, Coronado, although I doubt any gunmen will burst into the church and threaten everyone. Sorry to say that I believe that my cousin, Archie, will fill the best man role."

Coronado's large head drooped. "Oh, okay, Señor Graves."

Presently, the Graves *noblesse oblige* tapped the self on the shoulder. "Look at the poor chap," it said. "Allowing him to be your best man would thrill him beyond compare."

"You don't know him like I do," the grey matter replied.

"Of course, I know him, you nincompoop. Who do you think I am?"

"Then you surely know the damage he can and likely will cause."

"Well, granted, there is that. Nevertheless, what about the Graves code, *semper fidelis*? You've invoked it before. After all, Coronado has been a faithful friend."

"The Graves code does not require one to condone insanity. Besides, what about Loretta? As you well know, there already are sufficient pitfalls facing our impending nuptials."

"Ask her. I am confident she will approve of such a magnanimous offer."

I sighed. "Fine. Now, please just sod off," I said loudly.

"What did you say, Señor Graves?" Coronado asked.

"Eh? Oh, my apologies. I was, er, lost in thought. Now what were we discussing? Oh yes, the best man role. I, that is, I do appreciate your offer, Coronado. Allow me to take the matter up with Loretta and Archie. If they approve, then I should be honoured to have you as my best man."

"There's a good chap," said the *noblesse oblige*.

Coronado's eyes beamed. "Thanks, Señor Graves!" He extended his greasy right hand and wrapped it around mine, shaking it vigorously.

"You're, er, most welcome, Coronado," I said, wiping my now greasy hand on the trousers.

He returned to his lorry and swung the door open. It crashed into mine yet again, deepening the fissure. "Sorry, Señor Graves."

"Never mind, Coronado. The lorry is used to it by now."

"Oh, okay." After hoisting himself into his seat, he shut the door and started the lorry's motor. "Señor Graves?" he shouted.

"Yes, Coronado?"

"Should I bring a gun to the wedding in case a bad guy shows up? I could bring my shotgun."

"Are you mad? That is, I doubt any bad guys will burst into the church. Besides, Tiny will be at the wedding. Was there a sheriff at the wedding in your film?"

Coronado hesitated as a mesmerised visage engulfed him. "Uh, I guess not," he said after a long pause.

"Then I believe we may entrust our safety to Tiny. No need for you to be armed."

"Okay, Señor Graves. I like to help." He smiled, then roared off in a cloud of dust, leaving me to ponder this latest guilt-ridden decision.

"Bloody *noblesse oblige*," I coughed, whilst pulling the self into the lorry.

Chapter 14

I resisted the urge to set course for Rudy's and remedy the now reeling grey matter with several bracing doses of Dusty Trail. Instead, I hurried back to raise the issue with Loretta. I walked up to the house and knocked on the door. Loretta opened it and Chata rocketed outside, crashing into my legs. She wagged her tail and began barking.

"Good dog," I said, patting her head whilst attempting to prevent her from jumping up.

"Hi, Bennie," said Loretta. "Is everything okay?"

"Er, well, that depends."

Her ocular daggers readied for firing. "On what? Do you want to get *Tío* Joe drunk, too? Or maybe you want to be drunk?"

"Eh? No, nothing like that, although that might—Gah! My shoulder!"

"Nobody else is going to be drunk at my wedding, Bennie," growled Loretta.

"No, I mean, that's not why I wished to speak to you again. It was Coronado. Espying my lorry, he screeched to a halt. I thought he would crash into me, but Fate somehow intervened on my behalf. Anyway, Coronado wishes to be the best man at our wedding, and I am inclined to grant his request."

"Coronado? Why?"

"I gather his request has something to do with a film he watched several years ago in which the best man at a wedding disarmed an intruder who had burst in."

Loretta scratched her head. "Huh? How is that—"

"I long ago abandoned any pretence of comprehending the logical structure underlying Coronado's reasoning. I did stress there would be no need for him to bring a gun to the ceremony."

Loretta's jaw dropped. "Gun? You mean that huge shotgun of his, the one he almost destroyed the cafe with?"

"The same," I said.

"Who does he think will burst in?"

"I thought it best not to enquire. However, I assured him that because Tiny will be in attendance there will be no need for him to bring any weapons. Granted, if an intruder were to burst in, Tiny would be the first to crush anyone who stood between himself and the door."

Loretta laughed. "That's our Tiny." She placed her hand on my arm and kissed me gently. "That's really sweet of you, Bennie, but are you sure?"

"The Graves *noblesse oblige* was rather insistent that I offer Coronado the role."

Loretta pondered my rationale for a moment. "What about my ring?" she asked.

I eyed the third digit of her left hand, which bore the ring Uncle Bill had provided the self for the engagement. "It appears to be on your finger."

She rolled her eyes. "That's my engagement ring. You do know what a wedding ring is, don't you?" She raised the digit in question. "You are supposed to place it on this finger at the ceremony."

"Yes, I am aware of that. The wedding ring is safely at the ranch, in the top drawer of my bureau. Why?"

Loretta shook her head in exasperation. "Traditionally, the best man holds the ring and hands it to you when it's time to put it on the bride's finger."

I eyed her blankly. "Well, yes."

She tapped my shoulder sharply. "Don't you think letting Coronado keep the ring until the wedding is, um, risky?"

"Ah, I see. Sorry, my encounter with Coronado has addled the grey matter. I thought I would give him the ring in the church immediately before the ceremony. Surely he could not lose it whilst seated in the church."

"I guess that would work. But what about Archie? Won't he be disappointed?"

"Archie is not the sentimental traditionalist type, but I will ask him. I expect he will be delighted to be relieved of the responsibility."

Loretta shrugged. "Okay. But *Tía* Esperanza won't like it."

"True. Then again, your aunt dislikes everything about the wedding, especially the groom. Doubtless, she would be delighted if an armed intruder burst in and shot the self. Perhaps she will engage Hector for the task."

"Stop it. She doesn't hate you, Bennie."

Presently, Chata emitted a loud "woof."

"Chata disagrees," I said.

Loretta pursed her lips tightly. "Well, *Tía* Esperanza won't be armed."

"One can only hope," I said to myself. "Now, I must return to the ranch and discuss the matter with Archie."

Loretta kissed me again. "Will I see you this weekend?"

"Will your mother allow it?"

"Of course. You just can't see me in my wedding dress."

"Right, then. Dinner at the ranch and perhaps a private stroll around the countryside afterwards?"

"I would like that." Loretta paused, then pushed me playfully. "Now, get out of here so I can get my dress altered."

"It's your wedding, old chap," said Archie later that afternoon, whilst he, Uncle Bill, and the self slowly drained our glasses of Dusty Trail. "What was it MacArthur said about old soldiers fading away? If you desire that rodent-eyed hippopotamus to be your best man, I shall fade into the back of the church."

"Are you sure, Archie?" I asked.

"Pah," he said, with a dismissive wave of his hand. "Honestly, I would prefer a more anonymous role in the audience."

"You sure about this, Bennie?" asked Uncle Bill. "We're talkin' about Coronado."

I signed deeply. "Yes, I know, Uncle Bill, but he displayed that plaintive, downtrodden puppy look. The Graves *noblesse oblige* was rather insistent."

Uncle Bill laughed. "That got a lot of your ancestors in a heap of trouble, pard'ner. How you gonna keep him from losing Loretta's wedding ring? Or eating it?"

Archie frowned. "Eh? The chap has eaten a wedding ring?"

"No," I said. "Coronado has a well-deserved reputation, of misplacing objects . . . and letters. I doubt he would consume the ring, well, not intentionally." I shuddered as a vision appeared of an iguana with Coronado's head shooting out its tongue and ingesting a *burrito*. "Anyway, I intend to maintain possession of the ring until Coronado is seated in the church. Only then will I entrust him with the ring."

"That seems relatively foolproof," said Archie.

I emptied my glass. "We can only hope." I glanced at the watch. "Don't you think Mother and Rudy should have returned by now, Uncle Bill? It's half five."

He shrugged. "Guess they're having a good time, pard'ner. No need to send out a search party yet."

By half eight, Rudy and Mother still had not returned. Dinner was long past, and Archie and I had finished the evening chores. I left him in the sitting room, reading one of Uncle Bill's Zane Grey novels, and walked to the barn. I checked to ensure Marjorie was safely latched into her stall, and espied Uncle Bill underneath his newly purchased tractor, undertaking an unknown repair. "I say, Uncle Bill, perhaps we should organise a search?"

He slid himself out from under the tractor and sat up. "Eight-thirty, huh? Yeah, I guess it's gettin' kinda late." He paused. "Maybe they stopped at the bar. Rudy probably wanted to check on his grandson, then offered your mother a glass of wine."

A wave of relief washed over me. "Yes, of course. I had forgotten about the bar." Drops of fluid were dripping from underneath the tractor onto the dirt floor. "Was it leaking when you first saw it?"

Uncle Bill placed a small container under the leak. "Nope. Must be a bad washer in the drain plug. Probably the drive back jostled it. I'm gonna drive to Española tomorrow and get a new one."

"Anything I can do to be of assistance?"

"No thanks, Bennie." He stood up, retrieved an old rag, and wiped his hands. "I'm gonna call it a night. It's gettin' too dark for me to see much. You want a nightcap? I sure could use one."

"An excellent suggestion, Uncle Bill."

Presently, as we walked back towards the house, we heard an approaching vehicle. It slowed and pulled into the driveway, revealing itself as Rudy's lorry. I dashed over to the lorry and opened the door, espying Mother quickly removing her hand from Rudy's. "M-hem. How was the sightseeing, Mother?"

"Oh, it was wonderful, dear," she chirped. "So different from home. The mountains are quite spectacular. We drove through a mountain pass covered in snow, and at this time of year! Later, we stopped in a small town and had a wonderful lunch. And Rudy treated me to some charming wine."

"It was a bottle of pinot," he said sheepishly. "I got a small cellar hidden at the house. That's where I keep the good stuff. Not many folks in town would appreciate it. They sure wouldn't want to pay for it at the bar."

"Special occasions, only, eh?" I said. "We shall have to invite you here for dinner more often, Rudy."

"Anyway, your mother was real nice to put up with me all day, Bennie," Rudy said. "But I probably tired her out and wore out my welcome."

"Not at all, Rudy," said Mother, patting his hand. "I cannot thank you enough."

"Well, uh, I should be getting back home, Dorothy," said Rudy.

Mother exited the lorry. "Goodbye, Rudy," she trilled, shutting the door. "I'm looking forward to tomorrow."

"Uh, yeah, that is, I don't want to take time away from you visiting Bennie and Bill."

"Nonsense," Mother said. "They are probably happy to be rid of me."

I glanced at Archie, who replied with a slight nod.

"Oh, c'mon, Dorothy," said Uncle Bill. "I know Bennie's delighted you're here for the wedding."

"Couldn't be happier," I said.

"Well, see you tomorrow," said Rudy. "Bye, Dorothy." He waved, then turned the lorry around and sped off into the twilight.

"Such a charming man," Mother sighed. "He asked if he could escort me to your wedding, Benjamin. Would either of you mind?"

"What? He wasn't supposed to do that until—that is, no, not at all," I said.

"Fine with me, Dorothy," said Uncle Bill. "I'll drive Archie. More room for you if you go with Rudy. I wouldn't want your dress to get all mussed squeezed into my truck."

"Well, I've had quite a day," said Mother, "so I shall say 'goodnight' to all of you."

She walked onto the portal, paused to pat Daisy's *sombrero*, and disappeared inside the house.

"Well, old chap," said Archie. "The plan appears to be working. Perhaps too well."

I sighed. "Surely you're not suggesting anything improper," I replied.

"I dunno, Bennie," said Uncle Bill. "She does seem a might smitten with Rudy. And he does have a way with the ladies."

"Mother always has been a paragon of virtue," I said anxiously. "I mean, Father is a Member of Parliament, after all."

"Perhaps, old chap," said Archie. "But sometimes even a paragon flies too close to the Sun."

"Gah," I muttered.

The next morning, Uncle Bill and the self were breakfasting when Mother glided into the kitchen, humming something the grey matter vaguely recognised as an old show tune. "Good morning, William," she chirped. "Good morning, Benjamin." She was wearing one of those whitish jungle safari outfits, together with a pearl necklace.

I raised an eyebrow. Uncle Bill put down his mug of coffee and goggled the outfit. "Mornin', Dorothy," he said. "You and Rudy headin' out for the African savannah?"

"Heavens, no," William," she replied. "He is taking me out for a picnic," she replied. "He told me there is a small park in the mountains north of here where one can luncheon next to a beautiful creek that is surrounded by fluttering aspens."

"Bloody fluttering aspens," I thought.

"That so, Dorothy?" replied Uncle Bill. He stood up and stretched. "Well, that sounds real nice."

"Shall you return in time for supper?" I enquired.

Mother giggled softly. "I'm not sure, dear." She paused. "No, probably not. If today is like yesterday, the time will just fly."

"M-hem, what time will Rudy be arriving this morning?" I asked. "I must ask him about, er, supplying a few bottles of refreshment after the wedding ceremony."

Mother eyed her watch. "Oh, I believe he said around eight-ish. He should be here any moment."

As if on cue, I heard a vehicle coming up the road. I arose from the table and headed towards the front door. As I stepped onto the portal, Daisy raised her head and grunted. I looked up as a lorry pulled into the driveway and rolled to a stop.

Rudy stepped out, wearing a similar outfit to that he had worn two nights earlier, except his shirt was a pale blue. "Mornin', Bennie," he said. "Looks like it's gonna be a real nice day."

"Indeed," I said. "Mother informed us you are escorting her for a picnic in the mountains."

Rudy blushed. "Uh, yeah, I know a nice place up in the San Juans. You ought to take Loretta there sometime."

"Perhaps I shall." I paused. "Now, Rudy, I realise that part of the plan was for you to endear yourself to my mother. It appears you have succeeded, so much so that, well, I mean—"

"What's wrong, Bennie?" Rudy asked quickly. "This is what you asked me to do."

"Yes, of course, but Mother seems rather, well, smitten. Perhaps overly so."

Rudy's eyes narrowed. "You think I'm trying to take advantage of your mother, Bennie?"

"No, of course not," I said. "It's just that, well, she is a married woman. Granted, my father can be rather churlish at times, especially after a poor round of golf, but he would never, er, to my knowledge—"

"I get it, Bennie," Rudy interrupted. "Nothing's going on. Before I met her, I thought she would be—um, more like you. At least, like you except when you were sniffing around the Sunflower gal."

"Eh? What is that supposed to mean? And I most certainly did not 'sniff around' Sunflower, as you put it. She was merely rather, er, tactile."

"Uh-huh. I've been around the block a few times, Bennie. But you're real formal and proper. Remember after Joe had thrown that rattlesnake into the cafe? You were afraid to ask Loretta out on a date and came to me for advice."

I shuddered. "I remember the rattlesnake bunging only too well."

"I told you to talk like you lived here, and not some British snob."

I glanced towards the ground and sighed. "Yes, I recall your advice. I have tried."

"I know, Bennie. All I'm saying is that your mother is a pretty down-to-earth gal. I had a good time with her yesterday. Somebody to talk to."

"What about Maria? Is she not still your *querida*?"

Rudy shrugged. "I dunno. I always liked Maria, but she's not real talkative. And I never know whether she likes me."

"I believe she does, although one doubts Maria would ever admit to it, at least not publicly."

He laughed. "Nope, she wouldn't. Anyway, you can put your mind at ease."

Presently, the front door opened. Daisy raised her head and grunted as Mother stepped outside carrying a basket. "Hello, Rudy," she warbled. "Did you speak with Bennie about providing wine for after the wedding?"

"What?" Rudy asked, glowering at the self before eyeing Mother. "Oh, yeah, we talked about it. All set, Dorothy."

"Good. Now, are you ready to take me on that picnic? I've made us some sandwiches."

"Uh, yeah, that's great. Thanks, Dorothy," Rudy said. "We can stop at Joe's store and get some sodas."

"Aren't you going to bring that bottle of champagne?" asked Mother.

I eyed Rudy. "Champagne? A *Dom Pérignon* '52 perhaps?"

"I don't have that kind of money, Bennie," he replied. "But I've got a good California vintage."

"California champagne, Mother?" I said, turning towards her.

"Oh, stop being such a snob, Benjamin," she said. "I am sure Rudy's choice of vintage will be excellent." She walked up to Rudy and wrapped her arm around his. "Well, are we going on that picnic or not?"

"Well, sure," Rudy said. He doffed his cowboy hat. "See you this evening."

"Right-ho," I said.

Mother laughed. "Don't wait up, dear."

Rudy opened the passenger door of his lorry and Mother sat down. He walked around the front, opened the driver-side door, sat down, and started the motor. Mother waved as they drove off.

I stood silently for a minute as the lorry disappeared down the road, then walked up the steps of the portal. Daisy stood up, eyed me from beneath her *sombrero*, and grunted loudly.

"Porcine intuition, eh?"

She grunted again, then walked down the steps and around the house. I stood motionless for several minutes whilst the grey matter contemplated what Fate had planned regarding Mother's budding relationship with Rudy, before returning inside.

"So, old chap, Aunt Dorothy has gone off with Rudy again," said Archie, who was standing in the kitchen devouring a tortilla.

"Rudy assures me nothing untoward is taking place," I replied. "Rather, he is merely doing what we have asked."

"Well, speaking as one with extended experience with the fairer sex, I should be alert to danger signs."

I goggled him. "Such as? This is my mother we are discussing, after all."

"Do you consider Rudy to be an honourable chap?"

"Yes, although I have never enquired about the specific particulars of the four marriages."

"You should keep a weather eye out, old chap."

"How, exactly? Insist I ride in the back of the lorry? Contact MI-5 to ask whether they might spare a few hidden microphones?"

Archie paused. "Afraid espionage is not one of my specialities, although I did perform rather careful surveillance before nicking the Head's Jaguar. Besides, I've always been the chap in Rudy's position, not yours. Perhaps you should have one of those heart-to-hearts with Aunt Dorothy after she returns this evening. Remind her of her filial duties, the Graves code of honour, and all that other rot you believe in. You could even invoke the Seventh Commandment. Aunt Dorothy is a devoted Church of Englander, after all."

The jaw rocketed downwards. "One does not discuss adultery with one's mother. I mean, one recoils at the very, er, underlying concept in the parental context."

Archie smiled. "Desperate times, old chap. Desperate times."

"Gah," I muttered.

Chapter 15

B y nine o'clock, Mother and Rudy still had not returned. Several of the fingers were worn down from drumming them upon the kitchen table and the arm of the sitting room sofa. Uncle Bill and Archie had finished their evening doses of Dusty Trail, whilst mine sat untouched.

"I wouldn't worry about it, Bennie," said Uncle Bill, after closing the Zane Grey novel he was reading. "I'm sure they're fine." He yawned cavernously. "Well, I got to get me some shut-eye." He stood up, emitted a low groan, and yawned again. "I suppose you could drive down to the bar. That's probably where they ended up. If they ain't there, you could always head on over to Josefa's and call Tiny. She's got a phone."

I raised the untouched glass of Dusty Trail and downed a small dose. "Sound advice, Uncle Bill." I stood up and walked into the kitchen to retrieve the keys to my lorry.

"Would you like me to accompany you, cousin?" asked Archie. "Happy to provide moral support and such."

"Thanks, Archie."

"Do you really think something happened to them?" asked Archie, as we motored slowly down the dark road. "An accident of some sort?"

"I hope not—Gah!" I shouted as a deer ran across the road, narrowly avoiding the lorry.

"Such as crashing into a deer, for example," he said, clearing a few drops of perspiration from his brow.

I released a large breath. "Hitting one can do quite a bit of damage." I lowered the lorry's speed and proceeded down the road.

"One imagines the deer draws the short straw, though," said Archie.

Presently, we arrived at the bar. A lone streetlight nearby cast a dull, yellowish glow. We exited the lorry and walked to the front door, which was locked.

"Right, then, not at the bar," said Archie. "Next stop, Loretta's mother's house?"

Before I could answer, I felt a sharp blow on the cranium. "Gah!" I shouted, as I turned around and observed the rotund, macintosh-wearing silhouette of Porfiria raising her umbrella for a second blow.

"*Diablo!*" she screamed. "Get away from me!"

"Stop it, you madwoman!" I shouted. I lunged at the umbrella, but she skilfully withdrew the weapon beyond my reach.

"*Diablo!*" she screamed again, wielding the umbrella like a broadsword and striking a horizontal blow to my left leg.

"Bloody hell!" I shouted.

Archie stepped in front of the self and raised his hands. "I say, Porfiria, do you recall me from the cafe?" he said in a soothing voice. "I brought you a Coke and some lunch?"

Porfiria lowered the umbrella and goggled Archie. "Yeah, I remember. You're the nice-looking *gringo*." She pointed the umbrella at the self menacingly. "Not like him."

"You're most kind to say so," Archie replied, oozing calmness. He took her gently by the right arm, from which the weapon dangled. "Now, what brings you to town on this lovely evening?" He waved his left hand stealthily, signalling for the self to retreat. I backed away slowly until I was able to slide around the building to safety. I leaned against the wall and sighed, then perceived a sudden dampness on my left trouser leg. Glancing down, I espied Paco trotting away victoriously. "Bloody cur," I muttered.

After shaking off the now sodden trouser leg, I peered around the front of the building. Archie was still speaking quietly with the umbrella-wielding nemesis. Sensing the danger had passed, I walked to the back of the building, whereupon

I espied Rudy's empty and undamaged lorry. A dim light emanated from the window of Rudy's office. I walked up to the back door and knocked loudly.

"Hullo!" I shouted. "I say, Rudy, are you there?"

I heard muffled voices inside and thudding footsteps. The light was extinguished, followed by a minute of silence. Presently, the light over the back door was switched on. I placed a hand over the eyes as the door opened.

"Uh, hey, Bennie," a dishevelled Rudy said, rubbing his eyes. His shirt was untucked, and a strong odour of alcohol enveloped him. "Uh, what's up?"

I raised an eyebrow. "Er, well, as you had not returned, we were all rather concerned about you and Mother. Uncle Bill suggested I motor here to see if you and she were having a nightcap." I paused momentarily. "I gather you have."

"Uh, yeah," he mumbled absently. "Sorry, I guess I forgot about the time."

"Well, you appear to be in no condition to drive, so I shall return Mother to the ranch. May I come inside?"

"No!" he shouted. "I mean, I think your mother might be in the bathroom."

Presently, I heard what sounded like a glass breaking. "Mother?" I called. "Are you all right?" Not hearing a response, I attempted to navigate around him and into the bar.

"Hold on, Bennie," he said, capturing my arm.

"I say, Rudy!" I pulled my arm out of his grip.

"Just hold your horses, Bennie," said Rudy. "I'll tell your mother you're here to take her home." He turned around and disappeared inside.

Presently Archie appeared. "Everything all right, cousin?" he asked. "I heard raised voices."

I glanced anxiously behind him. "Where is Porfiria?"

Archie responded with a dismissive wave of his hand. "She walked across the road and disappeared like a yellow-macintoshed apparition. I must say, she does seem to dislike you rather intensely, old chap."

I rubbed the knot on the back of the skull. "M-hem, yes," I said. "Well, thank you for despatching her into the night. How she can locate herself precisely where I alight is a mystery I shall never solve."

"No matter, old chap. Soothing the savage beast is one of my specialities, especially that of the fairer sex."

Before I could respond, Mother came to the door. Her hair was dishevelled, and she appeared to be listing to port.

"Gah! I mean, are you all right, Mother?" I asked.

She straightened up and cleared her throat. "Yes, yes, I'm fine, dear," she replied, smoothing her hair. "Why? Were you worried?"

I raised an eyebrow. "Yes, rather. We expected you to have returned hours ago."

"I'm sorry, dear," Mother said. "We must have lost track of the time."

"Amongst other items," I thought, as images too horrible to contemplate roiled the grey matter. "Well, the lorry is parked in front. Archie and I can return you to the ranch if you are ready."

"All right, dear." She turned to Rudy, who was now beside her. "Well, goodnight, Rudy," she said awkwardly as she extended her hand towards his. "Thank you for a lovely picnic."

"Um, yeah," he muttered, shaking her hand. "I, um, I'm real glad you enjoyed it, Dorothy."

Mother turned to the self. "Can you just give us a minute, dear?" she asked.

"Er, yes, of course," I said. "Goodnight, Rudy."

He raised his hand and waved dully. "Yeah, sorry about the time, Bennie."

Archie and I retreated to the lorry. We stood next to it, waiting for Mother. "Heh," Archie said quietly. "If I had to guess, cousin—"

"Please don't! This is simply too horrible to contemplate." I leaned my head against the lorry door. "Gah," I moaned softly.

"Steady, old chap," said Archie, patting my shoulder. "Nothing untoward may have occurred, even if the evidence—all circumstantial I might add—suggests otherwise."

I raised my now throbbing head and glanced at him, espying a rather sordid smile. "You're enjoying this, aren't you Archie?"

"No, of course not, cousin," he said, smiling wryly. "A most serious business. You must admit that your plan has succeeded, perhaps more than you envisioned."

I perceived a rising emetic urge. "We are speaking of my mother. I doubt you would be as sanguine had Aunt Constance emerged from the bar like that."

"My mother? Sorry to disappoint, old chap, but that ship sailed some years ago."

"Good God! You must have been horrified. With whom?"

Archie shrugged. "A London barrister, whom I gather was a silk."

"Did your father know about it?"

"He may have, although I did not wish to enquire. Besides, one of the chaps I knew at Oxford informed me that he had seen the old coot with a rather fetching young bird in a pub near the Financial District. All's fair in love and war, as they say."

"What, what about the Graves code?"

"Your code? Why, broken, old chap, broken, as least for my branch of the family tree."

I was about to respond when Mother exited the front door of the bar and walked up to the lorry. "Are you sure you are all right, Mother?" I asked. "You seem dishevelled."

"Of course, dear," she said, whilst smoothing her hair. "I'm just a bit tired, that's all."

"Did you, er, enjoy the outing?" I asked.

"What? Oh, yes, the picnic area was quite lovely. It was next to a stream with aspen trees along its banks, just as Rudy described it."

"Planning another outing this weekend?" I asked warily.

Mother sighed. "No, I don't believe so, dear," she said, with a slight shake of her head. She slid into the middle of the front seat. "Mr. Salazar is, how shall I say, a robust gentleman. I would not wish him to get any wrong ideas. I am a married woman, after all. Now, please take me back to the ranch."

"Er, yes, of course," I said.

The next morning found me assisting Archie with the four-leggeds. After feeding and watering Marjorie, who was in her usual obstreperous mood, we stood outside the barn, contemplating the consequences of last night's events.

"Now, what?" I moaned. "Rudy must have behaved in an ungentlemanly manner and now Mother wishes to have nothing to do with him. What about the plan?"

"Best not jump to conclusions regarding anyone's behaviour," replied Archie. "As for the plan, perhaps discussing last night's events with Rudy himself before abandoning ship would be best."

I grimaced. "The events, as you call them, are quite clear."

"Not necessarily," said Archie. "I can personally attest that I have found myself in situations where appearances were rather deceptive."

"No doubt," I grunted, whilst lifting a heavy bale of hay. "However, one suspects the situations in which you found yourself are dissimilar to Mother's."

Archie shrugged. "Which is why you must speak with Rudy."

"What am I to say? Do I call him a cad and demand satisfaction for dishonouring my mother?"

"How very eighteenth-century of you, cousin," Archie chortled. "Do they still have duels in this country?"

"Well, Uncle Bill's Zane Grey novels frequently involve combatants telling one another, 'Draw, pard'ner,' which I gather was the western equivalent."

"May I suggest a modicum of discretion before discharging your pistol?"

"If discretion is called for, then perhaps it would be best for you to speak with Rudy. I don't know if I could maintain a calm demeanour."

"Me? I barely know the chap. Do you expect me to walk up to him and say, 'What-ho, Rudy, did you shag my aunt last night?'"

"Which is why I cannot speak to him," I moaned. "I am desperate, Archie."

Archie sighed deeply. "Very well. 'The course of true love never did run smooth' as the Bard wrote. Little did he know. But you will accompany me, cousin. She is your mother, after all."

"What if I cannot remain calm?"

"You've mentioned your verbal jousting with Esperanza, whom I gather is wont to insult you in various ways."

"I have turned the other cheek numerous times for Loretta's sake and am generally immune to Esperanza's vituperative eruptions."

"Well, you may have to turn it again so as not to offend Rudy. That is, if you wish the plan to remain in effect. Perhaps you should dose yourself with that Farm Calm concoction before we confront him."

I sighed. "Even if Rudy remains willing, Mother may not be."

"One crisis at a time, old chap," said Archie.

After completing the morning feedings and waterings, we returned to the house for a second dose of cowboy coffee.

"Howdy, boys," said Uncle Bill, who was sitting at the kitchen table with his cuppa. He glanced at his watch. "I guess Dorothy must be real tired. Eight o'clock and she's still asleep."

"I gather she and Rudy had a long day picnicking and, er, whatnot," I said.

"Yep," Uncle Bill said, nodding. "Gotta hand it to you, Bennie. I didn't think this plan of yours would work. Guess I was wrong."

"Er, no need to apologise, Uncle Bill," I stuttered, envisaging Fate rubbing its hands in glee. "Sometimes, one succeeds against long odds."

"Indeed," said Archie. "It may have worked rather too well."

"Huh? What's that mean?" Uncle Bill asked.

Before I could provide a synopsis of the previous evening's events, Mother strolled into the kitchen. "Good morning, everyone," she said brightly. "Goodness, look at the time. I was rather fatigued."

"M-hem, good morning, Mother," I mumbled.

"Good morning, Aunt Dorothy," added Archie.

"Benjamin, I must again apologise for your having to retrieve me last night," said Mother. "Rudy was in no condition to drive."

"He did appear to be several sheets to the wind," I said. "I hope he did not, er, embarrass himself in any way."

"Not overly so, dear," replied Mother. "I must admit to being flattered by the attention. Your father could learn something from that man."

"God help us," I muttered under my breath. "I mean, we, that is Archie and I, will be motoring to town soon to discuss some wedding-related matters with Rudy."

"What sort of matters?" she asked.

"Er, he agreed to supply some of the liquid refreshment, bottles of champagne, and the like," I said hesitantly.

"Well, make sure he provides a decent vintage," she said. "We shared an excellent bottle of wine at our picnic and a respectable champagne last night."

"Of course, Mother," I replied. "About last night, I am sure Rudy regrets his excessive alcohol consumption. I hope you will not let that colour an otherwise favourable opinion of him."

She eyed me warily but remained silent.

"Yep, I wouldn't take it real serious, Dorothy," said Uncle Bill. "Rudy sometimes hits the sauce a little too hard like the rest of us, but he's harmless. I wouldn't be surprised if he apologises to you."

Mother sighed. "I suppose you are correct, William."

"One must be prepared to turn the other cheek, Mother," I added. "Glass homes, stones, and so forth."

Mother glowered at the self. "What is that supposed to mean, Benjamin?" she asked.

I raised my hands in mock surrender. "Er, merely that I observed Father on several occasions to have, one might say, overindulged." In fact, I had observed my father being poured out of a cab numerous times after a golf outing with his colleagues, which invariably ended at his club. In one incident, he staggered through the front door and, espying the self, shouted "Sod off, wench." Subsequently, after Mother appeared, he pawed at her dress before vomiting profusely over it. Mother refused to speak to him for almost one week.

"Very well," she said. "I shall accept Rudy's apology should he choose to offer one."

"You always were a good sport, Aunt Dorothy," chirped Archie.

"Quite," I stammered. "Well, Archie and I should be off now. Doubtless in the light of day, Rudy will be horrified about any, er, indiscretions or ill-chosen words he may have uttered in his inebriated state."

"Thank you, dear," she replied. "Will you be seeing Loretta, as well?"

"Yes, as a matter of fact," I said. "Still various i's to be dotted and t's to be crossed wedding-wise."

"Would you like my help, Benjamin?" asked Mother. "I did plan your sister's wedding, after all, which was a rousing success."

My sister's wedding had been one of those lavish affairs attended by several hundred guests, including several members of the Royal Family, the First Lord Admiral, and many of the Tory Members of Parliament. After the ceremony, the bride and groom departed in a gilded horse-drawn carriage for the post-ceremony reception, which was held at the Savoy. The groom, then a captain in the Royal Navy, drank himself silly before collapsing onto the dance floor, ripping my sister's gown in the process and exposing some of the more intimate parts of the female anatomy. Had my sister possessed one of my father's shotguns at the time, I suspect she would have concluded the evening, and many thereafter, in gaol.

Not wishing to remind Mother of the particulars, I replied, "A most kind offer, Mother. However, the ceremony will be quite small and informal. Far beneath your organisational talents, I should think."

"Very well, Benjamin," she said. "But if you need my help, you have only to ask."

"I shall indeed," I replied falsely, as Mother's help would be akin to asking her to set the marital ship's course for the nearest iceberg.

"Tell Rudy I hope he ain't too hungover," said Uncle Bill, who was smiling. "Hell, I remember when he fell into a water trough and slept it off. Another time—"

"Er, no need to recall the particulars, Uncle Bill," I interrupted, espying Mother's widened eyes and look of horror. "We've all of us engaged in the occasional laddish behaviour. Now, if you will excuse us, Archie and I shall be off."

After leaving the ranch, I breathed a sigh of relief, having escaped both Mother's potential for laying waste to the wedding and Uncle Bill's description of Rudy as a staggering inebriate in the manner of Nestor Martinez.

"I recall a few of the lads launching themselves into the canals after a particularly festive evening," said Archie, as we motored into town. "I do hope Uncle Bill's description has not soured Aunt Dorothy," "Is he, by the way?"

"Is who what?"

"Rudy. Is he a drunkard?"

"No, of course not. Well, not as far as I know. Besides, you saw him at dinner several nights ago. He maintained an entirely lucid and dignified demeanour throughout."

"Falling into a water trough is not what one would consider dignified, old chap."

"Er, no. However, unlike Nestor Martinez, Rudy never crashed his lorry through the front door of a bar nor, unlike Coronado, vomited on my trousers."

"I suppose one must maintain certain standards," said Archie, laughing.

Presently, we arrived at Rudy's. As the bar did not open until eleven, we walked around to the back door, whereupon I knocked heavily and shouted, "Rudy, are you inside?"

A minute or so later, we heard footsteps nearing the door and a lock disengaging. The door opened, revealing a barefoot and shirtless Rudy.

"I say, Rudy," Archie chirped, "you look rather worse for the wear."

He eyed Archie, shook his head and muttered, "M-mph."

"We've all been there, old chap," chortled Archie. "Though it's a bit easier to recover for someone my age."

"You gonna yell at me about last night, Bennie?" asked Rudy. "Because if you are, I'm gonna get my shotgun and shoot you."

I shook my head and raised my hands apologetically. "I do not intend to cast aspersions, Rudy. In fact, Mother seems to be rather nonchalant about what took place."

"I told you, nothing happened," he said.

"Er, yes, I mean, no," I replied. "However, our plan may be on the verge of foundering."

"What plan?" Rudy asked.

"The plan in which you ply Mother with champagne and then escort her to the wedding," I replied.

Rudy rubbed his chin. "Yeah, well, I think that ship has sailed. Isn't that what you would say?" He blinked again. "I need some coffee. You can come inside while I make it if you want."

Rudy turned around and walked down the hallway towards the bar, whilst we followed. Once the coffee was brewing, he sat down at one of the tables and groaned.

"So, your mother must be pretty mad at me," he said. "Guess I deserve it."

"What happened?" I asked. "On second thought, I would prefer not to know the details."

"I tried to kiss her, okay?" Rudy growled. "I know it was stupid. She enjoyed the picnic by the creek. Under that British exterior, she's funny. Told me some great stories, including about you and about some of the difficulties she's had with your dad."

"M-hem, yes," I muttered.

"Anyway," Rudy continued, "when we returned here last night, I brought out a bottle of champagne for a nightcap. I was drinking a second glass. I toasted her, but my glass broke. Spilled champagne on both of us. I got a towel and tried to clean up her blouse. That's when it happened. I leaned over to kiss her. She slapped my face and ran into the bathroom. Then I went into my office to get a clean shirt." He paused, then stuck out his chin. "You want to belt me, Bennie; you've got every right."

"Eh, what? I have no wish to engage in any fisticuffs, Rudy," I said. "I appreciate your candour. As I said, Mother is not overly distressed about last night. She described you as a 'robust gentleman' and said that my father could learn something from you."

"Robust, huh," said Rudy. "I guess that's okay for somebody my age. So, what now?"

"Flowers," said Archie, who was grinning. "And chocolates. Works every time, whether a wounded bird or the iciest of matriarchs. Of course, a grovelling *mea culpa, mea maxima culpa*, cannot hurt."

"Yeah, I get it," said Rudy. "I was married four times, not that *mea culpas* helped much. I guess I can drive down to Santa Fe and pick that stuff up. Should I come around tonight?"

"A capital idea, Rudy," I responded. "Mother always responded favourably to flowers offered by my father. Granted, she once launched a flower-filled vase at him at a speed that would have impressed W.G. Grace."

"Who?" Rudy asked.

"Ah, sorry," I said. "England's greatest cricketeer."

"Don't know anything about the game," said Rudy.

"No one else does, either, old chap," chirped Archie, "even the ones who play it."

Rudy laughed and then glanced at his watch. "Look, if I'm gonna get back here in time for dinner, I should leave soon. Could one of you open the bar at eleven?"

"At your service," said Archie, offering an exaggerated bow.

"Thanks, Archie," Rudy said. "I'll ask Anthony to come over this afternoon, so you don't have to stay long."

"I shall be the very model of a modern barman," replied Archie.

"You may wish to batten down the quality alcohol under lock and key, Rudy," I said, "in case Archie attempts to imbibe the profits."

Rudy eyed Archie suspiciously. "You can help yourself to the stuff on the shelves," he said, "but if you break into my stash, I'll shoot you."

"No need for concern, Rudy," Archie said, smiling. "Although perhaps you would be willing to grace us with another bottle of that cabernet you provided before?"

Rudy nodded. "Okay. You gonna grill another steak?"

"Duly noted," I said.

"Okay," replied Rudy. He reached into his trouser pocket and retrieved a set of keys, then removed a gold-coloured one and handed it to Archie. "Here's the key to the front door. Try to keep Paco outside when Nestor Martinez shows up—probably by noon. Otherwise, you'll be cleaning up his mess. God, I hate that damn dog."

"Wise counsel, Rudy" I added.

"And make sure Coronado pays," growled Rudy. "He owes me too much money as it is. That goes for anybody else who asks you to put their drinks on a tab. Cash only."

"Understood, Rudy," said Archie, saluting. "No scroungers."

We exited the bar and returned to the lorry, having first reconnoitred for any signs of my umbrella-wielding nemesis. As we motored back to the ranch, Archie turned to the self. "What do you think, old chap? Will Aunt Dorothy accept Rudy's apology?"

I sighed. "One hopes so, otherwise we will be forced to draft Uncle Bill into service for 'Operation Inebriate.' One doubts he would succeed."

"Why not, old chap?"

"Uncle Bill lives by the cowboy code, which prohibits one from taking advantage of the fairer sex with drink and duplicitousness."

Archie sighed and shook his head. "You and your bloody codes."

Chapter 16

T he regulars had already begun drifting in when I left Archie in command of the bar later that morning. I decided to call on Loretta, whom I had only briefly seen the prior two days. As I rolled to a stop in front of her mother's home, Chata exploded off the porch and raced towards the lorry. After opening the door, I was engulfed immediately by a canine attempt to defenestrate the face with her tongue. Of all the Vaca Seca inhabitants, two-legged and four, Chata seemed the most accepting of my presence.

"Good girl," I said, pushing her away. She emitted a loud "woof" and then bounded towards the front door. As I stepped onto the porch, she emitted another loud "woof." Presently, it opened and Chata muscled her way through and disappeared inside.

"Oh, hi, Bennie," said Loretta, who was wearing an apron and holding a greyish rag in her right hand. A lock of her hair draped itself lazily over her forehead. "Sorry, I wasn't expecting to see you this morning. We've been cleaning house. C'mon in."

Presently, the dog pushed herself through Loretta's legs, turned hard to starboard, and raced off. "Has Chata been assisting your efforts?"

Loretta laughed. "Not exactly, unless spreading mud around the house counts as helping."

"I suppose not. Once, Daisy pushed her way into Uncle Bill's house and left a porcine typhoon's level of destruction, including his bed, which collapsed under her 25-stone weight.

As enamoured as Uncle Bill is with her, he nearly converted her into bacon afterwards."

"I guess Daisy has nine lives like a cat."

"Perhaps, although I suspect if such an incident occurs again, she may find there are none remaining." I paused. "I do apologise for the unannounced visit. It has been rather a stressful morning wedding-wise."

Loretta scowled. "Your mother again? Is she still going on about the Catholic ceremony?"

"No," I replied. "Well, she has not said anything more, if that is what you mean. The plan we devised may be foundering."

"What do you mean?"

I sat down on the small sofa under the sitting room window. "Rudy," I sighed.

"Did he change his mind? I thought he and your mother hit it off. Didn't he take her sightseeing?"

"Er, yes. Yesterday they motored into Colorado and enjoyed a picnic by a creek. They returned to Rudy's in the early evening for a nightcap and, well—"

"And what, Bennie?"

"Mother said that Rudy became a bit too 'robust' for her."

"What does that mean?"

"He attempted to kiss her."

Loretta's eyes widened. "Really? Your mother? What did she do?"

"Rudy claimed that his romantic entreaties were met with a vigorous slap to the face."

Loretta began laughing uncontrollably. Finally, she stopped to catch her breath. "I guess your plan worked a little too well."

"It is no laughing matter. If she doesn't accept his apology, then the plan is dashed."

"Sorry, Bennie," Loretta said. "I just can't imagine— anyway, what will you do now?"

"Rudy has voyaged to Santa Fe to procure flowers and chocolates. I have invited him to dinner this evening so that he may apologise profusely to Mother."

Loretta shook her head and smiled. "When do I get mine?"

"Eh?"

"My flowers and chocolates."

"Why should I—gah!" I exclaimed as I parried a fist launched towards the shoulder.

Loretta smiled. "Because a girl always deserves flowers and chocolates, and not just on Valentine's Day."

"Er, yes, I shall endeavour to remember that. I believe your uncle sells chocolate bars in his store, unless of course, Coronado has devoured them all. Shall I purchase one for you?"

"No, of course not," she said, before kissing me lightly. "You really are gullible, Benjamin Graves. That's one reason I love you."

"M-hem." I paused, as the grey matter whirled. "Speaking of your uncle, have you discussed his providing refreshments for the party after the wedding? Maria will provide the comestibles, but we shall need various supplies."

"Yeah. He said, um—"

"There was still time for you to come to your senses and abandon ship?"

"Something like that. He doesn't really mean it, Bennie."

I exhaled deeply. "You said the same thing about Esperanza. Fortunately, I can negotiate your uncle's acquiescence for a price. I shall voyage there presently and discuss the butcher's bill."

"Okay. Do you want me to come with you?"

"A capital idea. Shall we?"

"I just have to tell my mother." Loretta dashed into the house. She emerged several minutes later. Mrs. Alvarez stood behind her, holding Chata and looking displeased.

"Is your mother upset about something, too?" I asked as we motored to the store. "She appeared to be scowling."

"It's nothing, really. I think she is still mad at your mother."

"And reciprocated by mine. Hence, the importance of the plan's success. Speaking of which, would you come to dinner, too? If Mother baulks initially at Rudy's apology, perhaps you could negotiate on his behalf and explain to Mother that Rudy is an upstanding sort of chap."

"Sure."

"Excellent."

Presently, we arrived at Joe's store and walked inside. I espied several individuals trolling through the aisles and several others queued behind the cash register, which appeared abandoned. We continued towards the back of the store until arriving at a door with a sign that proclaimed "Manager." I proceeded to knock stoutly and waited. There was a loud crash behind the door, followed by more silence, until the door opened and revealed Coronado's rounded visage.

"*Hola*, Señor Graves. *Hola*, Loretta," he said, nodding absently.

"Er, yes, good afternoon, Coronado," I replied. "I say, what was that noise? Did something break?

Coronado shrugged. "Uh, sort of, Señor Graves."

Reasoning that ignorance was bliss where Coronado was concerned, I decided not to enquire about the breakage. "We are looking for Joe. Is he here?"

Coronado turned around and appeared to scan the office. "Sorry, Señor Graves. Joe left."

"Do you know where he went or when he will return?" I asked.

Coronado shrugged. "Can I help, Señor Graves?" he asked, nodding expectantly.

"Er, thank you, no, Coronado," I said. "We can return later. You do realise customers are waiting at the cash register. Should you not be there assisting them?"

"Yeah, I guess so," he said.

"Actually, there is one thing you can help me with, Coronado," I said.

"Sure. I like to help," he replied.

"Do you have any chocolate bars?" I asked.

Loretta laughed.

"They're up front," said Coronado. "I ate one a little while ago because I was hungry. Are you hungry, Señor Graves? When is the cafe gonna be open again? I sure miss Maria's *enchiladas*." He patted his ample stomach.

"Er, no, the chocolate bar is for Loretta," I said. "And the cafe shall reopen after Loretta and I return from our honeymoon."

"Do you like the one with nuts in it, Loretta?" Coronado asked. "That's my favourite."

"Mine, too," said Loretta. "But you better get to the cash register now."

"Okay, Loretta," Coronado said. He waddled towards the front of the store before disappearing around the aisle.

"Did you tell him about being the best man, yet?" asked Loretta.

"Er, not yet. I need to muster sufficient courage. Now, about that chocolate bar."

Loretta laughed. "I guess I am hungry."

As we walked towards the front of the store, we heard another crashing sound and then someone cursing loudly in Spanish. Quickening our pace, we arrived at the cash register, where Coronado stood, devouring another candy bar. The contents of a milk container were spread across the floor where he stood. I spotted the two individuals who had been waiting when we came inside walking towards their car.

"What happened?" asked Loretta.

"I kinda dropped Señora Flores' milk," Coronado said. "It splashed all over her dress and face, too. Then Señor Flores got real mad."

"Well, er, accidents happen to us all, Coronado," I said. "Doubtless Joe has spilt the occasional bottle of milk."

"I dunno, Señor Graves," he said. "Only Joe's gonna be real mad because they didn't pay for her groceries. Señor Flores grabbed the bag and walked out."

"Ah," I said. "Tell you what, Coronado. I shall pay for them."

"Thanks, Señor Graves." He extended a somewhat chocolate-covered hand towards mine and shook it.

I withdrew the now chocolate-infused hand and attempted to keep it a safe distance from my trousers. "I do want to ask you one favour, Coronado," I said.

"Sure, Señor Graves. I like to help."

"How would you like to be best man at the wedding?" I muttered, reluctantly.

"Like in that movie? Thanks." He extended his hand again and further covered mine in a chocolate residue. "I'll bring my gun to the wedding in case somebody attacks you."

"What? No!" I shouted. "I mean, we shall be perfectly safe, Coronado. No need for firearms of any type at the ceremony." From the corner of my eye, I espied Loretta stifling a laugh.

"Okay, Señor Graves," he said. "But if you change your mind, I can bring one. The guy in the movie had a pistol, but I think my shotgun would be better."

The grey matter recalled the image of Coronado's shotgun unleashing a fusillade that nearly destroyed the cafe whilst he attempted to despatch Señor Apestoso.

"God no!" I cried. "No shotguns, no carronades, no weapons of any sort . . . please."

"Okay," he said. "Señor Graves?"

"Yes?" I sighed.

"What does a best man do?"

"Er, well, it is quite simple, really. You merely give Loretta's wedding ring to me when Father Castillo asks for it," I said.

Coronado goggled the self blankly. "Can't I just give it to Loretta?"

"Er, afraid not. After you give me the ring, I place it on Loretta's finger. Father Castillo will then say a few words and pronounce Loretta and I married."

"Oh, okay, Señor Graves," he replied, nodding. "But I don't got Loretta's ring."

"Not to worry, Coronado," I said. "I shall entrust the ring to you immediately before the ceremony."

"Huh?" he said.

"I will give you the ring right before the wedding starts when we are all in the church. You shall then place the ring in your pocket and leave it there until Father Castillo asks for it. Then you give the ring to me and Bob's your uncle."

Coronado goggled me silently, then slowly reached for another chocolate bar.

"Something wrong, Coronado?" I asked.

"Is Uncle Bob gonna be at the wedding, too, Señor Graves?"

"Gah," I moaned softly, espying Loretta, who had turned around to avoid bursting into laughter. "No, Uncle Bob is in London and cannot attend. Now, if you will excuse us, we must be off. Can you please remember to tell Joe we need to see him?"

"Okay," said Coronado. "Do you know where he is?"

The jaw dropped. "We just asked you that—"

"We don't know where Joe is, Coronado," interrupted Loretta. "That's why we wanted your help."

"Oh, okay, Loretta," said Coronado. "Maybe he's at Rudy's." Coronado's face turned blank, and he stared out the store window. "I'd sure like a beer now."

"We must have just missed him," I said to Loretta.

We motored to Rudy's and found Archie holding court behind the bar. The regulars appeared to be noisily enjoying themselves, presumably thanks to Archie providing more stimulating conversation than Anthony, who tended towards a more Captain Bligh-like manner, along with larger drinks.

"Quiet everyone," Archie shouted above the noise. "The prospective bride and groom have arrived." The regulars turned towards Loretta and the self, raised their glasses in unison, and cheered, before resuming their conversations.

Loretta waved shyly to everyone. "Thanks," she said. She then spotted her uncle and walked to his table.

As the regulars' reaction nonplussed the self, I motioned to Archie to step over to the end of the bar. "What was that about?" I whispered.

"Oh, nothing really," Archie said. "They all know about the wedding."

"Yes, I know," I said, "but I believe most of them would prefer if I were tarred and feathered, then bunged out of the nearest aeroplane, rather than marry Loretta."

"I did notice a certain, how shall we say, ambivalence towards the upcoming nuptials. I thought 'Why not provide them with something tangible to change their opinion?'"

"Something tangible?" I hesitated. "Have you been providing free drinks to the locals in exchange for their support?"

"Heavens, no, old chap," Archie replied. "Rudy entrusted me as his temporary barman. I would never dishonour that."

"Then why the sudden burst of enthusiasm amongst the locals?" I asked.

"I invited them all to the wedding and the reception afterwards."

"Gah! You did what? We are supposed to have a small, quiet family ceremony. God knows that will be bad enough owing to the attendance of Esperanza and Joe, but an event for the entire town? Sheer madness. Given some of the long-running, internecine disputes amongst some of the locals, I imagine the reception will degrade quickly into a rugby scrum . . . or worse."

"Ah, but think of the goodwill already engendered," he said. "'Hussah's!' instead of tar and feathers for Benjamin Graves."

"All well and good, but we cannot afford a town-wide celebration."

"Surely Aunt Dorothy will help defray the expense," said Archie.

I sighed. "Mother's finances are rather dependent on Father's generosity of spirit, which even Scrooge would find wanting. Then again, as this is your doing, perhaps you can fund it with your trust."

"Er, yes, about that, old chap," Archie said, grimacing. "Afraid it is rather depleted. There was an, er, incident involving several large bells at Christ Church."

"Yes, I am familiar with that 'incident,' as you call it."

"Ah. Well, the repair bill was rather substantial. Consequently, the trust fund is, shall we say, rather moribund. And what remains is off-limits until I turn thirty. Damned inconvenient."

"Then you must rescind the invitation," I said.

"I would counsel against doing so, cousin. When I first mentioned the wedding and reception, there was a noticeable grumbling amongst the patrons. I fear a withdrawal of the invitation so soon afterwards, especially a withdrawal at your behest, would be met with extreme displeasure. Of course, I may be mistaken. They may be quite understanding and magnanimous, even after learning you have disinvited them."

A vision of the self in a cocoon of tar and feathers being bunged into a pit of rattlesnakes with Joe and Esperanza looking on eagerly arose in the grey matter. Maria could not possibly feed the entire town, nor would Rudy have sufficient supplies of spirits to quench its rapacious thirst. Then there was the slight issue of the cost. "Gah," I moaned softly.

"Cheer up, cousin," chirped Archie. "I shall think of something."

"That frightens be even more, as does informing Loretta the small family wedding she wants will be a town-wide affair."

"Pshaw. You're far too pessimistic. What bride doesn't wish to be treated as a princess with throngs of admirers? The birds at Oxford certainly do."

"I would not describe Loretta as a princess and advise you to avoid doing so, especially if she is in earshot. Loretta is a kind-hearted, level-headed girl. As for the girls at Oxford, you may recall I was previously married to one. I do not care to repeat that."

"Er, point taken, old chap," said Archie. "Would you like me to speak to Loretta? She may be more inclined to forgive my trespasses, after all."

"No," I sighed. "I shall do so. And then I shall speak with Joe about securing the necessary supplies. If nothing else, an opportunity to exercise his inner rapaciousness will muffle his disapproval of the wedding."

I left Archie behind the bar and walked to the corner table where Joe and Loretta sat. As I approached, Joe eyed the self icily and drained the beer bottle he held in his hand.

"What do you want, *Pendejo*?" asked Joe.

I shrugged. "I have become inured to that particular epithet, Joe. Besides, I have some good news for you."

Joe sat up and his eyes brightened. "You and Loretta call off the wedding? Or maybe she told you to get the fuck out of town."

"*Tío* Joe," Loretta said loudly. "Stop it before I tell *you* that."

"Okay, okay," Joe said. "So what's your good news, *gringo?*"

"You now have an opportunity to earn a substantial sum," I said.

"How?" he asked suspiciously. "I don't trust you."

"We need you to supply comestibles and drinks for the wedding reception," I said.

Loretta looked at me quizzically. "What for, Bennie? *Tía* Maria will cook and Rudy will provide the drinks."

"Er, yes," I said. "I understand there will be some additional guests at the wedding and reception afterwards."

"Who?" asked Loretta. "It's just our families."

"Yes, about that," I stammered. "It seems the entire town shall be in attendance."

"What? We agreed on a small ceremony with just our families." She poked her finger sharply into my chest. "When did this happen and why didn't you tell me?"

"Yeah," said Joe. "What the fuck did you do now, *gringo?*"

"Please, Loretta," I pleaded. "I only just found out. Apparently, the regulars at the bar were grumbling about the wedding, so Archie invited them—and the entire town—to participate in the festivities. I gather the prospect of free food and, especially, drink caused a favourable change in their collective attitude."

"Archie invited the entire town?" Loretta spluttered. "To my wedding? Then he can uninvite them." Her ocular daggers made ready to fire.

"M-hem, yes," I said. "As much as I would prefer a private gathering, discretion may be the better part of valour in this instance. If we disinvite them, their disapprobation towards the self is likely to increase markedly, and I should like to avoid tar and feathering."

The daggers in Joe's eyes had given way to dollar signs. "Look, Loretta," he said, "I hate to say it, but the *gringo* is right. You don't know some of them like I do. Things could get ugly and both of you could get hurt."

Loretta shook her head. "*Tío* Joe, all I wanted is a quiet little wedding. Now, the entire town will show up and ruin everything." She began to sob.

I placed an arm around her shoulder. "I'm sorry, Loretta. I really am. Archie meant well."

"Yeah," said Joe. "It's still gonna be a real nice wedding, Loretta. I'm gonna go to Santa Fe and get everything for the reception. Real good stuff, too." He looked at me and put his hand out. "*Mucho dinero*," he mouthed silently.

I nodded to him discreetly and mouthed, "Not now."

Presently, Loretta wiped her eyes. "Okay," she said. "I just want it all to be over."

I took Loretta's hand and squeezed it gently as the grey matter catalogued the upcoming horrors yet to be inflicted on the self: the initial meeting with Father Castillo, the confessing of sins, real and imagined, the baptismal dunking, and the now teetering plan to thwart maternal violence during the ceremony itself. "You have no idea," I thought.

"Oh, there is one other small item, Joe," I said. "You may wish to return to the store with all haste. Señor and Señora Flores left the store without paying for their groceries."

"Huh? Carmina and Rudolfo didn't pay?" He stood up quickly. "How come?"

"I believe the proximate cause may have been Coronado dropping the bottle of milk they wished to purchase onto the floor. Upon contact, the bottle erupted, spraying the contents over her dress and face. Señor Flores then yelled obscenities at Coronado, picked up the bag of groceries, and left."

Joe pounded his hands against his forehead. "Idiot. ¡*No más!*" he shouted. He stood up, pushed past us, and ran out the door.

"Everything all right, cousin?" Archie said from behind the bar. "Joe seems to have departed rather hurriedly."

"I believe he is returning to the store to admonish Coronado, if not worse."

"Has Coronado been hoovering up the profits?" asked Archie.

"Er, something like that," I replied.

Presently, Antonio came through the front door and stepped behind the bar. Then, turning towards the various patrons, he shouted, "Everybody pay up unless you want me to get tough," whilst ritually grinding his right fist into his palm.

Archie raised an eyebrow. "No need, Antonio," he replied. "Several requested I keep a tab, but I refused. Strictly cash on the nailhead. I must say, they are rather a thirsty lot."

"Yeah, we got some real boozers," said Antonio, nodding. One would have thought he had tended bar for decades.

"Well, I leave the bar in your hands," announced Archie. He turned to the assembled regulars at the bar and saluted. "Good day, all. I hope my efforts as your publican were successful." The regulars grunted their affirmation as Archie stepped around the bar and glided over to where Loretta and I stood. "Right, then, old chap. Shall we prepare for tonight's *rapprochement?*"

Chapter 17

Wesoon docked at the ranch and were greeted with a noncommittal grunt from Daisy who resumed her afternoon siesta after discovering we had not brought any comestibles. The ears perceived some sort of metallic pounding coming from the barn, followed by a string of epithets uttered by Uncle Bill. I suggested Archie and Loretta repair to the house and entertain Mother, whilst I investigated the source of Uncle Bill's duress.

I entered through the open barn door and spotted Uncle Bill standing at the small workbench at the rear, raising the hammer in his right hand and bringing it down onto a metallic object.

"I say, Uncle Bill, something the matter?"

He turned around and eyed me. "God damn, Marjorie."

"Has she not been gentle as a lamb?" I said innocently.

"See for yourself." He pointed towards her stall. The upper door hung obliquely from one remaining rusted hinge. The lower door, along with a sizeable portion of the entire door frame, lay in pieces scattered on the ground. I walked over to the stall to inspect the damage more closely. Besides the damaged hatch, daylight streamed through the wall where several boards had been vanquished, presumably by one of Margorie's hooves.

"I gather Marjorie did not wish to be confined."

"Yep," he hissed. "Broke the door and kicked a big hole in the wall."

"Hmm. What precipitated her outburst?"

"You know that big horse Manny Obrador got last year?"

Manny Obrador was an unusually gregarious chap who owned a large ranch that bordered Uncle Bill's to the west and north. "Do you mean Sampson, that chestnut gelding?"

"Check Sampson's caboose, Bennie. He ain't a gelding."

"What do you mean?" I asked. Presently, the grey matter tut-tutted at my ignorance. "Oh, ah, quite," I muttered. "Er, where is Marjorie now?"

"How the hell should I know?" yelled Uncle Bill. "She must have been in season. Sampson must have jumped the fence and come over here. I was way in the back field when I heard loud neighs and then a crash." He paused to point at the wreckage. "I ran over here and saw Marjorie running off with him."

I resisted a strong urge to shout, "Good riddance" and "God is in His Heaven, all's right with the world." I cleared the throat. "M-hem. Well, one presumes we shall hear the patter of little hooves in future."

Uncle Bill grunted. He turned back towards the work-bench, raised the hammer again, and brought it down onto what had been the bottom hinge.

"Anything I can do to assist, Uncle Bill?"

He turned towards the self. "Yep. You know that pile of wood by the back fence? Go fetch a few pieces and patch up the back wall."

I saluted and exited the barn. As I rounded the corner towards the house, I spotted Loretta accelerating towards me like an enraged grizzly.

"Take me home, Benjamin," she commanded. "Now!"

"What?" I stammered. "Why? Has something happened?"

"Your mother happened," she growled. "Again."

I shook my head in despair. "What did she say this time?"

"That it was all *my* mother's fault because we insisted on a Catholic wedding and that I was pig-headed."

"Say no more," I interrupted. "I will speak with her."

"Don't bother. I had a glass of water in my hand and I threw it at her. Archie tried to intervene, but your mother screamed at me to get out."

"Gah," I moaned.

"I'm sorry, Bennie, but if this is what things will be like, we can't get married. Now, take me home."

I envisioned Fate wagging a finger at the self whilst singing "tra-la-la." "No, Loretta. I mean, yes, I shall take you home. I promise to resolve this once and for all."

"How?" she asked. "It's hopeless."

The grey matter envisioned binning Mother into the barn with Porfiria the morning of the wedding. But as Archie was wont to remind the self, the Graves code would not allow such treatment of the *materfamilias*.

"Well, several options we have discussed come to mind."

Loretta placed her hands on her hips and glowered. "I refuse to elope. Besides, she'll still be my mother-in-law."

"One presumes decamping to the Australian outback is out of the question."

"I don't think so."

"No, I suppose not. Rather too many poisonous snakes anyway. Perhaps I should mention that to your Uncle Joe." I paused and took Loretta's hand. "I shall have words with Mother and enquire of Uncle Bill, who may have some suggestions. After all, he faced a similar situation with his disapproving mother-in-law."

Loretta crossed her arms stiffly. "If you want to marry me, Benjamin Graves, you'd better deal with her. Tonight. Come to the house on Monday and let me know. I've got things to do tomorrow."

"Er, no cause for alarm," I pleaded. "Mother may be stubborn, but I know she will accept the marriage and welcome you into the family. On my honour as a Graves."

Loretta eyed me sceptically. "Uh-huh."

"By the way, do we not need to, how do they say in the movies, 'get our alibis straight' for the meeting with Father Castillo on Tuesday?"

"He just wants to meet you before the wedding and ask a few questions about your conversion." Loretta's eyes narrowed. "You *are* still converting, aren't you? Or has your mother said you can't?"

"Eh? No, that is, yes, Mother has accepted the forthcoming conversion, just as she will our marriage. You must believe me, Loretta. Mother's outburst was utterly out of character. I am confident that, upon my return, she will express her sincerest wish to apologise to you personally."

"She needs to apologise to *my* mother, too."

"Yes, of course," I stammered, clueless about how to produce the required *mea culpas.*

After returning Loretta to her mother's home, I hurried back to the ranch, in part to avoid the stream of invective that surely would have been launched at the self by Mrs. Alvarez. The grey matter pondered how best to approach Mother regarding this most recent outbreak of hostilities. When I arrived, I espied Rudy's lorry. "Damn and blast," I muttered, as I did not wish to address Mother in his presence. I dashed through the front door and into the sitting room, where Rudy, Mother, Archie and Uncle Bill were conversing.

"Ah, there you are, dear," Mother said. "I must speak with you about your fiancée's shameful behaviour. You cannot marry such an inconsiderate and ill-tempered girl."

I sighed loudly and glanced at Rudy, who was shaking his head softly whilst stifling laughter. "Must we have this conversation again?" I asked. "You cannot expect Loretta to accept you denigrating her mother. Surely, you would not want me to accept *her* mother's denigrating you. They are both owed apologies."

"You expect me to apologise?" Mother growled. "Perhaps your father was correct, after all."

"What do you mean?" I asked.

"If you insist on marrying that, that, trollop, then you *are* a nincompoop," she snorted. "And I shall not attend the wedding."

Upon hearing her utter those seven words, I resisted the urge to dance wildly about the room shouting "Hallelujah!"—the

Graves code would not allow one to accept my mother's refusal so eagerly. Besides, I surmised it to be an empty threat; Mother would not miss the chance to attend, if only to complain even more bitterly before, during, and after the ceremony.

"Perhaps we should postpone this conversation whilst Rudy is here," I said dryly.

"Oh, very well, Benjamin," Mother grumbled.

"Hey, I don't want to get in the way of a family, um, discussion," said Rudy. "I can leave if you want."

Mother patted Rudy's hand. "I do apologise for Benjamin's behaviour, Rudy. Of course, you must stay for dinner."

I raised an eyebrow but remained silent. Perhaps Archie was correct about my embrace of the Graves code, although I doubt the Royal Navy would have condoned keelhauling one's mother.

"Yeah, Rudy," said Uncle Bill. "You don't want to pass up those steaks we're gonna cook."

"Thanks," said Rudy. "I'm sure everything will work out fine."

"My son needs the wisdom that comes from age," Mother said, patting Rudy's hand again. "Now, how about a glass of that wine you brought?"

"Uh, good idea," replied Rudy, as he glanced at his watch. I suspected he was counting the minutes until he could escape the verbal daggers. He stood up slowly and walked towards the kitchen. I quickly followed, as did Archie.

"What's going on?" Rudy whispered. "When I got here, I heard your mother shouting about Loretta from her bedroom. What the hell happened?"

"Well," Archie began, "Loretta and I were chatting rather aimlessly about the weather and such when Aunt Dorothy brought up the wedding and asked Loretta if she would settle for a civil ceremony. Loretta shouted, 'No!' and stood up rather defensively. Aunt Dorothy then asserted it was a reasonable compromise, far more so than forcing Bennie to become a Catholic and obey the edicts of, and I quote, 'a dim-witted clod wearing a pointy hat.' I mean no offence, of course, Rudy."

Rudy shrugged. "None taken. My parents were Catholic, like most everyone around here, but they didn't take it real seriously."

"Did you have church weddings?" I asked.

He laughed. "Heck, no. My first wife was Jewish. You think what you're dealing with is tough. We never told anybody. The rest were civil ceremonies. The last one was in Vegas to a cigarette girl. You know what they say, 'Marry in haste, repent at leisure.' That last one cured me for good."

"Er, yes," I muttered.

"Anyway," continued Archie, "the remark about the Pope proved to be rather too much for Loretta, who tossed the contents of her glass into Aunt Dorothy's face, followed by several rather choice epithets that would have gladdened the heart of any sailor."

"Gah," I moaned softly.

"Are you going to stay in the kitchen all night?" shouted Mother from the sitting room.

"Er, no, Mother," I replied. "The, uh, cork is proving to be rather recalcitrant. Shan't be a moment."

"Look on the bright side, old chap," Archie said. "The earlier rift between Aunt Dorothy and Rudy has faded in importance." He glanced at Rudy. "She does not appear at all nonplussed by your presence."

"Yeah, I guess that's good," said Rudy. "You think she won't come to the wedding, Bennie? That would make things a lot easier for everybody."

"Alas, no," I said. "Merely one of those maternal efforts at effectuating guilt. To use one of Uncle Bill's expressions, wild horses will not keep her from attending."

"Too bad," said Rudy. "I was hoping I didn't have to go through with your little plan."

I shrugged and eyed Archie. "Any suggestions, cousin? You seem to be more experienced in the art of deception than I."

Archie grimaced. "Though I have experience dodging the jilted bird and various parental types, afraid this sort of Montagues and Capulets battle is rather beyond my experience."

"Well, perhaps you can engage that devious mind of yours," I said. "Anyway, we should return to the sitting room."

I dispensed glasses around the room, followed by Rudy who poured. After everyone was seated, I raised my glass to shield the self from the ocular daggers Mother was firing towards me. "A toast to Rudy's excellent choice of wine," I said with strained cheerfulness.

"Here, here," added Archie.

"Yep, real good stuff, Rudy," said Uncle Bill.

"Nincompoop," Mother mumbled, just loud enough to reach the ears.

The remainder of the evening was uneventful, and it appeared that the rift between Mother and Rudy had been sufficiently repaired to restore our original plan. After Rudy departed, Mother turned towards me and resumed her fusillade of ocular daggers.

"Well, Benjamin, what do you intend to do about this?" she growled.

"About what, exactly, Mother?" I replied.

"You know perfectly well what I mean," said Mother. "Your fiancée lacks the necessary social graces to be part of this family."

"Such as hurling crockery?" I asked dryly. "Really, Mother."

"How dare you!" she yelled.

"Everybody quit your hollerin'," shouted Uncle Bill, as he stood up from the sofa and hitched up his belt. "Dorothy, you're yammering isn't going to change anything. Bennie's gonna marry Loretta. I've gotten to know her. She and Josefa are good people. And this ain't London high society. Damn good thing, too."

Mother remained silent.

"And, Bennie," he began, turning towards the self, "your mother just wants the best for you. Disrespecting your elders, well, that ain't the cowboy way."

"M-hem," I muttered.

"Now," Uncle Bill continued, "this is my house, not the OK Corral. I don't want any more dust-ups between you two." He eyed Mother and then the self. "Well?"

"Understood, Uncle Bill," I said. "I apologise, Mother."

"Very well, dear," she said. "I shall say no more about it."

Uncle Bill eyed Archie, who shrugged apologetically. "Your wish is my command, Uncle. I am merely your humble servant."

"Good. That's settled then," said Uncle Bill. "Now, I'm gonna get me a whisky. Anybody else?"

"Do you have anything besides Dusty Trail, Uncle?" asked Archie hesitantly.

"Nope," replied Uncle Bill. "Cowboys drink it. That's good enough for me and it ought to be good enough for you."

"Oh, ah, quite," said Archie. "Well, Dusty Trail it is then."

"What about you, pard'ner?" Uncle Bill asked.

"God yes," I said.

Uncle Bill turned towards Mother. "Dorothy?"

"No, thank you, William," she said. "I've never cared for whisky." She stood up and smoothed her dress. "Now, if you will excuse me, I will retire for the evening."

We bid Mother goodnight, then decamped to the kitchen and poured ourselves bracing doses of Dusty Trail, which the shell-shocked Graves nerves cried out for, before returning to the sitting room.

"Thank you, Uncle Bill," I said. "But even as this particular battle may be over, there remains the war."

"What do you mean?" he asked, obviously pleased with his earlier diplomatic efforts. "Dorothy knows nothing's gonna prevent you from marrying Loretta."

"Er, yes," I said, "but Loretta must still be mollified sufficiently to accept Mother as her in-law.

"Oh, hell," replied Uncle Bill. "That won't be a problem. Me and Cecilia survived it. After a few years, her mother came around and accepted me. 'Course, I didn't see her much, which helped. Dorothy will come around, too, especially if you tell her she's gonna be a grandmother."

"Gah!" I spluttered, whilst the contents of my glass spilt over the gunwhales. "That is, well, all in good time."

"You and Loretta discussed having kids?" asked Uncle Bill.

"Indeed, cousin," laughed Archie, raising his glass. "I should enjoy being an uncle. Shall we soon expect the patter of miniature Graves ready to uphold the familial code? Besides, aren't Catholics commanded to be fruitful and multiply."

I shuddered, downed the remaining Dusty Trail in my glass, and mopped the moisture that began to flow off the brow. The concept of small copies of the self, running hither and yon, filled me with dread, as did their being surrounded by the likes of Esperanza and Joe. One imagined the Graves children gleefully binning rattlesnakes into school rooms, addressing their father as "*Pendejito*," and possessed of a fondness for waving about large knives. "Er, the subject has not been first of mind recently, what with the wedding preparations."

"That reminds me," said Uncle Bill. "How are you two comin' along with your secret plans?"

"Well," Archie began, "as Rudy and Aunt Dorothy appear to have reconciled, or at least reached a *modus vivendi*, one presumes that part of the plan remains in force."

"What about Josefa?" asked Uncle Bill.

"I have spoken with Maria and Esperanza," I replied. "That aspect of the plan is rather high risk, to say the least. Unfortunately, we have no better alternatives unless Archie's innate deviousness discovers a better strategy."

"Sorry, old chap," Archie said. "Some things are beyond even my powers."

Uncle Bill grunted and shook his head. "What about Porfiria?" he asked.

"Benjamin believes that aspect to be straightforward," replied Archie. "I merely abscond with that nasty cur—what's its name again?—then find Porfiria, convince her to rescue the bloody dog, and finally lock her in your barn."

"I dunno, boys," Uncle Bill said.

"Superior alternatives would be most welcome, Uncle Bill," I said. "Otherwise, I suspect Fate will ensure that Porfiria breaches the church door, cries havoc, and lets slip Vaca Seca's dogs of war."

"Yeah, I suppose," Uncle Bill muttered. "You ought to elope like me and Celestina. It would sure solve a lot of problems."

"An excellent suggestion, Uncle Bill," I replied, "if only the bride-to-be and her family would accept it.".

"Birds do rather like the ceremonial aspects—gowns, bridesmaids, flowers, and such," added Archie. "Well, so I have been told."

Uncle Bill drained his glass and stood up. "Well, I'm off to bed myself." He paused and looked disapprovingly at the self. "I'm gonna be glad when this is all over. Everything always seems to get real complicated with you. Bennie."

"Sorry," I mumbled. "It is not by choice, I assure you."

He emitted a last, reproachful grunt, then walked into the kitchen, deposited his glass, and strolled down the hallway to his bedroom.

Archie eyed me and smiled. "They do seem rather complicated, old chap."

"If only you knew."

Chapter 18

The next morning found a gloomy and dull-witted self, sitting at the kitchen table with hands folded around a steaming mug of cowboy coffee. Whilst the rest of the household slumbered, I pondered the current situation. Mother's resistance was as untrammelled as a mass of icebergs, despite Uncle Bill's admonition, whilst Loretta insisted on apologies for both herself and her mother, lest she disembark the marital ship. "Gah," I moaned softly.

Presently, Uncle Bill shuffled into the kitchen, grey hair dishevelled and still in his pyjamas. He rubbed his unshaven chin and eyed me. "You're up mighty early, pard'ner. Everything okay?" He retrieved a mug from the cupboard and filled it with my brew. "Not bad," he said softly, after imbibing a large swallow. "Almost strong enough. You still upset about last night?"

"Well, Loretta demands Mother apologise to both her and her mother, but I rather doubt Mother will comply."

He sat down heavily at the table. "Hell, Dorothy's all show, Bennie. It's what they say in Texas: 'All hat and no cattle.' She'll come round soon enough."

"Soon may be too late, Uncle Bill. The wedding takes place this week. I know Mother's threat not to attend is an empty one. As for apologies to Loretta and Mrs. Alvarez, one suspects Mother is the veritable immovable object."

Uncle Bill drained his mug and grimaced. "Yeah, you got a point about that." He stood up, walked to the stove, and poured another mug of the thickening brew. "Tell you what.

You leave Dorothy to me. I'll get her to ease off the reins. And I'm gonna talk to Josefa, too."

"Any assistance would be much appreciated," I replied. "Perhaps Rudy is correct about marrying in haste."

Uncle Bill laughed. "He told you about that cigarette girl he married in Vegas?"

"Well, none of the details."

"Let's just say, you ain't marrying a cigarette girl, Bennie. Loretta's a fine filly. You know it, too."

"Indeed, she is. I wish to marry her, but Fate appears to have other ideas."

"Oh, hell, Bennie. Did I ever tell you about Celestina and me?"

"Yes, you explained how you eloped. Alas, Loretta is adamant about a church wedding."

"Yeah, well I didn't tell you the whole story. We were in her parent's house, standing on the porch because I had been out all day and was covered in dirt. Her father was out on a round-up, so it was just her mother. She was hollerin' that she wasn't gonna let her daughter marry some dumb foreign cowboy who talked funny, and she sure as hell wasn't gonna let me step foot in her church.

"Celestina tried to reason with her. Said she was gonna marry me, whether her mother liked it or not. Her mother listened. Finally, she said 'Okay' and walked inside the house. We were surprised, but glad that her mother had finally accepted the marriage. I told Celestina I wanted us to get married as soon as we could, and she agreed."

"What about her father?" I asked. "Did he approve?"

"I don't think any father ever fully approves of the fellow who marries his daughter, but he liked me because I worked real hard. We both wanted to wait for him to return."

"Anyway, there was a local cafe that we both liked, so I suggested we go there for some dinner. As we were walking to my old Model T that was parked nearby, Celestina's mother came out of the house carrying a rifle. 'You ain't marrying my daughter, you goddamn foreigner,' she yelled. She raised the rifle and shot at me. The first shot hit the back window of the car and shattered it. 'Next one's not gonna miss,' her mother shouted.

"Well, we both started running towards the car. Celestina ran behind me so her mother wouldn't shoot again. But she did. Hit the left rear tyre. 'Goddamn, Celestina, get out of the way,' her mother shouted. She fired again and hit the right rear one. We got to the car and scrambled inside. I drove off with two flat tyres, telling Celestina to keep her head down. We heard another shot, but I don't think her mother was aiming for the car. Once we were out of range, I stopped, changed one tyre, and then drove slowly with the other flat to the nearest gas station, which was about 10 miles."

"Good Lord! What did you do then?"

"We kept driving until we got to Tucson. Found a justice of the peace and got married right then and there. The next day, we drove back to my little place."

"Did you ever dare set foot at her parents' home?"

"Yep. About a week later, we drove there so Celestina could get her things. Her dad had returned. I got out first, but Celestina insisted on walking in front, in case her mother still had any ideas about shooting me. Her dad was sitting on the porch. After Celestina told him what happened, he just shook his head and laughed. Said her mother always was hot-tempered. Then he shook my hand, told me to take real good care of his daughter, and gave me ten dollars for the two tyres." Uncle Bill sighed heavily. "Damn I miss her, Bennie. Don't you dare let Loretta go."

The Graves pride surged. "I shall not, Uncle Bill. As Nelson insisted, I shall go straight at 'em."

"Good, boy. Now, we got us some chores to do this morning. Then, after everybody's fed, we'll hook up the trailer and go fetch Marjorie from Manny's. I'm sure she followed Sampson home so she could get some grub."

"Er, yes, of course," I said, hopes dashed that my equine nemesis would not return.

206 | J.A. LESSER

Just before ten o'clock, we returned to the ranch with Marjorie trailered and recalcitrant as ever. After Uncle Bill opened the trailer door in front of the barn, she walked out haughtily towards her stall and, upon seeing my presence, kicked a nearby bucket, which narrowly missed my shin.

"Still believe she is as gentle as a lamb?" I asked. "As you observed, that was a thoroughly unprovoked attack."

Uncle Bill laughed. "That's just her maternal instinct."

"No doubt, Medea would approve."

"You just got to be nicer to her, pard'ner. Now, we better get inside and see what's goin' on with your mother and cousin."

I grunted an affirmation, cursed Marjorie silently, and followed Uncle Bill, who had already disappeared inside the house. Presently, a car screeched and turned into the drive, horn blaring. It stopped suddenly, raising a cloud of dust, and I feared Coronado had acquired another vehicle with which to destroy my lorry and anything else of value.

To my surprise, the front passenger door opened, and Loretta emerged. "C'mon, let's go," she said, motioning towards the self with her hand.

I espied Esperanza and Maria sitting in the rear seat. Esperanza wasted no time raising her middle finger at the self. The horn blared again. "C'mon, *gringo*," Joe shouted. "I gotta get to the church."

"Loretta," I said hesitantly, goggling her. "Church? I don't understand."

"It was *Tía* Maria's idea," said Loretta. "She said that, before we meet Father Castillo, you should see what a Catholic service is like."

"Eh? Surely Father Castillo will be upset if he sees me sitting in a pew having not yet converted."

"Oh, no, he won't be there today. *Tío* Joe is leading the service."

The jaw dropped. "Joe?"

"That's right. He's a lay priest."

The jaw fell to the ground and hoisted a white flag. "Joe?" I repeated dully.

"C'mon, Bennie. You can sit up front." She laughed and motioned me towards the car. "I promise not to make you sit between my aunts."

The grey matter reeled. "I, er, I suppose I should change."

"That's okay. You don't have to. Besides, *Tío* Joe can't be late."

I ran inside, bid my mother good morning, and found Uncle Bill sitting at the kitchen table with a cuppa.

"What's up, pard'ner?" he asked. "Whose here?"

"Er, Loretta, actually. She insists I accompany her to church this morning."

"That's a good sign, ain't it?"

"Not with Maria and Esperanza attending, and her uncle serving as this morning's substitute priest. I suspect he will charm various snakes as part of his sermon." The horn blared again. "That would be Joe. Please say nothing to Mother."

"Okay," he replied. "Uh, maybe you ought to have a bath and change into some clean clothes first. You don't look or smell real church friendly."

I glanced at my shirt and trousers, which were stained with manure I had acquired when I fell into a large mound near the corral where we had cornered Marjorie. "M-hem, yes," I sighed. "But Joe insists on departing immediately."

"He may change his mind when he gets a good whiff of you," said Uncle Bill. "Maybe you better sit by yourself in church. I don't think folks will want you nearby."

"M-hem, yes," I repeated. As I walked through the sitting room, Mother glanced up from the book she was reading. "Are you leaving, Benjamin? I thought we would spend some time together today."

"Eh? Oh yes, I am sorry, Mother. Must dash. The, er, cafe, is, er, taking on water. Several feet in the well and rising," I mumbled as I sailed through the front door.

"What?" she said.

"Cheer-o" I shouted from outside the house. I walked over to the front passenger door, opened it, took a deep breath, and sat down.

"About time, *gringo*," Joe said. He put the vehicle into reverse and backed up onto the road, then quickly accelerated towards town.

"What stinks?" Esperanza grumbled. "Where you been, *Pendejito*? Rolling around in horse shit?"

"As a matter of fact, we've just retrieved Marjorie from Mr. Obrador's ranch. During my efforts to lead Marjorie into the trailer, I, well, encountered, some recent manure that had been deposited."

"That's what El Vaquero's horse thinks of you." Esperanza laughed again. "Maybe God's punishing you, too."

I turned around and glared at her. "I can assure you, Esperanza, he is at this very moment."

"*Tía* Esperanza, stop," said Loretta. "Maybe you should sit in the back of the church, Bennie. You do stink."

I grunted, wondering if I might sit outside the church. "Yes, well, had I known—"

"I remember when you first tried to make *tamales, Pendejito*," interrupted Esperanza. "They looked like horse shit," she said, emitting a hyena-like laugh. "Now you smell like horse shit."

"*Hermana*," Maria growled. "*No más*. I told you before."

"Yeah, okay," Esperanza said. She retrieved a cigarette, ignited it, and blew a cloud of smoke that enveloped the cranium. I rolled the window down and coughed.

Between Esperanza's chimneying and Joe's serial complaints about the cafe needing to reopen so he could sell us more supplies, the ride into town was excruciating. Once we arrived, Joe sprinted through the door, saying he needed to put on his vestments.

Maria walked into the church and disappeared. Esperanza, who was behind Maria, dropped her cigarette onto the ground and crushed it angrily, then turned to face me. "Maybe you're gonna get struck by lightning, *Pendejito*," she muttered. "God don't like the Devil inside His house."

"Stop that, *Tía* Esperanza," said Loretta. "Go inside. I'll be right there." Loretta turned to me. "I'm sorry, Bennie."

I shrugged. "Rather tame by Esperanza's standards. Is the equine odour too overpowering for me to come inside?"

Loretta grimaced. "No, not really, especially if you sit in the back. Do you mind?" she asked gently. "I can sit with you if you like."

"Quite all right," I said, waving her away. "I have no wish to expose you to the unpleasant odour," I said. "I shall be a contented backbencher."

"Okay. I'll see you after the service." She patted my arm and walked inside. Several other congregants walked past me, sniffing the air and grimacing. One muttered, "Stupid *gringo.*"

I sighed, inhaled deeply, and walked towards the door. Presently, a pudgy hand fell heavily onto the shoulder and held me back. "*Hola,* Señor Graves," said Coronado breathlessly. I turned around to face him and goggled. Instead of the usual greasy jeans and dirty shirt, he wore grey slacks, a pressed white shirt, and a blue tie that was askew. The tie had a large reddish stain that resembled Maria's *enchilada* sauce.

"I never seen you here before, Señor Graves," said Coronado. "Did you come so you could hear Joe preach? He's real good. Last time, he pointed right at me and shouted that God must be protecting me. Maybe he's gonna say the same thing about you."

"Eh? How, er, Christian of him to say such a thing," I replied.

Coronado grinned and nodded blankly. Then he sniffed the air. "You kinda smell like a horse, Señor Graves. Joe told me I gotta wear clean clothes to church and take a bath the night before."

"Er, yes, Coronado. I had not planned on attending this morning and had been assisting Uncle Bill. We had to retrieve Marjorie—"

"Am I still gonna be your best man at the wedding, Señor Graves? Can I wear this?"

"Perhaps a different tie, Coronado. That one has a large stain on it."

Coronado grasped the tie, eyed the stain, and sniffed at it like a hungry dog. "Sorry, Señor Graves. I spilled some *enchiladas* on it last time because I had lunch at the cafe after church."

"Quite all right, Coronado. Do you own another tie?"

"I don't think so, Señor Graves." He scratched his head. "I had a black one, but I used it to tie the mirror on my truck to the door after I hit a tree. Otherwise, I would have hit a deer that jumped into the road."

I shook my head and sighed. "That's quite all right, Coro—"

"You ever hit a deer, Señor Graves?," he said almost gleefully. "I did once. It was a three-point buck. Joe helped me gut it and then we—"

"Yes, thank you, Coronado," I interrupted, not wishing to hear any more about the ultimate disposal of the deer. "I will be happy to lend you a suitable tie."

"Thanks, Señor Graves." He shook my hand and smiled, then waddled into the church.

As I entered the church, a strong, musty odour invaded the nostrils. There were ten wooden pews, separated by a narrow nave down the middle. The wooden floor creaked ominously. On the right side stood two small doors on what looked like old telephone booths, which I took to be the confessional. To the left of the altar, there was another small door, with a small wooden sign reading "Private," which I took to be the good Father's office.

I sat down heavily in the last pew. A few more stragglers wandered into the church, all of whom eyed me suspiciously, sniffed, and hurried towards the front. Presently, the congregants stood when Joe came out from behind the small door. Esperanza turned around and motioned me to stand, albeit with an extended middle finger.

Joe walked to the alter. "Please be seated," he said. I drummed my fingers softly on the wooden seat. "We got a special guest today. In the back." Joe pointed a crooked finger at the self. "The *gringo*. He's supposed to marry my beautiful niece, Loretta."

Everyone turned around and eyed me suspiciously, and I wondered if they would attempt one of those old west hangings in the Zane Grey novels. There arose a general muttering, sounding like distant thunder, and the ears perceived Esperanza's shrill voice emitting her favoured epithets.

I raised my hand and offered a small wave. "Gah," I moaned silently.

"I'm gonna talk about unbelievers today," Joe continued. "We gotta be real careful around them, because they may be in league with Satan." The congregants again turned around. I slumped lower in the pew, wondering what the good Father would say when I met him the day after tomorrow.

"Please turn to Corinthians 1:7," Joe intoned. "It says, 'If a woman has a husband who is not a believer—' he paused in midsentence, allowing everyone to turn around and glare at the self yet again. 'If the unbeliever leaves, let him do so.' That's real good advice, *¿que no*? But I say, let's encourage the unbelievers to leave."

He eyed the self coolly whilst the congregants nodded their approval. Several could be heard muttering about the *gringo*. Joe closed his Bible. "Okay. Now, please turn to—" He broke off suddenly and uttered "Oh, shit."

Presently, I heard an odd, shuffling sound and turned towards it. "Gah!" I shouted at the yellow-macintoshed, umbrella-wielding intruder who stood beside me.

Porfiria's eyes widened. "*Diablo!*" she shouted, raising her umbrella and bringing it down on the forehead. "*Diablo!*"

"Ow! Bloody hell," I shouted, feeling a sharp pain as I grasped for the weapon.

"*Diablo!*" she shouted a third time. "Get out! This is a holy place. God's gonna strike you down." Apparently believing she was His righteous agent, she swung her umbrella towards my abdomen. I parried the strike, grabbed the umbrella, and pulled it out of her hands.

"Enough!" I shouted as I stood up.

"Give me my umbrella!" Porfiria screamed, thrusting her hand towards it.

"Get away from me!" I yelled, waving the umbrella menacingly. I brought the umbrella down on my leg, hoping to snap it in half like a twig, but was unsuccessful.

Porfiria repeated her attempt to retrieve her weapon, but I quickly raised it over my head and outside her grasp, before escaping from the church. "Stay away, all of you," I yelled, as I exited the church. I set a rapid course towards the nearest refuge whilst glancing over my shoulder to see if the yellow peril was in pursuit.

Chapter 19

"Rudy, are you inside?" I shouted as I pounded on the bar's front door. I twisted around repeatedly, umbrella at the ready, in case Porfiria attempted any further attacks. "Rudy!"

The door opened slowly, revealing a bleary-eyed Rudy. "Bennie? What's going on?" He paused and his eyes widened. "Jesus, what happened? Your head's all bloody and it's running down the side of your face."

"That madwoman just attacked me in the church."

"*La Loca* came into the church and attacked you? What were you doing there anyway?" He sniffed the air tentatively and stared at my shirt and trousers. "I smell horseshit. Jesus, did she throw horseshit at you?"

"Eh? I mean, no, Uncle Bill and I retrieved Marjorie this morning from Manuel Obrador's ranch and—" I took a deep breath and groaned. "May I please come inside?"

"Yeah. Let's get you cleaned up." He glanced at my forehead. "I think it looks worse than it is. Go into the bathroom in the back hall. There are bandages in the top drawer to the right of the sink. I'll get you some clean clothes."

Ten minutes later, after a wash and brush-up and application of a sticking plaster to the dented forehead, I was seated at a table in the small kitchen located behind the bar. Rudy had brewed a fresh pot of coffee and offered me a cuppa, which I accepted greedily.

"So, why you were at the church this morning?" asked Rudy.

"I was dragooned by Loretta. I gather Maria thought it would be best for me to experience a Catholic service before meeting Father Castillo. I was sitting in the back pew when Porfiria arrived. She espied the self and immediately set upon me like a baying hound."

Rudy began to laugh heartily. "Sorry, Bennie. You sure do set her off."

"M-hem, yes," I replied, gingerly touching the forehead, which throbbed. "Before she attacked the self, Joe was reading from Corinthians about unbelievers. Of course, one would never credit Joe for subtlety."

Rudy laughed. "Yeah, I guess not. Well, I guess *La Loca's* sticking around here," said Rudy. "Too bad. You really think your plan's gonna work?"

I groaned softly. "As Loretta refuses to elope, I see little choice in the matter, unless Tiny removes her to the nearest loony bin."

"That's ain't gonna happen," said Rudy.

"Is there no one else? Uncle Bill's Zane Grey novels often feature fearless United States Marshalls. Are any of those nearby? Or perhaps a squadron of grenadiers?"

Rudy shrugged. "Sorry, Bennie. You just better hope your plan will work."

"Indeed."

"How's your head?"

"Throbbing," I said. "Might I ask for you for a ride back to the ranch? You could see Mother again if you wished."

He gestured with his thumb. "Sure. Let me get my keys. My truck's parked out back."

Before I could exit through the back, I heard a loud knocking at the front door. I walked silently towards a window in the bar and espied Loretta. She raised her arm and knocked again.

"Loretta," I said, as I opened the door. "How did you know I was here?"

She eyed my forehead and stepped inside. "Where else would you go? Are you okay? Everyone was worried about you after you ran off."

The grey matter envisioned a cackling Esperanza, cheering on each blow of Porfiria's umbrella, and the other lynch-happy congregants. "I doubt *everyone* is concerned," I said. "Doubtless your aunt is disappointed that my injuries were not fatal." I touched the sticking plaster. "A bit of a blow to the forehead. The weapon is in Rudy's office."

"This is all my fault," she said as she put her arms around me.

I bent down to kiss her but was interrupted by Rudy. "Hey, you two," he said. "I run a clean bar. No hanky-panky."

Loretta laughed. "It's not hanky-panky. When I was a little girl, if I got hurt, my mother would say 'I'll kiss it and make it better.'"

"Uh-huh," said Rudy. "So, where's *La Loca?*"

"After Bennie ran out of the church," replied Loretta, "she kept screaming about her umbrella. *Tío* Joe ran back to Father Castillo's office. Most everyone else ran out of the church, even *Tía* Esperanza. *Tía* Maria walked over to Porfiria and said, '*No más*, Porfiria.' Porfiria turned around and sat down in a pew. Then Coronado came over. '*Hola*, Porfiria,' he said. 'Are you hungry?' He took out a candy bar from his pocket and offered it to her. She just stared at him at first. Finally, she took the candy bar and ate it. Then she walked out the door. *Tía* Maria even thanked Coronado afterwards."

"He does seem able to soothe the savage beast," I remarked. "Odd, that."

"Maybe she was just hungry," said Loretta.

"Perhaps. Although when I feel peckish, my first reaction is not to biff everyone within firing range."

"Yeah," said Rudy, "but you're not crazy. Well, not like that."

I was about to respond when there was another knock on the door. Fearing it was Porfiria sniffing out her umbrella like a crazed bloodhound, I ran into the darkened hallway towards Rudy's office. Rudy glanced out the window. "It's okay, Bennie. It's Coronado and Maria." Rudy opened the front door. "*Mi querida*," he said. "Come in."

Maria shook her head in disavowal and walked inside, releasing a flurry of cigarette ash onto the floor. Coronado followed.

"*Hola*, Rudy," Coronado said. "*Hola*, Loretta. Is Señor Graves here?"

I walked back into the bar. "Hullo, Maria," I said. "Thank you for intervening."

Maria eyed the sticking plaster on my forehead and pointed her cigarette at it. "I'm real sorry about church this morning," she said. "You okay, Bennie?"

"Dented, but unbowed, Maria," I replied. "It seems I am in your debt, as well, Coronado. Your confectionary soothed the savage beast."

"Huh?" he replied.

"The chocolate bar," I said. "Loretta tells me Porfiria stopped screaming after you gave it to her."

"Oh, yeah," Coronado said, nodding. "I can tell when somebody's hungry. I wish I had another candy bar. I'm real hungry." He patted his ample stomach.

"Er, perhaps we can remedy that. What do you think, Maria?"

Maria sighed. "*Sí*, okay." She stared at Coronado. "You want a *burrito*? I got some *carne adovada* in the fridge."

Coronado's eyes widened. "Thanks, Maria."

"Do you mind, Maria?" I asked.

She shrugged. "I got enough for everybody. You and Loretta can help cook."

Rudy looked at Maria. "*Gracias, mi querida*. It's been too long since I had some of your cooking."

"I ain't your *querida*," Maria growled, menacing an imaginary chef's knife at him using her cigarette. She turned around and walked outside. Coronado hurried behind her. I held the door for Loretta and Rudy, then surveyed the nearby region thoroughly for any signs of Porfiria, who at least was now disarmed. Seeing none, I followed the others quickly towards the cafe. The front steps and door displayed ample evidence of visits by Paco. Maria cursed under her breath, and we followed her to the back door that opened into the kitchen. Inside, I retrieved a small shovel and bucket from the storeroom, filled the bucket with hot water, and scoured the front porch.

"You still want me to give you a ride back home, Bennie?" asked Rudy. "If Loretta can take you, I'll stay here and help *mi querida* with the dishes."

I glanced at Maria. Whilst she admonished Rudy about calling her his *querida*, it was evident she enjoyed the attention. "Thanks, Rudy," I said. "Loretta, would you mind?"

"Of course not," she replied.

"You want me to wash dishes, Maria?" asked Coronado. "I like to help."

"No!" Maria and Rudy replied simultaneously. Although we had engaged Coronado to wash dishes after the cafe had opened, he had proved himself adept only at dropping crockery. "Uh, thanks for the offer, Coronado," Rudy continued. "You were a big help at the church. I'll help Maria. Maybe you better take a *siesta* or something."

"Okay, Rudy," said Coronado, who had hoovered up two huge *burritos*. "I am kinda tired. Those sure were good, Maria." He stood up and patted his stomach, which now seemed visibly distended, then waddled out the front door.

"My God, he puts Daisy to shame," I said absently. Maria grunted in agreement. "Loretta and I can assist with the washing up, if you like, Maria."

"That's okay, Bennie," Rudy said quickly. "You let Loretta take you home. I'll help here."

I nodded. "I, er, do feel a trifle unsteady. Very well, if neither of you have any objections, Loretta and I shall take our leave. Er, before we go, might Loretta and I have a private word with you Rudy?"

"Okay, sure," Rudy said, before turning to Maria. "I'll be back in a minute." He stood up from the table and we walked outside. "What's up, Bennie?" he asked.

"Well, it concerns Maria," I said. "I, that is, we know you care for her—*de gustibus non disputandum est* and all that—but if you arrive at the wedding with my inebriated mother as planned, won't that cause Maria distress?" I knew from experience that a distressed Maria was not someone to be trifled with, especially when she brandished one of her chef's knives. Nor was she one who could be pacified with a large dose of Farm Calm or its alcoholic equivalent, unlike many of the locals.

Rudy's jaw fell slightly. "Uh, I hadn't really thought about that," he said. "I'll just tell Maria that Bill ran into some sort of ranch problem and that he asked me to take her. That should work. I hope."

"I don't want you to hurt *Tía* Maria's feelings," Loretta added.

"Yeah, I don't either," said Rudy.

"A Maria with hurt feelings is a dangerous beast," I added.

"Uh-huh, yeah," mumbled Rudy. "Is there anybody else?"

"I rather doubt Mother will accept a stranger barging in with a bottle of champagne and declaiming, 'Right-ho, inebriation awaits!' or something to that effect."

"What do you think I should do?" he asked. "I don't want to upset *mi querida*, but I promised I would help with your crazy plan."

"Does Maria expect you to escort her to the wedding?" I asked.

"We haven't really talked about it," he said. "I just assumed she would go with the rest of Loretta's family."

"Perhaps you can act as an intermediary, Loretta," I said.

"Me? I'm the bride, or had you forgotten that?"

"No, I mean, of course not," I stammered. "I merely thought—"

"Stop thinking," commanded Loretta. "If she plans on going with my family, then it's no problem. If she plans on Rudy taking her, I will let you know. This would be a lot easier if you just told your mother she can't attend the wedding."

I sighed. "It would be far easier if we eloped—gah!" On hearing the word "elope," Loretta's arm shot out and scored a direct hit to the beleaguered Graves shoulder, followed by the inevitable ocular daggers.

"Hey, you two," said Rudy. "I don't want to mess up your wedding. I'll take care of it."

"Are you sure?" I asked.

"I'm the guy who's had four wives, remember? I'm an expert."

"Er—" I began.

"Thanks, Rudy," interrupted Loretta. "I'm just going to assume everything will be fine. Right, Bennie?"

"Er, yes, of course," I said, wondering what new horrors Fate would surely unleash.

"I'm sorry about this morning," Loretta said, as we motored towards the ranch. "Tuesday, it will just be Father Castillo and us in his office."

"Not your fault, Loretta," I said. "Although, I would like to know if the good Father owns any umbrellas, broadswords, or daggers."

Loretta shook her head. "I told you, he's very nice. You'll see."

The Trojans thought the same about the "nice" equine statue the Greeks gave to them, but discretion suggested I not mention that to Loretta. We soon arrived at the ranch. Daisy, in a fit of porcine exuberance, raised herself off the front porch and trotted over to Loretta's car.

"Would you care to come in?" I asked.

Loretta scowled and shook her head. "I don't want to see your mother."

"She's actually very nice," I blurted, instantly regretting the words.

Loretta offered up a look that would have terrified an enraged cobra. "Nice, huh," she said finally. "Nice as in throwing dishes at my mother? Nice as in yelling at me for wanting you to convert?" Nice as in telling me I'm not worthy of her son? Just be at the church Tuesday at two o'clock to meet with Father Castillo. And don't bring your mother!"

"Of course," I said soothingly. "Shall see you there then?" Loretta did not answer. Instead, she slammed the car into reverse, turned around, and left the self in a cloud of dust.

I walked inside the house, enveloped in dejection, and immediately encountered my mother. "Well, Benjamin, did you repair the leak at the cafe?"

"Eh, what?" I eyed her absently until the grey matter recalled my having told her the cafe was taking on water. "I mean, yes, all ship-shape now."

"Whatever happened to your forehead?" she asked, eyeing me with more suspicion than concern. "You have a lump the size of an egg."

I placed a hand gingerly on the spot where Porfiria's umbrella had struck and winced. "Er, yes, that. A spot of bother at the cafe. No need to concern yourself."

"She hit you, didn't she? I am not surprised."

"How did you know?" I stuttered.

"I could see it in her eyes, Benjamin. How can you possibly marry her if she is so unbalanced."

"What? That is, no, Loretta didn't do this, Mother." My shoulder ached an objection.

"Then who did?"

"That madwoman roaming around town. I told you about her. The one who wears the yellow macintosh. She biffed me with her umbrella."

"You mean she walked into the cafe and attacked you? I distinctly recall seeing a 'Closed' sign on the front door when I was with Rudy."

"Er, yes, we do have a 'Closed' sign on the door." Beads of perspiration began to appear on the Graves brow.

Mother cocked her head. "Benjamin, you are perspiring, which means you are not being truthful. It was that hussy who hit you, isn't it?"

"No! Loretta witnessed the attack on my person, as did several dozen others. She did not instigate it."

"Do you expect me to believe that two dozen people were in the cafe helping you effect repairs?" she asked, shaking her head in disbelief. "You never were an accomplished liar, Benjamin."

The grey matter felt itself slowly sinking into the web it had woven and I sat down heavily on the sofa. "Very well, Mother. Porfiria attacked me whilst I was sitting in church listening to Loretta's uncle's sermon on unbelievers."

Mother's eyes widened and her jaw dropped. "Church? You were attacked in church?"

"Yes."

"Why?"

"Porfiria believes I'm the Devil incarnate."

"Not why were you attacked. Why were you in church and why did you lie about the cafe?"

"Loretta's Aunt Maria thought it would be useful for me to listen to a service before meeting Father Castillo Tuesday. I had no time to explain this morning."

"Well, if you convert, one sin you can confess will be lying to your mother. Goodness knows how many more there are."

"I did not wish to upset you, Mother."

"Well, you have, Benjamin. That girl has had a terrible influence on you. You should be ashamed of yourself. I'll have nothing further to say on the matter. Good morning." She stood, emitted a loud "harrumph," and launched herself towards her room.

Presently, Archie and Uncle Bill walked through the rear door and into the kitchen.

"What-ho, cousin?" chirped Archie. He eyed the bandaged forehead. "I say, that's quite the robin's egg. It looks rather painful."

"Whoa, pard'ner," Uncle Bill added. "How did you get that?"

"Porfiria," I said. "She biffed me in the church this morning. Scored a direct hit on the forehead."

"What did you do to incur her wrath this time?" Archie asked.

"Nothing. I was sitting in the back pew, listening to Joe spew codswallop about unbelievers or should I say, this unbeliever."

"That chap we saw in the bar yesterday is a priest?" Archie asked, nonplussed.

"Well, he is a lay priest of a sort. I did not know that until this morning. Anyway, Porfiria walked inside, espied me, called me the Devil, and launched her attack. Then she began swinging the bloody umbrella like a cricket bat. I was fortunate to disarm her, else she would have otherwise struck me amidships."

Uncle Bill laughed. "How the hell did she know you were there, Bennie?"

"I can only surmise Fate has endowed Porfiria with some sort of Devil's radar. Anyway, I managed to disarm her and retreated, with the umbrella, to the safety of Rudy's. Loretta returned me here a few minutes ago." I paused and sighed. "Unfortunately, we had another row about Mother. Loretta remarked that Father Castillo was 'very nice' and I responded with the same description about Mother. Rather a tactical error, that. Loretta departed immediately thereafter, but not before reciting a litany of Mother's transgressions."

"You do have a way with words, old chap," laughed Archie.

"Where is your mother?" asked Uncle Bill.

"Er, she retired to her room. She assumed Loretta had biffed me, giving her yet another reason to oppose the wedding. I admonished Mother for her erroneous assumption, which was another tactical error. I would describe Mother's current mood as somewhere between the apoplectic and the merely volcanic."

Archie clapped me on my sore shoulder and laughed. "Well, old chap, it shall all be over soon, eh? You do seem to be a magnet for these sorts of things."

The vocal cords emitted a sound somewhere between a groan and a sigh, after which I glanced at the watch, which read half one. "I say, Uncle Bill. Would you mind if I poured myself a whisky? It has been rather a trying morning."

"Sure," he said. "Maybe I'll have one myself. How about you, Archie?"

Archie grimaced. "Well, 'when in Rome,' as they say, although I shall never understand why anyone would ask for your Dusty Trail."

Uncle Bill muttered something about "high horses" and retrieved three glasses. "Let me speak to Dorothy a little later,'" he said after pouring out a large dose of Dusty Trail into each glass. "I'll smooth things over with her." After saying "cheers" and emptying his glass, he eyed the bandaged forehead. "You ought to put some ice on that, Bennie. It looks mighty angry."

Soon thereafter, I was relaxing on the sofa. The combination of a bracing dose of Dusty Trail and an application of ice had successfully appeased the injured forehead.

"What remains to be done, wedding-wise, cousin?" asked Archie.

"Assuming there will be a wedding, I must speak with Joe tomorrow about his catering efforts. And he will expect me to provide the necessary brass beforehand. We should review our plans for Porfiria, too. Her appearance at the church this morning was most worrisome. She must be locked in the barn before the ceremony begins."

"I meant to ask you about that, old chap. As I recall, I must first abscond with that nasty little cur. What if we cannot find him?"

"No need to worry about that, Archie. Nestor will surely be at Rudy's bar, and he always brings Paco along. A few beef strips to distract the dog will be all that is necessary. And, if Paco is not with Nestor, we can always voyage to Nestor's home. I have been there before."

Archie grimaced. "I hate to imagine the smell, given the dog's proclivities."

"The dog is smart enough not to waste ammunition at home when there are numerous doorways, steps, and trousers to be attacked repeatedly."

"The voice of experience, presumably?"

"Far too much, experience," I sighed. "Not five minutes after I stepped off that same bus you and Mother rode, Paco struck both of my valises. Then, when I arrived at the ranch,

Daisy finished them off. She grabbed the handles and tossed them about like some world-champion shot-putter, destroying a fine bottle of single malt I had brought. I suppose it was a signal from Fate about the travails she intended to bestow upon the self."

"Stiff upper lip, eh, old chap? Isn't that part of the Graves code, too?

"M-hem. I believe the upper lip solidified long ago." I roused myself off the sofa. "Uncle Bill mentioned additional fence wanting repairs. Care to assist me, cousin?"

"Never let it be said that Archibald Graves shirked his responsibilities. Well, not always, at least."

The remainder of Sunday proved uneventful. During the afternoon, we repaired various portions of the fence that the herd had defenestrated. Mother reappeared before dinner, her internal lava having cooled to a mere condemnation of the self. She was further mollified by a surprise visit from Rudy, who arrived with an excellent vintage to share, along with an invitation to luncheon in Santa Fe the next day, plus a guided tour of the Plaza. Privately, Rudy explained that he intended to take Mother to see Loretto Chapel to see the Miraculous Staircase, in hopes of softening her aversion to all things Catholic. He also reassured me of his honourable intentions. After Mother accepted the invitation, Rudy requested that Archie again provide temporary barman services to slake the Monday crowd of regulars, which Archie agreed to cheerfully.

The following morning, soon after Rudy and Mother had departed, found the self in the barn, attempting to effect repairs on a small wire gate. When I heard a screech of tires signalling the arrival of a vehicle, I assumed it was Coronado. Fortunately, I had parked my lorry behind the house, hoping it would be safe from his failed brakes and errant doors.

"Hey, *gringo!*" the grasping and penurious voice of Joe shouted. "I gotta talk to you."

Groaning internally, I walked out of the barn to speak with him. "Good morning, Joe. Planning to sermonise a bit more about unbelievers and such?"

"Huh?"

"Never mind," I replied. "What brings you here today?"

"Money. You gotta pay me so I can buy stuff for the wedding."

"Ah, yes, I planned to meet you later today to discuss that. Er, how much do you require?"

His visage transformed into one of tranquillity. "Gonna be real expensive. All those supplies, more food, and lots of beer for everybody. I wrote it down for you."

I sighed, wondering what level of rapacity would manifest itself. He handed me a folded sheet of paper with the requested disbursement, which I then opened. "Gah!" I shouted, goggling at the total. "Are you mad? This is robbery. The Queen's wedding surely cost less."

Joe shrugged. "Sorry, *gringo*, you want me to cater? That's how much it's gonna cost. I got to buy enough for everybody in town. 'Course, you could tell Loretta you don't want to get married. Then you don't got to spend nothing." He offered a smile that would have put the Cheshire Cat to shame.

"Fine," I growled. "I shall write you a check for the amount."

"No check, *gringo*. I want cash."

"What? I cannot possibly obtain that much cash today. It will have to be wired from London." I glanced at the watch. "My bank is closed for the day. Even if I contact them tomorrow, they will not wire the funds until Friday at the earliest, and more likely not until next week."

Joe crossed his arms "No money, then no food and no booze. Everybody's gonna be real mad at you. Loretta's gonna be mad, too, at the cheapskate *gringo* she's supposed to marry."

The Graves countenance stiffened whilst the grey matter arrived at a Hobson's choice-like solution. I raised my hand and waved the piece of paper in the air. "What would you prefer, Joe: the money or the wedding to be cancelled? Well?"

"Don't matter to me, *gringo*. I win no matter what."

"Are you quite sure?"

Joe crossed his arms and laughed. "Don't try to trick me, *gringo*. Sure, I'm sure."

I sighed with an artificial heaviness. "Perhaps you are correct. If you will excuse me, I must speak with Loretta. I will explain the situation, including the rapacious amount of brass you have demanded. I will also explain to her that, although I could arrange to have the money wired from London, you refuse to wait. Therefore, the wedding must be cancelled."

"Sounds real good to me," said Joe with a laugh.

"No doubt. However, allow me to finish. I will suggest to Loretta that, given her uncle's recalcitrance and naked greed, we marry on Thursday in a civil ceremony and reschedule the formal wedding in the church when I have sufficient funds to arrange for a proper caterer, which will be both less costly and surely of superior quality. And I will inform Maria of the situation. No doubt she will wish to, er, discuss the matter with you."

Joe's countenance turned a deep crimson. "You can't do that," he shouted. "You promised."

I shrugged. "*C'est la vie.* Oh, there is one other matter. After we return from our honeymoon and reopen the cafe, we will no longer purchase any supplies from you, regardless of the number of snakes you bung into the kitchen or attempts you make to set fire to the cafe. *No más.*"

Joe's jaw dropped. In seeming affirmation, Daisy emitted a loud grunt from the porch.

"Now, if you will excuse me, I must inform Loretta of the change in wedding plans. Good day." I began to walk towards the back of the house, where my lorry was parked.

"Wait!" Joe shouted. "You promise you'll keep buying supplies from me?"

"No," I said calmly. I reached into my trouser pocket, retrieved a fifty-cent coin, and tossed it towards him. "A small token of my appreciation." I turned around and resumed walking towards the lorry.

Joe retrieved the coin from the ground and then ran after me. He grasped my left arm and pulled. "C'mon, *gringo*—I mean, Bennie. Let's talk about this, huh?"

I turned to face his surprised countenance. "There is nothing to discuss, Joe. You have triumphed and I raise the white flag in surrender. Of course, it may prove a pyrrhic victory for you."

He released my arm and blinked. "Huh?"

"*Adiós*, Joe." I waved, turned away from him, and resumed walking towards the lorry.

"Okay, okay," he shouted as he trotted after the self. "Forget what I wrote. How about a hundred dollars so I can buy supplies tomorrow? I can cover the rest until after the wedding."

"How much will 'the rest' be?"

"Uh, just what it costs me, plus gas for the truck. I, uh, I'll show you the receipts, too."

"What about your opposition to the wedding? Do you wish your niece to be happy or is the thought of her marrying a *gringo* a bridge too far?"

"Okay, okay," Joe muttered, raising his hands in mock surrender. "But you gotta keep buying supplies for the cafe from me."

"Only if you stop charging such exorbitant prices. I am willing to pay somewhat more than what Sabrosa Foods charges, but not double, which is what you have been charging us. Unless, of course, you wish the cafe to close permanently."

Joe sighed. "Okay. How about forty percent? It costs me more to buy stuff than Sabrosa and I gotta make some money for the store. It needs a new roof. And you know what Coronado does."

I extended my hand towards his. "Eminently reasonable. Shall we shake hands on it?"

Joe extended his hand reluctantly and shook mine. "I guess you ain't as stupid as you look."

"Neither are you, Joe; neither are you. Now, shall we discuss the specifics for the post-wedding *fiesta*?"

I invited Joe inside the house, and for the next hour we discussed the items he would purchase for the wedding reception.

Satisfied, I gave him the promised one hundred dollars, which he accepted hungrily. We walked outside to his lorry. He opened the door and stepped inside. "One more thing," he said, leaning out the window.

"Yes?"

"You promise to treat my niece real good? She deserves it."

I raised my right hand. "You have my solemn word as a Graves. I shall always treat Loretta with honour and respect."

"Okay, *gringo*—Bennie. I gotta go before Coronado destroys anything else at the store."

"I understood you had fired him . . . again."

Joe shook his head and muttered something unintelligible. He started the motor, turned the lorry around, and drove off hurriedly.

I stood motionless for a minute, surprised that sanity had won out, or at least what counted as sanity in Vaca Seca. I walked over to the house and onto the porch, whistling a happy tune. Daisy raised her head and eyed me from under her *sombrero*. "There's a good pig," I said, patting her head.

Stepping inside and still whistling, I espied Archie, who was in the sitting room, reading one of Uncle Bill's Zane Grey novels. "I say, cousin, you look like the veritable cat that ate the canary. Why the sudden good cheer?"

"I just had a favourable encounter with Joe Garcia, whose avarice finally exceeded his grasp."

"How so?"

"He asked for an exorbitant amount of brass to provide food and drink for the post-wedding festivities." I retrieved the piece of paper Joe had presented and gave it to Archie.

Archie's eyebrows rocketed upwards as he read the amount Joe had proposed. "Bloody hell! I suspect the Ritz would charge less. What did you do?"

"I refused, of course. He was quite pleased, reasoning that I would be either forced to accede to his extortion or to call the wedding off. Instead, I offered him an alternate strategy, involving an immediate civil ceremony and a rescheduling of the formal wedding. I also informed him the cafe would no longer purchase any supplies from him."

"A direct assault on the chap's wallet, eh?"

"Yes, but I also deployed another weapon, one which he did not expect: Maria."

"Maria? I don't understand."

"Maria favours the wedding. When confronted with the prospect of my informing her the wedding was cancelled because of him, Joe hastily retreated. Moreover, he agreed to charge less for supplying the cafe in future. A Graves victory all around, I should think."

"Right-ho, old chap. Well done. Perhaps a small tipple to celebrate."

I poured out two doses of Dusty Trail and we raised our glasses. But as I drank, the initial euphoria soon evaporated, for I knew that Fate would not accept defeat graciously, if at all.

Chapter 20

T uesday morning dawned freakishly cold and blustery, causing me to wonder if it were an omen for the inquisition I would face before Father Castillo that afternoon. After the morning care and feedings, I returned to the house for a cuppa, where I encountered Mother breakfasting in the kitchen.

"Hullo, Mother," I chirped as I opened a cabinet to retrieve a cup. "Did you enjoy the tour of Santa Fe?"

"I did, thank you," she replied curtly.

I swallowed. "M-hem, I trust there were no, er, issues, with Rudy?"

"He was a perfect gentleman. We had an excellent luncheon. We also encountered several Indians selling jewellery." She thrust out her left hand, displaying a small silver bracelet inlaid with a turquoise oval. "Rudy purchased this for me as an additional apology for his behaviour."

"Did you see anything else?" I asked.

"Yes. He showed me—what was it called?—the miracle staircase in a small Catholic church."

"I believe it is called the Miraculous Staircase. A most endearing little chapel."

Mother harrumphed softly. "They'll believe anything, won't they. I am quite sure any competent British carpenter could build it."

"Er, yes. Well, the important thing is you enjoyed yourself." I poured out a large measure of coffee, which seemed more tar-like than usual. "If you will excuse me, I should, er, speak with Uncle Bill about Malcolm, the bull."

"Don't think I have forgotten about your meeting this afternoon with that priest, Benjamin."

"Eh? Oh no, merely routine I am assured. Father Castillo wishes to speak with me. I suppose to discuss the particulars of the wedding vows and such."

Mother did not respond. Instead, she retrieved a piece of toast from her plate and bit into it savagely.

"Yes, well, enjoy your breakfast, Mother. Cheer-o." I quickly escaped through the kitchen door and encountered Archie.

"What-ho, cousin?" he said. "Ready for your priestly chinwag?"

"I suspect it will be more of an inquisition. I would not be surprised if he tells Loretta that marrying the self means she will be condemned to eternal damnation."

"Pshaw. The good Father merely wants to ensure you are not some sort of Jack the Ripper type before baptising you tomorrow."

"I remain sceptical. What does one wear to an inquisition?"

Archie laughed. "I'm not sure it mattered during the original, old chap. Sackcloth and ashes, perhaps?"

"Quite. However, as I do not expect to be burned at the stake, although such an event would be well-attended, with Esperanza in the front row cheering, I believe a jacket and tie shall suffice."

"Don't be so glum, cousin. Simply utter many 'Yes, Father's' and a 'Thou shalt' or two, and Bob's your uncle."

"Gah," I replied with a heavy roll of the eyes.

"There's no need to be nervous, Bennie," said Loretta, as we walked up to the church door precisely at two o'clock that afternoon. "Father Castillo is very nice."

I wiped the sweat that had formed on my brow, despite the cold weather. "No doubt Torquemada would have said the same about himself."

"Benjamin Graves, you're impossible. He just wants to get to know you, explain tomorrow's baptism and confession, and ask you a few questions about your commitment to the faith."

"And then burn me at the stake," I thought.

I opened the door for Loretta and we entered the church.

"Do we go in there?" I asked Loretta whilst pointing at the door marked "Private."

"Yes. That's his office."

We walked up to the door and knocked softly.

"*Venga*," a voice boomed.

I opened the door slowly and espied a grey-haired, slightly roly-poly chap leaning back in a wooden office chair behind a small desk. His feet, shod in dusty brown cowboy boots, sat atop the desk. He was chimneying on a cigarette and reading a *LIFE* magazine. He wore jeans and a white shirt sans priestly collar. A pair of black-framed reading glasses was perched on his nose. To the left of the desk was a small window, on the sill of which stood a bottle of what appeared to be whisky. He motioned us to sit down in the two small chairs in front of the desk.

I eased myself into one of the chairs, feeling rather like I was in first form again.

Father Castillo removed his feet from the desk, sat up in the chair and goggled the self suspiciously over his glasses. "*Buenos días*, Loretta," he said. "So, this is the *gringo* you want to marry, huh?" What's your name, *señor*?"

"Er, Benjamin Graves. Father," I mumbled.

"Graves, huh? You related to El Vaquero?"

"El Vaquero, as you call him, is my uncle."

Father Castillo shook his head gently. "I remember his wife, Celestina. She was a good Catholic. Always came to church." He paused and pointed his cigarette menacingly towards me. "Your uncle isn't Catholic, is he?"

I stiffened. "No. He was brought up in the Church of England, as I was."

"He should have converted," the priest said. "I could never bless their marriage. I told Celestina that, but she told me he was stubborn. Said he didn't like priests, either."

The jaw tightened. "What does my uncle have to do with any of this?"

"Maybe the *gringo* apple doesn't fall far from the tree," he said dismissively.

The blood pressure had begun rising to stratospheric levels and the grey matter suggested I inform the good Father that he was a self-righteous prat. I glanced over towards Loretta who, apparently having read my thoughts, covertly gestured with her hand to urge calm.

"I say, Father," I began in a tone that strained to be civil, "I am sorry that my uncle was a source of disappointment for you. However, I can assure you that he was devoted to Celestina."

"That don't matter in the hereafter," he said. He opened one of the desk drawers, retrieved a small glass, and pulled the bottle of whisky off the sill. He filled the glass, then downed the entire contents in one swallow. "Okay, you know how this works?"

"Er, no. How what works exactly?" I asked.

"If you're gonna convert, you gotta mean it. Otherwise, I can't bless a marriage between you and Loretta. And if I can't bless the marriage, I can't perform the ceremony."

"I do wish to convert," I said dryly.

His eyes narrowed. "I need to make sure you're serious before I baptise you tomorrow. *¿Comprende?*"

"M-hem, yes, I believe I do," I replied.

He turned to Loretta. "Loretta, normally, you can't get married in the church if you're divorced. But I know that Jaime was a *cabrón*, so this time it's okay."

"Thank you, Father," Loretta replied softly. "Benjamin isn't like Jaime at all. He's a gentleman."

The priest eyed me suspiciously again and grunted. "So, *gringo*, you been married before, too?"

"Well, I, that is—"

"So, divorced," he said with a tone of disgust. "Tell me what happened."

"Er, the ex-wife ran off with a Spaniard with whom she became enamoured because he communicated with various flora."

Father Castillo tilted his head. "Huh?"

"Well, I never met the bastard—sorry, Father—but that is what she told me when she asked for a divorce."

The priest rubbed his chin, which was covered with grey stubble. "Jesus," he muttered, before turning to Loretta. "You know about this Spaniard?"

"Yes, Father. Benjamin's been very honest about his previous marriage and so have I."

"*Madre de Dios*," he said softly. "You sure you want to marry this *gringo*, Loretta? Even if he does convert?"

Loretta bowed her head. "Yes, Father, I'm sure."

He shrugged, poured himself another glass of whisky, and downed that. "Okay, *bueno*," he said. "What did you say your name was?"

"Graves," I replied through tightened jaws, "Benjamin Graves."

"Okay, Señor Graves, I need to ask you some questions about your faith to make sure you're gonna be a good Catholic like Loretta."

I groaned softly. "Fire away, Father."

He gave the self a sideways glance, then shook his head again. "You believe in the Holy Trinity?"

"Er, yes."

"Are you a Christian, Señor Graves?" he asked.

"Well, the Graves have always been Church of England members, if that is what you mean."

He grunted. "So, you believe in that fat *pendejo*, Henry the Eighth? He wanted a divorce like you, so he ignored the Pope and created his own church."

"That was over four hundred years ago," I stammered.

"We got long memories, Señor Graves," replied Father Castillo, waving an accusatory index finger. "Real long memories."

I stiffened. "Really, you can no more hold me personally responsible for the actions of Henry the Eighth than I can blame you for Torquemada." I felt a sharp, sudden pain in my right ankle. "Gah!" I yelped, before turning towards a scowling and narrow-eyed Loretta.

The priest removed a package of cigarettes from his shirt pocket and slowly extracted one. He retrieved a small gold lighter on the desk, lit the cigarette, inhaled deeply, and breathed a large cloud of blueish smoke—Esperanza-like—towards the self. "I ain't holding you responsible for nothing . . . *gringo*."

"I'm sure Benjamin didn't mean it, Father," said Loretta. "Did you, Benjamin?"

"What? I mean, no, of course not," I said meekly. "Merely engaging in an, er, historical comparison."

The chimneying Father blew another large cloud of smoke towards the self. "You even understand what it means to be a Catholic, especially here?"

Suppressing the desire to shout that it meant listening to a deranged priest, I said, "Well, one supposes it has something to do with the Pope, his supremacy over the Church, and so forth." The priest eyed me warily, then reached for the bottle.

I eyed the bottle. "I say, would it be inappropriate to ask you for a small tipple?"

"What? You want a shot of whisky?" he asked incredulously. "Now?"

"Well, as you are imbibing, I thought I might—gah!" Loretta's foot scored another direct hit on the ankle.

"I'm sorry, Father," Loretta said loudly. "Benjamin didn't mean that. He's just nervous about tomorrow's baptism and confession. Aren't you, Benjamin?"

I nodded meekly as the beleaguered ankle throbbed.

"I understand, Loretta," said Father Castillo. He turned to the self and asked, "You worried you're gonna drown?"

"Eh?" I said, mouth agape.

"Some people are afraid that I'm gonna hold them underwater. It's just for a couple seconds. I tell them to hold their nose."

"How reassuring," I muttered softly. "I mean, I am not concerned about the requisite submersion."

"Okay, that's good," he said as he ground the depleted cigarette into the overfilled ashtray on the desk. "Now, how well do you know Loretta?"

"Well, we met three years ago here, that is, in the cafe."

"I mean do you know Loretta in the Biblical sense?" He raised his forefinger and I thought he might repeat the rude gesture Esperanza was fond of using.

"What?" I stuttered, swallowing anxiously. "I mean, m-hem, that would violate the Catholic faith, would it not?"

"Yeah, but you ain't Catholic yet," said Father Castillo dryly. He then turned to Loretta. "Is this true? You and the *gringo* haven't—"

"No!" Loretta shouted, her visage turning a bright crimson. "Benjamin has a strict code."

"Code?" the priest asked. "What kind of code?"

"The Graves code," I replied haughtily. "*Semper fidelis*. Do you even know what that means?"

Father Castillo blinked. "Yeah, as a matter of fact, I do. Everyone in seminary learns Latin. And before I went to seminary, I was a Marine. Were you?"

"Eh?"

"*Semper fidelis*, always faithful," he said. "It's the Marines' motto." He rolled up his sleeve, revealing a tattoo on his forearm with the motto, then pointed the accusatory cigarette in my direction. "My younger brother was a captain in the Marines. He fought at Guadalcanal. You don't look like a Marine to me, Señor Graves."

I swallowed anxiously. "Er, no, that is, I merely meant it is the family motto. In this instance, it means a Graves is always an honourable gentleman."

"Uh-huh," he grunted. He leaned back in the chair, which emitted a loud squeal. "You intend to have children, Señor Graves?"

"Excuse me? That is not your concern—gah!"

"Yes, lots!" interrupted Loretta, who had struck a third blow to the ankle. "We want a large family."

"Er, yes, that's correct," I added hastily. "A cricket-team's worth!"

"What's cricket?" asked the priest, lighting another cigarette. "Never mind, I don't want to know." He looked to the ceiling and mouthed several words silently.

The interrogation continued for another half-hour, by which time he might as well have announced, "The prosecution rests," so thorough was the good Father's defenestration of the self's religious beliefs, such as they were, and my entire life in general. Though he may have been a Marine, I was convinced that the good Father had been trained in interrogation by the Gestapo.

"Well, Father," I mewled, "do I, er, pass the examination?"

He lit another cigarette, then reached for the whisky bottle and poured himself yet another glass. Ignoring the question, he turned to the intended. "Loretta, I've known you since I baptised you. I watched you grow up and always thought you were real smart. I also know Jaime did you wrong and I'm sorry for that. God forgives us, but He wants us to learn from our mistakes. ¿Que no?"

Loretta nodded meekly. "Um, yes, Father," she said.

"You sure you aren't making another mistake by marrying this *gringo*?" he asked, jerking his thumb towards the self. "If you ask me, he's a *pendejo*, but I'll marry you if that's what you want."

I stood up abruptly upon hearing Esperanza's preferred epithet. "How dare you!" I shouted. "I shall not remain here and be subjected to your insults. I will not tolerate such an attack on my honour. No Graves would."

Loretta sat silently. She looked straight ahead at the priest, who had leaned back in his chair.

"Loretta," I cried, "surely you are not rethinking our impending marriage because of what this cassock-wearing Cassandra has said."

She lowered her head and remained silent.

"Why don't you sit down, Señor Graves," he said calmly.

"Gah," I moaned, before falling into the small chair.

Finally, Loretta spoke up. "I do want to marry him, Father. I know Benjamin is different from people around here. The way he talks sometimes drives them crazy, including me. But he's a good person. He worked hard to rebuild the cafe and works hard to keep it running. The cafe would never have reopened if it weren't for him and his uncle. Plus, he really is a gentleman, almost a throwback to the last century with his talk of honour and his family's code, I guess." She turned towards me and took my hand. "Please, Father."

Father Castillo sighed, drew on his cigarette, and unleashed another cloud of smoke. "*Bueno*, Loretta." He then eyed the self. "Okay, Señor Graves, I'm gonna baptise you tomorrow at two o'clock. Then, I will hear your confession. Maybe we can finish that before dark."

"Yes, er, thank you, Father," I replied meekly.

"Don't thank me, thank Loretta. She's a candidate for sainthood." He shook his head in seeming exasperation and muttered under his breath.

As soon as we had exited his office and closed the door behind us, I walked over to a nearby pew and collapsed. "Very nice, eh?" I grumbled. "Well, thank you for coming to my defence."

"I'm sorry about the interrogation, Bennie. Father Castillo isn't used to people like, um, you."

"Eh? You mean English or *gringo*?"

"Both," laughed Loretta. "The important thing is he agreed to marry us."

"You are correct, of course. At least the baptism should be painless. I recall my nephew's baptism lasting only five minutes. As for confession, what, pray, am I supposed to confess."

"Uh, Bennie, maybe you shouldn't confess *everything*."

"M-hem, yes."

We walked outside and hurried towards the lorry, as the wind had risen, and we were being lashed with cold rain. I returned Loretta to her home, then sped towards the ranch, desperate for a large Dusty Trail.

"Well, old chap," said Archie after I sat on the sofa and had drained a bracing dose of Dusty Trail. "Did you charm the good Father?"

"Not exactly. Torquemada is a choir boy compared to the good Father. One is surprised he did not suggest I be subject to the rack or other assorted tortures. Plus, he had the temerity to suggest Loretta call off the wedding."

Archie raised an eyebrow. "Rather a low blow, that. Don't you officially convert tomorrow?"

"Well, I am supposed to go through baptism and confession, after which I shall be deemed a Catholic. I was rather surprised when Father Castillo used Esperanza's favourite epithet to describe the self. One should have turned the other cheek, but the Graves honour was at stake."

Archie nodded. "Well, although one doesn't expect a priest to curse, I would not be surprised if priestly epithets were uttered after the, er, incident with the bells at Christ Church. So, is the wedding off?"

"Thankfully, no. Loretta salvaged the meeting. Despite Father Castillo's suggestion that she turf me out, Loretta insisted she wanted to marry me."

"Right-ho, old chap! Good on, Loretta. All that matters, eh?"

"Well, given Father Castillo's opinion of the self, one suspects the next two days shall be unpleasant, even without the additional complexities of capturing Porfiria and ensuring our respective mothers do not engage in open warfare."

Chapter 21

I slept little that night. Instead, I lay awake contemplating a variety of horrors that Fate would surely conjure for the afternoon's baptism and subsequent confession, assisted by a screech owl living up to its name. Staggering into the kitchen at half five that morning, I reached for the still boiling cowboy coffee.

"Whoa, pard'ner," Uncle Bill said all too cheerily. "The coffee ain't finished yet." He eyed the self. "Tough night?"

"Quite," I mumbled. "Bloody screech owl."

"Yeah, I think I heard it, too." Uncle Bill walked over to the stove and checked the coffee pot. "Yep, done now. Give me your cup. You don't look like you could pour it."

"Thanks, Uncle Bill." I took the steaming cup from his hand and inhaled deeply, then began sipping the contents.

"You ready for your baptism? At least it's gonna be warmer today."

"I'm not sure, given yesterday's debacle with the good Father." The previous evening, I had informed Uncle Bill of the events, although not in Mother's presence to avoid any further eruptions.

Uncle Bill waved a dismissive hand. "You worry too much. Besides, Loretta's gonna be there with you to keep Father Castillo in line."

"I suppose so. You are most welcome to attend, Uncle Bill. I did not mean to suggest you could not do so."

"Thanks, pard'ner, but if you don't mind, I'm gonna skip it. Never much liked being in any church. 'Course, I'll be there for the wedding. What about Josefa?"

"Eh? One presumes she will attend if only to ensure the self becomes a Catholic in good standing before marrying her daughter."

We finished breakfast in relative silence, after which I took care of the morning care and feedings. Perhaps owing to her equine sympathies regarding my forthcoming conversion or her recent mother-to-be state, Marjorie was unusually acquiescent and did not even attempt to fire a hoof into the self.

Afterwards, when I returned to the house, Archie and Mother were in the kitchen; Archie was drinking coffee, and Mother was having her tea.

"Good morning, all," I said, mustering as much cheer as possible.

"What-ho, cousin," said Archie. "Ready for the big day? Well, biggish, at least. Will Uncle Bill be attending the sacred ceremonies today?"

"No. He, er, has other plans."

"Well, I shan't attend," said Mother. "This entire conversion is ridiculous."

"Quite all right, Mother," I said. "It will be a brief ceremony. Loretta and her mother will be in attendance. Archie, of course, if you wish to attend—"

"Thanks, cousin," he interrupted, "but I must decline. When he was here Sunday, Rudy asked if I would oversee the bar this afternoon. I gather his grandson is attending some sort of camp and will be unavailable."

"Baptism," Mother muttered. "Well, I hope that trollop is worth it, Benjamin, although Heaven only knows why."

"She is, Mother," I said, "and I would be most grateful if you would not refer to her in that way. As I have told you before, the baptism is a mere formality. I shan't be undertaking any pilgrimages to Rome or taking Holy Orders."

Mother harrumphed loudly, rose, and left the table.

I sighed. "Perhaps we should tell Rudy that Mother must be at least four sheets to the wind tomorrow before stepping inside the church, rather than the usual three. Better yet, perhaps you can lock her in the barn with Porfiria."

"Aunt Dorothy is rather headstrong," said Archie.

"They all are. Rather like a sack of enraged tomcats. I shall be grateful when it is over."

At half one, I arrived at the church and awaited Loretta and her mother. Not knowing what one wears to a baptism, I had donned the suit intended for tomorrow's wedding. The nerves were on edge owing to the uncertainty of how Father Castillo intended to proceed, including whether he would further interrogate the self. Upon entering the church, I noticed a half-dozen townspeople seated and chattering amongst themselves. I walked to the front pew, closely followed by every pair of eyes.

I turned to an older, heavyset woman sitting in the pew behind me, whom I recognised as an infrequent customer in the cafe. She laughed. "Josefa told me you're gonna get baptised and convert, *gringo*," she said. "I never seen a grown-up get baptised. Father Castillo holds babies in his arms, but he ain't gonna hold you."

"I'm sorry, madam, but this a private ceremony. Only myself and Loretta's family are invited."

"Huh? Joe Garcia said everybody in town was invited. Said we could all watch the *gringo* get baptised."

"He did, eh?" I replied angrily. "I am afraid that Joe is mis-informed. This is not a circus performance, and I shall thank you to leave."

"I ain't going nowhere, *gringo*," she said angrily, crossing her arms across her chest.

I sighed, the grey matter rehearsing various responses. Additional locals were entering the church, which was filling rapidly. I lowered the cranium into my hands. "Gah," I moaned softly. Presently, I felt a finger tapping on the shoulder. I lifted my head and beheld Coronado's rotund form.

"*Hola*, Señor Graves," he said. "Are you ready for your baptism? Can I sit here with you?"

"Er, I believe Loretta and her mother will sit beside me, Coronado."

"Oh, okay," he said, extracting a grease-stained package from his trouser pocket. "You want some of my *burrito*, Señor Graves?" He extended the package until it was directly beneath the olfactory, which reeled at the strongly malodorous item.

"Er, thank you, no, I have already eaten." Coronado shrugged, stuffed the package back into his trouser pocket, licked his fingers, and sat down. I leaned towards him. "Is every one in town planning to attend?"

"I guess. Joe said he was gonna invite some friends of his from Española, too."

"He did, eh?"

"*Sí*. Joe said everybody who bet had to attend if they wanted to win."

"Bet? I stammered. "Bet on what?"

"How long Father Castillo is gonna hold your head under-water. I bet ten seconds. Joe said it would be longer."

"What?" I exclaimed. "Do you mean that Joe is collecting bets on how long I shall be submerged?"

Coronado nodded. "I bet a quarter."

The jaw dropped. Not only was the self's baptism to be a public spectacle, but it was also to be a summer carnival event.

Presently, Loretta and her mother arrived.

"*Hola*, Loretta. *Hola*, Josefa," Coronado said. "Are you here 'cause you bet, too?"

Loretta and Josefa both looked at him quizzically. "Bet?" asked Loretta. "On what?"

"Joe told everybody to bet on how long Father Castillo would hold Señor Graves' head underwater for the baptism. I bet a quarter on ten seconds." He smiled and nodded.

Loretta brought her hand to her mouth to stifle a laugh, whilst her mother guffawed. "We didn't hear about that, Coronado," said Josefa. "Is it too late to bet?"

"I dunno," he said. "Joe's gonna be here real soon. I guess you can ask him. How long do you—"

"This is outrageous!" I shouted. "It is supposed to be a private ceremony I have undertaken voluntarily, not some Roman circus."

"Sorry, Señor Graves," said Coronado. He shrugged, then moved his bulk towards the far edge of the pew. Loretta and Josefa sat down, and Loretta took my hand. "It's okay, Bennie."

"It is not okay," I growled. "Has your bloody uncle also arranged for jugglers and dancing bears? Or perhaps he has invited the United Nations to observe the adequacy of the baptismal submersion? The mind boggles at the endless possibilities."

"Okay, Bennie," Loretta said softly. "Calm down. It will be over in just a few minutes."

"I doubt he will hold you under for more than 15 seconds," added Mrs. Alvarez. "You can hold your breath that long, can't you?"

As the grey matter debated whether to demonstrate my breath-holding abilities, Esperanza and Maria sat down immediately behind us. "So, *Pendejito*," Esperanza chortled, "I bet a dollar for two minutes. If I win, that means maybe you're gonna drown."

I turned slowly towards Esperanza, ready to engage in verbal battle. Maria eyed me and shook her head. "*Hermana*," she said coolly, "*no más*. Bennie's doing a good thing today."

Esperanza nodded. "Okay," she muttered, slowly raising her middle finger towards the self.

Presently, Father Castillo, wearing a white cassock and biretta, opened his office door and strode to the pulpit. He scanned the parishioners and then eyed the self. "Okay, everybody," he said loudly, "let's get this baptism started so I can take the gringo's—Señor Graves' confession after." He turned to the self. "You ready, Señor Graves?"

"Er, yes, Father, I am."

"Okay, good. You got any questions about this?"

The grey matter wished to ask whether the good Father had participated in Joe's betting scheme, but the vocal cords thought better of it. "No, Father," I said haltingly.

"Okay, everybody go around back. That's where we got the water tank."

I stood up and observed as the congregants began exiting the church. "Gah," I moaned softly.

Loretta took my arm and began to pull me towards the door like a recalcitrant puppy. "C'mon, Bennie," she said. She pulled me outside and around towards the back of the church, where I espied a water tank easily as large as the one Uncle Bill used for the cattle. "Gah! I thought Father Castillo would merely pour a spot of water on the self's head and mutter the blessing."

Esperanza, who must have noticed my shocked countenance, strode up besides me. "Better hold your breath, *Pendejito*," she laughed.

Presently, Father Castillo reappeared. Over his cassock, he wore a pair of fishing waders, which stretched to his waist. He walked over to the tank and stepped over the side as water sloshed over the top. "Okay, gri—Señor Graves, get in the water."

I stepped towards the water tank and began removing my jacket and tie.

"No time for that," Father Castillo shouted. "Just get in. *¿Comprende?*"

"Yes, but the jacket is wool and it shall be ruined—"

"God don't wait and neither do I," growled Father Castillo. "You want to be baptised or not?"

As I could not shout, "No, I bloody well don't!" without jeopardising tomorrow's wedding, I shook the cranium in defeat and stepped over the side.

Father Castillo motioned for me to move towards him. "Stand next to me."

I heard and obeyed. He grasped my shoulder with his right hand and placed his left hand behind my head. "I baptise this gringo—uh, Benjamin Graves, in the name of the Father, the Son, and the Holy Ghost." He then pushed my head into the water and held it there. I heard muffled voices and struggled to rise against the good Father's vice-like grip. I grabbed his arm as panic set in, wondering if Esperanza had been correct that I was to be drowned. Finally, he pulled me out of the water. I coughed and gasped for air as water streamed into my eyes.

"Only six seconds!" someone shouted.

"Who won the bet?" someone else asked.

"You look like a drowned rat, *Pendejito*," shouted Esperanza.

Joe spoke up. "Okay, everybody. Coronado bet the shortest time, ten seconds." He looked at a beaming Coronado. "You win, Gordo," he muttered.

Coronado waddled up and extended his right hand, into which a reluctant Joe deposited several dollars. Coronado then turned to me. "Thanks, Señor Graves!"

I espied Loretta and walked over to her. "Would you have a towel I might use?"

She brought her arm from behind her back and offered a largish one. "Here, Bennie," she said. "It's all over."

"Thankfully, yes," I replied. "I suppose I must now go back inside for my confession." I dried my scalp and face, handed the towel back to Loretta, and began to walk towards the door of the church.

"Don't go nowhere, Señor Graves," said Father Castillo. "I got to take your confession."

"Eh? Yes, I know, Father," I said. "I was going inside to the confession."

Father Castillo shook his head. "No, it's gonna be right here."

The brow rocketed upwards. "What? Where?"

Presently, two folding chairs were set down before Father Castillo. "Right here," he said.

"You cannot be serious," I stammered, as I sat down. "Confession is a private matter between priest and supplicant. Do you expect me to shout my confession to the entire town?"

"Of course not, Señor Graves. You can whisper it to me. Everybody else is just gonna watch. When you're finished, I will pronounce you a convert to the Church." He sat down on one of the chairs and motioned for me to be seated in the other.

Then he withdrew a flask from his cassock, unscrewed the lid, and raised it to his lips.

"Don't worry, *Pendejito*," shouted Esperanza. "Father Castillo won't tell us nothing. But maybe God's gonna strike you down when He hears." She emitted a hyena-like laugh.

The jaw dropped and searched for any nearby holes in which to bury itself. "Fine," I growled and sat down beside him. "What do I say first?"

Father Castillo rolled his eyes in apparent disgust. "You say, 'Bless me Father, for I have sinned. It has been'—you say how long it's been since you last confessed—'since my last confession.' Then you tell me all your sins."

"I have never confessed," I said.

"Okay, then say 'I have never confessed my sins.'"

"Bloody hell," I whispered under my breath. "Bless me Father, for I have sinned. I have never confessed before."

"Tell me your sins, my son," he replied, lifting the flask to his lips a second time.

"Liar!" screamed Esperanza. "Don't believe nothing *Pendejito* tells you, Father."

Father Castillo eyed Esperanza severely. "*¡Cállate!*" he shouted. "Sorry, Señor Graves," he said softly. "Don't pay any attention to her."

"Difficult not to, Father, although I have learned to turn the other cheek, and to keep turning it."

Father Castillo laughed. "Yeah, I've heard Esperanza's confessions a few times. She doesn't like you, that's for sure."

"M-hem, yes," I said.

"Okay, what are gonna confess?"

I leaned over to him and whispered in his ear. "I have murderous thoughts regarding Marjorie and Paco."

He goggled me and whispered. "Paco? You mean Nestor's dog?"

"Yes," I whispered.

He shrugged. "That's not a sin. Everybody hates that stupid dog. He ruined my best cassock."

"Sorry, Father," I whispered. "He's ruined several pairs of my trousers."

"Now, wanting to murder your ex-wife Marjorie is different," he said. "You must forgive her so I can forgive you."

"How can I forgive her? She has hurt me many times," I said with feigned sadness, not wishing to disabuse Father Castillo of his mistaken conclusion.

Father Castillo sighed. "You are going to marry Loretta. You must leave Marjorie in the past, even if she hurt you."

"But Marjorie will still be there after Loretta and I are married.

"Forgive her, my son, and then forget her."

"All right, Father."

"Anything else you wish to confess, my son?"

"Er, nothing I can think of. Perhaps next time."

"Okay." He sat up, made the sign of the cross in front of the self, and offered his blessing. Then, turning to the audience, said, "In the eyes of the Lord, Señor Graves is now a Catholic." I espied Loretta clapping softly, whilst Esperanza booed like an opposing football fan.

Father Castillo stood up, shook my hand lightly, and then rocketed back into the church. Loretta, Josefa, and Maria walked up to the self. "Thank you, Bennie," said Loretta. "This means a lot."

"Was the confession difficult?" Loretta asked.

"Surprisingly not," I replied. "In fact, he told me that one of the sins I confessed was not a sin at all."

"What was that?" asked Loretta's mother.

"I am afraid that must remain between priest and supplicant," I said. "Now, I believe I have earned a large whisky."

Chapter 22

I spent a fitful night, between lying awake listening to the noisy crickets and nightmaring about a macintosh-wearing Esperanza and a pink-robed Porfiria beating the self with umbrellas during the wedding, whilst shouting "¡*Pendejito*! and "¡*Diablo*!" I awakened at half five to the usual cacophony of birds and wondered if they were preparing their unique form of ammunition to deposit onto my suit jacket before I entered the church this afternoon.

I staggered out of bed, dressed, and shuffled into the kitchen. "Morning, pard'ner," said Uncle Bill. "Coffee's fresh." I grunted an affirmation and retrieved a cup. The hand shook as I filled the cup with the always tar-like brew, spilling a good portion onto the stove. "You all right, Bennie? Looks like you got pre-wedding jitters."

"I was either awake or suffering from various nightmares," I replied.

"Pretty normal, I imagine. Everything's gonna be fine."

"There is much coordination to be done. I should awaken Archie, as our first task is to nick Paco, which will allow him to capture Porfiria."

Uncle Bill shook his head. "I sure hope you know what you're doing, Bennie. Seems like it would be easier to just post a guard and keep her out of the church."

"It might if our local rotund constabulary was not so terrified of her. Esperanza and Joe would surely usher her inside and ensure she had an ample supply of umbrellas with which to beat the self."

"Well, I gotta admit Tiny wouldn't be much use. I could stand guard if you wanted."

"A kind and generous offer, Uncle Bill, but I insist you attend, as I am sure Loretta and her mother will insist. Besides, you could suffer a knock on the head. That madwoman is surprisingly strong."

He shrugged. "Okay, pard'ner. When are you going to send Archie out for Paco?"

I glanced at the watch. "Well, Nestor usually arrives at the bar when it opens, so Archie can begin his reconnaissance at nine o'clock. Paco may be outside by then. He has already secured several brands of canine biscuits, a serving dish, and a bottle of Farm Calm. Once he has captured the dog, he will bring it here and lock it in the barn."

"Did I hear my name to start this fateful day?" a dishevelled-looking Archie asked as he entered the kitchen.

"Good morning, Archie," I said. "Uncle Bill was enquiring about the schedule for the dognapping and the subsequent imprisonment of Porfiria."

"Still intent on pursuing that strategy, eh cousin?" asked Archie.

"Would you prefer to stand athwart the church and prevent Porfiria from entering?" I asked.

"I think not, given her girth and proficiency in wielding an umbrella," Archie said. "Of course, she might not show up at all."

"If Fate has anything to do with the wedding," I said, "she will. Fate has undoubtedly encouraged Porfiria to practise her thrusts and parries, and has booked her to arrive at the church at two o'clock sharp."

"Very well, cousin," said Archie. "I take it I am to dognap the mangy cur and return it to the confines of the barn, then find the madwoman?"

"Yes," I replied, noticing Uncle Bill shaking his head.

"When should I undertake the mission?"

"I suggest you depart no later than nine o'clock. Nestor should be awake by then and Paco will have been let outside. You have the Farm Calm and the bowl?"

"In the lorry as we speak," said Archie.

"I hope you boys know what you're doing," said Uncle Bill. "Meantime, I got work to do this morning. When's Rudy coming to get your mother?"

"Er, I suggested he arrive before one o'clock," I said. "That should afford him ample time to render Mother—"

"Render me what, Benjamin," Mother said, eyeing the self from the doorway.

"I say, Mother," I stammered, "You are awake rather early."

"I could not sleep," she said, walking over to the table where we were sitting. "I spent half the night thinking about your wedding. It's bad enough that you are now Catholic. Now, answer my question, Benjamin."

"Eh? What question would that be, Mother?"

"What is this about rendering? I am familiar with the term as it applies to the making of lard. Are you planning to turn me into lard before the wedding?"

"What? No, of course not, Mother," I said. "Er, I meant 'rendering' in terms of rendering you to the church, like 'render unto Caesar' and such."

"Your eyes are darting back and forth, Benjamin," she said, raising an eyebrow.

"No, really, Mother," I stammered again. "We were discussing, er, transport to the wedding. Yes, that's it. I must be there no later than one o'clock for a rehearsal and Archie's presence will be required, as well. You will be bored silly. Uncle Bill has some important business out of town this morning and just informed us that he may need to motor directly to the church afterwards. As a precaution, he will bring a pair of trousers, a suit jacket, and a tie with him. Isn't that right, Uncle Bill?"

"What? Oh, uh, yeah," Uncle Bill mumbled. "I'm real sorry, Dorothy, but that's ranching sometimes."

"Well, then," Mother said sternly, "how am I to get to the church this afternoon?"

"Uh—" Uncle Bill began.

"Uncle Bill has already spoken with Rudy," I interrupted quickly, "who will be delighted to escort you to the wedding."

Mother pursed her lips and glanced at her watch. "You say William has already spoken with Rudy? It's not yet six o'clock." She eyed the self warily over her reading glasses.

"Uh, I spoke with Rudy yesterday after I found out," said Uncle Bill. "He'll take real good care of you, Dorothy. If I finish up early, I'll come back and get you."

"I don't believe either of you," growled Mother. "Benjamin, if you do not wish me to attend this afternoon's abomination, you have merely to say so and I shall not. And you, William, I expected better. This place—" she paused and waved her hand through the air, "has caused you both to behave no better than savages."

Uncle Bill stood up. "Now, hold on, Dorothy," he said. "If it weren't for your—"

"Gah!" I shouted, terrified that Uncle Bill would reveal the real reason for the transport-related machinations. "I mean, it is true, Mother, that life in this small and isolated outpost is the antithesis of yours in London. I rather suspect that, when I arrived here, my shock was greater than yours. However, it is a life Uncle Bill has long embraced, as have I now."

"A noble speech, Benjamin," Mother said. "I apologise for implying you and William are 'savages.' But even a Scot could see through this façade you and William have erected. Now, perhaps one of you will have the decency to tell me the truth."

Although I espied Archie's eyes grow large as he drew his forefinger across his throat, the Graves code, which placed a high value on truth, rose within the grey matter. "Very well, Mother. It is you."

"Me? What do you mean?"

"I cannot have you engaging in a verbal or physical altercation with Loretta's mother," I said. "Or have you forgotten the incident in the cafe?"

"The woman insulted me, as you well know, Benjamin," she replied indignantly.

"Whether or not she did, it was owing to the same shameful arrogance you have displayed towards my impending marriage. We, that is, Archie and the self, arranged to have Rudy arrive this afternoon and ply you with sufficient champagne to neutralise any potential outbursts."

Mother goggled the self. Her jaw dropped as if attempting to reply, but she said nothing.

"I am sorry, Mother," I continued. "You, however, demanded the truth."

She closed her jaw, which then dropped again like a confused grouper. Then she sat down at the table. "I don't know what to say, Benjamin. I am in a state of shock. She turned and eyed Archie, then turned back towards the self. "Do you two truly believe I would have disrupted your wedding?"

I nodded cautiously. "You have already expressed your disapproval in *extremis*, as it were."

"You could do so much better, Benjamin," she said softly.

"I rather doubt that. I love Loretta and intend to marry her, with or without your approval. Therefore, I will not permit you to endanger the wedding. Does it not strike you as ironic that several of Loretta's relatives themselves wish to sabotage the wedding because they believe *I* am not good enough for *her*."

"Did you know about this, William?" she asked.

"I knew the boys had hatched a plan, Dorothy," said Uncle Bill. "You may want Bennie to marry some high society girl again. He tried that. Heh, I met the gal when she came out here a couple of years ago. Now, Loretta, she ain't a high society gal at all. But she's kind and a real hard worker. That cafe wouldn't exist if it hadn't been for her, too. So, put that high-falutin' pride of yours away and let those two marry with your blessing."

Mother placed her hands in her lap and sighed deeply. "You are both right. I am sorry, Benjamin. I hope you and Loretta will forgive me. May I attend the wedding?"

"Yes, of course, Mother," I said. "I would be honoured to have you present. You do know it will be a Catholic ceremony. Can you accept that?"

"Yes," she said, sighing. "I won't like it, but I suppose I must accept it." She rose and straightened her dress. "So, will you be taking me after all, William?"

"If you want to go, I will," said Uncle Bill.

"Would you be terribly offended if Rudy still escorted me?"

Uncle Bill offered a sly smile. "Heh. Sure, Dorothy. I know how much you enjoy his company."

"Really, William," she huffed. "There is nothing improper about my request. Rudy is a gentleman. Now, I must prepare my tea."

I glanced at Archie, who offered a slight nod. Mother's desire to be chauffeured to the wedding by Rudy and her likely pre-wedding consumption of the champagne Rudy would offer beforehand, would, I hoped, neutralise any potential eruptions, regardless of her promise of good behaviour. Even if Esperanza failed in her mission to inebriate Josefa, there was solace in knowing Mother would be in no condition to engage in open warfare.

Whilst Archie helped the self with the morning care and feedings, we reviewed the plans for capturing Paco and Porfiria. I had previously drawn a map showing the location of Nestor's and Porfiria's dwellings, which I had placed in the lorry, as well as a small portion of hamburger from the deep freeze for Archie to use as bait, presumably for Paco, but potentially Porfiria, depending on her appetite. I also put the collar and leash I had purchased from Joe's store inside.

"Ready to carry out the mission, Archie?"

He replied with a mock salute. "Aye, aye, cousin. Er, what happens if I cannot find the bloody dog?"

"I suppose one could set down a valise or suit jacket in Nestor's yard as additional bait. The dog is drawn to objects that it can ruin."

"Wouldn't it be easier to tell Porfiria about the dog, cousin? I mean, once she's locked up in the barn, it shouldn't matter if the dog is with her."

"Yes, well, if Paco is not himself secured, Fate will ensure he arrives at the church and wreaks urinary havoc, starting with my trousers."

"I could biff the dog with the lorry, if you wish."

I shook my head. "No, one must live up to RSPCA standards. Besides, as I said before, many of the locals have tried that without success. The dog possesses some special form of canine radar that enables it to dodge even the speediest of vehicles."

Archie shrugged. "Very well, capture and imprison then. I suppose I should be off. Are you sure you would not rather do the honours?"

"You have the advantage of relative anonymity. Did you not say you had fed the dog crisps in the bar? In any event, Paco knows me far too well to succumb to any lures I might offer. Although, if I dangled the trouser leg in front of him—"

"Very well, cousin." Archie offered another mock salute and climbed into the lorry. He shut the door and leaned out the window. "Was it General Montgomery who said, 'I shall return?'"

"I believe it was the Yanks' General MacArthur, although the sentiment is appropriate." I returned Archie's salute and watched as he turned the lorry around and motored away, wondering what spanners Fate had prepared."

An hour later, Archie returned. I walked outside and spotted him opening the lorry's door. He slid out slowly whilst emitting a groan. I ran over to him. The leash was wrapped around his right hand and attached to Paco, who was still sitting in the lorry. Archie's left hand was wrapped in a cloth, which appeared to be soaked with blood, and his face was pale.

"Gah!" I exclaimed. "What happened?"

Archie pulled on the leash, which caused Paco to exit the lorry. "Bloody cur bit me is what. Rather a nasty one, too, as you can see. There was a towel or some such thing on the floor, which I used to stem the bleeding. I have read that rabies is a problem in the States. Has the dog been vaccinated?" Archie's eyes bulged. "God, what if I must undergo rabies shots? They are supposed to be excruciating." His head slumped down.

I took the leash from him. "First, we must Florence Nightengale your hand. I will lock the dog in the barn and return to administer aid. Did you give him the beer and Farm Calm?"

"He bit me before I could. I was tempted to biff the dog on the head with the bottle."

"Well, once I have him in the barn, I will administer the entire contents."

"What will Aunt Dorothy say? She will want to know what happened."

"Er, yes." I paused. "Tell her you were assisting the self with some barbed wire, your hand slipped, and—Gah!" I looked down and saw that Paco had scored a direct hit on my trouser leg, which was dripping onto my boot. "Bloody cur, I ought to strangle you."

"Remember the RSPCA, cousin," Archie replied, laughing. "Right then, inside for bandaging."

"I shall join you after I lock Paco in the barn," I said.

Archie strolled towards the house. I pulled on the leash, which Paco's jaws had latched onto. The dog growled and shook his head vigorously, attempting to escape. I pulled harder. Paco held his legs stiffly against the strain. Finally, I reached down and gripped him by the scruff of his neck. Paco growled violently, but I remained steadfast. I trotted to the barn and used my foot to push the door open, bunged a still-leashed Paco inside, then closed and secured the door.

Paco barked, scratched, and began to howl. I strode over to the lorry and retrieved the Farm Calm, bottle of beer, and the bowl. I filled the bowl entirely and slipped it under the small gap between the door and the ground. Paco growled again, after which I heard lapping noises. Secure in the knowledge that the dog would soon be asleep, I returned to the house to attend Archie.

Inside, Archie was being attended by Mother at the kitchen table, who had wrapped a large piece of gauze around his hand and now was taping it securely. "How is the patient?" I asked, noticing that the colour had returned to his face.

"Really, Benjamin," Mother said, "your cousin should not be working around such dangers."

"Quite all right, Aunt Dorothy," said Archie. He held up the now bandaged hand. "Good as new, what?"

"You should rest, Archie," said Mother, who then turned towards the self. "Make sure you drive slowly to the church, Benjamin, so as not to jostle his hand."

"Er, yes, of course, Mother," I said.

"Very well," she said. "Now, I must get dressed before Rudy arrives." She walked out of the kitchen and disappeared into her bedroom.

When her bedroom door had been shut, I turned to Archie. "Sorry. I am surprised you could not pacify the dog with a biscuit."

"I offered him one, but rather than taking it like a civilised dog he bit my entire hand. I grabbed him by the scruff of his neck with my other hand, then secured the leash around his neck, which I then tied to the window crank." Archie paused to inspect the bandage. "Afraid the lorry's seat is a bit of a mess, old chap. I used a rag on the floor to wrap my hand with, but not before some of the red stuff dripped onto the seat."

"I shall clean it up. Are you able to carry out the remainder of the mission?"

"Does one have a choice?"

"Well, a Graves always endeavours to do his duty."

"Your silly code again?" he asked. "Right, well, don't let Aunt Dorothy know I've gone out. Where should I look first?"

"I would start in town, then proceed along the road to where she lives. You can use your injury to embellish the dognapping story. Tell her you valiantly fought the fiends off, and so forth."

"Right-ho," he said dully.

After I retrieved a cloth from the kitchen, we walked out to the lorry. I cleaned off the blood that had dripped onto the seat. "Thank you for doing this, Archie. It is most appreciated."

"As the Bard said, 'the course of *true love* never did run smooth.'"

"Shakespeare would never have imagined a path strewn with broken glass and land mines underneath." I checked the watch, which read half ten. "If you cannot find her, please return before half twelve. I must be at the church by one o'clock. You will have to lock her in the barn yourself. She must not see the self."

"Aye, captain, return no later than half twelve. With luck, I will spot the yellow madwoman soon and return forthwith."

At half twelve, Archie still had not returned and the Graves nerves were becoming increasingly agitated. I poured a large glass of Dusty Trail to soothe them and downed it forthwith. I then returned to my bedroom to change into my wedding attire, only to discover that the suit jacket had reacted to yesterday's baptismal submersion by shrinking to a size more appropriate for a dwarf. The sleeves reached halfway between my elbows and wrists and the back made a tearing sound if I moved my arms forward. The trousers had reduced themselves similarly, with the legs several inches shy of the ankles.

I walked back slowly to the sitting room and found Mother, who was awaiting Rudy's arrival. She eyed me and emitted a laugh that would have startled a half-deaf hyena. "Good heavens, Benjamin, why on earth are you wearing that jacket and those trousers? You look like Frankenstein's monster."

"Bloody baptism. Father Castillo submerged me entirely. As you can see, the suit reacted poorly."

"Well, you cannot wear those clothes."

"This is my only suit. I cannot be married wearing blue jeans and a grease-stained cowboy shirt."

"Why not?" Mother grumbled. "Surely those are what the natives are more accustomed to."

"They are not some undiscovered African tribe, Mother."

"Well, perhaps William has something you can wear. Have you checked?"

"No. However, you may have noticed Uncle Bill is rather shorter than the self."

"Suit yourself, Benjamin," she chortled. "I have no sympathy for your predicament, which is entirely the result of your decision to convert."

I sighed. "Yes, Mother. I will check Uncle Bill's closet. Perhaps he has something not quite as ill-fitting as my ruined suit." I walked into his bedroom and began examining the contents of his closet. It contained one green jacket, which looked appropriate for an overgrown leprechaun. Nevertheless, I donned it. The sleeves were too short, although not as short as those on my jacket, whilst the body was almost too large. I continued my search for suitable trousers but found none. Fate, it appeared, has consigned me to be married looking like a circus clown.

I returned to the sitting room for Mother's amusement. She eyed me over her glasses and shook her head. "Too short black trousers, a blue shirt, and a green jacket. How appropriately appalling."

"Yes, thank you, Mother. I am glad you are amused." I looked at the watch again. It was now ten minutes before one o'clock. Presently, I heard the lorry turning into the driveway. I peered out the window and beheld Archie driving, together with his yellow-macintoshed quarry.

"That must be Rudy," said Mother. She stood up and straightened her dress.

"No, it is Archie."

"He went out? With that injured hand? Where?"

"I, er, do not know. Now, if you will excuse me, I must be off to the church." I dashed outside before Mother could say anything else and crouched behind a bush so as not to be seen by Porfiria. Archie gestured towards the barn and Porfiria pointed at it with her umbrella. Presently, he opened the door. Paco lay beside it, asleep. Porfiria turned around.

"Is that the dog?" she asked. "I've seen that dog before." She walked towards Paco, bent over to retrieve the somnolent canine, and then started to walk back towards the lorry.

"I'm afraid you cannot leave, madam," said Archie, as he grabbed her macintosh and pulled.

"Let go of me!" she shouted. "¡*Diablo!*"

Archie gripped her tightly and pushed her back towards the barn door. "Sorry, madam, but in you go." Porfiria raised her umbrella and attempted to bring it down on Archie's head whilst still holding Paco, but he parried the blow, grabbed the umbrella from her hand, and tossed it aside. Then he pushed her again, which caused her to fall backwards into the barn, still clutching Paco. As she sat up, he slid the door shut and locked it.

I rose from my hiding spot. "Good work, Archie," I said.

"What an ordeal," he replied, panting heavily. "That was truly above and beyond the call, cousin. My God, she is strong. When she raised that umbrella, I thought it was all over."

"Well, she is safely locked away now," I said. "I must depart for the church. Loretta and family will be there waiting. Can you ride with Mother and Rudy?"

Archie examined my raiment from head to toe and began to laugh. "I say, cousin, the Yanks have a most interesting standard of suitable wedding attire."

"My suit shrank from yesterday's dousing. The jacket is unwearable. This one"—I pulled at the lapel, "belongs to Uncle Bill. It is the only jacket he has, apparently."

"Hmm. I hope Loretta appreciates your peacock-like plumage."

"Yes, yes, enough of that," I said. "Mother will question you as to your whereabouts. She assumed you were resting your injured hand."

He glanced at the bandage and shrugged. "Not to concern yourself, old chap. I will think of something." He took a deep breath, exhaled, and set course for the house.

As I walked towards the lorry, Rudy arrived. He stepped out of his lorry, retrieved a bottle of champagne, then looked at the self. His eyebrows rocketed upwards. "Jesus, Bennie, you gonna get married wearing that?"

"As I explained to Mother and Archie, the near drowning Father Castillo attempted ruined my trousers and suit jacket. This jacket belongs to Uncle Bill. I have no other suitable trousers."

Rudy laughed. "Well, everybody's gonna make fun of you, but I guess it doesn't much matter unless Loretta calls off the wedding." He paused. "I hope Esperanza doesn't wear her pink robe."

"Gah! What a horrible thought. In any event, I shall explain to Loretta what happened and I already anticipate a severe cheek-turning once Esperanza sees the outfit."

Rudy nodded.

"By the way, Mother knows about the plan."

"She does? How?"

"Er, I informed her early this morning."

"Why? What do you want me to do?"

"Nothing, that is, proceed as planned. Surprisingly, she accepted my explanation and still wants you to escort her to the wedding. I suspect she will happily down the champagne you have brought. Now, I really must dash." I returned to the lorry and sped off towards the church, ready to battle Fate's slings and arrows.

Chapter 23

I arrived at the Church, espying Josefa, Maria, and Esperanza standing outside. Loretta's mother swayed, apparently from the effects of the beer Esperanza was supposed to have plied her with. Esperanza, who also appeared intoxicated, scowled whilst chimneying away, and Maria appeared expressionless. I exited nervously, preparing for the onslaught of criticism about the self's appalling wedding attire. I exited, shut the lorry's door, and walked towards them. Five jaws dropped as I approached.

"Apologies for the delay," I muttered.

"What the fuck are you wearing, *Pendejito*?" slurred Esperanza. "This is Loretta's wedding, not some fucking clown show. You expect her to marry you when you're wearing that shit?"

Mrs. Alvarez smiled obliviously and said nothing.

"Sod off, Esperanza," I said. "If it weren't for that priest trying to drown me, my suit would not have shrunk. I cannot even wear the jacket. This one belongs to Uncle Bill."

"I got Josefa drunk like you asked, *Pendejito*," said Esperanza, pointing an accusatory finger at the self.

"What did you say?" asked Loretta's mother, sounding fully sober. "You asked Esperanza to get me drunk?"

"Eh? I mean, no, of course, not," I said.

"Yeah, he did, Josefa," said Esperanza. "*Pendejito* didn't want you gettin' into no fights with his fucking mom."

"How dare you speak of my mother in that way," I said.

"¡*Vete a la chingada, Pendejito*!" Esperanza shouted, raising her middle finger.

"Why would I want to fight your mother, Benjamin?" asked Mrs. Alvarez.

"Well, there was the incident at the cafe," I said.

She folded her arms across her chest. "You think I would start a fight in church? At my Loretta's wedding?"

I began to perspire. "Er, no, that is, of course not," I said meekly.

Mrs. Alvarez shook her head and raised her middle finger. She then walked into the church.

"Good work, *Pendejito*," Esperanza laughed. "Now Josefa hates you, too."

"*No más, hermana*," Maria said. She looked at the self and shook her head. "It ain't gonna matter to Loretta, Bennie."

"I hope not, Maria," I said. We proceeded into the church and sat down on opposite sides of the two front pews, waiting for the ceremony to begin. The church began to fill slowly with townspeople. At fifteen minutes before two o'clock, Archie came inside, followed by Uncle Bill. They walked over and sat beside me.

"Well, old chap," Archie said, glancing around the room, "ready to take the plunge, as it were?"

"Plunge is the operative word," I replied, "especially given yesterday's dousing."

"How many of the townspeople will be in attendance?" Archie asked.

I turned around and goggled at the growing crowd. "Thanks to your invitation, I suspect many are in attendance for the free food and drink. Doubtless Esperanza has convinced them to arrive bearing pitchforks, tar, and feathers."

Archie laughed. "I shall defend you from the marauding hordes, cousin," he said. "Besides, you shall have Maria at your side. I gather she can repel any army."

I laughed. "I would not care to challenge her."

I noticed Uncle Bill eying the self. "That my jacket, pard'ner?" he asked.

"Er, yes, Uncle Bill," I replied. "Mine was ruined by yesterday's baptismal submersion, so I borrowed yours. Whatever possessed you to purchase a jacket of this colour?"

"Hell, I didn't buy it," he said. "Won it in a poker game about twenty years ago. Fella ran out of money. Said his jacket was genuine silk, worth twenty-five dollars. With that blue shirt, you look kinda—"

"Yes, I know," I interrupted. "When Loretta casts her eyes on the self, I shall not blame her for abandoning the marital ship, as it were."

"Oh, hell, Bennie," said Uncle Bill. "Loretta's got more sense than that. 'Course, it's a good thing she's gotta pretty good sense of humour, too."

"M-hem," I mumbled. I turned around and eyed the now almost full pews. Presently, Coronado came inside and waddled up to the front pew. "*Hola*, Señor Graves, *Hola*, Señor Archie," he said, offering a rodentary smile. "Did I miss the wedding?"

"Er, no, Coronado," I said. "The ceremony begins in several minutes."

"Oh, okay," he replied. "Is Loretta gonna be here, too?"

"Of course she will be here you—" I said, "that is, she is rather an integral part of the ceremony, Coronado, being the bride."

"Oh, okay," he said. "I never been to a wedding before."

"Never been married, Coronado?" asked Archie.

"I don't think so," said Coronado. "There was a girl I liked in Española, but I don't think she liked me so much."

"You don't think—," Archie said, before I grabbed his arm and shook my head.

"Trust me, it is not worth the bother," I whispered to Archie.

"Well, it's never too late, Coronado," I said. "Perhaps you will meet the woman of your dreams in Española. Who knows, perhaps she awaits you here in Vaca Seca."

Coronado shrugged. "You think so, Señor Graves?"

"Er, well, one should never abandon hope, Coronado."

"Okay, Señor Graves, I won't." He paused and nodded at the self. "I'm kinda hungry. Do you think Maria would make me a *burrito*? I saw her in the cafe a while ago."

I pointed to the opposite pew. "Maria is sitting there, Coronado. She was likely in the cafe earlier preparing refreshments for after the ceremony."

"What are refreshments?" he asked.

I groaned inwardly. "Food and drink, Coronado. There may even be a *burrito* for you."

Coronado's eyes widened and I detected a spot of drool at the corner of his mouth. "Thanks, Señor Graves. Do I got to pay for it?" He reached into his pocket and retrieved the contents, including the ever-present mousetrap, and began to count several coins. "I got a dollar."

I waved my hand. "No need to pay, Coronado. You will be our guest. Everything will be free of charge."

"Thanks, Señor Graves," he said. "I guess I'll see you later." He turned around and began to waddle away.

"Coronado, wait," I shouted. "Have you forgotten?"

He waddled back and looked at the self blankly. "I dunno."

"You are my best man, Coronado," I said, "which means you must hold the ring for Loretta and give it to me when Father Castillo asks."

"Oh, I forgot," he said. "Sorry, Señor Graves."

I retrieved the ring from my trouser pocket. "Now, take the ring and place it in your pocket."

"Which one, Señor Graves?" he asked. He held out a pudgy hand and encircled the ring.

The blood pressure was now rising steadily. "Well, your right trouser pocket has the mousetrap," I said, "so perhaps your left trouser pocket would be better."

Coronado deposited the ring into his left pocket. "Okay, Señor Graves," he said, before walking away.

Archie shook his head. "Not the brightest bulb, eh?"

"No," I sighed. "Rather exasperating, really, which is why I must remind the self that he is a kind-hearted chap." I glanced at the watch, which now read two o'clock. "I wonder where Father Castillo is. He should be here by now."

"I can reconnoitre the local environs if you wish," said Archie.

"Thanks, Archie. You might check Rudy's. During Loretta's and my meeting, he downed several glasses of whisky. And during my confession, if one wishes to call it that, the good Father withdrew a small flask from his cassock. I rather doubt it was filled with sacramental wine."

"Indeed. One always joked about Irish priests. Then again, if one takes a vow of celibacy, perhaps one needs a bit of bracing now and then."

"M-hem," I gargled. "Best not to discuss that amongst the locals. They might take offence."

"Not to worry, cousin," he replied with a wave of his hand. "I shall return shortly."

Archie offered a quick salute, then marched out the front door, leaving me alone in the church.

"Gah," I muttered.

Presently, the silence was interrupted, as Uncle Bill entered the church, followed by Loretta, whose arm was wrapped around Joe's. She appeared radiant wearing a light blue wedding dress and holding a small bouquet of white flowers in her hands. Joe escorted her to the front of the church, where she sat down on the pew next to her mother.

Loretta looked over towards the self and gaped. "What are you wearing, Bennie? You look ridiculous."

"Yesterday's dousing ruined my suit. These belong to Uncle Bill."

She shook her head in disbelief, then began to laugh quietly. "Good thing I'm not marrying for your fashion sense."

"M-hem, quite," I muttered.

"You and Loretta ready, pard'ner?" Uncle Bill asked.

"I believe we are," I replied. "However, we require Father Castillo's presence."

"Where is Father Castillo?" asked Loretta.

"Archie has gone in search of him," I said.

Loretta furrowed her brow. "You don't think that because of your confession—"

"Of course not," I said. "That is, I do not believe so, despite Esperanza's shouting 'Liar!' He absolved my sins, real and imagined."

Uncle Bill laughed. "I'm sure he's heard worse. Don't you and Loretta worry."

The church door opened again, admitting a stream of townspeople. The entire church was now full, with several dozen locals standing against the walls. Coronado returned, accompanied by his equally rotund sister, who worked at the local bank and was equally dim.

"*Hola*, Señor Graves," said Coronado. "You remember my sister, Isabella, don't you?"

I glanced at the scowling figure before me. "Ah, yes, I remember her," I said with gritted molars. "How nice of you to attend."

She scowled and muttered something, which sounded like "Stupid *gringo*," before waddling towards one of the pews near the back.

Presently, Luis Chavez stood before me, resplendent in a brown jacket and red tie. "Hey, Bennie," he said, shaking my hand vigorously. "¡*Felicitaciones*!

"Thank you, Luis," I replied. "I don't think I've ever seen you wearing a tie."

Luis laughed and pulled at the tie. "Nah, I hate these things. I got one a long time ago for my sister's wedding. I think that's the last time I wore it. No, wait, I wore it at my Dad's funeral."

"Er, yes," I said. "Well, I do hope today is a more pleasant occasion than your father's funeral."

He laughed. "Dad always said he wanted us to have a big party to remember him, so we did. I just remember waking up at the station the next morning. I dunno how I got there."

"Well, I'm delighted you are here, Luis," I said.

As Luis turned into the nearest pew, Joe Romero approached me. "You gonna marry my niece wearing that?" he asked. "What the hell's wrong with you?"

"Yesterday's baptism is what is wrong," I snarled. "If you don't like it, sod off."

Joe shook his head. "Okay, okay. I don't suppose Loretta has changed her mind?"

I sighed. "Not to my knowledge, Joe. Although I am quite sure you did your best to convince her of the error in her ways."

"Yeah," he grunted, "but she's always been stubborn." He then looked at me suspiciously. "You better do her right, *gringo*," he growled. "I ever see you around another *chichona*, I'll cut your *cojones* off."

"How noble of you," I replied acidly. "Do you have everything ready for the party afterwards? Oh, and Loretta told me that she thought you're charging far too much, so we shall be purchasing more supplies from Sabrosa Foods in future."

"Hey, we agreed," Joe hissed.

"Well, surely you would wish me to listen to his wife's advice," I said, smiling.

"Fucking *gringo*," Joe muttered under his breath, before taking a seat.

As the minutes passed, the crowd was becoming increasingly boisterous. They began clapping loudly and shouting. The watch read almost three o'clock, and there still was no sign of either Father Castillo or Archie. Presently, I espied Mother and Rudy enter the church. Mother was clinging to Rudy's arm, and both appeared to stagger as they walked to where Uncle Bill and I sat.

"Are you quite all right Mother?" I asked.

Mother goggled the self, then began laughing hysterically. "Perfectly fine, Benjamin. Are you married yet? Did we miss the cere-ceremony?" She swung her head around, eying the attendees. "Is everyone here a bloody Catholic except me?"

"Mother, quiet please," I hissed. "Rudy, perhaps you should take Mother outside."

"I guess we had too much champagne," he said. "I had a second bottle in my truck. Your mom sure likes it."

"Did you say 'champagne' Rudy?" Mother said. "Be a dear and fetch me another glass."

"Rudy, please," I implored.

"Sure thing, Bennie," he said. He dragged Mother down the aisle like an anchor.

"I guess there won't be much trouble between Dorothy and Josefa," said Uncle Bill. "Hell, she can barely stand."

"One hopes Rudy will escort her somewhere far from the premises," I said as I checked the watch again. "Where is Father Castillo?"

As if on cue, the door to the good Father's office swung open, and the glassy-eyed priest stepped through, followed by an equally glassy-eyed Archie, who walked over to our pew and sat down heavily.

"Where have you been?" I asked. "Do you know what time it is?"

Archie looked at his wrist, despite not having a watch. "I dunno, cousin," he said with a noticeable slur. "I found Father Castillo at the bar. I told him he needed to get to the church to perform the wedding, but he said you and Loretta could wait. Well, he didn't say it quite like that. I didn't know priests swore."

"I am sure he was well taught when he served in the Marines," I said. "Judging from the quality of your speech, you happily joined him."

"One doesn't wish to be unsociable, cousin," said Archie.

Father Castillo climbed the altar, grasped it with both hands, and shouted, "Okay, everybody, sit down and be quiet. We got a wedding to perform." The crowd murmured and obeyed. "Loretta, you come stand over here." He pointed to the front of the church between the pews. "Where's the *gringo*—groom?"

I raised a tremulous hand and stood. "Er, here, Father."

"You got a best man?"

"Er, yes." I motioned to Coronado, who was sitting at the end of the pew.

Coronado waddled over and stood between Loretta and me. "Thanks, Señor Graves," he said.

"Er, you need to stand on the other side of me, Coronado," I said, whilst pulling him to starboard.

"Oh, okay. Sorry."

Father Castillo waited impatiently as Coronado repositioned himself. He then eyed my colourful attire and shook his head. "What the hell are you wearing? You look like a clown."

"Well, Father, if you had not attempted to drown me yesterday, my trousers would be a proper length, and I would be wearing my suit jacket—gah!" My left ankle had suffered a direct hit from Loretta's shoe.

"It's called a baptism," the priest growled. "Loretta, you sure you want to marry him?"

"Don't do it, Loretta," shouted Esperanza. "Don't ruin your life marrying *Pendejito*." Several of the attendees applauded.

I turned around. I recognised one, an elderly woman who frequented the cafe and would dash off without paying. As I started to shout, "Sod off," the ankle suffered a second direct hit. "Gah!" I yelled again. I eyed Loretta, who raised an index finger to her mouth, imploring me not to respond. I drew a deep breath and turned back to Father Castillo.

"Yes, I want to marry Benjamin, Father," said Loretta calmly, before hearing Esperanza whisper, "*Vete a la chingada, Pendejito.*"

"Okay, but no more divorces, Loretta," said Father Castillo. ¿*Comprende?*" He then began the ceremony, droning on about the sanctity of marriage and quoting extensively from the Bible. There were several prayers, in which those sitting in the pews stood.

"*Bueno*," he muttered, as he retrieved the small flask from his cassock and raised it to his lips. "Do you, Loretta, take this *gringo*—sorry, man, to be your husband, to uh—" He paused and reached into his cassock again, retrieving a small piece of paper. "Oh, *sí*," he muttered and began to read. "To have and to hold, for richer or poorer, in sickness and in health, until death do you part?"

"I do," said Loretta.

Father Castillo cleared his throat and took another drink from the flask. "And do you, Benjamin Graves, take this woman to be your wife, to have and to hold, for richer or poorer, in sickness and in health, until death do you part?"

"I do—gah!" I shouted as a heavy object crashed down onto the cranium.

"*¡Diablo!*" shouted Porfiria. "*¡Diablo!* She brought the umbrella down on my head a second time. "Don't you marry him! His brother kidnapped me and locked me in a barn."

"Get her out of here," I yelled. I turned to face her. She pointed the umbrella at me and thrust it back and forth like a knife-wielding assassin. "Stop!" I shouted, attempting to grab the umbrella from her hand.

She raised the umbrella again and I braced myself for another blow. "*Hola*, Porfiria," Coronado said calmly. "You remember me, don't you?"

Porfiria lowered the umbrella. "*Hola*, Coronado" she muttered.

"Are you hungry?" he asked, retrieving what I presumed was a *burrito* from his pocket.

"*Sí*," she said. She took the *burrito* from him, unwrapped it, and took a cavernous bite.

"No, you keep it, Porfiria," Coronado said, as she attempted to return the now half-eaten *burrito*. "If you wait outside, there's going to be a *fiesta*. Maria's making *enchiladas*. I can come find you after the wedding."

"Okay," she said. "What about him?" She pointed at the self.

"It's okay, Porfiria," said Coronado. "I like Señor Graves. He's not the Devil."

Porfiria shrugged, adjusted her macintosh, and then walked towards the door. She opened it and disappeared.

"Thank you, Coronado," I said.

"Sure, Señor Graves," he said. "I like to help."

"You and Archie locked her in the barn?" Loretta asked, goggling me.

"Er, rather an involved story," I muttered. "Perhaps we should continue with the ceremony."

"Where was I?" asked Father Castillo.

"I had just said 'I do,' Father," I replied.

"You sure, Loretta?" he asked again. "Last chance."

Loretta nodded, tightening her grip around the bouquet of flowers she held.

"You got the ring, Señor Graves?" asked the priest.

I turned to Coronado. "May I please have the ring?"

"Okay." He reached into his right trouser pocket and retrieved the contents, which included the used mousetrap.

"Uh, I dunno, Señor Graves. It was here."

"Try the other pocket, Coronado," I said.

"Oh, okay, Señor Graves." He reached into the other pocket. "It's not in this one, either, Señor Graves."

The jaw dropped. "What? I gave it to you several minutes ago," I wailed. "How could you possibly lose it?"

Coronado thrust his hand into the pocket again. "There's a hole in it," he said with a shrug. "Sorry, Señor Graves. Does this mean I can't be your best man?"

"Worst is more like it," I muttered silently. "Well, it cannot have travelled far," I said, as I began to scan the floor.

"Okay, everybody," Father Castillo shouted. "We got to find Loretta's ring. Everybody look around."

The crowd murmured and began to search the floor. After five minutes of searching unsuccessfully, I had become increasingly agitated. "*No está aqui*," an elderly man announced.

"It must be here," I shouted. "Please, please look again." I lowered myself onto the floor and began slithering under the front pews. I heard a low growl and felt a sudden dampness on my ankle. I turned my head and espied Paco, leg raised, and unleashing a torrent of urine onto my sock. "Bloody cur," I screamed, raising my head and banging against the pew. "Gah!"

Paco barked and ran to the door, where Nestor stood. He opened the door and they both exited. The church erupted into laughter, including Father Castillo.

"Now we know what Paco thinks of you marrying Loretta, *Pendejito*," Esperanza chortled.

"It's okay, Bennie," Loretta said, stifling a grin. "I don't need a ring now. Why don't you get off the floor so we can finish the ceremony."

I stood up, brushed the dust off my jacket, and pressed my hands tightly against my forehead. "It is most certainly *not* okay," I moaned loudly. "This entire wedding has been a disaster. I mean, I look like a circus clown. I've been beaten over the head by a madwoman who thinks I am the Devil incarnate. Your wedding ring has vanished. And Paco has struck again. What comes next? Swallowed by a snake-filled pit? Plagues of locusts and frogs?"

"Calm down, Bennie," Loretta said sternly. "You're making a scene."

I walked over the front pew and sat down heavily. "I'm sorry, Loretta. Perhaps this is Fate's way of saying we should not be married."

Uncle Bill placed an arm around my sagging shoulders. "C'mon, pard'ner," he said. "A cowboy's got to face adversity and keep going. Giving up ain't the cowboy way. You ought to know that by now."

"I'm no cowboy, Uncle Bill," I said. "I mean, look at me."

"Oh, hell, that's enough stewing," he replied. "Now stand back up and finish marrying the best gal you've ever known."

"If she will still have me," I muttered.

"She will, pard'ner," he said. He looked at Loretta. "Ain't that right, Loretta?"

"Of course," said Loretta, extending her arms towards the self. "Now, stand up and finish marrying me, goddammit. Oh, sorry, Father."

"Next time you confess, Loretta, don't forget to say you took the Lord's name in vain," said Father Castillo.

I stood up slowly. "I still cannot understand how your wedding ring vanished."

"I don't got it," said Esperanza loudly.

"*Hermana,*" said Maria, extending her hand. "It's not yours and Loretta is going to marry Bennie anyway. *Damelo ahora.*"

"Fine," said Esperanza, who tossed the ring towards the self. It clattered on the floor and was retrieved by Coronado, who groaned as he stood up.

"Here you go, Señor Graves."

"Thank you, Coronado. You are a best man indeed."

"Thanks. I like to help."

Father Castillo motioned for everyone to sit down. "Okay, so now maybe we can finish. Señor Graves, put that ring on Loretta's finger before something else happens to it." I placed it on her finger as instructed. "*Bueno.* I now pronounce you husband and wife. You can kiss the bride." We kissed and the room broke out in cheers, except for Esperanza, who booed. Father Castillo retrieved his flask and drained it dry. He then shook Loretta's and the self's hands. "¡*Felicitaciones*! he said. "God help me if I ever have a wedding ceremony like this again."

"Thank you, Father," said Loretta.

"M-hem, yes, thank you," I added.

Mrs. Alvarez walked over and embraced Loretta. "I hope you will be happy, Loretta," she said, casting an aspersive glance at the self.

"I will, mother," said Loretta.

Her mother then pointed at me. "You better be real good to my daughter, Benjamin, or I'll cut your *cojones* off. ¿*Comprende?*"

The eyebrows rocketed upwards. "Er, yes, Mrs. Alvarez. Joe already promised the same."

"I'll see you at the party, Loretta," Josefa said. She embraced Loretta a second time, then walked away. Joe Romero embraced Loretta and congratulated her, offered me a look of disgust, and then disappeared.

Archie approached. He kissed Loretta on the cheek and then shook my hand. "Well done, old chap. Well done. You make a fine couple."

"Thanks, Archie," I said. "God, I am sorely in need of a drink."

"Right-ho," he said. "Where is the post-marital party to take place?"

"At the cafe," I said.

Uncle Bill embraced Loretta. "Welcome to the family," he said. "I'm real glad you're a part of it now." He handed me an envelope. "Here's a little wedding present for you."

"I say, Uncle Bill, that is most kind of you."

"Well, open the damn thing up," he said.

I did as he asked. Inside were two aeroplane tickets to Paris, along with a week's reservations at the *Hotel d'Angleterre*. On the return, we were to stay in New York City, at the Plaza Hotel. I showed the materials to Loretta.

"Oh my God!" she shouted, embracing him again. "Thank you! Paris! New York!"

"I'm staggered, Uncle Bill. This must have cost you a bloody fortune."

He shrugged. "I may have been the black sheep of the family, but your grandfather forgot to cut me out of his will. I was gonna buy me a bigger ranch with the money, but I decided to stay right here. It's plenty big enough. You two enjoy your honeymoon. You earned it." He slapped me on the back and walked out.

Maria had been standing behind him. She embraced Loretta. "*Felicitaciones*," she said with an uncharacteristic smile. "I'm sorry about *mi hermana*, Bennie."

I sighed. "I doubt she will ever change, Maria. Nor will Joe. But as Uncle Bill said, one must trundle onwards whatever the obstacles."

Maria shrugged. "Okay. I gotta get back to the cafe to get everything ready. Joe brought some stuff earlier and Rudy brought more cases of beer."

"Would you like some help?" I asked.

Maria shook her head. "No. It's for you and Loretta."

"Thank you, Maria," I said, shaking her hand. "Now, I must locate my mother."

Loretta clutched my arm. "Paris, Bennie! And New York! I can't believe it."

"And two weeks away from this loony bin," I replied. "Now, *Mrs. Graves*, shall we set course for the cafe and the celebration?"

"It's going to take a while for me to get used to that," said Loretta.

I laughed. "I doubt anyone here will ever refer to you in that manner. The *gringo's* wife, perhaps, but not 'Mrs. Graves.'"

For the next half hour, a dozen or so more individuals congratulated Loretta and offered her advice. Several repeated the warnings about the awaiting defenestration of the self's *cojones*. Others expressed their condolences to her about the presumed forced marriage and enquired as to the arrival date of the presumed forthcoming infant. One older gentleman gave Loretta a loaded pistol in case the "*gringo* don't behave, or you just want to get rid of him" and said he knew of a great place up north where a body could be disposed. I thought it best not to enquire as to how he had made that determination.

Finally, after listening to them, we stepped outside. I scanned the area carefully, fearful that Porfiria was waiting to biff me yet again, and we proceeded to the cafe. I espied Paco, who appeared overwhelmed by the numerous tyres ready to be marked and who had already christened the cafe's front door.

Inside, the scene was boisterous. Music blared from a radio and the natives were busily helping themselves to the comestibles and, especially, the beer. When they espied Loretta, they raised their bottles in congratulation. "Perhaps I should disappear into the kitchen," I shouted to her above the din. "May I get you anything?"

"No thanks," she said. "I just want to go to Santa Fe like we planned. Can we leave soon? Do you think we will be missed?"

I scanned the crowd and said, "I rather doubt it. They seem quite content to eat and drink themselves into oblivion. I should look for Mother before we depart. She must be here some-where—ah, near the corner, with Rudy. Shan't be a moment." I made my way through the horde until I stood behind Mother, who seemed quite animated. "Excuse me, Mother," I said.

She turned around, a glass of wine in her hand. "Benjamin. Congratulations, my dear. I hear you will be honeymooning in Paris and New York. How marvellous!"

"Yes, it was most generous of Uncle Bill. We will be depart-ing soon for our originally planned honeymoon in Santa Fe. We should return on Monday. When do you and Archie depart?"

"Archie will be leaving Monday morning. You should say good-bye to him before you leave."

"I don't understand, Mother. You said Archie is leaving Monday? Are you not returning together?"

"Oh, no," she replied. "I'm staying."

"Eh?" I asked.

"I have decided to divorce your father."

"What?" I spluttered.

"Rudy and I are to be married." Rudy raised his glass. "Great news, huh, Bennie. We're gonna be family."

"Gah!"

THE END